jennie

jennie

douglas preston

André Deutsch

First published in the UK in 1995 by
André Deutsch Limited
106 Great Russell Street
London WC1B 3LJ

Design by Junie Lee

CIP data for this title is available from the British Library

ISBN 0 233 98918 8

Printed in Finland by WSOY

For Selene

Despite appearances to the contrary, *Jennie* is a work of fiction. However, there is no *science* fiction in this book. The scientific and behavioral experiments described here actually took place, under different circumstances, with the results as reported.

preface

Many readers of this book, no doubt, will have heard of Jennie Archibald or will remember the details of her life as reported in the press during the period of 1965 to 1975. As a boy growing up in Wellesley, Massachusetts, I myself recall reading about Jennie in the *Boston Globe* and other papers. The stories I read had a special meaning to me, since the town of Kibbencook, where she lived, lies only eight miles from Wellesley. I remember my parents discussing Jennie at the dinner table. When I egregiously misbehaved, my mother more than once compared my behavior to Jennie. Jennie became, in a small way, a symbol of willful disobedience in our household.

I decided to write a book about Jennie three years ago, while working on a story for *Massachusetts Magazine* about the Boston Museum of Natural History. I had the pleasure of interviewing Dr. Harold Epstein, a retired curator at the Boston Museum. During the course of the interview the conversation shifted abruptly to the subject of Jennie, and it required a considerable effort to return to the topic of my article. This was when I first learned many of the unpublished details of Jennie's life. I was intrigued. Dr. Epstein was anxious to talk and so I scheduled a second interview with him later that month. That was the genesis of this book.

Why write a book about something that was already extensively covered in the press? The answer is quite simple. The more I delved into the subject, the more I realized that what was reported in the press was at best only a small portion of the story. With few exceptions the articles were rife with inaccuracies, distortions, sensationalizing, and, in several cases, actual falsehoods. Most "science reporters" for newspapers and magazines did not have the scientific background to understand the ramifications of the story. Those involved with the story of Jennie's life were anxious to correct the record.

Finally, the results of the "Jennie" research have been attacked by a group of cognitive scientists who (in my opinion) did not look at the results of the project as a *whole*. None of these ethologists actually met Jennie. Their attacks have been based on a detailed analysis of a two-hour segment of videotape. This book tries to present the other nine years of Jennie's life.

At first I planned to write a straightforward book with the usual omniscient authorial voice. As I compiled my interviews and read through the Archibald papers, I began to realize that the major players in this drama were not average people. They were highly educated, intelligent, and almost without exception very articulate. As their words unfolded and the full dimensions of this extraordinary story were revealed, a conviction grew on me: there was no need for *me* to tell the story. Instead, in this book, I have let the people themselves speak. I have merely acted as an editor. I have kept my interpolated comments, which appear in brackets, to a minimum.

My first source was the posthumously published memoirs of Dr. Hugo Archibald, Harkison Curator of Physical Anthropology at the Boston Museum of Natural History and Adjunct Professor in the Department of Zoology at Harvard University. I did not have the opportunity to talk to Dr. Archibald. He tragically passed away in 1991, not three weeks before a scheduled series of interviews with him were to begin. His memoir, *Recollecting a Life,* was evidently based on an extensive journal that he kept for much of his life. Unfortunately, extensive efforts to locate this journal failed, and, in fact, there is reason to believe he destroyed it shortly before his death. I might also add here that it is not the intention of the present work to explore or even address the somewhat puzzling circumstances surrounding Dr. Archibald's untimely death.

The extracts from Dr. Archibald's memoirs have been supplemented by interviews with his colleagues and family members. All interviews were taped by myself and have been reproduced with editing only for clarity and economy. With the exception of the description of the home movies at the end, none of the words herein are my own.

It is important to point out that not everyone involved with the story agreed to be interviewed.

During the course of the interviews, several people expressed doubt regarding my motives or "point of view." Let me say that I, personally, have no point of view. Those who read this book must judge for themselves what really happened and why. I am aware there are several instances where interviewees contradicted each other's accounts. Many hours of interviews did not resolve some of these contradictions, and I therefore can make no claim to know where the real truth lies, or whether, in fact, this book indeed presents the truth.

I am grateful to Harvard University for permission to quote from the Archibald papers; to the Boston Museum of Natural History; to the Center for Primate Studies at Tufts University; to the Tahachee Center for Primate Rehabilitation; and to the Archibald family, particularly Lea Archibald and Alexander Archibald.

jennie

one

[FROM *Recollecting a Life* by Hugo Archibald, Ph.D., D.Sc., F.R.S., published by Harvard University Press. Copyright 1989 by The President and Fellows of Harvard College. Used with permission.]

The Cameroons, April 15, 1965

I will not soon forget the day the two Makere men brought the chimpanzee into camp. The animal was slung over one man's shoulder and a thin rivulet of blood trickled down the shining hollow of the man's back, black blood glistening against black skin. I watched him through the half-open flap of the tent. He stopped in the clearing in front of the tent and slid his burden sideways on to the hardpacked dirt, where it lay with arms crossed. His friend stood next to him. Both their feet and legs were white with dust to the knees. The man straightened up and clapped his hands twice, sharply, to announce their arrival. I waited. The men knew I was in the tent, but to show myself too quickly would make negotiations over the price more difficult. I soon heard Kwele shouting at the visitors in Pidgin, the lingua franca of the Cameroons.

"Whah you done bring, hunter man? Na bad beef dis!"

Kwele was a fine negotiator. We had worked out an excellent system of softening up the seller.

"Masa no want dis beef! Masa done get angry too much. Go away!"

All this was part of the routine, and Kwele relished his role a great deal, perhaps a little too much. Naturally, I was excited by the prospect of acquiring the skull of a female chimpanzee. A small group of camp assistants had dropped their work and converged on the scene, with that look of boredom mixed with the faint hope that something unexpectedly unpleasant might happen. The two men stood behind the animal, stubborn and silent.

I moved aside the flap of my tent, without getting out of my chair. The shouting stopped and Kwele stood there grinning, holding a shovel.

"Eh!" he said. "Dese hunter man got um beef. Masa no want dis beef?"

I smiled and clapped my hands softly, as etiquette required. "Iseeya, hunter man," I said.

"Iseeya, sah," they said in unison. They were thin, with a delicate tracery of tattoos on their abdomens and around their nipples. One carried a tiny crossbow with a fascicle of darts.

"Thank you, Kwele," I said. Kwele grinned again, then scowled at the men.

The men shuffled their feet in the dust.

The animal was a female *Pan troglodytes,* a lowland chimpanzee, and she was very pregnant.

"You kill this beef with poison arrow?" I asked the two men.

One of the men stepped forward. "He go for stick, sah, shoot um with arrow." He held up the crossbow for me to inspect. ("Stick" is the Pidgin word for tree.)

I knelt by the animal and looked at her face. The eyes, which were half open, suddenly widened. It gave me quite a fright; the bite of a chimpanzee can break one's arm.

"Whah! Na alive, dis beef!" shouted Kwele accusingly, delighted to find one more thing wrong with the specimen. "Mebbe 'ee go hurt Masa! Den *you* go pay!"

"Poison be working," said one of the men placidly. "Ee go die one time." Then he added, firmly: "Masa gone pay twenty-five shillings."

"Na whatee!" cried Kwele. "Masa no go pay twenty-five shillings. Mebbe 'ee no go die attall!"

" 'Ee go die one time," the man repeated stolidly. He knew the efficacy of his poison, and so did I.

The dying animal stared at me with round dark eyes, and a gurgle sound issued from her throat. Her mouth opened, exposing a row of worn, heavily caried incisors. The hairs around her muzzle were gray, and one ear was in tatters, torn and healed long ago. She was old, and I remember thinking, Better to die old after a full life. And, of course, they would have killed her for food anyway.

"Go get my pistol," I said. Kwele ducked into the tent and came back with the holster carrying my Ruger .22 magnum. I checked the barrel to make sure it was loaded and leveled the gun at the animal's heart. A shot to the head would have destroyed the thing I needed for my taxonomic studies: the skull.

Then a movement began to take place, a quick even movement of the animal's body. I backed up, thinking she might be reviving. But then I realized something far different was going on. The animal was aborting her fetus.

"Roll her on her back," I shouted.

There was a sudden sharp murmur from the crowd; this was turning out to be far more interesting than yet another bargaining session for a dead specimen. The female chimpanzee began to shudder, and a whitish head, slick with thin black hairs, appeared. In a second it was over. The fetus lay on its side in the dust, and the afterbirth was sliding out. The mother's eyes were still open, looking.

Then I heard it: a tiny whistle; a thin simian cry.

"This thing's alive!" I said. "Kwele, go get a basin of water. You, hunter man, get back."

The crowd shoved forward and for a moment I thought the baby would be trampled.

"Back!" I cried.

I picked it up and, not knowing what else to do—and feeling more than a little foolish—I whacked it lightly on the back. The thing whistled and squeaked. I called for a machete and one was thrust into my hands; as I cut the umbilical cord a great "Ahhh!" rose from the crowd.

"Help me," I said to Kwele, who had returned with a sloshing basin. "Help me wash it. And you all, get back! You no go push, you hear! Go back to work!"

The crowd backed up, jostling each other. No one went back to work.

We washed it in the basin and Kwele held it while I carefully towled it dry. The baby chimpanzee had a white face, and fine black hair covering its body. It was a female. The hair was very long and as it dried it fluffed out from the chimp's body. When the animal was dry I wrapped her in the towel and cradled her in my arms. She had an impossibly tiny face, wrinkled and owlish, and her eyes were open. In a curious way her face looked both sorrowful and wise, as if she had seen a great deal of the world and its troubles. Which was amusing, since the only thing she had seen so far in the world was my unshaven face hovering over hers. It cried again, a very small sound, and the eyes widened and looked into my face. A wobbly arm, no bigger than a twig, reached up with five little fingers spread wide and groping, and it touched me on my chin. It was a sweet gesture, and in that brief moment, I was hopelessly entranced.

I have been asked many times why I took such a fancy to this little animal. My only answer is this: if you had been there, if you had seen this tiny little animal, with the pot belly and the surprised beady eyes peering at the world for the first time, and heard its helpless voice, you would have been won over just as I was. Perhaps this sounds overly sentimental coming from a scientist whose career had been collecting dead chimpanzees and examining their skeletons. I cannot, in the end, defend my sentimentality, except to say that scientists are human beings too. It was an utterly enchanting little animal.

When I recovered my senses I heard the sounds of an argument. Kwele was sweating and gesturing broadly at the two men, but the two men were not even looking at Kwele. They were looking at me. What they saw had, apparently, encouraged them to raise the price.

"Na whatee!" Kwele was shouting. "Masa done hear? Hunter man want de bigger dash! Fifty shillings! Hunter man no palaver with Masa no more. Get out! Go away!" He advanced at the men, flapping his arms like a big buzzard. They stood their ground, their faces without expression. The female chimpanzee lay on her back on the ground, momentarily forgotten, but still looking with strange terrible eyes at me and her baby.

The look in those dying eyes will never leave me. They stared upward like two cloudy gemstones, colorless, without light. The poison in the arrow that had struck her was, in chemical structure, like curare; it paralyzed first, killed second. It is not a merciful death: one dies fully conscious and aware of one's surroundings. The Africans call it *chupu*. It is a high-molecular-weight globulin protein, and as such it could not penetrate the placental barrier, which is why the infant was spared its effects. Looking back across nearly twenty-five years, knowing now what I did not know then— it seems to me it was a prophetic look, a gaze not at the present but into the future. I have always wondered: what was she thinking, as she hovered between life and death, when she saw this strange, white, hairless primate gently cradling her baby?

If this sounds like strange talk from a scientist—so be it. If there is one thing I have learned from a lifetime study of science, it is that the world is not a place we human beings will ever comprehend. Understand, yes; comprehend, no. The reason for this—like the reason for almost everything in the way we think—is evolution: our brains did not evolve to help us comprehend the true meaning of things, only to understand their mechanical workings. Knowing the *true* meaning of reality does not contribute to one's ability to survive, and thus this kind of understanding was not addressed by evolution.

I averted my eyes from that intense dying stare, and found myself looking at Kwele. "Fifty shillings!" he repeated. "Hunter man be robber man!"

"We don't want the female," I said, and then to make sure I was understood, repeated it again in Pidgin: "Masa no want dis beef. Kwele, shoot dis beef and tell hunter man to take it and get the hell out. Tell hunter man go for bush. Give him the fifty shillings."

"*Ndefa mu!* Fifty shillings! Up de twenty-five! Masa!"

"For God's sake, be quiet and give the man fifty shillings," I said, and went back into my tent, pulling the flap shut, with the baby in my arms. I could hear more shouting, a chorus of voices raised in discussion. Then there was a sudden hush, the sharp crack of the Ruger, and another swell of argument. After a while the talk died away and the camp became quiet.

As I thought about the events of the morning, I knew that my excellent relationship with Kwele had suffered possibly irreversible damage. I had allowed him to lose face in front of strangers, bush men of no status. Some repair work was in order. I opened the flap of my tent and called for Kwele.

The man arrived, after an appropriately insolent interval, and stood in the shade of the flap, his face uncharacteristically inscrutable.

"Kwele, I owe you an apology. Masa feel sorry. Kwele done good work."

A small quantity of disappointment leaked into Kwele's face. "Fifty shillings," he said. "We go pay five, ten shillings, Masa. Hunter man be nekkid bush man."

"I know," I said. "You savvay, Masa like dis small beef too much."

"Na fine ting dis *big* beef too. Why Masa no want big beef?"

"I know," I said. "We should have bought it." It had been a foolish thing not to acquire the female chimpanzee. I had to get one for my research project, and chimpanzees were becoming increasingly rare. I could not shake that look out of my memory.

There was a small silence.

"Kwele, would you mind bringing me some warm milk, please?"

The African spun around on his flat feet and flicked open the tent flap. He was still angry. I would have to think of something to bring him back around.

As I sat at my camp desk, the baby chimpanzee continued to look into my face with slitted eyes, her tiny arms bumping about. She said "oo oo oo" and grasped one of my fingers with both hands, her fingers closing on mine with surprising strength.

I suddenly felt quite strange, flooded with an unexpected surge of fatherly feeling.

I was searching for several species of pongid—chimpanzees, bonobos (pygmy chimpanzees), and gorillas, to be specific—for my major project at the Boston Museum, which was a reclassification of the primates. Because expeditions like this are extremely expensive, I was also collecting certain species of mammals for the Department of Mammalogy and lizards for the Department of Herpetology. The Ornithology Department had asked me to keep an eye out for a rare genus of raptor they were anxious to obtain.

During the next months we crossed the vast Batuti forest on wide forest trails, my camp assistants trailing me with bundles of equipment balanced on their heads. I had found this a much better method of travel than by Jeep, which in the mid-sixties in west Africa was infuriating. Jeeps broke down, sank into swamps, ran out of gas, and had their tires and batteries stolen. There were no spare parts to be had. The rapid population growth had pushed the really rare pongids into the deeper forests that were still largely inaccessible by Jeep anyway.

The news of my coming always seemed to precede me. As soon as we had set up camp, the natives would begin arriving with specimens. The government of the Cameroons had issued me with a permit to collect a specific number of specimens in each genera of the primates. Since the Africans hunted most of these species for food, it was easy (as well as ethical) to collect them. If the natives were going to kill and eat an animal anyway, I felt my efforts would not affect the rapidly dwindling populations of these animals. All I needed for my research was the skull, pelvis, and skin; the natives could still have the "beef." Certainly, the benefits to science outweighed other considerations.

I made a very wide circuit of the Batuti, planning to arrive back in Lukemba shortly before the monsoon season. A spacious wattle-and-daub house, built in the colonial style, awaited me there, where I could prepare my specimens and renew my acquaintance with the Mololo of Lukemba. The Mololo was the charming and vivacious leader of the area, a man I'd known since my first trip to the Cameroons as a graduate student.

The baby chimpanzee slipped into this life without even a ripple. When we traveled, I carried her high on my back in a baby carrier provided by one of the camp wives. It was woven from pounded and separated vines, and padded with soft, dry *bangi* grass, which acted as a kind of diaper. I had to carry her close to my head, because she had conceived a fondness for my hair and clutched fistfuls of it with amazing force, as she would have clung to her mother as she climbed through the trees. Otherwise, she was completely helpless and unable to walk.

At first she was terribly distressed when she was separated from me. Her little arms would wave about and her face would screw up into a wrinkled mask of unhappiness while she made an "oo oo oo" distress call. Baby chimpanzees must cling to their mothers while they climb trees and run along the ground, and as a result evolution had given her a shockingly tenacious grip. Where she held on to my neck or shoulders, tiny bruises developed. Sometimes when I put her down, her hands would wave about and find each other in a crushing clasp. Then she would squeak and cry, unable to understand what was gripping her hands so painfully.

I was deeply attached to the lonely life of the forest, the smell of the *ika* wood burning, the forest cave about me humming and crackling with the electricity of life. I loved especially the long, soft green light of evening, with only the distant flash of gold in the upper canopy indicating the presence of a sunset. During these evenings, I would sit in my camp chair smoking my pipe, with the chimpanzee nestled in my partly unbuttoned shirt, sleeping quietly, or sucking and pulling on my chest hairs. I have never quite been as contented as I was during those four months in the Batuti forest.

I had made peace with Kwele. I had told him that the little chimpanzee was a very rare specimen indeed, for which fifty shillings was an absurdly low price. The poor ignorant bush hunter men had been royally snookered. Kwele was to be congratulated. It was terribly important to keep the specimen alive, I said, and to that end I was putting Kwele in charge of it, with a salary supplement equal to the gravity of his new responsibility.

As I had anticipated, Kwele immediately subcontracted out the work of caring for the chimpanzee to two of the camp wives, paying them only a fraction of his supplement, and loudly directing every operation with imperious gestures and references to the terrible anger of the Masa should any mistakes be made. The two women took excellent care of the chimpanzee, treating her just like a child, heating her milk, feeding her every four hours. When the chimp began to look peaked they had a discussion and found her a wet nurse—a woman whose own baby had died of diarrhea. The chimp seemed to thrive on human milk, although I could not overcome my astonishment at seeing an animal sucking for all she was worth at a human breast, clamoring and pawing around and raising a racket whenever she felt deprived of the tit.

We supplemented the chimpanzee's human milk diet with powdered milk. Every morning the squeaking, gurgling chimpanzee sat in my lap and sucked on a bottle.

During my four-month circuit of the Batuti forest, the chimpanzee grew fast. Faster, it seemed to me, than my son, Sandy, had when a baby. Her skin remained white (white skin is not uncommon among lowland chimps) but the hair thickened and shortened, and the face grew rounder and more appealing every day. The eyes, which started off blue, began to darken into blue-black. She learned to grab, and while she suckled on the bottle one hand would wave about and finally snag my button or a wrinkle in my shirt—which she would yank.

She walked for the first time just before we reached Lukemba. She was about four months old. The forest had begun to darken every afternoon, the sky filling with unseen clouds. Sometimes a wind shook the upper canopy and distant thunder rolled through the muffling trees, bringing with it a whiff of humidity and ozone.

The chimpanzee had been crawling around under my camp desk, patting the dusk and crooning softly to herself. I felt her fist on my pantleg and looked down in time to see her launch herself across the room, taking four or five quick wobbly steps before pitching forward onto her knuckles and then facedown in the dirt. This performance was followed by a triumphant gale of high-pitched hoots and cries, while she bounced up and down holding on to a table leg.

The rains began early. A few heavy drops slapped down through the leaves, the chimpanzee began screaming with displeasure (she hated rain), and soon it was as black as night. We arrived in

Lukemba in a warm downpour, the mud streets running with water. Steam and cooking smoke rose from the conical thatched roofs. A wet chicken strutted around, and a tethered goat with a swollen udder forlornly watched us.

The peace lasted only a moment. Pouring out of the huts came the naked village children, their bellies swollen with *kwashiorkor*, their white teeth flashing, their pink throats showing behind their shouts. Incredibly enough, almost every child already had a dead specimen in hand, a toad, a spitted cane rat, a bird, a salamander, a big beetle, or splay-winged cricket. They hopped up and down and grabbed at my shirt, flapping and waving the dead animals in front of me, hollering out in Pidgin the most outrageous sums. Kwele immediately went into action, perhaps too enthusiastically, scolding, pushing the children back, waving about a big stick, grimacing and slapping down hands as they thrust dead specimens in my direction.

"Masa no want dis beef! Ha! Masa gone be angry! No want dis beef! Dis bad beef! Whaaaa!"

A group of men had gathered in the village square—a pool of mud surrounded by ancient *bala* trees—behind a large man in a white robe and embroidered skullcap, thatch umbrellas clustered over his head. He was the Mololo, the Lukemban chief. He met me with a large, wet hand and a brilliant smile, while his men rushed to shield me from the downpour, jostling each other and arguing as they held the umbrellas over my head.

"Na foine!" said the Mololo, in his rich, rolling voice. "Na foine ting dis! Welcome!" The crowd echoed "Welcome!" and he linked his arm with mine and we proceeded toward the big house at the edge of the square.

It was a welcome sight, an old colonial house with a large porch, a pitched roof, and an airy interior of small cool rooms opening one into the other. A heavy mass of bougainvillea twisted up the adzed tree trunks that supported the porch roof, and inside sat an enormous stone fireplace, an atavism of some turn-of-the-century colonial official.

After we went inside, Kwele took a stand at the doorway, brandishing his stick, poking back the children, while the rest of the expedition filed inside and piled their gear and specimens in the back. As most of the skeletal material was still "dirty," the house soon filled with the smell of decaying flesh, augmented by the odor of wet people. It was a smell I had grown accustomed to years ago.

The Mololo seated himself opposite the fireplace and opened his palm toward a chair, giving me leave to sit. The officials stood in a respectful circle around us, steaming and dripping water. A bottle of Bombay gin appeared from underneath someone's robe and was placed on the rattan table with a loud thump, along with two tumblers.

"We drink!" the Mololo said, filling each glass with care. While this was going on I had freed the chimpanzee from her carrying sling and she now climbed over my head and down my face, dropping into my lap.

We drained our glasses, as courtesy required, and the Mololo refilled them.

"Welcome!" he said again, immediately echoed by the men around him. "You get um good beef?"

"Yes, sir," I said. "Lots of good beef. It's been a good trip."

"Na foine! We got um many hunter mans here, get you all good beef you want. We done been waiting."

"Thank you, sir." The Mololo had been very helpful on my previous trips, encouraging his people to comb the forest for specimens.

"Na whatee dis ting?" he said, leaning over at the chimpanzee. The animal sat up in my lap and peered at the Mololo.

"Wheee!" she said, and ducked down.

"I found her in the forest," I said. "Her mother was killed by hunter man."

"You savvay dis beef? When he go big, he done cause trouble, you watch um good!" He laughed and tossed back his glass. "Na whatee dat palaver for dis beef?"

"We call it a 'chimpanzee.'"

"Timpansee! Na foine name." He leaned over and looked at the little animal. With a solemn expression on her face, the little chimpanzee reached out and he enveloped her tiny hand in his and shook it.

"He shake um hand, like all de Masa!" The Mololo exploded with laughter. ("Masa" is the Pidgin term for any white man, and does not necessarily connote rank or respect.) "Dis beef gone grow into Masa for true!"

My work in Lukemba proceeded smoothly. Kwele organized the buying of the specimens. Every day at four o'clock, those villagers with dead animals would fill the dirt area in front of the house, and Kwele would wade through, swagger stick in hand, dismissing most of the people but sending those with unusual specimens up to the porch, one at a time, where they would lay their catch on the table.

As soon as a deal had been made the specimen would be carried around to the back, where it was immediately skinned and de-fleshed; the meat was given back to the seller, the skin pegged for tanning, and the fleshed-out skeleton dumped in one of several old bathtubs I kept as maceration vats.

The chimpanzee played under the table while the bargaining sessions went on, climbing the legs, dropping back to the floor, rolling around and hooting softly. Sometimes she would climb into my lap and suck on my buttons, and once in a while she would climb to the top of my head and sit there, surveying the world like a diminutive Chinese emperor. Her appearance on my head always caused an uproar from the ubiquitous crowd, who laughed and stamped their feet. Sometimes she would sneak under the table and lie in wait, ready to grab the feet of some unsuspecting African, usually with lively results. Then she would scream and retreat behind my chair.

We spent two months in Lukemba. It was remarkable to me how fast the chimpanzee grew and how quickly she lost her shyness. During the second month of our stay the children of the village would come by the house in the morning and squat outside the door calling out a word in Nala that I couldn't quite understand. The chimp would be up and tumbling out the door like a bullet, and later I would see her running through the village with a laughing crowd of children.

When we first came to Lukemba, I had worried how the chimpanzee would fare with the dozens of vicious dogs that slunk and skulked around the town. But the village children teased the dogs mercilessly and I noticed that the chimp was a most enthusiastic participant in this game. The dogs, for their part, reacted to the chimpanzee as if she were a human child, whining and groveling whenever she swaggered by. I once saw the chimp threaten a dog with a stick and take away a piece of garbage it was eating.

One morning I asked Kwele what it was the children chanted at the chimp every morning.

"Dat be dis beef's palaver," Kwele said.

"What is the word? What does it mean?"

"*Jen ikwa si go*. It say, dis little beef, he stick out de hairs, make himself look bigger den he is."

"I don't understand."

"You see dis beef, when he have de fear? Or he be angry? He stick out de hairs. Whoof! Like dis." Kwele hunched up his arms and hunkered down in an imitation of a chimpanzee display of aggression.

"I see."

"*Jen ikwa si go*. Dat be his palaver."

I thought about this. I had been having some difficulty thinking of a name for the animal. I have always had trouble with names, and it was my wife, Lea, who had to choose names for our two children, Sarah and Alexander. For six months I had struggled to name the animal, but they all sounded awkward and flat and in the end I'd been too embarrassed to voice any of them out loud. Jen-Ikwa-Si-Go. Little-Animal-Who-Bristles-Herself-up-to-Look-Big. It sounded like a fine name to me. I called her Jennie.

[FROM interviews with Mrs. Hugo Archibald, January 1991, October 1991, and September 1992 at her apartment in Kibbencook Lower Falls, Massachusetts.]

Is that really necessary? I don't like tape recorders. They make me nervous. Well, if you insist. Yes, I talked to Dr. Epstein. What a clever, sly old man he is, the way he stares at you with those beady eyes. He's always been a wrinkled old man, as long as I've known him. He was one of those people born old. I'm not sure I altogether trust his judgment of people. He's too clever for his own good. I hope he's right about you. He said you were going to set the story straight.

Where shall we begin? It's such a terribly long story, I'm not sure I'm up to going through the whole thing. Oh dear. I'm just an old lady now. How long is this going to take?

We lived in Kibbencook proper, about a mile from here. Our house? It was a rambling, seedy old place. Hugo loved it. I found it nearly impossible to keep house. It wasn't a nice suburban house by any means. It was too big and rambling. And not very chimp-proof. When we bought it we weren't exactly thinking about having a chimpanzee. The yard was full of dandelions. How the neighbors hated that! It was enclosed by the most awful hedge. A diseased-looking thing, all gapped and yellow. We tried everything, but every year a little more of it died. The lawn had big brown patches all over it. And the rhododendrons! They were so overgrown they grew up to the second story windows and when the wind blew we could hear the scraping noises from inside. It used to scare the children. Hugo told them it was a bear outside. In the side yard was a marvelous old crabapple tree, with sagging limbs propped up on sticks. Behind that was the Kibbencook golf course. Our yard was not the envy of our neighbors, to say the least. [Laughs.] Hugo was not exactly interested in lawn care. And I certainly was not going to start pushing around a lawn mower.

Kibbencook was a lovely town. Very quiet. Not like it is today. Those horrid town houses along Washington Street hadn't gone up, and the bandstand was still in the square. Kibbencook had once been an Indian settlement along the Charles River. You can still see their shell heaps down by the river. Do you know Route 9, that dreadful strip with all the gas stations? That was once the Kibbencook Trace, the old Indian trail that went to Boston Harbor. The Indians had villages along the brook, where the golf course is today. Once in a while a golfer would lose a ball in the brook and find an arrowhead where the bank was eroding. Every golfer seemed to have an arrowhead. Sandy, our son, used to trade golf balls for those arrowheads. Golf is a ridiculous game. My father, who was of English descent, used to call it a Presbyterian game. Of course I married a Presbyterian, but thank goodness he didn't golf.

I don't suppose this has anything to do with Jennie. If I get off the subject you just interrupt me and set me back on track. Don't you let me wander about.

Our house had once been the old farmhouse of the area, before the suburbs sprang up. In the woods behind the house you could still see the farm's old stone walls. It was never good land. The glaciers dumped too many boulders on it. When the Midwest opened up, all the farmers left and the woods grew back. Now, of course, they're cutting them all down again to build more houses.

There is a great deal of history in this town, only most of the people here are ignorant. The only thing they know is real estate values. They could tell you to the dollar what any one of these houses is worth. Half of the women here are real estate brokers. Real estate is what you do if you have no talent or education. Is that tape recorder still going? Perhaps you should edit my comments; I'm just a crabby old lady, you know. I can scarcely believe what has happened to the price of real estate in this town. I don't know where people are getting the money.

They tore down the town hall, a lovely example of Romanesque Revival architecture, and put up that concrete cube. Appalling. The things they've done to this town. Why, only ten years ago they tried to blast out that big rock down by the brook. They thought it was an eyesore. So I went down there and I sat on that beautiful rock. For three days. And I said, "If you touch me, I'll call my lawyer!" I outlasted them. It made them hopping mad, but then the papers took it up and—

Now you've let me get off the subject again.

The name of the town? Now that has a curious history. It originated with an Indian ruler named Kibenquot. He held court right here at this bend of the Charles River. But when the white men came he was corrupted by whiskey and money and sold the land out from under the tribe. They all died out. The only thing left were those arrowheads they'd find along the brook.

It was a lovely place back then. The woods and fields were endless, not like it is today. It was a wonderful place to raise children. Or a chimpanzee, for that matter. [Laughs.]

Our house was number sixteen Hawthorne Lane. It was angled to the street, not facing it like the other houses. It was a rickety old thing. The roof sagged, the porch was rotten, and it had been painted so many times that once in a while a piece of paint the size of a dinner plate would fall off. Long after the farm was gone, the farmer's widow lived in it until they hauled her off to the nursing home. Hugo and I bought it in 1957, for $22,000. Now I expect it's worth half a million. I wish them luck, whoever lives in it now. Probably some stockbroker. I wonder if they know a chimpanzee grew up there?

We were not popular in the neighborhood. We didn't join the country club, we didn't have barbecues in the backyard, and we had friends from Cambridge who looked Jewish. They say Massachusetts is a liberal state, but the only people we ever met in Kibbencook were Republicans. It was a very narrow-minded town.

When Jennie arrived, we became famous. Or perhaps I should say infamous! It was all great fun, in the beginning anyway.

Yes, indeed, I remember when Hugo returned from Africa with Jennie. He was supposed to come home on a Thursday and he arrived on Tuesday. I heard the cab in the driveway, gunning his engine, and there was Hugo, standing there with those two great ugly suitcases of his and a canvas sack slung around his neck. Sandy shot out the door with the two dogs on his heels. Such a commotion. I had the baby in my arms. She was squirming around like a coiled spring, trying to see what all the excitement was. She was only two months old when Hugo left, and this was six months later, mind you.

Hugo gave me a big kiss and he stepped back with a silly grin on his face. And he said he had a surprise for me.

He looked just like a mischievous boy when he reached into that bag. I thought he was going to pull out a snake. Instead out came this tiny thing, dangling by its arms. For the life of me I didn't know what it was. The little thing blinked, looked around, hooted, and swung up into the crook of his arm. I was never so surprised in my life. It was Sandy who figured it out first.

He started screaming, "A monkey! Daddy brought us a monkey!"

Hugo explained that she was not a monkey, but an ape, and her name was Jennie. Sandy was just wild to hold her.

I remember Hugo looking at me with this nervous, boyish look, and he asked me what would I think of having a chimp as a pet. He was afraid I might disapprove.

I didn't know what to think. The little thing was peering around with tremendous interest. Her little black eyes were so round. She always looked astonished.

Well, the dogs were barking, Sandy was hollering, the baby was crying. Those dogs were in an absolute frenzy. I was frightened. I remember that all I could say was, "Won't the dogs bite her?"

Hugo just smiled a wicked smile. And then he put this helpless little chimp—why, she was no bigger than a baby!—on the grass in front of the two snarling terriers. Frick and Frack were their names. Well! You know how fierce terriers can be. Oh, my goodness I will never forget what happened next. She bristled up her hair, which made her look twice as big, and she rushed at the dogs with a great screech. Straight at them, running on her knuckles! The dogs turned to run, but she grabbed Frick's tail with both hands and pulled back hard. The poor dog scrabbled on the lawn, desperately trying to get away. Then she released it and the dog fell all in a heap, collected itself, and ran through a hole in the hedge. Jennie was so proud of herself! She whirled about on the lawn like a dervish, hooting and screeching, her pink mouth open. You've never seen such a large mouth on such a small creature.

What a homecoming!

Hugo had spent nearly eight hundred dollars in bribes and permits to get Jennie out of Africa. At the time, I thought of it as one more of Hugo's impulsive actions. He was always doing something outrageous. In his quiet way, of course.

I was worried about Jennie getting along with Sarah, our baby girl. I was also worried about germs. Who knew what horrible diseases she might have brought back from the jungles of Africa. Hugo wanted to introduce Jennie to Sarah right away, but I said not on your life, not until that ape is clean!

The next thing I knew, Sandy had his bathing suit on and Hugo was sitting on the front stoop, smoking that terrible pipe of his. Ugh! How I hated that dirty old thing. He dropped ashes everywhere and all his shirts had burn holes in them—

What was that? Oh yes, Hugo was sitting on the stoop, spraying the hose across the lawn. When Jennie saw the water she screamed and hid in the hedge, but Sandy dragged her out, and soon the two of them were running and jumping through the spray of water. Sandy was in front, while Jennie scooted along behind, screaming with delight. With her hair plastered down by the water she looked so small, just an itty-bitty black thing with big ears and that enormous mouth. When she ran along on her knuckles she looked like a bowling ball with ears. And the *noise* that came out of that mouth! Heaven help us, no human could have made that noise. It sounded like something out of a Tarzan movie.

While this was going on, I could see old Mrs. Wardell staring out her kitchen window. She was the dentist's wife. What was going through her mind heaven only knows. And then I realized that all up and down the street, there were faces in the windows. Only Reverend Palliser across the street had the nerve to come out to see what unholy creature was making such a row. It's odd how clearly I remember him now: standing there in his shirtsleeves, with the funniest expression of bewilderment on his round face. He looked just like a big Charlie Brown. The poor man, he was gassed at Ypres, you know. I don't think he ever quite got over it. And then he went senile, wandering all about the neighborhood, and—

Oh yes. The story. Well! Hugo finally brought Jennie in to meet Sarah. I sat on the sofa with Sarah in my lap, while Jennie squatted on the floor, watching. She was terribly interested in the baby. Sarah had grown so in the six months Hugo had been gone. She had a potbelly and big fat cheeks. Cute as a button.

Jennie hopped up on the sofa and stared at Sarah. The baby looked back at the chimp and stretched out both hands. The chimpanzee didn't scare her in the slightest. Nothing scares her, even today. She was always a fearless little firebrand.

Hugo introduced them. Jennie looked right into Sarah's face and laid a hairy hand on her head. They stared at each other, fascinated. Neither one had seen anything like the other! And then Jennie said "Oooo" and stuck Sarah's hand into her mouth.

Oh my goodness. You can imagine my reaction. I shrieked and snatched Sarah away. You see, I thought Jennie had tried to bite Sarah. Hugo explained everything. This was just Jennie's way of greeting, he said. She took your finger and put it in her mouth.

That was fine and good in Africa, but not in America! Later I put an end to that unsanitary habit.

Poor Jennie was terrified at my reaction. She crouched on the sofa, covering her head with her hands and rocking back and forth. You would have thought I had just beaten her. She looked so pitiful. I comforted Jennie and gave her my hand. She guided my pinky into her mouth and I gritted my teeth while she sucked on it.

And then Sarah, dear Sarah, held out her arms to the chimp. She wanted a hug!

Hugo told Jennie she could hug the baby. And I was so surprised, she shuffled over and gave Sarah the sweetest hug. I could hardly believe it when I saw this hairy animal cradling my baby Sarah. She rocked her just like a mother. The baby looked at me and began flapping her arms, her little bald head bumping against the hairy chest of the chimpanzee. Isn't it odd how clearly I remember that first meeting? Oh dear . . .

Even at that age, Jennie understood some English. Now some of these primate researchers will tell you that chimpanzees cannot really understand spoken English. That's ridiculous. That chimp understood almost anything you would say to her. You had to live with her to see what I mean. When she learned ASL—that's American Sign Language—you could ask her a question in English and she'd answer in ASL. Honestly, I'd never met a more awful group of people in my life than those primate researchers. That horrible Dr. Prentiss—

Yes, I know, one thing at a time. I'll save that for later. Thank you.

Hugo built a house for Jennie in the old crab apple tree in the side yard, and he gave her a pile of old army blankets. Hugo was a terrible pack rat, and he saved everything. The attic was full of his papers, fifth grade report cards, college essays, you name it. They were a dreadful fire hazard in that wooden attic. We had terrible fights. I thought we were going to have a divorce over those papers. And now that he's gone, I don't have the heart to throw them out. There you go. [Long pause.]

Where was I? Hugo built Jennie a little tree house in back. Every evening Jennie gathered up her blankets and climbed into her tree and arranged them in her treehouse. In the morning, at first light, her head poked out, and then she dropped each blanket, one by one, to the ground.

Jennie had her own tin cup, plate, and spoon given to her by the captain of the ship that brought them back from Africa. The captain insisted that she and Hugo eat at his table every night. It made the other guests hopping mad to have this ape in a diaper sitting in the seat of honor! But that's another story.

When she finished dropping her blankets she threw down the cup, plate, and spoon. Then climbed down, collected her tableware, and banged on the back door, giving her "hungry hoot" at the top of her lungs. That was her "food" sound. I think the primate researchers call it a "pant-hoot." It was sometimes a grunt and sometimes a howl, depending on how hungry she was! Mind you, this was five, six o'clock in the morning. The dogs would start barking hysterically, even though they knew perfectly well who it was, and I would have to get to the door as fast as possible to keep Jennie from waking up the neighborhood.

When Jennie came in, the dogs hid under the sofa. They were

afraid to death of her. Jennie sat at the kitchen table and carefully arranged all her tableware. And then she would sit there for an hour or more, waiting to be fed, fretting and hooting and chattering away. When she got older she got more impatient. She screamed and hooted as if we were starving her to death. Jennie just loved her food.

At first we fed her baby food. But it wasn't long before she insisted on eating what we ate. She wanted to do everything we did. The food on her plate was never good enough; she had to eat ours. Most every morning, she ate a slice of buttered toast, a banana, and a bowl of oatmeal and honey. Once in a while she would eat a piece of bacon, but she didn't like meat that much. Chicken and pork she would eat, but nothing else.

She looked so funny when she ate! You should have seen her, with her little black eyes peeping above the tabletop. Oh my goodness. And her wispy hair stuck up from the dome of her head in the funniest way, and she made these little crunching noises as she ate her toast. And those jug ears! They stuck out and looked like big pink Christmas lights when the sun was behind them. [Laughs.]

She was always suspicious about her food. Once in a while, you see, she would bite into something she hated. She sniffed at her food constantly. I suppose she was never sure when that piece of toast might turn into, say, a hamburger with ketchup. She loathed hamburger with ketchup! And pickles. If there was pickle in there somewhere, watch out! When she got something she didn't like, she picked it up and threw it as hard as she could into the dining room. Tomatoes, baked beans, lobster, steak—all got thrown into the dining room at one time or another. I think she got that idea from watching the Three Stooges on television. They were always throwing food on that horrid program. Jennie could be so trying at times. There was a streak of ketchup on the kitchen ceiling from one of Jennie's hamburgers. It stayed there for years, long after Jennie was gone. It used to make me feel so sad, but I could never bring myself to get a ladder and scrub it off. It was like a memory; you hate to see them go. Memories, I mean.

Jennie looked so solemn when she was eating that you couldn't help laughing. When she chewed, the little hairs on her chin moved up and down and her eyebrows contracted as if she were thinking great thoughts. Well perhaps she was! After us, food was the most important thing in her life.

When she finished eating, there was no separating Jennie from her plate, cup, and spoon for washing. Heavens no. She guarded those with her life. She thought she would starve to death if those disappeared. She had a fit when I tried to wash them. They got so dirty, so absolutely filthy, that I was positive Jennie was going to get salmonella poisoning and spread it to the whole family. Finally Hugo waited under the tree one morning and stole them when Jennie dropped them. You should have heard her screaming. After that she let us have them, but she always kept her beady eyes fixed on them while I rinsed and loaded them in the dishwasher. Then she would wait right next to the dishwasher until they were done. The minute it was opened she would be reaching in there, rummaging about and rattling things around to get her precious tableware.

After three years she began rinsing the dishes herself. She wasn't exactly the most thorough dishwasher, but she had her style. First she licked the plates clean, and then she washed them. I can't begin to tell you how many dishes she broke. But when we had guests, the highlight of the evening was when Jennie cleared the table and rinsed the dishes. People could not get over the fact that an animal could do such a thing. They would always say, Will you look at that! We have to get one of our own! And then Jennie would drop a stack of dishes. Or take a bite out of a bar of soap. And that would be the end of that kind of talk! Hugo took a marvelous picture of her washing the dishes. Now let's see, where are those pictures? Do you want to see any?

Those first few years with Jennie were blissful. It was a happy period in our lives. Jennie made it a great adventure. Not that it was easy; toilet training Jennie was the hardest thing I think I've ever done. Oh my goodness! That ape was not going to be toilet trained, if it was the last thing she did. She tried, but it wasn't in her nature. When you live in the trees all day, I don't suppose it really matters where you go. I developed a system where I'd give her candy when she did it "right." She would do anything for a piece of candy. She tried so hard. It was so dear. She'd be playing in the kitchen, and I'd see this expression on her face. And she'd run for the bathroom! And on the way there she'd stop and stick her hand in the candy jar. That was fatal. Sometimes her reward was a little premature, and— oh dear—her diaper would be all soggy. And then do you know what she did? She'd put the candy back. All by herself. Jennie was so human, so utterly human. You had to see it to believe it.

[FROM *Recollecting a Life* by Hugo Archibald.]

Jennie settled into suburban American life as if she had been born to it. She quickly developed a taste for television. We owned one of the latest models, a Vision-Aire De Luxe, molded in space-age brown plastic, with a bulbous screen and silver-painted dials. It cost $99.95, a large sum in those days. Jennie became an addict, and as long as the television was on she was content for hours at a time. In retrospect, I often wonder what effect the violence and aggression of television might have had on Jennie. In the mid-sixties, however, television was more benign than it is today, and it was even thought to be educational. Children were considered deprived if there was no television in the house.

Jennie's consumption of television was on the vocal side. While she watched, a stream of grunts, hoots, and squeaks issued from the den, punctuated by stamping or pounding during particularly exciting scenes, such as car chases and gunfights. She also favored programming that involved canned laughter. Human laughter fascinated her.

We first had an inkling of Jennie's fondness for television one Saturday shortly after my return from Africa. I woke up to the faint sounds of the television set floating up from the den. Watching the television was an early Saturday morning ritual with Sandy. It was an oddly comforting sound, one I had not heard in six months.

I found the two of them sitting cross-legged, Indian-style, on the carpet, watching the Three Stooges. Even after all these years I remember that particular program. The action was taking place in an elegant drawing room filled with people in formal dress, and the Three Stooges, themselves dressed in evening clothes, were throwing pies and food and rapping each other on the head and poking each other in the eyes, to the usual sound effects of squawking horns and pizzicato violins. I asked Sandy what the point of all this was, and I remember him explaining that a professor, as an experiment, had tried to make gentlemen out of the Three Stooges. This was the unhappy result. It was a takeoff on Pygmalion and it was particularly apt that Jennie found it amusing.

Jennie was transfixed, staring at the screen. Her little eyes glittered. I wondered what her simian brain was making of the program.

"Dad! Jennie likes to watch TV!" Sandy cried, as if reporting a revelation. "Watch!"

He turned off the television set and sat back. The screen contracted to a point. Without missing a beat, Jennie scooted over and turned it back on.

"He he heee!" she said as the picture slowly focused. She gripped the sides of the television and hopped up and down, her face inches from the screen.

"See, Dad? She can turn on the TV." Then he added, "Jennie, I can't see."

Jennie looked around at the sound of her name but continued to block the screen.

"Move over!" Sandy shouted.

An advertisement came on. It depicted a ruggedly handsome man inhaling a cigarette to a chorus of voices singing about smoothness and taste. He exhaled with a sigh of satisfaction and the singing crescendoed. "Hooo heeee heee," Jennie said, as if singing along.

"Jennie! No! Dad, make her get out of the way," Sandy said.

The Three Stooges returned to the screen, to the theme song of "The Three Blind Mice." Under Sandy's protestations Jennie finally went back and sat down next to him and held his hand, with a worried look on her face. Already Sandy was becoming her best friend. She admired him and wanted to do whatever he did.

"What rubbish," I said jokingly. "Maybe we should have left that poor animal in the jungle."

But Sandy and Jennie were so engrossed in the unfolding drama that they did not hear me at all.

Jennie's arrival had shaken the complacency of our suburban neighborhood. The first to show his interest in Jennie was our neighbor, the Episcopal minister from across the street. His name was Hendricks Palliser. He came calling on orders of his wife—a formidable woman. At the time neither Lea nor I knew Palliser well at all, and not being religiously inclined we had not cultivated a relationship with him. In one way, at least, he had intrigued me: in World War I he had volunteered for the French ambulance corps and, it was said, had known Hemingway. I had not been able to reconcile the cheerful, round-faced suburban rector across the street with the heroic volunteer who was, apparently, wounded at the second battle of the Ypres salient. This was the battle in which the Germans first used poison gas, and (it was said) he rescued a group of men from the gas with his ambulance.

The door chimes rang. The Reverend stood on the stoop, gray Borsalino hat clasped in hand, a nervous and apologetic look on his round face. Lea invited him in. He vigorously shuffled his feet on the doormat and ducked into the house.

Jennie was invariably excited by the arrival of strangers, but she was also shy. I saw a flash of black as Jennie shot down the hall toward the kitchen. Normally we did not allow her in the kitchen, but it seemed prudent, at the time, to pretend Jennie did not exist. We both instinctively felt that the subject of Jennie might be on the Reverend's agenda, and the later that subject was introduced the better.

We settled into the living room. Lea offered him tea "or something else?" and he asked for sherry. His voice was soft with a slight stammer, and he had an air of embarrassment about him. He was bald, in his mid-seventies, with several large moles on his nose. His blue eyes were nervous and squinty, as if he were in bright sunlight. He was not a handsome man. And yet there was something pleasing about the face.

As Lea poured the sherry, we heard a thump in the kitchen. I remember the Reverend's eyes darted toward the kitchen and back. We all knew there was a chimpanzee in there, but none of us wanted to be the first to mention it.

"Thank you kindly," said the Reverend, accepting the glass, while laying his Borsalino on the coffee table. "How was your trip?" he asked me.

At that moment there was another thump in the kitchen, and the Reverend's nervousness seemed to increase.

I chatted about the trip, how successful it had been, and what we hoped to achieve in terms of further research. I could see that the Reverend was having trouble concentrating on the conversation. Clearly his wife had put him up to this visit, just as she made him weed the dandelions out of our yard when she believed we were not home. I felt quite sorry for Palliser, with such a wife.

In the middle of our awkward and halting conversation, a tremendous crash sounded from the kitchen, the merry sound of broken glass. The chimpanzee could be ignored no longer.

"Oh dear," said Lea, and went off to see what had happened. There was a momentary silence and then a black form moving at high speed tore into the living room and disappeared under the chaise lounge. We could hear Lea calling for Jennie in the kitchen, in a scolding tone of voice.

"She's in here," I called out. I turned to the Reverend. "She's still adjusting to life in America."

"Yes, indeed," he said, very nervously.

I then added: "I think that crash may have been the punch bowl Lea's mother gave us as a wedding present."

"How unfortunate," said the Reverend.

It sounded so insincere that I couldn't help adding, "At least I *hope* so."

To my surprise the Reverend issued a loud and most undecorous laugh. Lea came in, looking flushed.

"She got into the refrigerator and broke the milk pitcher," she said, and turned to the Reverend. "She loves milk."

"Yes, indeed," said the Reverend.

"Whooooo," said Jennie from under the chaise lounge.

"Jennie," I said, hoping to draw the visit to a close as soon as possible, "come out and meet Reverend Palliser."

The Reverend could hardly disguise his curiosity. He leaned forward as two hairy hands and the top of a fuzzy head came out from under the chaise lounge and stared up at us.

"Jennie, come here," I said in a firm tone of voice.

The chimp slid out, stood up, pursed her lips, and strolled over, as coolly and nonchalantly as a movie star.

"Shake hands," I said.

The chimp condescended to hold out a limp hand, looking more like she expected to have it kissed than shaken.

"Why, how nice to meet you," said the Reverend, his face wrinkling with delight. "What a charming animal you are!" •

"He he," said Jennie.

"That's a good girl," I said.

Quick as a flash she swept the Reverend's hat off the table and whipped it onto her own head.

"No, Jennie," Lea said. "No."

Jennie picked the hat off her head and looked inside, sniffing loudly.

"Jennie!" Lea said, standing up abruptly. Lea had that peculiar ability to freeze you with a certain tone of voice.

But it was too late. Jennie reached inside the hat, and with one swift movement tore out the silk lining, tossed it like a piece of garbage into the Reverend's lap, and clapped the hat back on her head.

"Whoops!" said the Reverend. "Oh my!"

"Jennie! *No!*" I cried, and lunged at the chimp while making a grab at the hat. But the ape was too fast for me, and she retreated under the chaise lounge.

To our great surprise the Reverend laughed, his face turning bright red. "Oh dear," he said. "Oh my. Oh my dear." The tears streamed down his face.

"I'm *so* sorry," Lea said. "I don't know *what's* gotten into her. We'll get you a new hat."

The *he he he he!* of chimpanzee laughter issued from under the chaise. I got down on my hands and knees and could see her in the corner, sucking her toe with the hat on her head.

"Jennie! Bad, bad girl!" I said. "Come!"

"It's quite all right," stammered the Reverend, recovering his composure. "She's such a sweet animal. The hat is nothing."

I called Jennie again and she finally poked her head out, still wearing the hat, which now had a large dustball clinging to the crown. The crease had been knocked out, giving it the look of a hobo bowler. The only thing visible under the hat were her lips and whiskered chin.

"Jennie!" I yelled again, and the chimp ducked under the chaise.

"It suits her quite well," said the Reverend.

Lea was busy convincing the Reverend that Jennie's behavior was out of the ordinary, not her usual shenanagins. "Isn't it terrible!" she said. "I just can't understand what's gotten *into* her. She's *never* acted like this before."

I saw no alternative but to sacrifice my dignity and crawl under the chaise myself to retrieve the chimp and the hat. I grabbed Jennie by the foot and dragged her out. Her piercing screams filled the room, sounding for all the world as if she were being stretched on the rack.

"The poor thing," said the Reverend. "She's frightened."

"With good reason," I said, seizing the hat from her head and dragging her toward the bathroom. I locked her in. Her pounding and muffled screams gave the house the air of a nineteenth-century insane asylum.

When I returned, I found Lea still apologizing while the Reverend turned his hat over in his hands. Jennie's five minutes with the hat had completely destroyed it.

"The poor thing," said the Reverend, almost to himself, and then it all came out in a stammered jumble. "My wife is afraid of animals. She isn't too keen on the idea of having a monkey in the neighborhood."

There was a silence. What he had been sent over to say had just been said.

"I, myself, have always liked animals," he added wistfully.

"I just can't understand Jennie's behavior—" Lea began again, not very convincingly.

"I'm sure," I said, "that as Jennie gets a little older she'll settle down."

As if on cue the screaming redoubled and the Reverend winced. "I hate for her to be in there on my account."

We talked some more, rapid exchanges of small talk spoken during lulls in the storm. Then, from upstairs, the sleeping baby woke and also began to howl. Lea went up to get her while I released Jennie from her imprisonment.

As soon as the door opened her cries ceased, and she looked up at me with the most pathetically sad and frightened little face. She waddled over and opened her arms to be hugged, looking contrite. I carried her back into the living room.

Palliser sat on the sofa, looking rather at a loss, his hands folded on the table. Jennie climbed down and laid her hand on his and made a low, mournful hoot. Lea came down with the baby.

"Oh," said the Reverend to Jennie. "You're sorry. You want to say you're sorry."

Jennie hopped up on the sofa and opened her arms for a hug. Palliser picked her up and hugged her, her furry head briefly nestling against his bald pate.

"What a darling," the Reverend said, a little breathlessly. "I do think she likes me. Yes, indeed, I do."

Jennie sat in his lap, playing with one of his buttons.

"Aren't you a nice girl," he said again, patting her back. "Here, a welcome-to-America present for you," and he gave her back the hat. Jennie snatched it and clapped it on her head. Then she gave a big hoot and jumped to the floor and began strutting around.

"You don't have to do that," I said to Palliser.

"Oh, but I *want* to. She's very cute in a hat. Every monkey needs a hat, right, Jennie?" He turned to us, beaming, as if he were the father himself.

Jennie spun around and came strutting back, clacking her teeth with happiness.

The Reverend finally rose to leave. "We won't say anything about this to Mrs. Palliser," he said, stammering slightly and turning red with embarrassment. "The hat was a gift from her. But I never really liked it; I'm not a hat person, you know. She feels I ought to be covering up my baldness. One doesn't, so she tells me, expose one's baldness these days. I'll say I lost it."

He scurried out the door.

"Oh no," said Lea, looking out the window, "there she is, on the stoop, waiting to hear the news."

I saw that the very thick Mrs. Palliser was indeed standing in the door, with a sour expression on her face.

"What an oddly pleasant fellow," said Lea. "Jennie seems to have won him over. He's not at all what I expected."

"I don't think there will be any winning over the wife," I said, watching her follow him into the house with a firm shutting of the door.

three

[FROM taped interviews with Dr. Harold Epstein, Curator Emeritus, Department of Anthropology, Boston Museum of Natural History, in his office at the museum in July 1991, November 1992, and January 1993.]

Do you know the expression "Words pay no debts?" There is, you see, nothing I can tell you that will change anything. Or pay any debts. We're here because almost everything that was written about this thing was a pack of lies. You're finally going to tell the truth.

The "Jennie period," as I like to call it, took place between 1965 and 1974. I was head of the department. Hugo was about twenty years my junior and was the Curator of Physical Anthropology. Hugo assumed the chairmanship when I retired in 1974. Until this Jennie business, he was one of the most capable and creative scientists the museum had the privilege to employ.

The museum? It hasn't changed its appearance in one hundred and forty years. It's like Churchill said, it was ugly yesterday, it's ugly today, and it'll wake up just as ugly tomorrow morning. I always thought it looked like a grim Crusader castle. When it rains, those rooftop gargoyles spout water. At dusk, bats drop down from the eaves and swoop about. They scare the secretaries. The museum park used to be surrounded by a great wrought-iron fence with spikes. They took it down when someone jumped off the roof and landed on it. They had to cut out a piece of fence, you see. The spikes had gone clear through the fellow's gut. It was one of those A.B.D.s finally giving up. A.B.D.? It means "All But Dissertation." The museum is full of them, graduate students who are incapable of finishing their dissertations. They stay on for years, living off grants, examining specimens, gathering data, wandering about the halls.

That statue out front is Thierry de Louliz, venerable founder of the museum. It is always covered with pigeon lime: pigeons love to defecate on his head. It is a perfectly absurd statue, the old man holding that fossil fish like Napoleon with his sword. He was much feared and hated during his lifetime, but I think he looks like a dotty old uncle, cutting a ridiculous figure among the sycamores. I have not, thank goodness, accomplished enough in my life to be awarded a postmortem statue. Louliz's great accomplishment was to dogmatically oppose Darwin's theory of natural selection to the bitter end. I mean, to the bitter end of *Louliz*. His last words were, "Zis Darwin, I tell you, iss a great fool." [Laughs.]

The building inside had a most peculiar smell. A combination of damp granite, cheap cleaning fluids, and old buckram. Plus a faint smell of mortification. Dead flesh. There were a lot of dead things in the museum. Some thirty million specimens. Two million in the osteological collection—that's bones—and another three million alcoholics. Alcoholics, my friend, is what we term animals preserved in jars of fluid. Millions of insects and spiders. Snakes, tortoises, frogs and salamanders, rocks and minerals, meteorites, you name it. Ten thousand human skeletons and several hundred mummies. Not Egyptian mummies, but Indians, Aleuts, Tierra del Fuegans, those sorts of people. The collection represents a history of graverobbing, murder, and mayhem stretching back one hundred and forty years. I am being facetious, of course. Don't print that.

I'm eighty-five years old, and I have gotten into the habit of saying whatever I damn well please.

To get to the old Anthropology Department, one had to walk through the African Hall, past an archway framed by a brace of elephant tusks, world record size. The elephant was bagged by some bloodthirsty trustee of the museum in the 1920s. Hugo Archibald was a physical anthropologist, a collector of dead specimens. I am a cultural anthropologist—I study the living. His research was on the phylogeny of the primates. He spent years in Africa, Asia, and South America, collecting specimens.

We are primates, you and I. Naked apes. His early work was brilliant. His idea, you see, was to look at human evolution from the phylogenetic viewpoint, rather than from the fossil record. He examined the morphology—the *shape*—of all the closest living relatives to man. Those would be the great apes: gorillas, chimpanzees, bonobos, orangutans, and so forth. He wanted to know: what are the relationships? Where does *Homo sapiens* fit in? In the end, Hugo put us in the same family as the great apes. He said we didn't merit a family all by ourselves. I'm not sure I would go that far, but it's an interesting thought. And an idea influenced, no doubt, by the existence of Jennie. In the end, you see, because of Jennie, he lost his objectivity.

To do the work, Archibald needed skulls. He measured them, and quantified the differences in their shape. From there, using a technique known as phylogenetic or cladistic analysis, he drew a family tree—a drawing of the relationships among the species. Which characteristics were primitive, and which derived? One has to look at many skulls from each species to smooth out the natural variations in shape. Uncle Albert, you see, might have a strange lump on his head that is unnatural. You can only know that by looking at several skulls. Hence, Hugo made many collecting trips after ever more rare animals. His legacy is a collection of physical anthropology that is second to none, a great scientific resource.

Hugo freed the study of human evolution from abject dependence on the fossil record.

I've no doubt I'm boring you. Perhaps at my age I'm no longer making any sense at all. I am a very foolish fond old man. By all means, edit what I say, make it sound comprehensible and even intelligent—if such a thing is possible. If your publisher works as fast as mine, I'll be dead by the time your book appears.

What was Hugo like? Physically, you mean? During the Jennie years he was a lean, bony man. His hair was black and unfashionably long. He had dark eye sockets in which lived two restless black eyes. My, that sounds good. Maybe I should be writing this book. He looked like a British schoolboy, with his hair flopping down over his forehead. He had shifty eyes, not out of guilt, but out of curiosity. His mind was always clicking away while his eyes darted about. His posture was bad; his mother never taught him to stand up straight. That's one advantage of a Jewish upbringing, you know, having good posture. My mother never would have let me get away with that slouch! Hugo's breathing was distinctly audible. We'd be examining a specimen and I could hear him wheezing next to me like a set of bagpipes. He was missing the very top part of his left ear. He used to say it was a machete cut, and he had a marvelous story to go with it, but in fact it was a small birth defect. He had inherited many fierce prejudices from his father—what an eccentric man *that* was!—but he was far too innocent to understand his prejudices, let alone understand himself. His prejudices included a dislike of businessmen, movie actresses, policemen, people who drove Cadillacs, people who voted for Goldwater, and the annual Botolphstown Cotillion. He would become excited, raving about one thing or another. And then in the next moment he'd have forgotten all about it. He licked his plate after eating. He picked his nose when he thought no one was looking. He had a bit of the exhibitionist about him. In a quiet way. He did what he pleased and the hell with 'em. I mean the rest of the world. What was it Voltaire said? "To the living we owe respect, but to the dead only truth." I honor Hugo's memory by telling the truth about him.

I have not, in my lifetime, had another friendship I valued as much as his. When I first met Hugo, he was thirty and very eager. And naive. He was going to do great things. He used to bemoan the fact that the Nobel Prize was not given in his field. And he did accomplish great things. By the time he was forty, he had done more than most scientists do in a lifetime. With Jennie and her celebrity, he was forced to grow up in a great hurry, and this was a terrible shock to him. It was a shock that something awful could happen to him. Most of us, as we launch into adult life, feel invulnerable, or at least puissant, but some of us are more ready for tragedy than others. Hugo was not at all ready. Or if he was ready, he was blindsided; he never thought it could come from the direction it did.

It changed him. It changed all of us; *she* changed all of us. But Hugo, in particular, was never the same. I will tell you what I think. After Jennie, his science was no damn good. You see . . . Excuse me, I believe I'm telling you the moral of the story before you've heard the story. I will only say this. He was like so many scientists: he thought he could separate object from subject. He ignored the human dimension of scientific work, the effect of the observer on the observed. And *vice versa*! You see, what we observe is not nature itself, but nature exposed to our questioning. And what we are, of course, is a response to what we observe. This is what tripped Hugo up.

To the story, then. We can moralize later.

Hugo returned from the Cameroons in the early fall of 1965. A few days later he brought Jennie to work with him. She caused a sensation. He got off the fifth-floor elevator and came down that hall, with that little black chimp riding on his neck. Everyone started coming out of their offices. Hugo's office was at the end of the hall, in the corner. It was smaller than most offices but had a splendid view. He had a hideous old Victorian wing chair, which Jennie promptly claimed as her throne. He plopped her down in that chair and she sat back like a princess receiving courtiers, her legs sticking straight out, her eyes half closed, extending to each visitor a languid hand. She was wearing only a diaper, a T-shirt, and a hat. That hat! It was absurd, and it sat like a crown on her head, nearly obscuring her eyes, propped only by her big ears. I remember shaking her hand while her eyes wandered about the room, looking over my head, at my feet—like a rude guest at a party.

Even at six months she was full of the devil. At one point she snatched a pair of glasses from some hapless secretary—one of those marvelous cat's-eye glasses decorated with rhinestones—and they had to be pried out of her hands while she screamed piteously. It was as if she were being deprived of her last possession in the world. The glasses arrived back to their owner in a sad condition. Poor Hugo was always paying for something that Jennie had broken.

Jennie was a terribly captivating animal. There is something fascinating in looking at a chimpanzee, seeing an echo of humanity in the thing. I stayed on after everyone had left. Hugo gave Jennie a *National Geographic* magazine while we lit our pipes; I my Dunhill with Balkan Sobranie; Hugo that drugstore pipe filled with rum-soaked Borkum Riff Ready-Rubbed. Ugh.

Jennie was so small, she had to drag the magazine by both hands across the floor. She hauled it to my chair and hauled it up, where she settled in my lap, turning the pages. She then made a grab for my pipe.

I raised it out of reach. I told her that she was too young to smoke.

She did not like to be crossed. She gave my tie a yank, and then pulled off one of my buttons. Hugo scolded her, but she paid no attention.

The chimpanzee went back to her *National Geographic*, and coming to an especially interesting and colorful page proceeded to tear it out. Hugo took away the magazine and there was a brief struggle for the page, while Jennie screamed again.

Hugo told me his wife, Lea, was adapting well. Now that is one fine woman, Lea. Very capable. Did you talk to her as I suggested? Quite an imposing figure, isn't she? She comes from an old Boston family. The Dickinsons. Emily was her great-aunt. And the first sexologist, before Masters and Johnson, was also a Dickinson. Very distinguished family. Of course, she is like all of those blue bloods, very diffident. You'll never get her to admit it. And, of course, the Dickinsons lost their money when the Boston and Albany defaulted on their bonds in '32.

There is one thing a good Brahmin upbringing gives to the women, and she had it: a voice that could freeze water. Only when she wanted to, of course. When she disapproved of something, and that tone of voice was directed at you, it was zero at the bone. [Laughs.] With that voice, she controlled Jennie better than anyone. Jennie respected her. Hugo, on the other hand, was a bit of a pushover.

They were an odd pair, Hugo and Lea. She was a good three inches taller than Hugo, but he slouched while she stood as straight as a queen. What a presence! And her hair. It was iron-gray when I first met her, some thirty years ago, and it turned snow-white after that. But she was very beautiful. In those days, it was almost scandalous to be thirty and have gray hair. She never wore much makeup, or ever dyed that hair, and still she was radiantly beautiful. She's still beautiful, but in a different way of course. They were an odd pair, but somehow just right.

Hugo asked me if he could bring Jennie to work from time to time. That was fine with me. I remarked that she was in a diaper and wondered how long that would last, but Hugo assured me they were working hard on her toilet training, and that already Jennie loved to flush the toilet. Now if they could only get her to go in it, he said.

I was very much interested to hear the story of her capture. As a cultural anthropologist, I naturally saw the significance of it before Hugo did. He was only a physical anthropologist, poor man. [Laughs].

I remember clearly that first conversation we had about Jennie. Let me see if I can recall it for you.

I said to Hugo something like. "So! You whelped the beast."

Yes he had. And he said it with a great deal of pride, as if he were the father himself.

I asked him if Jennie had any contact with her mother after the birth.

Hugo said she hadn't. The mother was paralyzed and dying. He didn't even think the chimp had noticed her mother, she was so busy clinging to Hugo and looking into his face.

I asked him if she had met any chimpanzees later.

Hugo thought about that for a minute. No, she hadn't.

So, I said, Jennie's never seen one of her own kind.

That's right, Hugo said.

So I asked Hugo if he had read any Konrad Lorenz.

I had finally aroused Hugo's suspicions. He wanted to know just what I was driving at.

I told him he should read Lorenz's work on the greylag geese.

This, of course, irritated Hugo, who certainly knew of Lorenz but had never gotten around to reading him. As I said, he was a *physical* anthropologist. Behavior did not interest him.

When Hugo was irritated, he became very dignified and formal. He said he would "look into it," but I don't know if he did. Until much later, of course.

I, of course, recognized immediately the significance of Jennie's birth and early upbringing. Konrad Lorenz, as any educated person knows, had discovered that a newborn greylag goose is imprinted with the first thing it sees moving. It will then follow that thing around thinking it is its mother. Normally, it is the mother. But Lorenz was able to show that anything would imprint the gosling—a football, for instance, or a vacuum cleaner. Lorenz himself offered his head for imprinting, and dozens of geese grew up following Lorenz's magnificent bushy white head around in a Bavarian lake, believing it was their dear lovely mother. The idea occurred to me right away that Jennie had been, in a more sophisticated way, imprinted by Hugo. Not only did Jennie believe she was human, but she had probably been imprinted to believe that Hugo was her mother.

I explained all this to Hugo. Might that, I suggested, be cause for concern? The idea seemed to irritate him further. He said he thought anyone who tried to extrapolate the behavior of a goose to a chimpanzee was an idiot. He was quite defensive about this chimpanzee and why he had brought it back.

"Harold," he told me, "this is purely an informal little experiment in primate behavior. An *experiment*. Let's not get all worried about this thing. She's like a pet, only I'm curious to see what will happen to a chimpanzee that is raised like a human child. That's all. An informal, anecdotal experiment. I can't see any harm in that, can you?"

I pointed out that in no way could this be called an experiment. What were the objectives? Where was the control? What was the hypothesis? And I said he was naive to think there might not be any harm in it. This was not like raising a puppy. But all he did was start shaking his head and smiling. "Harold, Harold, Harold," he said. "Okay, Harold, you win. You're right. It's not an experiment. It's just for laughs. Strictly for laughs."

Ah, but you see— Now who was it that said: "The joker loses everything when he laughs at his own joke"? Hmmmm. Well, it isn't important. Schiller, maybe.

At any rate, what even *I* did not realize at the time, although it is painfully clear to me now, is that imprinting can sometimes work both ways.

[FROM *Recollecting a Life* by Hugo Archibald.]

In his old age, my father, Henry S. Archibald, became interested in death. As he was an avowed atheist, this interest took a rather peculiar form. Instead of worrying about the ultimate disposition of his soul, he became obsessed with the family burial grounds. He had a brush with death when I was away at college—a minor bout with phlebitis—and by the time I returned for the summer his new interest had blossomed. He insisted on involving me. My father's family was originally from Newburyport, Massachusetts, and we made many trips to obscure and overgrown cemeteries there.

There were six graveyards in Newburyport and four of them contained the precious remains of an Archibald. There was a graveyard on Plum Island that had two Archibald graves. During the last years of my father's life I came to know all these graves and more.

My father took it upon himself to tend these graves. He waded in among the wild tea roses wielding a fearsome brush hook, carving a swath around each of the Archibald headstones. He scrubbed off the lichen, weeded and trimmed the grass, and laid down fresh flowers. I found the concept as strange as Japanese ancestor worship. But I was young then, and I found my father's excessive concern with death amusing.

My father had become increasingly cranky in his old age, and accompanying him on these trips was the only way I found to maintain a relationship with him. He complained frequently. "Your brother," he would say, "has no interest in the family graves. I'm glad that at least one of my sons has taken an interest in the family history. Tending the Archibald graves is hard work, and when I'm gone it's going to take quite a bit of your time. I hope you realize how much of a responsibility you have taken on."

I did not recollect taking on any responsibility, and I certainly had no intention of carrying on my father's work after he was gone. I did not, however, have the heart to set him straight.

During World War I, my father was an engineer first class aboard a ship in the U.S. Navy. During that time he had a small idea relating to an improvement in the science of refrigeration. He married my mother, who at the time was a sixteen-year-old girl from Cincinnati, and moved to Waltham, Massachusetts, where he developed and patented his idea. He licensed the invention to General Electric and made a small fortune.

My father then spent the rest of his life tinkering and practicing a kind of genial crankiness. The grounds around our house looked like a junk heap. There was a windmill connected to an electric generator that lit a bulb inside a turning fresnel lens acquired from the old Shadd's Rock Lighthouse. In short, it was a wind-powered lighthouse. No one was interested. Then there was the experimental air-cooling machine that my father built in the twenties. It weighed eight hundred pounds and sat in the corner of the barn like a square bull. It thumped and shuddered and issued a massive blast of chill air for three or four minutes before it blew the fuses. Whenever some naive visitor to our house introduced the subject of air-conditioning (and you would be surprised how often that subject comes up in normal conversation), my father would stamp off to the barn to prove that he, Henry S. Archibald, was the actual inventor of the air conditioner. My poor mother would cry out, "Henry, the fuse box," and he would answer in heroic cadence: "Damn the fuse box!"

As a boy, I never developed an interest in machines or tinkering. I was captivated by the far more complicated workings of animals. I loved bones, their shapes, the way they fit together, the puzzle of assembling them. I loved the play of sunlight through the hollows of a skull and across the parietals, giving the skull the mysterious glow of a Greek temple. I loved the curve of the orbit and the delicacy of the zygomatic process. It was a wonder to me that such structures could exist, formed in secret under the covering of flesh, exposed in their beauty only by death.

At that time, woods and pastures surrounded our house outside Boston, and I often collected dead animals and skeletons and brought them home in a wheelbarrow. The larger animals, such as cows and horses, I laid out on the roof of an old shed near our house, where they would be beyond the reach of dogs, but where the crows could peck off any remaining meat. The smaller animals I buried for a month or two. My parents, to their credit, allowed me the full indulgence of my hobby, although my mother often worried about germs and fire from the kerosene I used to degrease the bones.

My most exciting discovery of those years was finding a dead bull moose near the Sudbury swamp. I found him by tracking the smell for over a mile through the woods. He lay peacefully on a bed of sphagnum moss, a massive animal with a magnificent rack. He had expired recently and was in no condition to be transported, but I went back again and again, collecting the odd leg or antler as the dogs tore apart the carcass. Sometimes bones would be dragged hundreds of yards into the woods, and I had to search the under-brush for hours. In three months I had everything but the rib cage and pelvis, which needed more time, and those I was able to rescue in the spring, just as the snow was melting.

When the bones of one of my animals had been stripped of flesh and skin, I set to work. I boiled them in a kettle behind the barn, carved off the cartilage, soaked them in a tub of kerosene, and then washed that out with soap and water, bleached them, and laid them back on the shed roof for a final sunning. When the bones were a pure lovely white, and light as seasoned pine, I mounted the skele-ton. It was a tedious process of drilling, screwing, gluing, wiring, and hanging. The end result was never, to my great disappoint-ment, as elegant as the mounted skeletons in the Boston Museum of Natural History. Nor did my larger skeletons stay standing very long. The mounted moose lasted until I tried to set an antler in the pedicle. That was the proverbial straw, and the whole thing came tumbling down with a noise that sent my poor mother out into the yard in a panic, thinking I had fallen off the roof. It was a bitter blow and I never had the heart to rebuild it.

My father was a staunch atheist. In New England at the time, atheism was tolerated as an eccentricity, not like Unitarianism, which was much worse. He said he had been converted to atheism at the age of six, when his Sunday school teacher had described with relish the eternal fires of Hell. He trotted out his atheism with great pride, while everybody rolled their eyes. I always believed (at least until the end) it was a case of the lady protesting too much. "Mary and Joseph," he said, "turned a very embarrassing situation into one of the greatest coups in history. Clever, clever, clever!" And he wagged his fat finger back and forth in everyone's deliciously scandalized faces.

My mother took us to church every Sunday. This was fine with my father. He used to say: "Your grandmother sent me to church every day, and it did me no harm. It was in church that I was converted to atheism. Also, it's a wise hedge. I myself might take it up on my deathbed, just in case."

I once asked my mother, "Aren't you worried that Dad's going to go to Hell?"

"God doesn't send good people to Hell," she said with absolute serenity of conviction. She had a deep faith in the goodness of people, and by extension the absolute goodness of God. In my mother's cosmogony, if there were a Hell, it would be an empty place indeed.

I always believed my father would take up religion on his deathbed, if he were given the time. He died in St. Clare's Hospital in 1958, of congestive heart failure. St. Clare's is across the street from the Boston Museum of Natural History (I can see its facade from my window as I write), and when I got the call from my mother I was the only one of his children there. He was lying in a private room in the intensive care unit, tubes coming out from the most unlikely places, his face gray and his bulky body and fleshy face melting heavily into the bed. The wild, Einsteinian tuft of hair that usually stood out from his forehead was laid low, soaked with sweat. There was a look of panic in his eyes. When I came in he raised his hand and gestured for me to come over; he clearly had something he wished to say. This is it, I thought. He's going to send for the minister or the priest or (it was not inconceivable) the rabbi. I leaned over and he gripped my forearm with fingers of steel, his strength shocking.

"Listen!" he said, so loudly the nurse started and admonished him not to excite himself.

"Listen to me!" he hissed. "You've got to promise me something. I don't entirely trust your mother in this. You know she believes in *God*. She doesn't understand."

"Yes, yes, of course, anything," I said. "Anything you want." I was suddenly puzzled. This was not how I imagined the conversation to unfold. His voice resonated in the tubes coming out of his nose, making him sound like Donald Duck. It was not a dignified scene.

"No matter how bad it gets, no matter how sick I am . . ."

And he paused to catch his breath.

". . . no matter if I become a complete drooling vegetable, no matter if my EEG is flat as a pancake . . ."

Wheeze.

"Yes?" I said.

"Even if there is no hope at all, none whatsoever . . ."

Wheeze.

"Yes?"

Another wheeze.

"Don't you, don't you . . ."

Wheeze.

". . . let them pull . . ."

Wheeze.

". . . the plug." And his grip relaxed and he sank back, with a look of peace finally on his face. "Promise?" he croaked.

"I promise," I said. Mother, who had been hanging on to every word over my shoulder, was irritated.

"Henry, how many times do I, and the doctors and nurses, and now Hugo, have to make these promises? No one's going to pull any plug, for heaven's sake. I wish you'd find something else to worry about. I wish you'd just concentrate on getting better."

"I'm concentrating," he protested. "It isn't working."

And then he died.

My mother wept, mostly out of hurt and frustration. The old crank, in her mind, had wasted his dying breath without ever saying how much he loved us. Nor did he leave us with a touching farewell speech. But to me he had said as much in his own peculiar way, and shown his love just as fiercely, by demonstrating how afraid he was of leaving us. In fact, I never realized how much he loved us until his deathbed scene.

My father died just after I had graduated from Columbia University and had joined the curatorial staff at the Boston Museum of Natural History. His atheism gave me the freedom to reject Christianity without struggle or pain. It was at this time, dealing with my father's death, that I had a conversion of sorts myself: I realized that evolution was, in fact, my religion.

This may, perhaps, sound eccentric. Let me explain. There can be no doubt: life is a miraculous thing, and even more miraculous is human intelligence. Our world, this earth, is a surpassingly beautiful place, perfectly suited to our needs. It is *as if* the world were created for us, so perfect is it. But this is an illusion; in fact, *we* were created for the world. The world is just right for us because we've been adapting to it for millions of years.

Love, sex, family, the pleasures of food, intellectual delight, friendship, appreciation of beauty, the pleasure of exercise and good health, the excitement of sport and adventure—all these qualities were given to us, not by God, but by evolution.

There is a catch, however. Evolution extracts a price. What is the price? Sickness, old age, and death; tragedy, hunger, sorrow, pain, and suffering—all these must exist in order for evolution to operate. Without death there can be no evolution. Without sickness, pain, and tragedy there can be no adaptation and natural selection. All living things must pay dearly for the miracle of their existence. We human beings must pay the highest price of all, because evolution has given us a brain capable of understanding death. And death lies across all our lives like some hideous, vulgar joke.

Does this qualify as a religion? I believe so. It gives us rules to live by. It highlights the importance of the family, of protecting and nurturing our children, of passing along our values to future generations. It gives us license to fully enjoy the blessings of evolution—sex, love, food, family closeness, pleasure—without guilt. It encourages us to develop evolution's greatest gift to us: our intellects. It instructs us to appreciate this life as fully as possible, because we will never have another.

This, then, is my religion.

[FROM the unpublished journals of the Reverend Hendricks Palliser, former rector, Kibbencook Episcopal Church. Courtesy of Elspeth Palliser Wallace, New London, Connecticut.]

September 30, 1965

It was a splendid, blustery autumn day, the clouds racing across the sky, the shadows running through the houses of the street. The birch is now crowned in yellow, and every gust of wind carried its leaves past my study window and into the wood. It was a day of mystery and vigor.

I have not had occasion in here to mention the professor across the street. He has recently returned from Africa with a monkey. This morning, R. asked me to call upon the professor. R. is upset at the noise and possible spread of "jungle diseases," and she charged me with discovering how long it will be before the professor takes the monkey to his museum or the zoo.

Accordingly, I ventured across the street and rang the bell. During the course of the visit the monkey—it is a chimpanzee named Jennie—relieved me of my hat. Much confusion, hilarity, and high jinks. The monkey, as I understood it, is to stay indefinitely. I returned hatless. R. was much put out. I pray God bring her peace.

I must confess a peculiar thought. I had never had occasion to observe a monkey closely before. It is an extraordinary animal. As I was watching it romping about, I was struck by how *human* it was, how so like a child in its actions and understanding. I wondered if the animal might possess a kind of soul. It is a curious fact that the Bible, despite the asseverations of some, is more or less silent on the question. This Jennie, as they call it, was so absolutely like a human child in every way except speech that it was quite perplexing. I have turned to the Bible—as one seeking guidance— and perused various passages, without enlightenment. I do not know why the idea had not occurred to me before. Man, to be sure, occupies the paramount position in Creation and was given dominion over the beasts of the field. But what position do the beasts occupy? Were they created solely to serve Mankind? Or do they serve God in some other capacity independent of man? Does the animal consciousness, like the human, survive the death of the body? Are there animals in Heaven? And at this juncture I realized that animals surely *would* be in Heaven, otherwise Heaven would not be Heaven. What happens, for example, to the faithful dog whose master loves him? Does the animal rejoin him in Heaven? The idea had never entered my mind before, but the answer appeared obvious; would God deny a kindly aged pensioner the beloved companion of his last years? Of course not.

Naturally, the next line of logic is the question of whether animals are judged, to be saved or damned. I should think not; a creature which is incapable of understanding the grace of Jesus Christ cannot be damned for it. It would be a cruel God indeed to judge a beast who had not the ability to know the love of Christ. Therefore, the logic seems impeccable: at least the higher animals have souls, and they are inevitably saved. Only man, who has the capacity for good and evil, can be damned. A peculiar line of reasoning, and somewhat unsettling. And yet inescapable.

I do not, as the Baptists and even some of my fellow Episcopalians do, subscribe to the idea of literal creation. It is (to me) as miraculous that God created the Universe and Mankind in five billion years through the process of evolution as it is to believe that He created the world in seven days by divine fiat. Indeed, it is far more miraculous to contemplate the infinite patience, wisdom, and vision of God over such an immensity of time, and to comprehend with rigorous scientific equations the beautiful starry vastness of His mighty works. Was the chimpanzee, thus, a way station on the road to Mankind? Of course. At what point in evolution did man acquire the knowledge of good and evil, and thus the capacity to be damned? In this light, the story of Adam and Eve takes on deeper significance. It is a parable of evolution.

But, as I write, another thought occurs to me. Is Jennie capable of knowing the Lamb of Christ, in a simple way, through feeling rather than intellect, as I have often seen a child do? She appears capable of understanding a great deal.

These are profound questions indeed. Prayer and meditation will bring the answers in due course. And then there is the situation vis à vis R. and the chimp. She has been talking about the leash laws and getting the neighborhood together to "nip this thing in the bud," etc., etc. To put that dear Jennie on a leash would be criminal. I pray for R. I shall have to talk to the professor.

As I write this, I feel that God, in His unknowable wisdom, has opened a door into a darkened corridor. I do not know why, nor where this corridor will lead. I shall watch, and learn, and pray, and sooner or later this crooked winding hall will lead to a room with light and a view—and then I will know.

Roast beef for dinner.

four

[FROM an interview with Lea Archibald.]

Well! It didn't take long before Jennie and Sandy were as thick as thieves. Sandy bossed Jennie around, made her wait on him hand and foot. She trotted after him, just worshiping the ground he walked on. Sometimes she rode on his shoulders, gripping his ears. She looked so goofy up there, peering around! When Sandy went off to school, Jennie got upset. She climbed up to her tree house to watch him go off down the brook path with his books. She looked so miserable, rocking back and forth and hugging herself. During the day, she would keep climbing back up there to see if he was coming home. When he did show up, she gave a scream and went racing down the tree and just threw herself at him. When she got bigger she sometimes even knocked him down in her excitement. Her face was wonderfully expressive, and you could read it just like a human face.

Jennie was so affectionate and so loving. Of all her qualities, this was her most outstanding. She was always underfoot, begging for hugs or kisses—or to be tickled. That chimp lived for a tickle! Goodness! It was more important to her than food—and that's saying a lot. She needed affection more than any human child I've known.

And she just adored Hugo. Hugo was so gentle and kind . . . [long pause]. Excuse me. When he came home from work, she hugged him and kissed him, laughing and squealing the whole time, and making this "hooooo ooooo" sound. She would hear his car in the driveway, and she would pound and stamp on the floor, or whirl around and around! My goodness, the things she knocked over! She broke every vase in the house, my grandmother's Sung porcelain, Uncle Nat's ivories. And she once tried to eat the Olmec jade head and then broke it in a fury when it didn't taste as she hoped. Oh my goodness! She was always whirling! It was exhausting to have her around sometimes. She'd follow me around all day long, whimpering for a tickle or a hug.

Sandy never had a younger sibling to order around. Sarah was too young. And even when she got older, *nobody* was going to tell her what to do! So Sandy thrived when Jennie came. He became much more self-assured and confident. They played every afternoon in the backyard. I could see them out the kitchen window. Oh! I used to watch them for hours! It was endlessly entertaining. Sandy had her playing this game he called "Space Invaders." Jennie was the alien. Oh my goodness. Of course, Jennie was thoroughly confused, but she always muddled through. I'll never forget watching them play that game. I wished Hugo had that movie camera during those days. Have you seen his movies of Jennie? Well, you must. You simply must.

Space Invaders? It was something Sandy made up. Jennie was the alien invader from Alpha Centauri, and Sandy was the astronaut who saved the earth. Sandy had this "Lost in Space" ray gun that he got from some cereal package. He'd make Jennie stay out of the lawn, while he crept into bushes. She'd be standing there, looking so confused. Sometimes she'd try to follow him into the bushes. He was so impatient. He'd start lecturing her, "No, no! You stay there! Wait for me to come out!" And Jennie would stand there, a forlorn expression on her face! She hated to be scolded.

Then Sandy would come bursting out of the arborvitae, firing his gun. Yelling, "Die alien!" [Laughs.] Jennie didn't usually die when she was supposed to. She just hopped up and down, squealing and trying to grab his gun. They'd get in a terrific tug-of-war sometimes over that gun. Sometimes it was too much for Sandy. Jennie wasn't playing by the rules! Well, she never played by the rules, in anything she did.

So Sandy had to demonstrate how to die. Oh my goodness. He'd clutch his chest and keel over with a terrible scream and begin writhing on the grass. It always frightened Jennie so! He'd give out this awful, bloodcurdling scream, and he'd twitch and lie still.

Poor Jennie. She'd squat next to him, poking him and backing off. Then she'd make that horrible grimace of fear and creep under the bushes. When she was frightened, she made a horrid face. It was really *quite* grotesque, all her teeth and pink gums exposed in a diabolical grin. I could hear her miserable whimpers from under the bushes. Her little heart was breaking, the poor thing, thinking Sandy had died!

And then Sandy would jump up. He'd cry out, "Ha! fooled you!" and Jennie would hug him, try to kiss him. She was so sweet, so caring. Always so concerned.

Oh my goodness. I hope I'm not giving you the wrong impression about Sandy. I remember thinking at the time, doesn't he know he's talking to an ape? It seemed quite ridiculous. But right from the beginning, Sandy talked to Jennie like she was a little sister—or rather a little brother. In a funny way Jennie seemed to understand.

I was so surprised one afternoon, the afternoon Jennie figured out how to die. Sandy came rushing out of the bushes firing that silly gun . . . Jennie did a somersault, convulsed on the ground for a moment, gave a screech and lay still. Well! She could never lie still for long, but she could lie dead for a few seconds. And then she'd be up again. She'd leap on his back, while he shouted "Die alien!" or some such thing, spinning around and shooting his gun, while Jennie clung to his back and screamed herself. Or he'd cry out, "Help, men, it's got me! I'm being eaten!"

Oh, I just wish I could have filmed them playing! It was the funniest thing you've ever seen. They raced around, Jennie like a black bullet shooting out of the arborvitae and through the hedge. With Sandy in hot pursuit. Every afternoon they played that game.

Sandy was not the most popular boy in school. He was very smart, you know, but immature for his age. So he didn't have many friends. But when the neighborhood children realized he had a chimpanzee in his backyard! Well! He became the most popular boy overnight.

It happened only three days after Jennie arrived. Sandy came traipsing down the brook path with a big crowd of kids. It must have been half the children in his class! When Jennie saw them coming from her tree house, she could hardly contain her excitement. And nervousness. At that age she was very shy. She squeaked and hid in the bushes when they came through the gap in the back hedge.

Sandy started calling out for her. Calling up to the tree house, calling around. But no Jennie. And those kids started to laugh. One of them said, "Get out of here, there's no *monkey*!"

Now Sandy was very particular about that. Just like Hugo. Jennie was an *ape*, not a monkey. Monkeys were inferior! [Laughs]. So an argument started. I was about to go out there and send those awful children home when I saw Jennie creeping along the bushes next to the house. She was carrying that ratty old hat in her hand. It was quite disgusting. That summer she lost it in the woods, thank goodness.

Well! Sandy started calling for Jennie again, but those awful children started to tease him. "Monkey, monkey! Here monkey!"

they kept saying. Poor Sandy. I could hear the panic creeping into his voice. If Jennie didn't come out soon, he would never hear the end of it. But I could see Jennie getting ready to make her move.

Oh my goodness! Jennie burst out of the bushes with a screech as shrill as a buzz saw! Nobody, not even a circus freak, could make a sound that penetrating. Her hair was all puffed out, and that pink mouth of hers was wide open. And she charged right at them, flailing that horrid hat about.

Heavens! You should have seen it. They were terrified! They all turned tail and went crashing through our poor abused hedge. It was all they could do to get away from that horrible pink mouth and that awful sound. Some hysterical girl was shouting about being bitten. And for a moment I almost hoped Jennie would bite her. Most of those children were dreadfully spoiled, and their parents were awful. No wonder they dropped out and took drugs and burned the flag. Children can be so cruel, you know.

Most of the boys came right back. And then! There was utter pandemonium! They raced around the yard, Jennie screeching, the kids hollering. I'm surprised old Mrs. Wardell didn't call the police.

The kids came back the next day with a big red wagon. They hauled Jennie around the neighborhood. If Kibbencook didn't already know a chimp was in residence, they knew it then. She stood in the wagon, gripping the sides, swaying back and forth with that ridiculous hat on her head. For some reason she reminded me of that silly painting of George Washington crossing the Delaware. And the noise she made! They went up Benvenue Street and down Dover and all around. I could follow their progress through the neighborhood by Jennie's hoots and shrieks. How her voice carried. Hugo used to say that she had a loud voice because chimps needed to communicate in the jungle. I believe it. If you could hear her ten feet, you could hear her a mile.

Another time the kids came around on bikes. Well! Jennie was so excited to ride a bike. She hopped up and down and tried to wrestle a bike away from a boy. And then some fool hoisted her up on one and, of course, it toppled over. There was Jennie at the door, screaming and pounding. She had skinned her poor little knee! When I opened it she came rushing into my arms—just like a hurt child, looking for comfort. I washed it and put a Band-Aid on it. She immediately picked the Band-Aid off, like she always did, peering underneath with fascination. I don't know what she expected to find, but we never could keep a Band-Aid on that chimp.

When I told Hugo about the bike, that was when he got the idea of getting Jennie a tricycle.

The tricycle! Oh dear . . . Of all the memories I have, none stands out more than that hairy little thing riding around on her tricycle. I still have it, after all these years. I'm not a sentimental person, but I didn't have the heart to throw it out. It's in the barn in Maine. We have a summer place up there, you know. Not long ago I came across that trike, all rusted and useless. The bright red paint was all gone. It was so sad, so . . . so forlorn, that I burst into tears! Can you imagine?

Hugo had the idea of buying Jennie the trike. He wanted to do it right. Buying a tricycle, he said, is a great moment in a kid's life. He was so proud. Just like a father. Poor Hugo, he was terribly attached to Jennie. He never got over her, you know. So one glorious fall weekend, the kind when the air practically *sings*, we all went down to Kibbencook Cycle. As long as I live, I'll never forget that day.

It was the only bike shop in town and it was down there by the railroad bridge. Of course it's long gone. Now it's one of those dreadful pasta shops, selling the homemade spaghetti at ten dollars the pound. The dry cleaners next door is now a gourmet cookie shop, and the old Kibbencook Dry Goods across the bridge is some kind of fancy housewares store selling those two-hundred-dollar coffee machines. Can you imagine? Oh! But it isn't called coffee anymore, it's called espresso. Lord save us.

Kibbencook Cycle had two huge plate glass windows in the front, with the name in gold paint. Behind the windows sat a row of the most marvelous bicycles you ever saw, with fat tires and swept-back chrome trim. Powder blue bikes for the girls, candy apple red for the boys. They made bikes back then like they made Cadillac cars, big and shiny and goofy.

Anyway, the shop was run by old Sam Hoyt and his son. Old Hoyt! He was dry and silent, with a face as smooth as Buddha. That man never said a word. When you asked for something, he'd shuffle off and go get it. Not a word. I'll tell you, he could sure ring up a cash register fast enough. And try to get a refund out of the old skinflint! His wife ran away with the Fuller Brush man.

The Hoyt son was fat and he never stopped talking, and he always tripped over the bikes or the hockey sticks. I can't remember his first name. He enlisted to go to Vietnam and his father was so proud, and then he was blown to bits in some kind of booby trap, helping himself to souvenirs at some Vietnamese village. We felt so sorry for poor Mr. Hoyt. But he never said a word, just sold the shop and disappeared. We all wondered where he went.

Sandy went in first, dragging Jennie by the hand. Without even giving the Hoyts time to think, he announced: "We've come to buy a tricycle for my little sister Jennie!" and he shoved Jennie forward. My goodness! The sister business was, to say the least, a surprise. We asked him later why he said that. He said he thought it would sound *really dumb* if he said we were buying a trike for our pet chimpanzee. And anyway, she could easily be a sister; she didn't look all that different. We had started dressing Jennie in shorts and a little T-shirt. I have to admit, she was starting to look just like a little person. It took an effort to think of her as an animal. It really did.

Sandy was so proud. He had trained Jennie to shake hands, and so she shook everyone's hand. Old Sam Hoyt, he stood there without the slightest change of expression. He just shook Jennie's hand like it was the most normal thing in the world. After all, a sale is a sale.

Hugo and I didn't say a word. This was Sandy's show.

Young Hoyt, the fat one, stood there thunderstruck. He couldn't believe it. "What, your sistah?" he blurted out, spraying saliva all over the place. Hoyt and his son both had these appalling North Shore accents. Danvers, I think.

Sandy came right back at him. "Yeah," he said. "My *sister*. What of it?"

I'm sorry, it was just so funny. [She wipes her eyes.] Sandy was so . . . so *creative* in his approach to life. His sister! Oh dear . . .

Anyway, young Hoyt said "Oooh" as if everything had suddenly been made clear.

So Sandy told him in no uncertain terms that his sister wanted a tricycle. Poor Hoyt was so nervous. He led us over to a row of trikes, all the while trying not to look at Jennie. He must have thought her terribly deformed. Sandy told him that Jennie wanted a red bike, not a blue one. Hoyt rolled one forward with his finger. And then Jennie gave a hoot. Really, it was a perfect chimpanzee hoot. Young Hoyt jerked as if he'd been slapped. His nervous eyes were darting everywhere but at Jennie. And then he finally looked at her and said:

"Get outta here! That ain't no kid!"

[Laughs.] Oh my goodness! There was a shocked silence. Sandy turned on Hoyt with all the dignity he could muster, and said to him: "Shut your big mouth, fatso! She is too!"

Dear oh dear . . . Hoyt started apologizing all over the place. I don't know what the poor boy thought Jennie was after that. Sam Hoyt just watched from behind the cash register, ready to ring up the sale as if nothing out of the ordinary were going on.

So we rolled out the red tricycle for Jennie to try out, and Sandy picked her up and put her on the seat.

You must remember that Jennie's last experience on a bicycle had not exactly been pleasant. That chimp had a memory like a steel trap. She opened that pink mouth and let fly a shriek that fairly blew out the plate glass windows in the front of the shop. Poor Hoyt, he was just sweating with nervousness. Sandy lowered Jennie to the floor and she shut up. Thank goodness. Then she bent over and examined her knee. It was so touching; you see, she was worried she might have skinned her knee again!

Sandy got on the tricycle and pedaled around the shop, saying, "Look, Jennie, isn't this fun?" And Jennie started her usual hop of excitement and stretched her arms toward the trike. She wanted to do everything that Sandy did. Sandy gave it to her and she climbed aboard. There was a tense moment of silence. Young Hoyt was looking on, his eyes popping. You see, Jennie had opposable thumbs on her feet like all chimpanzees. Her feet were really hands. What do you call that? *Prehensile;* she had prehensile feet. So instead of placing her feet on the pedals, she actually grabbed them with her feet. She gave a push with one leg and the trike inched forward. Then she gave a big push and the trike moved a few feet.

Well! When she felt herself moving, did she get excited!

She stood up in the seat and gave a big hoot of triumph. And then she began pedaling furiously. She was much more dextrous with her feet than a human child. The trike shot forward and went careening around the shop. She knew how to pedal, but she didn't know how to steer. Sandy tried to grab the bars as she went by. Oh dear! She went straight into a row of bikes and they all came crashing down. Hugo whipped out his wallet and said we'd buy it right away, before any more damage was done.

But Jennie wanted to ride again. She grabbed the handlebars and began trying to pull the trike away from Sandy. A tug-of-war began. And Jennie began screeching with frustration. The noises she made when she was upset! Sandy wouldn't let her have it, and I started to yell at Jennie too. But of course nothing worked. She hung on to that trike with every ounce of her energy. Jennie never listened to me; I was just her mother. Hugo was the only one she would obey, and even then not always.

We tried to pry Jennie away, but she just gripped harder. When that chimp held on to something, she had four hands to do it with, and you couldn't get anything away from her. And her grip! So

Hugo, he just scooped her and the trike up together, carried them out to the station wagon, and shoved them both in the back. It was just one big tangle of shiny chrome and hairy limbs.

When we got home, Hugo pulled her out, still clinging to the trike, and put them on the lawn. We all backed off to watch. When Jennie saw that we were far enough away she untangled herself and got back on it. It wouldn't go on the lawn. So she gave it a few good whacks and when that didn't work, oh, did she get mad then! When Jennie had a tantrum, she would work up a screaming that was quite magnificent to hear, until she lost her breath and began to choke and gasp in her fury. At first I was positively frightened by her tantrums, but after a few of them I could only laugh. She was like the boy who held his breath until he turned blue. Chimps are just as silly and absurd as human beings. Thank goodness we're not the only ridiculous species in the world!

Well, she finally got it working on the driveway, and Sandy showed her how to steer. And then Sandy got out his bike, and the two of them went riding off into the sunset.

Anyway, that was how Jennie acquired her famous trike.

[FROM the journal of the Rev. Hendricks Palliser.]

October 25, 1965

A chill wind out of the northeast removed the last leaves from the birch. I watched the last one flutter and carouse in the gray morning light, and it filled me with thoughts of God. The clouds thickened at midday, a dreary rain began to fall, and the fog of the season closed over the brook. The garden in the back, with its vacant beds, the cherry tree blackened by rain and stripped of its leaves, the damp turf matted and brown, all reminded me of the great system of life and death. I opened the study window and breathed in the damp air. It smelled cold, but pregnant with dormant life, and it was a wonderful smell—truly a gift from God. And it also reminded me, in a peculiar way, of those still mornings in Belgium, before dawn, when the mist rose from the fields, so beautiful, just before the sounding of the artillery.

I thought that we are like the last leaf of autumn, the matted grass, the sleeping tree—all part of some great invisible plan, a plan as incomprehensible to us as the cycle of seasons is to the fallen autumn leaf. Perhaps, as the cells of the leaf freeze and turn glorious color and die, the leaf does suffer in a dim way. But the leaf, as it blazes its last glory, can no more know the source of its suffering than we can. Thus we human beings suffer for the glory of God, and know not whence the suffering comes, or why.

It is a powerful image. I shall work it into a sermon someday.

I continued laboring over Sunday's sermon until lunch, sketching out the main idea. I've called it "Predestination and Postum." The thought I am developing is how one goes about integrating the mystical side of Protestant Christianity with quotidien living. My church suffers from being too prosaic. We lack a sense of the mystical, the unknowable, the ineffable. When I walk to the pulpit on a Sunday and see my parishioners seated so properly in their rows, so neatly dressed, so assured and expectant, I am filled with a sense of panic. I have not done what I set out to do. In forty years, what have I given these people? Only a sense of complacency?

I am not satisfied with the title. "Predestination and Porridge"? They both have a bathetic sound. I am not, I regret, very facile with words.

This all leads me to an extraordinary occurrence that happened this day. For some days now, at three o'clock, the boy Sandy from across the street has come riding past on his bicycle with the monkey in hot pursuit on a tricycle. The professor must be training her for an act of some kind. They generally head down to the brook path and thence into the park.

As they passed the house, where the street slopes downhill, the poor monkey lost control of her tricycle and ran up on the lawn before ending up in a heap. I heard the most heartbreaking sound coming from her, so I rushed out to help. I bent over her, not quite knowing what to do. The poor thing held up her arms to me! And allowed me to pick her up! She hugged me in a most endearing way. She was terribly distressed.

Without even thinking, I invited them inside for comforting, cookies, and milk. I dabbed some Mercurochrome on the animal's knee, and she set up a loud whimpering. R. came downstairs from her afternoon nap. "What is all this caterwauling?" she said, etc., etc. Not an altogether felicitous scene followed, but mitigated by the presence of the Archibald child. But the dear little animal is so captivating that even R. was softened. She even went into the kitchen and fetched cookies and milk.

Jennie and Sandy sat at the breakfast table, the chimp with her hands folded on the tabletop and her bright happy curious eyes darting about. When the cookies came she took one as polite as you please, from the correct (i.e., near) side of the dish. She nibbled it daintily while Sandy grubbed about with dirty hands looking for the three or four biggest, cramming one after the other into his mouth. The contrast was amusing and not lost on R. Indeed, R. was speechless. Jennie drank the milk with a rather unpleasant sucking noise and when she lowered the glass her muzzle was dripping, but then she politely wiped her mouth with the napkin and so all was well. Sandy wiped his mouth with his hand, and not—I might add—before wiping his nose.

Jennie was wearing the hat. I had an uncomfortable moment when R. remarked on what a peculiar hat the ape was sporting. But I needn't have worried. The hat was much altered. It was quite dreadful and unsanitary, and Jennie did not remove the hat at the table. Her manners still need work. The professor and his wife, I hasten to add, would do well to start with Sandy, however, whose lack of the finer graces is appalling.

I made a grave error in referring to Jennie as a monkey; Sandy was quick to inform me that she is an *ape*, that monkeys are a much lower form of primate, and that any such reference to Jennie was as insulting as it was inaccurate. And apparently, she is with the family for good.

I watched Jennie as she ate. I had not forgotten my earlier feelings about the animal. She seemed so alert and intelligent that I once again wondered whether she could possibly comprehend the love of God, and the love of Jesus Christ. As children do, through feeling, pictures, and story, rather than ratiocination.

When Jennie finished her cookie and milk, she sat back in her chair and in the satisfaction of the moment she looked right at me. There was a flicker of something—a flicker of that questioning, wondering, hoping, seeking? It was that mysterious self-awareness that I see in the eyes of children as they start to understand the world. That questioning is the first step to God. Then the chimp laid her hand on mine! It seemed a kind of thank-you for my help. A brief, warm touch full of affection, while she looked at me with those *eyes*, as if she wished to ask something of me. It was a gesture of kindness that bridged the chasm between Man and Beast, a gesture which effaced millions of years of evolution. For the pressure of her fingers spoke to me not through the intellect but through the heart. It was a universal gesture of love, and in the electricity of that touch, I knew that Jennie had a soul. My question had been answered.

Sandy took Jennie's hand and they rose to go. I quickly asked them to stay for a moment, while I went into my study without really thinking what I was doing, knowing only that I desired to give Jennie something. There I found a silver Mexican crucifix on a chain, given to me by Henry Cruikshank after his dear wife's funeral. It is a lovely little hammered cross, intricately chased and decorated.

When I came to the foyer, Jennie looked up at me. I kneeled in front of her with my hands behind my back. "I've got a present for you," I said. I don't know whether she understood the words, but she stretched out her hand readily enough. I gave her the crucifix and she immediately inserted it in her mouth! I gently removed it and draped it around her neck. She picked it up and gazed at it, sniffed it, tasted it with her tongue, turned it around and around. Such fascination! I watched her with great care, thinking she would try to swallow it. Finally she let it drop and Sandy and Jennie departed.

I later found a lovely picture of the Baby Jesus that I will give Jennie on her next visit.

I have reached a curious resolution. There are many who would ridicule the idea. I am now resolved to see what I can do to help this animal experience the love of God. As I write this, seeing in my mind's eye those alert black eyes, I cannot help but think that the chimpanzee has a mind capable of understanding the love of God. For love is an emotion present across the animal kingdom, and combined even with a modicum of intellect can grow from the instinctual love between beasts to a higher love of the ineffable.

N.B. So charming was Jennie that after she left R.'s steady complaints about the animal subsided. We shall see. R.'s great gift to me has been forcing me to learn patience and kindness, two qualities which are all-powerful. Patience and kindness.

[FROM *Recollecting a Life* by Hugo Archibald.]

Jennie had been with us two months when the weather turned cold. No longer could she sleep in her little tree house; she would have to move inside, and the question naturally arose as to where she would spend her nights.

This problem, for the first time, made us see the full ramifications of having an ape in our lives. While she was living in the tree house, we could still, however improbably, think of her as a pet.

Once she moved into the house, it became clear that she did not regard herself as a pet and would not tolerate the assumption in others.

We first tried her in a nice dog bed in the kitchen. The very idea was an insult: the floor was where the despised dogs slept. The first night we tried to bed her down there, she was soon up and pounding on Sandy's door, hooting and screeching. Sandy did not take well to this attack on his domain.

"Get out of here! This is my room!" he shouted. "Go find your own room, stupid!" Then Jennie came to our door and started hammering on it with her tiny fists.

We tried her in one of the spare bedrooms, but she hated to be shut in an empty room. As soon as we had withdrawn for the night, she was up, out, and banging on our doors. We tried to lock her in, but the tantrum that resulted threatened to shift the foundation of our house.

We decided to try her in our room. We piled her blankets in the corner and cajoled her to bed down there, but Jennie would have none of it. As soon as Lea and I were in bed, Jennie hopped up and began bouncing around, laughing and smacking her lips.

"Jennie!" I shouted the first night. "Bad chimp! Get off!"

Jennie jumped off and jumped on and off again in a whirlwind of motion.

"Stop it! Bad, bad Jennie!"

She crouched in her corner, whimpering. I must have dozed off, for the next thing I remember were the covers being pulled off.

"It's that damn chimp," said my wife. And there was Jennie, braced at the corner of the bed, tugging the covers with all her might. She was determined to spend the night in our bed.

"Jennie!" I yelled. "No!"

She dropped to a crouch on the floor and covered her head with her hands, shrieking miserably.

"Jennie, goddamnit, stop screaming!" I hollered.

She rocked back and forth on her heels, screaming louder.

"Hugo, you *know* when you yell at her all she does is scream louder," said Lea.

I gathered Jennie up and put her outside, locking the door between us. She redoubled her efforts, pounding, snuffling, rattling the doorknob. When I got up I could see her fingers curling under the door, while she heaved and stamped on the other side.

"I don't care what you do," I heard Lea's muffled voice say from the bed. "Just make her shut up."

I opened the door to discipline her, but she shot past me and dove under the covers, burrowing madly.

"What!" my poor wife said, now wide awake, laughing in spite of herself. "Hugo! There's an ape in our marriage bed!" She found it very funny. It was impossible to be angry at Jennie.

Jennie was moving around under the covers, laughing and clacking her teeth.

"If we let her sleep in here once," Lea said, "we're done for."

I should have heeded my wife, but at the time, having fought battles with Jennie for four nights running, I didn't have the energy for another try.

"She'll be all right," I said. "If we can just get her to stay on one side and shut up. We'll put her outside again in the spring."

"Good luck with *that*," said Lea.

We tried to sleep. Jennie kicked and jerked and wriggled until Lea and I were huddled at the edges of the bed, while Jennie lorded the middle. Periodically, she reached out with a hairy hand to check if we were still there. Lea finally reached her limit. With a cry of frustration she got up and whipped the covers off Jennie, who sprang up with a hoot, thinking a wonderful new game was about to begin. Lea tried scolding Jennie, but the chimp began one of her whirling dervish acts, screwing the sheets around herself. Lea seized her and together we managed to get her deposited into a nest of blankets in the corner. She sensed that this time we were serious, and she went to sleep without further ado.

For three or four nights after that, Jennie slept in the corner, in her tangled nest. She never snored and we never heard a peep out of her, so we concluded that everything was going to be all right. Then one night I became amorous, and before I knew what was happening Jennie was on top of me, screaming and hitting, clearly distressed. When I tried to push her off, she bit my arm. It was not a serious bite, just a quick pinch, but it surprised me. As far as we knew, she had not bitten a human being before.

When I related this story to Harold Epstein, he asked if I was familiar with Dr. Jane Goodall's research on chimpanzees in Tanganyika. Goodall had made the interesting observation that infant chimpanzees become violently upset when males mate their mothers, and often try to interfere with and prevent the copulative act. Harold was deeply interested in Jennie's reaction and he felt that it showed this kind of behavior must be genetically programmed.

That was the end of Jennie's nights in our room. We forced Jennie to sleep in the spare bedroom. It was a long, painful process, entailing many sleepless nights while we listened to Jennie's muffled screams echoing through the woodwork. She felt she had been given shabby treatment indeed. She never did reoccupy her tree house, except during the day. The spare bedroom became Jennie's room forever.

Jenny, we came to understand, had a highly developed sense of justice. She sincerely believed that she was human and should enjoy all the perquisites pertaining thereto. She would not allow herself to be treated in any way different from how we treated our children. If she perceived a difference—if, for example, Sandy was given a candy bar and she wasn't—she took it as a great injustice. Her sense of fairness was almost as highly developed as it is among human siblings, who, as any parent knows, are ready to protest any hint of favoritism.

Not long after Jennie arrived Harold asked me whether Jennie had ever seen herself in a mirror. Harold took a scientific interest in

Jennie and questioned me at length about her behavior. In this case, I thought back and realized that, in fact, she had not. Much has been written about the chimpanzee concept of "self." Cognitive tests using chimpanzees and mirrors have proven, beyond doubt, that chimpanzees do have a sense of self.

That evening, Jennie saw herself in a mirror for the first time. We wondered how she would react, since it was clear to us that she considered herself human and probably never realized she looked any different from the rest of us. It was our first "experiment" with Jennie. I removed the dressing mirror from Lea's closet door and placed it at the top of the stairs. Then we called Jennie.

She came bounding up the stairs without a care in the world, but when she reached the top and saw her image in the mirror, she stopped dead. Her hair bristled up and she "displayed" by swaggering about, stamping her feet on the floor, and staring aggressively. When the image did not flee as expected she became angry and charged. Naturally, her double showed equal fearlessness and charged right back, and this frightened Jennie half to death. She skidded to a halt and backed off screaming and grimacing in fear. Then she turned and fled down the stairs. If she had a tail it would have been between her legs.

At the bottom she gathered her wits and crept back up. Again, she had the unpleasant experience of seeing this black, hairy creature staring at her from the mirror. She stood there transfixed. Suddenly her expression changed. What was this? The ugly brute was wearing a hat just like hers! Her hair gradually subsided as it dawned on her that the image in the mirror was of *herself*. She took the hat off her head and looked at it, and put it back on, and went up to the mirror and ran her hands all over the mirror's surface. Then she simply walked away.

After that, mirrors held no interest for her, and she ignored them. It was not until much later that other experiments showed just how complex an image of "self" Jennie had.

It snowed in late December, the first storm of the season. It was a big one, and we were curious to see how Jennie would react. It began in the afternoon. With the cold weather, Jennie had been spending much of her time in the library, where she could bang on an old upright piano, wait at the window seat to spot Sandy returning from school, or warm herself by the fire. There was scant potential for mischief in the library, since the books and other breakables were safely locked up behind screens. Lea eventually installed a big box in the library and filled it with Jennie's dolls and toys.

On this particular day, Jennie was sitting on the window seat, as usual, waiting for Sandy, when a few flakes wandered out of a leaden sky. As the snow became heavier she stood up and pressed her face to the window. As it fogged up from her breath she kept wiping a little hole with her finger, just large enough for her eye. She peered at the falling snow with fascination. Finally she went to the coat closet where we kept her jacket and booties, and drummed on the door with her little fists. This was her signal that she wanted to go out.

Lea and I dressed her and we all went outside. By this time, the snow was heavy. She looked into the sky and was startled and annoyed by the cold flakes striking her face. She began to shake her head and rub her face, swatting at the flakes as they swirled about her, becoming more excited, whirling about and flailing her arms. Her excited hoots echoed through the neighborhood.

The next day was bright and cold, and Sandy took her out on the sled. She sat while he pulled her along the snowy street in front of the house. Jennie would not stop eating snow. Whenever any snow got on her booties she would raise her foot to her mouth and carefully eat it off. Soon more children had appeared with their sleds, flying saucers, and toboggans, and they went off to a favorite sledding hill on the golf course. For hours, we could hear Jennie's excited screams drifting across the snow-covered course. After that, she often went sledding with Sandy and the other neighborhood children.

The library was Jennie's living room during the winter. She loved to roast apples in the fire. Eventually she was able to wrap them herself with tinfoil, chuck them in the fire, and fish them out with a poker when they were done. Then she would squat by the cooling apples, staring at them while issuing grunts of anticipation and clacking her teeth. Seized with impatience, she would often try to grab one before it had sufficiently cooled, burn herself, and screech with frustration while drumming a tattoo with her feet on the hearth.

When not in the library, Jennie spent most of her time in the den with Sandy, watching television. She was curiously attracted to westerns, and she loved the sound of the shooting guns and galloping horses. Most of all she liked the food advertising on television. Whenever food was depicted on the screen, she would start making her "hungry hoot" sound and crowd the television screen, poking it with her fingers, trying to get as close a look as possible. She always seemed to hope, against all odds, that some attractive morsel might suddenly fall out of the screen into her hands. There was one advertisement in particular that saturated the airwaves at the time. It showed a refrigerator opening up to the sound of a swelling orchestra, with a great mass of fruit tumbling out as if from a cornucopia. All her favorite fruits were there: apples, grapes, bananas, peaches, and oranges. Jennie erupted with delighted screams when the advertisement came on. Even hearing the music would start her pant-hooting or racing from an adjacent room into the den. The advertisement had an electrifying effect on her. As soon as it concluded she often headed straight for the refrigerator and hammered on the door. Jennie confirmed my suspicions that television advertising is directed mainly at people with the IQ of a pongid.

In a twinkling, Jennie changed our lives. If you think having a baby changes things, you ought to get a chimp. She had so many tricks up her sleeve. During dinner, she'd get under the table and untie all our shoelaces. Thank goodness she never learned how to tie knots, or we'd all have been tied together. And then there was that vulgar sound she made, that Bronx cheer. A razzing of the lips. Well! Hugo tried to tell me this was a natural sound they make in the jungle, but I happen to know he taught it to her. In secret. Hugo had a mischievous streak a mile wide. And those lips of hers! Hugo used to make this demonstration in front of guests. He would hold a piece of candy right in front of Jennie's mouth, and her lips would pucker to a point, right where the candy was. Then he would move the candy from side to side, and the little puckered point of her lips would travel from one side of her mouth to the other! It was the funniest looking thing!

Jennie imitated *everything* we did. When Hugo was finished with the paper in the morning, Jennie would pick it off the table and take it to the floor. It was so dear. She would go through all the motions of reading the paper, unfolding it, staring intently at it, turning the pages, and clacking her teeth. Occasionally she would stop to sniff a picture. Pretty soon the paper would start to fall apart. A page would drop out, or the top would collapse on her head. And she would start to get mad, and whack the paper. Well! That just made things worse. And she would shake it angrily, and paper would fly out, and pretty soon she'd be sitting in a heap of crumpled papers, screeching in frustration.

She watched me put on makeup. Just fascinated. As soon as my back was turned, white powder would be flying everywhere and there she was, looking just awful, like the creature from the black lagoon, her little black eyes blinking out of this horrid white face! Oh my goodness. She used to drag Hugo's briefcase around. Clomping around looking very important and officious. If Hugo left it unlocked, she'd reach inside and then the papers would be all over! Or she'd dump it out and stir up the papers to make a nest. Served Hugo right. He always had that briefcase. I'd come down when we were going to Maine for a weekend, and there it was sitting by the door. And he'd say that he just had a little bit of work to do. Then he'd work all weekend and we'd only see him at dinner! How I hated that horrid briefcase!

There, you see. I'm off the subject again.

[FROM an interview with Harold Epstein]

Simia quam similis, turpissima bestia, nobis! Write that down. That should be the motto of our book. "How like us is the ape, vilest of beasts, and how noble!" Cicero, I think. . . . Anyway, how true it was. Jennie displayed the worst and the best of all the human qualities. It was a revelation to watch her. I can't begin to tell you. It made me question our species' claim to some kind of special status.

During that first year and a half, Hugo brought Jennie into the museum several days a week. The museum has very long straight corridors. Jennie learned to ride a tricycle and she went wheeling down the halls, chattering and hooting, and making a hairy menace of herself. It used to startle visiting scientists. [Laughs.]

While Hugo worked, Jennie made the rounds. She stopped at office doors and knocked. This was no polite tap, mind you, but a pounding and kicking that threatened to separate the door from its hinges. She was an unruly child, like that bad girl in the children's books, Eloise. When she came swaggering into your office, man alive, you had better batten down the hatches, for anything loose was going to get broken, eaten, or stolen.

You may wonder why we all put up with her. The answer is simple: everyone adored her. I take that back; there was one fellow who did not like Jennie. He was the elevator man, a sour old

Scotsman named Will. To this poor man's sorrow, Jennie learned how useful the elevator was. She seemed to be under the impression that the more she pushed the elevator call button, the sooner the elevator would come. I'd see Jennie at the elevator, pressing the button, and I'd hear Will's voice echoing up the shaft (I hope I can do justice to his brogue): "All right, I'm coming, I'm coming! Knock off, you bluidy ape! Have done!" [Laughs.]

Jennie often stopped by my office. We were great pals, Jennie and I. I'd hear the rattle of the trike and a tattoo of pounding would shake the office. She immediately demanded a hug, her arms out-stretched. That vital business being taken care of, she wandered about, poking at papers, picking up things and putting them in her mouth, climbing on tables and chairs, making the odd snatch at my pipe. She was determined to have that pipe! But I was too quick for the hairy devil. I kept a stack of old *Natural History* magazines and she poured over those, turning the pages and running her fingers over the photographs. As if verifying their two-dimensionality. Very interesting. She had a bad habit of tearing out pages. She favored pictures of animals, but pictures of humans held no interest for her.

One issue had an article on chimpanzees, and I showed it to her as a kind of experiment. Her reaction was extremely interesting. The first picture stopped her cold. By this time she knew what she looked like, having seen herself in the mirror.

She scrutinized the photographs, turning the pages back and forth, holding the magazine up to her nose. She then touched her face. It was as if she were trying to see if the pictures were a reflection of her. She made a low "oooooo ooo" sound—a sound she made only when she was intensely curious. She spent a good half hour examining the pictures before moving on to something else. And my friend, half an hour for Jennie was quite a long time.

She lunched with Hugo in the staff dining room, at the curators' table. She occupied the seat of honor. Hugo and I often went to lunch together. As we approached the dining room Jennie became more and more excited, riding ahead on her tricycle, pedaling furiously, her maniacal hoots echoing along the corridor. There was a bump, a ridge, on the stone floor right before the dining room entrance. Most of the time Jennie would stop and carry her trike over the ridge, but in her excitement once in a while she forgot. She whizzed along, hooting away, her legs pumping, and she turned the corner and we heard a *clunk! crash!* and then an eruption of screams. We would try to warn her, calling: "Look out, Jennie! Don't fall!" But when she was hungry she never minded anyone. When she was *full* she never minded. She never minded, period.

When she heard the clatter of the dishes, and smelled the food, and saw the place crowded with people, she broke into excited screams of joy, and so loud and piercing! All conversation in the dining room ceased. Jennie had arrived! Those who knew Jennie, of course, were amused. But more than once I saw visiting curators or new employees spill food on themselves when Jennie screamed her arrival.

Jennie sat in a high chair at the curators' table, where she ate with impeccable manners. Well, perhaps not *quite* so impeccable. When we finished eating, many of the curators took out their cigarettes. Jennie loved to light cigarettes. She went around the table with a box of kitchen matches and lit each curator's cigarette. These were the days, mind you, when everyone still smoked. One day a curator offered Jennie a cigarette, and she tried to smoke it while sitting in his lap, but it didn't agree with her. The curator paid for his poor judgment with a lapful of ape vomit.

During that first year and a half, I found myself observing Jennie with growing interest, I mean *scientific* interest. *Simia quam similis.* She was so very *human*-like. She appeared to understand at least as much as a human child her age. She showed astonishing intelligence. I'll give you two examples. There was a woman who came in three days a week who did "public relations" for the museum. She was really quite marvelous, a real *type*, with the bouffant hairdo, high heels, long red nails, lots of makeup. When she first saw Jennie she screamed, which frightened Jennie and made *her* scream, which made the woman scream even louder. It was not a felicitous beginning!

Jennie knew right away this woman disliked her. Whenever she passed the woman's office on her trike, she would stop, quietly open the door, and issue a sudden hoot. You could hear the woman inside give a big shriek, and then her voice yelling, "Get out of here! Stop that noise! Somebody get that animal out of here!" When the woman began locking her office door, Jennie gave the door a kick on her way by.

Now I can see you think this is very funny. And it was. But stop for a moment and think, if you will, about what this behavior involved. Let us dissect what Jennie had to know in order to torment this woman. First, it showed Jennie had the ability to impute a state of mind to another human being. Forgive me, I mean *a* human being. She knew this person disliked her presence. This was sophisticated reasoning, my friend! This was not a dog biting an unfriendly man. Jennie deliberately tormented her, making her startled and angry. It showed that she had the ability to *manipulate* a human being's state of mind. It showed a mastery of human psychology that I found extraordinary.

The second incident was even more unusual. It occurred after Jennie had been at the museum a year. For a while she had a Barbie doll which she carried around, dressed, undressed, fed, kissed, and so forth. Sometimes she would hand you the doll for a hug, and then take it back. One day, Hugo called me down to his office. Jennie was there, sitting in her wing chair, apparently cradling her doll. Only there *wasn't* any doll. She'd forgotten it, left it at home. Instead, she was cradling an *imaginary* doll, chattering to it, stroking it. Hugo said, "Jennie, hug." Jennie got up, *still cradling the doll*, and came over to Hugo. Hugo hugged her and then Jennie *offered Hugo the imaginary doll to hug*. Hugo hugged it and Jennie took back the pretend doll.

Do you see the *significance* of this? I saw it immediately. I felt my skin crawl. You see, ethologists had always believed that one of the traits distinguishing humans from animals was the ability to imagine and to create. Creativity was supposed to be one of the defining characteristics of what it *means* to be human.

What we had just witnessed was nothing less than the toppling of this grand idea.

Let me get a little technical here. If it's too much for your readers you can edit this out.

There are people who continue to insist on the uniqueness of the human animal, who continue to feel that man stands in isolated splendor. They come in two types: religious zealots and ethologists. The religious bigots can be dismissed out of hand, but the ethologists require a serious response.

These ethologists—I will name no names—have criticized much of the research done on chimpanzees. They say that by using words like "imagination," we are *anthropomorphizing* the animal's behavior. We are attaching human traits to an animal's behavior. Their argument goes like this: How can you know the animal is using "imagination" or "creativity," when you can't really *know* the animal's state of mind? It could just as easily be elaborate imitative behavior. And besides, how do you define the word "creativity" anyway? Aren't you imposing human assumptions on an animal's behavior? Thus, they brand us with the sin of anthropomorphization, one of the egregious sins of ethology.

These objections came from people who were (and still are) insecure about the "hardness" of their science. They are afraid of the "softness" of ethology. They want to be like the physicists. Of course, the physicists have abandoned pure objectivity, but the social scientists always seem to be twenty years behind everyone else anyway.

These objections are absurd. I get so tired of these people and their whining objections. For heaven's sake, we don't know what "imagination" or "creativity" is, in humans or in chimpanzees.

And do these ethologists really think we can know our *own* state of mind? Shows how little they know about human psychology. The point is this: Jennie's behavior looked exactly like imagination as it would operate in a human child. If it waddles like a duck, quacks like a duck, and looks like a duck, well then, what the hell is it if it isn't a damn duck? Aha! We can even turn their argument around and say that perhaps human imagination and creativity are "elaborate imitative behaviors." You see my point?

What I'd ask these ethologists is: *show* me the sharp line between the human and the ape. *Show* me precisely how the two species differ qualitatively, rather than just quantitatively. The more you study chimps, the more you realize it can't be done. They use the label "anthropomorphization" as a cover, because they're *scared* that maybe we're all just animals after all! [At this point Dr. Epstein laughed for an extended period of time.]

Oh my. I am getting ahead of myself. In the mid-sixties, everyone believed there were profound differences between humans and all other species. When I saw Jennie with that imaginary doll, I *knew* I was witnessing an event of profound scientific importance. I knew that chimpanzees must be closer to human beings than I or anyone else had thought. "I felt like some watcher of the skies/ When a new planet swims into his ken"!

What I also saw at that moment was an extraordinary opportunity for research. Here we had a perfect subject. An animal perfectly socialized as a human being. Can you appreciate what an outstanding scientific opportunity this was? To me—a cultural anthropologist—it seemed a miracle. A chimpanzee that had *never* come in contact with its own kind, *never* been exposed to its own heritage; a chimp that believed it was a human being in every way. A chimpanzee *imprinted*—to use Lorenz's term—as a human being. Why, not even Yerkes had such an animal to work with!

That was how the Jennie project began.

Let me make two points right now. First, Jennie gave to us, and to science, information of incalculable value. What we learned from

Jennie not only caused us to reevaluate what it means to be an animal, but it caused me, personally, to reevaluate what it means to be human.

The second point is this: Jennie loved every minute of the research. It was conducted in a spirit of kindness and fun, without stress or coercion. The atmosphere the Primate Center researchers created for Jennie was equivalent to the atmosphere in, say, a playroom or kindergarten. Did you read that *Esquire* article on the research? It was a libelous piece of trash. Scratch-and-sniff journalism. Well, what can one expect from a fashion magazine for men. Good lord.

It was after seeing Jennie with the doll—I think it was February or March of 1967—when I first called Pam Prentiss at the Center for Primate Research. Prentiss was the director of the center, and I wanted to know if she had any interest in studying Jennie.

She was excited. Excited isn't the word; she was beside herself. I then talked to Hugo about my idea. He found it intriguing, but he was skeptical. I said, "Hugo, you're the one who talked about this being an experiment." Well he'd forgotten all about that. Being a physical anthropologist, he did not see the full implications. I explained to him that it would be like the kind of psychological and cognitive testing done on, say, a gifted child. Lots of fun and games. Jennie would learn ASL—that's American Sign Language—and participate in a variety of interesting learning situations. I said it would be like sending Jennie to school.

He was still skeptical but agreed to meet with Dr. Prentiss. He was genuinely concerned about Jennie. He laid down two conditions: no matter what, Jennie would continue to live at home. And then he said that he didn't want Jennie subjected to anything that I wouldn't be comfortable subjecting my own children to.

Looking back these years, I can say quite comfortably that Jennie experienced nothing that I wouldn't have my own children experience. Just the opposite. A rich and rewarding environment was created for Jennie.

Now this is important. Back then, there was still a strong feeling that nurture, rather than nature, is what determines what we are. Environment, not genes, determines the course of our lives. There was still the heady notion that we could remake ourselves and the world, that biology was not limiting. The field of sociobiology was in its infancy, and it was considered shockingly reactionary, a throwback to the social Darwinism of the nineteenth century. E. O. Wilson's great work wouldn't be published until 1975. We thought that because Jennie was socialized as a human, and had this astonishing intelligence approaching that of a human child, that she would always *be* human. We forgot that Jennie was *not* human. There were impulses and desires and aggressions programmed into her genes that neither we nor she had any control over. *Biology is destiny.*

So what happens when you're raised to think you're something you're not? I guess we found out, didn't we?

five

[FROM *Recollecting a Life* by Hugo Archibald.]

In April of 1967, Dr. Pamela Prentiss met Jennie for the first time. Jennie was an astute judge of human nature. When she first met a person, it did not take her long to make up her mind: either she liked him or she did not. She was particularly suspicious of over-done heartiness, pompousness, repressive people, and an excessive "niceness." Her ability to humiliate people who showed these qualities never ceased to amaze me.

We were therefore quite interested to see Jennie's reaction to Dr. Prentiss. We trusted Jennie's judgment even more, in some ways, than we trusted our own. In our minds, how Jennie reacted would be the determining factor as to whether we would allow her to participate in the research project.

We were playing with Jennie on the lawn when she arrived. Dr. Prentiss made a rather dramatic first impression. She whipped up in a mud-splattered Jeep, blond hair spilling over her shoulders, and a battered hat on her head that looked the twin of Jennie's old Borsalino. She was wearing blue jeans and a work shirt, and I immediately respected her for that. If she had appeared in a dress I would have been skeptical of her experience with chimpanzees.

Ignoring us, she came over to Jennie and crouched in front of her.

"Hi, Jennie," she said. "My name's Pam. Do you want a hug?" She had an easy, self-confident, unhurried way about her with Jennie that was exactly right, and Jennie responded by opening her arms wide. She took Jennie in and gave her a big hug. And then Jennie kissed her, an unusually affectionate gesture to a stranger—especially a woman. Jennie usually preferred men.

Only after introducing herself to Jennie did Dr. Prentiss shake our hands. I liked her priorities. She was awkward and even a little defensive with us, and I suspected that she was one of those animal behaviorists who related better to her subjects than to her fellow human beings.

We retired to the living room. Sandy joined us, since the entire family would have to be involved. Dr. Prentiss outlined what their research goals and methodology would be for Jennie. The Center for Primate Research at Tufts had a captive colony of chimpanzees, all of whom were learning American Sign Language for the Deaf, or ASL. They needed a "control"; and Jennie would be that control. They wanted to see if Jennie, who was species-isolated and thoroughly socialized as a human being, would learn ASL differently from the colony's chimps.

The focus of the research project was more in the area of linguistics than primate behavior. The actual linguistic problems being posed were quite esoteric and are beyond the scope of this memoir. Indeed, they were difficult even for me to understand.

I was impressed by the careful way that Dr. Prentiss and her team had framed their research objectives. This was no fuzzy, open-ended plan, no woolly-headed idea to "teach a chimp sign language and see what happens." They wanted to explore precisely how chimpanzees acquire "language" and how this compared to the theory of language acquisition in human children.

It was a fascinating idea and Lea and I saw the value of including Jennie in the project. I had my own hypothesis: I felt that Jennie, being raised in a warm, loving human environment, would learn much faster than a group of caged chimpanzees who were not socialized as human beings. After all, language, whether it is ASL or English, is a human invention.

I remember voicing my opinion to Dr. Prentiss that day.

She glanced at me with surprise. "Dr. Archibald," she said rather crisply, "in our research, we try to avoid forming premature hypotheses. There is always the danger of a biased observer skewing the data." This was a rather typical response from Dr. Prentiss. She was a scientist through and through, sometimes even at the expense of people's feelings.

Dr. Prentiss explained that both Lea and I would have to learn ASL. Then she turned to Sandy. Did he also want to learn ASL?

Sandy was more excited about the project than any of us.

"Yeah!" he cried out. "Does this mean me and Jennie'll be able to talk to each other?"

"Yes, if you both work hard," said Dr. Prentiss.

"Wow, cool," Sandy said.

Sarah was only two at the time, and we felt that she would probably pick it up naturally as she grew older. It would be a valuable experience for all of us.

Learning ASL would not be difficult, Dr. Prentiss explained, because Jennie would probably learn only five or ten signs in the first year. Over the course of the five-year project she could be expected to learn perhaps one hundred signs. She would never be able to communicate as well as a deaf person, she explained, and her signing would not be as crisp or as rapid.

Dr. Prentiss proposed to visit our home three days a week, where she would take complete charge of Jennie. They might play in the crab apple tree, they might go for a drive in the Jeep, they might take walks on the golf course or down by the brook. She would need a room in the house—we offered her the basement playroom—where she and Jenny could play and study. Our privacy would be respected and the rest of the house would be off-limits while she was here. Finally, she said, the Primate Center would furnish us with a stipend to defray some of our costs in taking care of Jennie.

Lea and I talked about the proposal. We were surprised to discover that we both longed to be able to communicate with Jennie. Jennie understood in a vague sort of way quite a few English words, but her inability to respond often left her frustrated. If she wanted something, she would tug on my pant leg, scream, point, and in extreme cases drum on the floor with her hands and feet. Her needs were not complex—food, toys, tickling, and hugging were her main concerns—and we felt that even a few signs would open up a whole new world to her, and to us. Our feelings were probably not very different from those of the parents of a deaf child.

The idea was appealing for another reason: Lea found Jennie to be an exhausting charge, and having a professional baby-sitter three days a week would be most welcome. Jennie seemed genuinely fond of Dr. Prentiss and we knew they would get along well.

Before making our final decision, however, we visited Dr. Prentiss's chimpanzee colony. We wanted to see how she was treating their other animals.

The Primate Center was a large estate in Hopkiln, Massachusetts, given to the university by, of all people, the circus impresario P. T. Barnum. The colony was unofficially called the "Barnum colony." It consisted of forty acres of gardens, fields, woods, and ponds, surrounded by an electrified, chain-link fence. The four chimpanzees lived in an enormous, heated barn, formerly a dairy barn. It had been converted to spacious and comfortable living quarters built into the biggest jungle gym we had ever seen, where the chimpanzees slept high up on shelves. In addition to having free run of the estate, the chimps had access to the first floor of the old

Barnum mansion, where they met with their teachers every day in a classroom setting of sorts. There were no cages.

The animals were visited regularly by the doctor, dentist, and nutritionist. The chimpanzees themselves were so obviously happy that all our lingering fears were laid to rest. I doubt there was anywhere a happier or more luxuriously pampered group of animals. A human being would be content to pass his life in such a place.

Dr. Prentiss was a new kind of primate researcher. She abhorred the intrusive and cruel psychological testing done by primate researchers such as Dr. Harry Harlow at the University of Wisconsin at Madison. Dr. Prentiss insisted on human standards of decency and kindness to her chimpanzee subjects.

Dr. Prentiss also explained to us that when the project was over, her colony chimpanzees were going to be sent to an island in Florida where she had founded a "rehabilitation" program for once-captive chimpanzees. One of the cruelest aspects of primate research, she pointed out, was that when the researchers were finished with them the animals were simply shunted to labs or zoos, to live the rest of their lives miserably caged. In the case of her project, she felt a responsibility to the chimpanzees for life.

We were deeply impressed and accepted Dr. Prentiss's research proposal, with a few caveats. We refused the stipend; we found the idea of taking money to put Jennie into a research project repulsive. We also reserved the right to observe Dr. Prentiss and Jennie whenever we wished and to terminate the project at any time, for any reason.

Dr. Prentiss accepted these requirements, and Jennie's momentous voyage into the world of language began.

[FROM an interview with Lea Archibald.]

Dr. Prentiss . . . Well! What can I tell you about Dr. Prentiss? Maybe I'm not the best person to talk to about her. She was not exactly a warm person. She was all business, and full of that jargon that makes even the most ridiculous thing sound intelligent. We did not see eye-to-eye. She didn't approve of the way we were raising Jennie—she who had never raised a child in her life. She never has married, you know. It makes one wonder, doesn't it?

She felt we were being inconsistent while raising Jennie. She wanted us to do all these experimental things, while I just wanted to raise a child.

Yes, I have to admit it, she loved Jennie—in her own limited way, of course. And Jennie loved her back. Jennie was so sweet and trusting, even with people like her.

What did she look like? Huh! Immaculate, poised, beautiful, a blond icicle. She was about thirty-five years old. Came from a rich old New York family, although you'd never know it from the way she dressed. Patched jeans and a work shirt and a silly hat. Plucked her eyebrows though; I could tell. She drove an old Jeep at reckless speeds through the neighborhood, endangering the neighborhood children. She was supposed to be brilliant, Ph.D. from Harvard, et cetera, et cetera. Perhaps she was; I've never read any of her papers on Jennie. Nor do I have the slightest interest, thank you.

Now isn't it funny, but I don't even know what they discovered from studying Jennie. Hugo tried to talk to me about it but I found it silly. Something about how they found out Jennie was smart! Well hallelujah! Any fool could have told them that.

Dr. Prentiss started giving us ASL lessons. It wasn't quite as simple as she had said. Although Jennie was supposed to learn only five or ten signs the first year, she wanted us to learn hundreds. *Give, drink, eat, tickle, hug, more, you, me, tricycle, sorry, dirty* (that really meant "I have to go to the bathroom!"), and many others. We made up signs for our names and Jennie's name. Her sign was an ASL "J"—the little pinky extended from a clenched hand—but pointing at her chest. [She proceeded to demonstrate the gesture.] Mine was an ASL "L" drawn through the air in a kind of "Howdy!" gesture. Like this. [Another demonstration.]

Dr. Prentiss's demands on us were excessive. She actually expected us to sign whenever Jennie was around, whether we were talking to Jennie or not. Can you imagine? It was a ridiculous imposition and I vetoed it immediately. I had to put my foot down on a number of occasions. After all, it was my house and my daughter. I mean my chimpanzee daughter, of course. She also wanted us to sign silently. I said, "Why on earth sign silently when Jennie understands spoken English already? No thank you," I said, "we will speak the words while signing them." I also pointed out to her that Sarah was just two years old and still learning how to speak. If we started this silent signing business, goodness knows how she would have turned out. Jennie wasn't the only child we were raising. With all her brains, Dr. Prentiss never thought things through. She didn't have any common sense at all.

Don't get me wrong: we were thrilled about the prospect of being able to communicate with Jennie. That was terribly important to us. We wanted to unlock her mind and her thoughts.

Sandy was the most enthusiastic of all. He picked up ASL just like that. We already knew he was a genius—I mean he scored at that level on IQ tests. You should have seen him after a few years, signing furiously all over the place, just as fluent as a deaf person. It was a *beautiful* thing to watch him sign. The physical movement, the fluidity, of ASL is so lovely and graceful. It's like a dance, you know. The whole body is involved. In a way it's even more beautiful than spoken language. I've forgotten most of it now, it's been so long.

So Dr. Prentiss started coming three days a week. I heard a lot of noise from the basement where they played, but I didn't see any evidence of signing. Some days they went outside and climbed around the crab apple tree, and I saw her signing away. But no response from Jennie. Hugo and I fumbled our way through signing, and clear wore out that ASL dictionary but Jennie seemed totally uninterested. It was so discouraging. She'd sit there on the floor playing with a stuffed animal or something, and Hugo and I'd be bending over her, signing away till we were blue in the face, looking up signs in the dictionary, arguing about what sign was what. And you know what? She'd just look at us with that what-the-heck-are-you-crazy-humans-doing-now expression on her sweet little face.

After a month of this I took Dr. Prentiss aside. "Now look here," I said, "what's going on? Why isn't Jennie learning anything? She's darn smart enough to learn these signs," I said, "so what's the problem?" What was wrong with her teaching?

Dr. Prentiss was a defensive girl. Woman, I mean. She got all huffy and said our expectations were too high. It might take six months for the first sign, she said. *Six months!!* I was furious. Why. This was the first I'd heard of six months. Well, I talked to Hugo and he tried to calm me down, but I was not going to have this woman in our house for six months. We had quite an argument about it, Hugo and I. Oh dear.

[FROM *Recollecting a Life* by Hugo Archibald.]

Dr. Prentiss began working intensively with Jennie during the late spring of 1967. She felt that a warm relationship was a necessary prerequisite to teaching a chimpanzee sign language. While this may seem obvious to the uninformed reader, in fact it was a highly controversial position in the field. Many primatologists felt that early efforts to teach chimpanzees ASL had been compromised by the strong bond that always developed between researcher and subject. They believed that such a relationship would destroy the researcher's objectivity and would cause unconscious "cueing" to the chimpanzee. This criticism of ASL teaching to chimpanzees, unfortunately, continues to this day. There are still a great many eminent ethologists who dismiss the validity of all ASL experiments done with chimpanzees for this very reason.

Dr. Prentiss, Harold Epstein, and I felt otherwise. Human infants need a close bond with their mothers and a great deal of love while learning language. There was no reason to suppose chimpanzees were any different. We could have introduced rigorous double-blind controls for teaching Jennie ASL, denying her direct human contact and therefore eliminating the possibility of cueing, but the end result would be a perfect experimental setup with a negative result. A human baby could not learn language under those circumstances, let alone a chimp.

Dr. Prentiss spent twenty-four hours a week with Jennie. After four weeks, to our surprise and disappointment, there were no results whatsoever. Jennie could imitate anything, and we expected her to pick up signs as fast as, for example, she had learned to wash the dishes, start the car when our backs were turned, light matches, unscrew light bulbs, and use scissors to cut all the hair off her tummy.

We expected it would take only a day or two for Jennie to pick up her first sign. Instead, we had been waiting a month, without any encouraging signs at all. Sandy in particular was very disappointed. He had studied ASL with enthusiasm and had learned dozens of signs, but after a month with no progress from Jenny his interest was flagging. Dr. Prentiss encouraged us, saying that imitation and communication were quite different. It would be simple to teach Jennie to *imitate* hand gestures; it was a different matter entirely teaching her to *communicate* with hand gestures. Looking back, I am amused by our reaction. We were typical parents, overly ambitious for our child, full of expectations, and ready to blame a lack of progress on the teacher.

[From an interview with Lea Archibald.]

Let's see now . . . About five weeks after Dr. Prentiss started, I was in the kitchen cooking dinner. Dr. Prentiss had just left, and Jennie was inside playing on the kitchen floor. She got bored and started banging her cup on the floor. I turned around and said, "No!" very crossly. She stopped for a moment and then started banging again. Except this time she was banging her cup and spoon. And she made that sassy noise, you know, the Bronx Cheer. That razzing noise with her lips, while sticking out her belly. Right at me!

She knew exactly how to get under my skin. I picked her up and swatted her on the fanny. Now don't be shocked. The truth is, it did no good to swat that chimp on the fanny. It didn't hurt her a bit. Chimpanzees don't have a nice cushioned tush, you know. It's all bone and hard as a rock back there. But it made me feel better. And of course it upset her, because she was very sensitive to our moods. Although sometimes when I spanked her she would laugh and pretend that we were playing and start swatting me back. Oh, that used to make me boiling mad.

Anyway, after I swatted her she sat on the floor rocking back and forth, going "Oooo oooo ooo." Very upset. I was still angry and I said, "Shut up!" And then, then she made a sign. I was stunned. I said, "What?" and then I signed *What?* She did it again, insistently. It was the sign for *hug,* like this. [She demonstrated the sign by crossing her arms over her chest.] I was startled, but then I thought, Oh well, that's a natural gesture. That's not a sign. She's done that before. You see, Jennie would sometimes hug herself in a way that was very similar. So I signed *Hug who?* just to see. And Jennie signed back *Hug, hug, hug, hug Jennie, Jennie!* She actually signed her name! *Jennie!* [Again she demonstrated the sign.]

I was . . . thunderstruck. I signed *Who are you?* and she signed *Me Jennie!* with both hands. Two signs altogether. Just like this. [Mrs. Archibald demonstrated.] *Me Jennie!* With this look of *triumph* on her face, it was unmistakable. . . . It was . . . excuse me . . . Please forgive me. . . . It brings back such memories. Oh dear . . . [Editor's note: At this point Mrs. Archibald broke down and the interview session was suspended.]

[FROM the journals of the Rev. Hendricks Palliser.]

January 15, 1967

Yesterday I called upon the Archibald household, to see Jennie. Jennie is now being instructed by a tutor three days a week who is teaching her sign language. I have seen the lady coming and going in a Jeep for some weeks now. She was there, and I regret to say she was a rather rude, inconsiderate person. She asked me to leave. Jennie, it seems, is actually *communicating* with various people using sign language.

I returned after the woman had departed and spoke with Mrs. Archibald. I have been giving a year or more of thought to this question, and I finally made her the proposition.

It sounds perfectly ridiculous on paper and I do not doubt it sounded equally absurd to Mrs. Archibald. I stated that, in my opinion, Jennie would benefit from religious instruction. I asked if I might be permitted to take her one afternoon per week.

I naturally received the reaction I expected: disbelief followed by ill-concealed mirth. I explained to Mrs. Archibald how and why I felt that Jennie might enjoy learning about Jesus and God. I talked about Jennie's intelligence, her capacity for kindness, and I recounted Jennie's interest in the cross. I reminded her of Jennie's unaccountable affection for the picture of Jesus I had given her. I explained that I would learn sign language myself.

Mrs. Archibald asked me what kind of religious instruction I was proposing. Episcopalian?

I chuckled at this and explained that the instruction would be nondenominational, that it would be the kind of teaching that I have done with very young children. I explained that it would not involve matters of dogma, but would merely help Jennie understand and *feel* the love of God and His Son Jesus Christ. All religious instruction, I said, begins with one simple feeling: love. Surely, I said, Jennie understands love. Yes, murmured Mrs. Archibald, she knows what love is. I said: then she can understand religion, because religion starts with love. Religion *is* love. Without first loving God and feeling God's love for us, there can be no religion.

She said she thought this kind of teaching would be confusing to Jennie and frustrating for me. I replied that I had been called to do this. I said I would consider it a great favor if she would permit me to give it a try, and that as silly as the idea sounded, it was only arrived at after a great deal of thought and prayer. I ended by reminding her that Jennie already visited the house at least once a week and that we had become fast friends; and I mentioned that Reba and I had never had children and that I had begun to consider Jennie as a kind of child to us. She seemed moved by this and said she would discuss it with her husband and the teacher, who is no less than a professor at Tufts University undertaking some kind of linguistical study.

[FROM an interview with Dr. Pamela Prentiss, former Director of the Center for Primate Studies and Throckmorton Professor of Linguistics, Tufts University, Malden, Massachusetts, in her office at Tufts, November and December 1992.]

Dr. Epstein explained everything. What you hope to do with this book. So what's your background? I would like to know what makes you such an expert in this subject that you can write a book about it. [Editor's note: At this point a lengthy discussion of the author's credentials followed, which did not entirely satisfy Dr. Prentiss. For the sake of the story we have omitted this discussion.]

The long and the short of it is, I'm only going to talk to you because Dr. Epstein told me to. Okay? Forgive my skepticism. All the journalists I've dealt with have been so poorly informed. They don't make the slightest effort to understand the *science*. Journalists are lazy and stupid. I won't mention any names. But take that young man from *Esquire* magazine. Did you know his journalism background was in celebrity profiles? He wrote about movie stars, so that gave him the authority to write about Jennie. Why, you see, Jennie was a celebrity. Make me laugh. And you'd think the *Boston Globe* would be concerned about scientific accuracy. That hapless reporter didn't even know the difference between an *ape* and a *monkey*. It would have been funny if it weren't so pathetic.

I've brought some things for you to read: papers, offprints, monographs. This'll be a start, and then when you need more—see those three shelves? That's *all* Jennie research. You'll have to read most of that stuff too. It's really very interesting, if you take the time.

Now, I want to make you understand. I'll talk to you on certain conditions only. [Editor's note: Again, most of this discussion has been omitted.]

Finally, you'll tell the *truth*. I've read so many lies about the project I can hardly stand it. If this book can set the record straight—well, you'll be doing us a service. And I hope you won't mind if I turn on my own tape recorder while we talk. It isn't that I don't trust you. . . .

I've brought some notes here. Whoops! Shit. Help me pick this up. For Christ's sake now everything's messed up. Let me see. . . . My work with Jennie began on May 1, 1967. She learned her first two signs five weeks later, on—let's see here—June 4, 1967. They were *hug* and *me*. On June 6, she spontaneously signed *Hug me*

Jennie to Mrs. Archibald, her surrogate mother. Mrs. Archibald was under the impression that Jennie's first sign had been directed at her. I didn't correct that misapprehension. Why? I should suppose the reason's obvious.

My technique was to mold Jennie's hands into the sign while speaking the word. We always *spoke* the words while we were signing them. Jennie already seemed to understand some English. I molded her hands into *hug,* and then gave her her reward, which was a hug. As soon as Jennie learned a sign, I wouldn't respond to her requests unless she used the sign. For example, when she learned *drink.* From that point on, in order to get a drink she would have to sign *drink.* Her reward was, of course, receiving the drink, or the hug, or whatever she wanted.

We didn't use food as a reward. As some previous ASL researchers did. Jennie's reward was making herself understood. That is, she was rewarded like a human child would be rewarded. We wanted to replicate the way a human child acquires language. You don't cram food into an infant every time she says something, now, do you? Of course not.

The conditions at the Archibald household were not ideal. It was chaotic over there. But Jennie made extraordinary progress anyway. Our Barnum colony chimps learned at less than half the rate Jennie did. Jennie's progress had a lot to do with the Archibald boy, Sandy. He learned ASL as fast as a deaf child and used it extensively with Jennie. Jennie's surrogate parents, Mrs. Archibald in particular, didn't participate in the project. Jennie's rate of learning could have been even faster had there been consistency in her training. And in her relationship with her surrogate mother.

We faced some big problems with this experiment. The Archibald family went away on vacation every August. This interrupted my work with Jennie. Then there was this peculiar old cleric who lived across the street, who interfered constantly. Interference that Mrs. Archibald *encouraged.* I would have understood it if she were a religious woman. But she was not. Mrs. Archibald was always undermining me. Very jealous of my relationship with Jennie. A very difficult woman. This priest or whatever learned the barest rudiments of ASL, which he combined with his own crude signs. It became a *serious* problem. I have never worked under such difficult conditions. Every week, I had to deprogram Jennie after a session with this terrible man. She never did learn the signs for *sky* or *clouds,* for example, confusing them with the cleric's crude sign for *God.* When she saw a bearded man, she would rub her head. I couldn't figure out what the hell she was doing. And then I learned that this rubbing was that priest's sign for *Jesus.* And one day she started making this gesture. It wasn't an ASL sign at all, and I realized with a shock—I'm sorry, but you won't believe this—that she was *crossing* herself. I can hardly believe it now when I look back, that this . . . this *man* was attempting to make Jennie into a Christian. *Why* the Archibalds put up with it is entirely beyond my comprehension. Dr. Archibald was a reasonably competent scientist but when it came to Jennie and family matters he deferred to his wife. She was—well, she was a difficult woman. A difficult woman. With a voice as cold as ice. You've met her. Need I say more?

There were other limitations. None of the children in the neighborhood who played with Jennie learned ASL. I feel this *must* have undermined her progress. It only proves how much *more* a chimpanzee could learn under better circumstances.

We expected her to learn five or ten signs the first year; instead she learned twenty-one. Let me check my notes here. . . . Shit, they're all mixed up. Where are my glasses? Here we are. . . . She learned forty-four the second year, sixty the third, fifty-one the fourth, and seventeen the fifth, for a total of one hundred and ninety-three signs. Now wait, is that right? I thought she learned more. Let me add this up. I always carry this calculator. What a godsend. Hmmmm. I guess it *was* one hundred and ninety-three. Well, still, that's a *lot.* More than any other chimp up to that time. Penny Patterson has taught that gorilla, Koko, six hundred signs.

Absolutely true. I've been there and seen it with my own eyes. I *know,* if I had been allowed to continue the project, I could have taught Jennie a thousand signs. Chimpanzees are *much* smarter than gorillas.

Anyway, of these one hundred and ninety-three signs, no less than twenty-five signs were of her own invention. No previous project had shown a chimpanzee inventing even a single sign. Our first paper was on Jennie's invented signs. Let's see, it's right there. In that volume. *Proceedings of the Thirty-third Annual Conference of the North American Association of Linguistics.* I think you've got an offprint of it in there somewhere. Is that it? No. Well it *should* be in there. Unless I've got it here. Let's see. . . . No, you must have it.

The four colony chimpanzees, on the other hand, learned ninety-one, one hundred and one, fifty-four, and sixty-six signs, respectively. None of them invented a single sign. During the course of the project, Jennie made over thirty thousand different utterances from these signs. That we know of. Of course, when I wasn't there no one kept track of anything Jennie said. We call them "utterances" because there's a question as to whether they are sentences. There's a big controversy whether chimps are creating sentences. Or whether they have language at all. Which is a bunch of shit, because they *do.* I mean, when Jennie says *Give Jennie apple,* what the hell is that if it isn't language? These people are full of shit. Excuse my French. That's another subject anyway. We're *still* analyzing this data.

Jennie's invention of signs was the first surprise. The first was the sign for *play.* It occurred in, let's see . . . April of 1968. April Fools Day. Aha! Here's that paper! I *knew* I had it in here. You'll definitely want to read this paper! It's only thirty pages. If some of the terminology confuses you, give me a call. Are you familiar with *Generative Grammar and Deep Structure: A Prolegomena to Future Linguistics?* What? It's a book, of course. An outstanding introduction to linguistics. Very readable. By the great linguist, V. R. Czerczywicz. You can borrow this copy.

It happened like this. We were having a study session in our basement study room. The sun was shining outside the window and Jennie started to become restless. She vocalized and tried to open the locked door. I ignored her. Our methodology was to pretend not to understand Jennie's requests unless they were signed. She didn't know the sign for *play*, but she slapped the floor. It was a deliberate movement that to me looked uncannily *like* a sign. As an experiment, I slapped the floor. She slapped it and rattled the doorknob. I signed, *Jennie want to go outside and play?* But I used her sign for *play*, slapping the floor. She slapped the floor three or four times in succession, signing in between *Yes, yes, yes.*

So I rewarded her with a play session down by the brook. Playing tickle-chase, her favorite game.

After that, she signed *play* by slapping the floor or ground. She signed it when she saw children. And she sometimes signed it when she saw a dog or a cat. Her idea of playing with a dog, however, was chasing it and pulling its tail.

When Jennie was given that kitten, she often signed *play* to it insistently before picking it up and playing with it.

Let's see. What else do you need to know. When she wanted to make a strong point, she signed with both hands. At first we tried to curtail this practice. But she persisted. We finally gave in. And then Sandy started two-handed signing, and I found myself doing it. For emphasis. Deaf children—now this is interesting—also sign with both hands for emphasis. The linguistic parallels between human being and chimpanzee were quite startling.

Now here's something interesting. Jennie quickly began to use language to mislead us. Or to manage a situation more to her liking. For example, Jennie would use the sign *dirty* to indicate a need to use the toilet. *Dirty* goes like this. [Dr. Prentiss demonstrated the sign, patting the back of her hand under her chin.]

Jennie discovered she could get out of a boring lesson by signing *dirty* when she didn't have to go. We'd rush her to the potty and nothing would happen. It happened again and again. Then we figured it out. She was lying to us. Of course, she sometimes *did* have to go. So when she *really* had to go, and we doubted her, she started signing *Dirty dirty dirty* with both hands, like this: [Dr. Prentiss made another demonstration with both hands.]

If she wanted a banana and signed *Banana*, and it wasn't forthcoming, she would often start signing *Banana! Banana!* with both hands, like this: [Again, a demonstration.]

Jennie used language much like a human child. I'll never forget when this was brought home to me. I was trying to end a play session and resume study in the house. Jennie refused to cooperate. I became increasingly frustrated and finally I clipped a lead around her neck, which for Jennie was the ultimate punishment. She rushed at me in full piloerection, and I was afraid she was going to bite me. Instead she violently signed *Bite, angry, angry, bite!* with both hands right in my face. It was an astonishing and very intimidating performance.

This occurred—where are those damn notes?—on October 5, 1968.

[FROM an interview with Lea Archibald.]

One of the oddest episodes in Jennie's life started about this time. Did I mention the Episcopal minister who lived across the street, the one who looked like Charlie Brown? Well, Jennie had been visiting him regularly. He fed her enormous quantities of chocolate chip cookies and milk. It's a wonder that that wife of his would let Jennie in the house. Anyway, he came to me with the idea of—I'm not quite sure how to put it—*converting* Jennie to Christianity. Giving her religious tutoring. He said—and I'm quite serious—that he felt God had called him to bring Christianity to the poor dumb animals or something like that. Can you imagine? I could hardly keep myself from laughing. But he was so serious, and so embarrassed, that I promised I'd talk to Hugo about it. He had been so kind to Jennie.

I thought Hugo would scotch the idea. You know, he didn't believe in God or anything like that. But he thought the idea was marvelously funny. He roared with laughter and said that he didn't see any harm in it. Oh my goodness. Jennie, he said, would love the attention. And it would get Jennie off our hands for an afternoon a week. Dr. Palliser was as kindly an old man as you could find, so earnest and gentle.

Well! I spoke to Dr. Prentiss about it and—you can imagine—she was horrified. I can't help but laugh when I think about it. Oh, she was just scandalized. She said, "What? This *cleric* wants to give Jennie religious instruction? How peverse!"

I explained that he was really a harmless old man who Jennie was quite fond of. Dr. Prentiss found the whole idea diabolical. It would ruin her experiment! Well, I thought about that for all of two seconds and decided that what was right for Jennie was not necessarily right for Dr. Prentiss and her experiments. There are times, you know, when a mother simply has to do what she thinks is right.

So Jennie started going to the Reverend's house once a week. She would come home with cookie crumbs *all* over her shirtfront. And a big white mustache from the milk she drank. He spoiled her terribly. I'm surprised his wife put up with it. He never had children, you see. I think that had something to do with it.

By this time Sarah had reached the terrible twos. But Sarah's terrible twos were mostly unterrible. Sandy had been an absolute horror at two. When he learned the word no it was the end. "No!" was a constant refrain in our house after Jennie arrived. Hugo told me I used to shout it in my sleep! Oh dear. Sandy got a mynah bird from his aunt once, and we kept it in a cage in the kitchen. That darn bird learned only two things. The first was an earsplitting chimpanzee scream, and the second was *"No! No! No! No!"* It seems so funny now, but I'm telling you when that bird started up with that, we got rid of it so fast! There was enough noise in the house, thank you, without a bird repeating it.

Let's see, now, where was I?

Oh yes. In the beginning, you know, Jennie took a great interest in Sarah. She carried her around and even fed her once in a while. She put her in the high chair, fed her, and then wiped up the mess. It was quite a sight, watching an animal feeding a baby with a spoon. But around two we realized Sarah didn't really like Jennie. She was a quiet child, and she liked an orderly house. She always put her toys away, even without being asked. She did not like a chimpanzee or anyone else getting into her toys. Jennie was always getting into things and creating a ruckus.

Jennie would take her toy and Sarah would sit there and burst into tears. And then Jennie would quickly give it back. That chimp just hated it when people cried. She was so concerned and would whimper and say "Oo oo oo" and try to pat away their tears. You know, chimpanzees can't cry. They don't have the tear ducts or whatever. Or is it they don't have the proper part of the brain? Maybe that was for speech. I get so confused sometimes about all these experiments they did.

When Sarah became mobile, she made it quite clear that Jennie's presence was a bother. If Jennie so much as looked in her direction she would clutch her toys in her little fists try to totter away with them. Poor Sarah! Growing up with a noisy, rambunctious chimp was not her idea of fun.

Sarah naturally picked up some signing. Not like Sandy, but she was quite capable of telling Jennie where to get off. In ASL. She'd sign *Go away!* or *Bad Jennie!* at two years old. Can you imagine?

In that first year Jennie must have learned fifty signs. She was really quite the genius. After a year, Jennie and Sandy were signing back and forth like pros. They had a ritual. When Sandy came home from school the two of them went straight to the kitchen, looking for food. Jennie was signing furiously that she wanted something to eat.

What? Demonstrate? Oh dear, I haven't signed in seventeen years. Let's see now. . . . [Editor's Note: At this point Mrs. Archibald stood up and demonstrated each of the signs as she told the story.]

So Jennie would say, *Me Jennie eat*, like this.

Sandy always had a snack when he came home from school, and Jennie knew she was going to get something too. On the rare days when Sandy came home late or went over to a friend's house to play, Jennie would fret and fret and finally come banging and hooting into the kitchen, demanding her snack.

Anyway, when Sandy came home they both went straight to the kitchen. Sandy would sign *What Jennie eat?* Sandy had to get her what she wanted, because Jennie was absolutely forbidden on pain of death to touch the refrigerator. When Jennie got older, we actually had to padlock the refrigerator. She had no self control.

Jennie might sign *Eat Jennie eat orange* or something like that. While Sandy was rummaging around in the refrigerator, Jennie would be signing furiously *Orange, orange, orange!* She had no patience, that chimp! And Sandy would get irritated and start telling Jennie to shut up, like this: *Jennie wait shut up!*

I found it a bother to sign all the time, especially when I had my hands full cooking dinner. Jennie could understand quite enough English. But Sandy, he signed all the time. He was hardly aware of it. Sometimes when he lost his temper at me he'd yell and start signing something right in my face. At the same time.

At first, Jennie's table manners were awful. Sandy took it upon himself to improve her. When she drank milk, he signed *Clean mouth*. If she spat her food out, Sandy signed *No Jennie eat food*. Jennie would sign back *Bad food, bad food*, like this, and Sandy would respond *Jennie shut up, no spit food, eat food*. On the rare occasions when she still threw food, Sandy would really let her have it. *No Jennie, no throw food, bad bad Jennie!* And Jennie would usually hang her head and sign *Sorry sorry sorry.*

Sandy sometimes became just a shade too zealous in scolding Jennie at dinner. Sometimes Jennie turned the tables on him! When Sandy drank milk Jennie would sign *Clean mouth, clean mouth!* even while he was still drinking. Well! Sandy did not like Jennie telling him what to do. He'd sign back *Shut up Jennie,* and she would hop up and down in her chair signing *Clean mouth! clean mouth!* Just like a brother and sister. It made Sandy so mad.

Ah dear. It was hard to stay mad at her though. She knew just what to do. I remember one day. I had scrubbed and cleaned the floor with a little bit of Babbo cleanser, and she was enthralled by the powder coming out of the can. She kept trying to get back in the cabinet to inspect the can. I said no and thought that was the end of it. I left the kitchen for a few minutes, and when I returned, there was Jennie in the middle of the floor, completely covered with Babbo, with the stuff all over the floor. She looked at me and before I could even say anything she was signing *Sorry, sorry, sorry, sorry!*

Now this made me even madder. Jennie knew perfectly well that she was doing wrong, and she thought that just by signing *sorry* she could escape punishment. I grabbed her by the ear and I hauled back to give her a good swat on the fanny, when she signed *Me Jennie! Hug Jennie!* That stopped me dead. How could I possibly hit Jennie when she talked to me like that? Crying out that she was Jennie and to hug her. She certainly had my number, that chimp.

You know, Jennie, for all her roughhousing, was very kind. She was always terribly concerned when someone got sick or hurt. When Sandy cried, she instantly stopped whatever she was doing and hugged him and touched his tears and tried to wipe them away. She was always concerned with our welfare.

I think it was the summer of 1969. I had never had chicken pox as a child, and that summer I came down with it. I was awfully sick.

I was in the kitchen cutting tomatoes from our garden, and Jennie was playing on the floor. I had been feeling under the weather all day and suddenly I felt nauseous. I ran into the downstairs bathroom and was sick. Jennie came running in, and she was upset. She hugged me around the waist and whimpered and laid her little palm on my forehead.

I was so surprised with what Jennie did next. She signed *Bad, bad!* at the toilet, and then actually struck the toilet with her hands! *Bad dirty dirty bad!* she signed, hitting the toilet again, as if somehow the toilet were at fault. *Dirty* was her sign for both going to the bathroom and the toilet itself.

She followed me upstairs and helped me turn down the sheets to the bed. When I got in it, she crouched on the bed, kissing my hand and wiping the sweat on my brow. She quickly noticed the spots developing on my forehead and shoulders. She touched them lightly with her fingers, hooted mournfully, and signed *Hurt hurt Lea hurt*.

By this time I was feeling simply dreadful. *Hurt* was one of Jennie's favorite signs, you know. She used to sign *hurt* when she saw a scab on you. She'd poke at it and sign *Hurt?* Or she'd bang her knee and rush over signing *Hurt!* frantically, and we'd comfort her. Until she started doing it again and again and we realized she wasn't hurt at all! Just faking, the little rascal!

Anyway, Jennie began rubbing the chicken pox spots and signing *Go away bad bad*. When I asked her to stop, she just sat there, looking so miserable and worried. The she signed *Hurt Jennie hurt*.

As sick as I was, this touched me. *Jennie hurt.* My being sick was causing her pain. I felt like crying I was so touched. She was so truly concerned about me, so deeply worried. Hugo put me in the guest room and Jennie stayed up with me the whole night, getting me a glass of water when I asked, stroking and grooming my hair, kissing me, and showing the most genuine concern. It was more than just concern: Jennie was actually scared. She even brought me her food. She was quite insistent, even though I couldn't even think about eating. She would sign *Eat eat* or *Eat apple apple* while shoving a disgusting half-eaten apple in my face.

For two weeks while I was sick she hardly ever left my room. Sandy might be outside, whooping it up with his friends in the yard. Jennie would go to the window and look out, but she wouldn't leave. It was a bit of a bother, her in the room day and night. When Hugo tried to get Jennie out, she screamed so frantically that we decided it was better for her to stay. During the two weeks I was bedridden, Jennie lost so much weight she began to look sick herself. That's how worried she was. Oh my goodness, she was such a kind little animal. . . .

Yes, Jennie was very kind; it was her most outstanding quality. It was just that sometimes she didn't know her own strength, and she didn't understand that people were a lot more fragile than she was. Sometimes she was rougher than she intended, you see. Did you know that a full-grown female chimpanzee is three to five times stronger than a man?

Her kindness wasn't only to humans. Did I tell you about Jennie's pet kitten? Jennie just loved looking at pictures of animals in magazines, and she particularly liked cats. One day Sandy and Jennie and I were looking at a magazine, I forget which, and there was a picture of two cute kittens peeking out of a mailbox.

Jennie signed, like this, *Cat, cat.* Sandy was there and he asked Jennie if she wanted a cat. Well! Jennie loved the idea. Jennie started signing *Give cat, cat give cat me.*

Well why not? So we went to the pound and brought Jennie a kitten. It was a little gray-and-white Siamese cross that Sandy named Booger T. Archibald. Please don't ask me why. We set it free in front of Jennie. Now was that a mistake. We should have known better. Jennie did not like surprises. If a package arrived and was put carelessly in the hallway, Jennie would sometimes be frightened of it and hit or stamp on the package. She managed to break a piece of Lalique glass my mother had sent, just stomping on the box. And this was after the post office had done their damnedest with it!

Anyway, when Jennie saw the kitten she signed *Bad cat bad cat angry!* and rushed at it, her hair all sticking up, and we barely saved its life. We were *horrified*. Then Jennie went and skulked in a corner while we talked about what we were going to do. Meanwhile, the kitten started wandering around. The next thing we knew it was heading in Jennie's direction. Sandy jumped up to fetch it, but Jennie reached out and tenderly picked it up and started stroking it. She'd just been frightened, that's all.

After that, they were inseparable. Jennie lugged that poor kitten around night and day. She put it on her back and Booger would cling for all he was worth while Jennie went about her business. At other times she would cradle it in her arms just like a baby and rock while it purred away like a little motor. She even tasted its food and made horrid faces. Cat food was the epitome of what Jennie considered bad food. All meaty and fishy tasting.

She showed real tenderness toward Booger. Booger wasn't quite so thrilled, I think, to be the property of a chimpanzee. If Booger was eating and Jennie heard something interesting going on in the other room, she picked it up and carried it with her, not thinking that maybe the poor little thing would like to finish its dinner first. That poor cat was carried around day and night. It was never allowed to just sleep on the sofa and be a kitten.

Jennie and Sandy used to argue about the kitten. There was no role in "Space Invaders" for a cat. Sandy would tell Jennie to put the cat down and Jennie would refuse, putting the cat on her back and taking up her position on the lawn. And Sandy would order her to put down the cat, and she'd sign *Jennie's cat!* Of course, while she signed she'd still be holding the cat, and the poor thing would be slung about. Once, when Jennie finally put down the cat, she signed *Stay, stay!* I could hardly stop laughing.

Jennie signed to everything: animals, people, pictures in books. She never figured out that animals couldn't sign and that only a few people could sign. I told you about how she signed to the toilet. She just couldn't stop expressing herself.

*   *   *

Jennie had Booger for only three months. Then one day, in the morning, we heard Jennie scream in her room and pound on the door. By this time we simply had to lock her into her room at night, or she would go wandering about and cause no end of trouble.

We rushed in and found Booger dead. His neck was broken. Jennie was simply terrified of the dead cat. She would reach out to touch it with a trembling hand and jerk away at the last moment. She was whimpering and hugging herself over and over again. With that hideous grimace of fear. *Cat, cat, cat,* she signed, and then *Bad cat, bad bad bad.* I think she had rolled over on the cat during the night. The cat used to sleep in her bed, you see. Or maybe she played with it too roughly. Anyway, that was the end of Booger T. Archibald.

I'll tell you a most interesting story. Years later, at least three years later, we were looking through some old photo albums. And there was a picture of Jennie holding her cat. She slapped her hand on the page and looked intently at the picture. She wouldn't let us turn the page.

Then, all of a sudden, she signed *Jennie's cat!* Like this, with both hands, *Jennie's cat!* And she fell silent—I mean she stopped signing, of course—and she just stared at the picture with the saddest expression on her face. Every time we tried to turn the page, she'd put out her hand to stop us. She looked at that picture for a good ten or fifteen minutes and then started signing, very slowly and clumsily, as if to herself, *Sorry, sorry, sorry.* It was awfully sad.

[FROM *Recollecting a Life* by Hugo Archibald.]

In the late 1960s, when it seemed as if the country were falling apart, my work at the museum was proceeding apace. My phylogenetic analysis of the primates had allowed me to construct a revision of the "evolutionary tree" of the primates, *Homo sapiens sapiens* included.

There are many popular misconceptions of the evolutionary tree—or, as I prefer to call it, a phylogenetic schema. It is not, as many believe, a diagram showing how "man evolved from the apes"—for, in fact, man did *not* evolve from the apes. Man and the great apes all evolved from a common ancestor, each species taking its own evolutionary pathway.

The most controversial result of my work—still not generally accepted—was to eliminate the family *Pongidae* entirely and place the pongids in with the family *Hominidae*. Thus the genus *Homo* shares the same family with the genus *Pan* (chimpanzee), the genus *Pongo* (orangutan), and the genus *Gorilla* (gorilla). Put in simpler terms, I grouped man with the other great apes. Man, clearly, does not merit a separate family all to himself. Man is a mere variation of the great ape pattern—in morphology, genetics, and basic behavior. Cultural development—which is where humans differ from the apes most dramatically—is not biologically based and should not be taken into account in a classification.

We humans, even human scientists, are still suffering from that disease known as *egocentria*. One primatologist, my good friend Stephen I. Rosen, stated it best when he wrote that "man and ape are separated more by ego than anatomy." This is the affliction that once caused us to place the earth at the center of the universe, and it still infects some taxonomists who wish to award mankind its own exclusive genus. I, personally, do not see the danger in sharing our family tree with a few of the more intelligent apes. It would be a small step in recognizing our relatedness to all life on earth, something we must do in order to survive as a species. We are not the result of a special creation.

My preliminary reclassification of the primates used only skeletal morphology as the basis for determining the relationships among the apes. I wanted to extend this work to DNA and blood protein analysis. How closely related are the apes using these methods? I received a generous National Science Foundation grant to make these studies. My graduate students, Ellen Bitterbaum and Giancarlo DiLuglio, did much of the work on this project and I wish to acknowledge their fine contributions here. Ellen is now at the Institute for Advanced Study at Princeton, and doing splendid research there on isolating antibodies from human archaeological remains. Giancarlo was tragically killed in a car accident some years ago, and the world lost a promising young scientist.

Many readers of this memoir will already be aware of one "startling" conclusion from this research: humans and chimpanzees share roughly 98 to 99 percent of the same DNA. This fact was widely reported in the press, but—as is usual with popular journalism—it was reported out of context and with no understanding of what the numbers meant. For example, humans share 40 percent of the same DNA with termites. Extremely small differences in DNA sequences can mean very large differences in morphology and behavior. The conclusion that we share up to 99 percent of the same DNA with chimpanzees alone was not all that startling: what mysteries lurk in that 1 percent!

What was more significant from a biological point of view were the many similarities between humans and chimpanzees in brain structure, the endocrine system, chromosomes, blood albumen proteins, and the immune response. This is what makes chimpanzees so important in medical research, especially for studies of human pathogens such as the Human Immunodeficiency Virus (HIV). Chimpanzees are susceptible to almost all the same diseases as humans. When Dr. Jane Goodall was studying the chimpanzees of Gombe, a terrible polio epidemic, introduced from a nearby African village, swept the chimpanzee community; and only through administering the human polio vaccine to the chimpanzees was she able to prevent a worse tragedy.

To me the most startling result of the research was that we found the differences between humans and chimpanzees were much smaller than had been supposed. To put it another way, chimpanzees are more related to humans than they are to gorillas and orangutans.

In a curious way I was discovering this same conclusion in my own home, with Jennie. By 1968 Jennie was signing fluently, using almost a hundred signs. Being able to communicate with Jennie changed our family in a profound way. I am not exaggerating when I say that it changed Sandy's life. He became extraordinarily fluent in ASL and he and Jennie carried on conversations together, he signing so fast that one could hardly see his fingers move, while Jennie watched spellbound, and then fumbled her reply, always eager to keep up.

I have always been a verbal person, and when I began to communicate with Jennie using ASL it carried my relationship with her to a new level. Not that we discussed anything profound; Jenny's utterances usually revolved around such necessities as food, play, and bodily functions. Nevertheless, it seemed so natural that I found myself thinking of Jennie as my own daughter, and when I looked at her, I did not see an animal; I saw a child. Anyone who has lived with a severely handicapped person knows that the handicap, so shocking when first seen, eventually becomes invisible. In just this way Jennie's "animalness" became invisible to us—so much so that I will relate a rather embarrassing story illustrating this.

It was a snowy Sunday during the winter of 1968. I was in my study going over a grant proposal. Sandy and Jennie had gone sledding on the golf course, and Lea was out with Sarah. Toward late afternoon, I heard a loud simian screaming coming from a distance, and I looked out the window. I saw Sandy jogging along, pulling a toboggan on which Jennie sat, screaming her head off. These were not normal screams. I rushed downstairs as they arrived at the back door.

Jennie had sledded into a tree and was badly hurt. I immediately got her inside and on the sofa. She had a bloody nose, which had bled over her clothing. We got her jacket and shirt off but she screamed every time we tried to remove her pants. I then slit her pants off with a knife and felt her leg. To my horror I discovered a badly displaced double fracture of the tibia and fibula. The broken ends of the bones had not pierced the skin but I could feel the broken end of the tibia pressing into the calf muscles. Jennie was frantic with pain.

Sandy was also upset, so I told him to stay put and I would bring Jennie to the emergency room. He insisted on coming, so we bundled her up and roared off to the Newton-Wellesley Hospital. By the time we got there Jennie had quieted down somewhat. I was even more worried, because she had a glassy look showing the beginnings of shock. But she was still coherent, and as I carried her into the emergency room she feebly signed *Jennie hurt, Jennie hurt*. I bundled her up on an empty cot and a nurse came over with a clipboard to sign us in. She was an older woman, stout, one of those unflappable nurses who had seen just about everything. I was immediately reassured.

"What's the problem?" she asked.

"Displaced fracture of the tibia and fibula," I said. "Sledding accident."

She looked up with a slight raising of the eyebrows and asked, "Are you a doctor?"

"No," I said.

She lowered her head.

"Patient's name?"

"Jennie Archibald," I said. I gave her the address and signed the release.

"Let's take a look," she said, and we went over. The nurse bent over the cot and let out a very short scream. She spun to me.

"What is *this*?" she demanded.

"What? What's wrong?" I said.

"Is this some kind of *joke*?" Her voice was ice cold.

"What the devil are you talking about?" I said. I could not understand what had suddenly come over her.

"*Get* this animal out of here," she said. "This is not an animal hospital."

I remember stammering "What?" It still took me a few seconds to understand what she was exercised about. Jennie, of course, was an animal, and this was a human hospital. When I realized this I became angry.

"You mean you're going to *refuse* her admission?" I cried. "Can't you see—"

"*I* see an animal," the nurse said. "We have a strict rule against animals in the emergency room. I'm sorry, if you don't remove her immediately I'm going to call Security."

Jennie signed *Jennie hurt* to Sandy. Sandy signed back, in his wonderfully fluent way, *No worry, Sandy love Jennie, Jennie feel good soon.*

Jennie then signed *Jennie hurt, Jennie hurt, hug.*

The nurse was staring at the two of them, and a peculiar expression developed on her face. She asked, "Are they speaking ASL to each other?" It turned out she had done work with deaf children and knew some ASL.

"That's right," I said. "Jennie is a member of our family. She speaks ASL."

"Oh lord," said the nurse. "I can't believe it."

I finally collected my wits. "May I speak with the admitting physician?" I asked.

"I'll get him," she said.

He was a young nervous intern, short and stocky. He followed the nurse on stumpy legs with a worried expression on his face. He looked so young and earnest that I girded myself for a big fight. There was no chance I was going to take Jennie to another hospital, let alone a veterinary clinic. She was in serious shock.

"This is Jennie," I said. "She's a member of our family. She has a very badly broken leg."

The doctor stared. Sandy was signing comforting words to Jennie, while Jennie was still signing *Jennie hurt*.

"What's this?" he said. "A talking chimpanzee?"

"In a way," I said.

"Why did you bring it here?" he asked.

I replied, not altogether truthfully: "Because a chimpanzee's physiology is a lot more like a human than a dog or cat. A veterinary hospital wouldn't know what to do with her."

The doctor nodded. Emergency room doctors are trained to make fast decisions, and he was no exception. "Okay," he said, "let's go."

"Doctor, how should I admit her?" the nurse said.

"As Jennie . . . Jennie . . ."

"Archibald," I said.

"Archibald. We don't have to say what she is. There's no line for 'species' on that form of yours, is there?"

And that was that.

six

[EXCERPTS from the journals of the Rev. Hendricks Palliser.]

February 12, 1968

Last week I purchased, somewhat belatedly, a book on American Sign Language for the Deaf. It is a textbook with many instructive pictures. It is indeed great fortune that Jennie has begun learning ASL and can now communicate with people. I have wondered about the fortuitous series of events that have led to this juncture. It is too much to believe in coincidence; indeed, I am once again reminded that there is no such thing as coincidence.

I practiced my signs all week, and when Jennie arrived I greeted her with a big "Hello!" (in sign language, of course). Jennie signed something in return, but I am afraid I missed it. It is possible she was scratching herself. Her signing is rather sloppy and sometimes I wonder if it is signing at all. We sat down for the morning's lesson.

I brought out a picture book of the life of Jesus, which had been my favorite book as a child. It is much dog-eared but the pictures are still fresh and colorful. Jennie perused it with much grunting and poking. When we came to the picture of the Baby Jesus in the manger, surrounded by the animals, Jennie stopped and made some more signs, at least I think she did, looking into my face with a hopeful, questioning expression. I could find no sign for Jesus in the textbook so I signed *baby* and Jennie immediately signed it back. Such an intelligent creature! When we arrived at the Sermon on the Mount, I created a sign for Jesus, which I thought rather clever: the hand placed behind the head, tracing out in circular motion a halo. This Jennie did not understand. I pointed to the picture and made the sign, and pointed again. Then I helped Jennie fashion the sign with her hand. By the end of an hour she almost had it, placing her hand on her head and rubbing it vigorously. She did not, however, seem to connect it to the image of Jesus. These things perhaps take time.

R. has blossomed under Jennie's influence. It breaks my heart to watch her walking with Jennie, hand in hand, around the room, thinking how much she wanted a child. Thinking that she might have had a daughter of her own but for me. R. brought out cookies and milk. We perused the book slowly, and Jennie became restless. She finally stood up and wandered about the house, picking up objects. R. became cross and slapped her hand. Jennie crouched on the floor screaming and holding her hands over her head, and it was a rather upsetting scene. I brought Jennie back to the Archibalds' and R. later felt very sorry and even wept a little. A child would have made such a difference in her life.

February 19, 1968

Jennie is now signing *Jesus*, making an unmistakable connection between the image and the sign! We were perusing the picture book, and when we arrived at the Sermon on the Mount she rubbed the dome of her head while pointing at the picture. I think we shall leave the head rubbing as our sign for Jesus; the halo seems beyond her now. I have been endeavoring to inculcate in her some concepts, simple ones naturally. Such as God as a man who inhabits the sky. Of course, I am not one of those who believe God is a bearded man seated on a throne in the clouds, but as a *concept* it is appropriate for children and those with weak intellectual faculties. I have adopted as a sign for God the "one way" sign of the Christian evangelists; that is, the index finger pointing upward. Really, it is surprising that the books on ASL do not address religious words. It is perhaps another sad indication of the increasing secularization of our society, as if deaf people do not need to speak or know of God.

My approach is this: all good things come from God. Therefore, when Jennie receives anything that delights her, such as a tickle or cookies and milk, I make the God sign and point upward. I have also been "explaining" to her who God is, using other signs, such as *person* and *good* and *beautiful* and *love*. I do not know which, if any, of these signs she knows, except *love,* which she uses in its earthly sense, as in "affection." Is she capable of understanding a higher "love"? Only time will tell.

March 15, 1968

Our progress is slow. Jennie is often distracted, and she has begun to tease R. She will behave like an angel until R. enters the room, and then she will be up and about touching things, which she *well* knows R. abhors. Today R. shouted at her and Jennie, cool as a cucumber, deliberately let fall a knickknack she was holding, which fortunately bounced unharmed on the carpeting. Then she signed *Sorry* in a manner that I can only characterize as insolent, although R. does not, fortunately, understand American Sign Language. Jennie had been frequently employing another sign that had a rather vulgar air, and which I looked up and discovered was "Phooey!" Imagine teaching an animal to speak like that. I was shocked and amused at the same time. Jennie is very like a human child in challenging and testing her elders. I feel that R. wants to love Jennie, and wants Jennie to love her. She does not, I fear, have the right touch with Jennie. She is too cross and nervous, and she is overly attached to material objects. Jennie is very sensitive and has a mischievous streak in her. The combination is not good.

It has, indeed, been a trying day. Jennie tore pages from *The Life of Christ* and attempted to eat one. She signed *God* over and over again, indiscriminately, at everything, and I simply was incapable of making her desist. It was redolent of blasphemy, of taking the Lord's name in vain.

No one promised this would be easy. Some of my most devout congregationals are often those who came to God through adversity and sneering doubt.

[FROM an interview with Harold Epstein.]

I'm sure you've heard from Mrs. Archibald all about the subject of Dr. Pamela C. Prentiss. Now Mrs. Archibald is a strong-minded, capable, smart woman, sharp as a tack, and cranky as hell. In almost any marriage there is a dominant partner, and she was the dominant partner in that marriage. This is not to say Hugo was weak. I think you know what I mean.

Dr. Prentiss, in many ways, was just like Mrs. Archibald. More intellectual, perhaps, but not smarter. More defensive. Wrapped up in her science, and not aware of much else. As often happens when two strong women meet, they clashed. I want you to take what Mrs. Archibald said with a grain of salt, you understand?

Now these two women respected each other, and that's what kept the project going. Hugo and Lea were both excited by Jennie's progress. Lea, as a good mother, recognized what an important force Dr. Prentiss was in Jennie's life. Dr. Prentiss, for her part, may not have approved of Lea's relationship with Jennie, but she recognized that, for all intents and purposes, Lea was Jennie's mother. You don't second-guess a mother.

Dr. Prentiss took herself very seriously. Ah! You see, she was compensating for her looks. Beautiful blond women are supposed to be dumb, and she was, shall we say, a little overanxious to correct that misapprehension. The Jeep, the old clothes, the absence of makeup, all this was by way of compensation. And back then women were discriminated against in science. No doubt about that. So she was a bit defensive.

It is no mystery where the real source of conflict with Mrs. Archibald came from. The feminists are going to jump down my throat, but Dr. Prentiss, like most women, had a strong maternal instinct and this she directed to Jennie. All subconscious, of course. This put her in subconscious conflict with Lea for Jennie's love and attention. Two mothers, one child. This is not to say both individuals were undisciplined neurotics. To the contrary. They handled their relationship quite well, considering. I don't believe the conflict affected Jennie. Of course I wasn't there when they were together.

Let's talk about the science for a moment. Can you stand it? Just a little bit? If it gets too dull you can always edit it out. Young man, I'm going to make you understand the scientific issues here whether you like it or not.

Dr. Prentiss came 'round my office from time to time, to discuss her findings. We had an informal arrangement. As a psycholinguist, she lacked a sense of the human context of the experiments. I, being a cultural anthropologist, was able to provide this.

I felt that we were seeing results that had wide implications. The colony chimpanzees weren't learning at anywhere near the rate of Jennie. Dr. Prentiss therefore concluded that language acquisition in chimpanzees was dependent on their degree of human socialization. We know that language acquisition in human children is also dependent on their degree of socialization. The link between human culture and language is so tight, and so complex, that—Pam reasoned—even an animal requires some degree of human socialization in order to learn language. Astounding! Happily adjusted chimpanzees, no matter how pampered, just can't cut it the way a home-raised chimp could. This was her conclusion.

Now I detected a flaw in this hypothesis. What if Jennie were a genius? Dr. Prentiss saw my point immediately. Jennie's fluent signing ability might not be the product of human socialization; she might just be smarter than the Barnum chimps.

However, a solution suggested itself to me rather quickly. Why not devise a chimpanzee IQ test? We agreed this was a brilliant idea.

Little did we know where it would lead us, and what astounding results would emerge.

We devised a set of tests that were not dependent on language. This was to equalize Jennie's advantage over the Barnum chimps. We created a number of "problems" and set the chimps to solving them. The details are complicated, but I will describe a few. You see, it was the results from these cognitive "problems" that so startled us. To the point where Dr. Prentiss greatly expanded the Jennie project. It was these IQ tests that finally (in my mind) erased the dividing line between human and animal.

The problems ranged from simple to very difficult. The simpler ones were mechanical, the more difficult ones cognitive. The problems required only the minimum of signing ability, well within the range of the colony chimps. Dr. Prentiss and I had a great deal of help from an ethologist at the museum named Alfred R. Jones, and a psychologist at Tufts by the name of Murray Sonnenblick.

I'm going to describe some of the tests and their results. The conclusions were *astounding*. I can see you are nodding off already. Bear with me; I promise you will not be disappointed. This is not boring.

We tested Jennie in the museum. In an empty storage room in the basement, which we painted with bright colors and turned into a playroom. We built a one-way mirror in the door, visible from the corridor outside. It wasn't the most comfortable observation point, sitting out there in the filthy basement corridor, with the steam pipes rumbling—but it sufficed.

The first tests involved mechanical problem solving. Many of these tests we adapted from earlier primate researchers.

The first test was called the "banana in the tube" test. It was originally thought up by Yerkes. We bolted a tube to the floor, open at both ends. Then we put a banana in the middle, out of reach. The only way to get the banana out was with a pole, by poking it through the tube and pushing the banana away from you and out the other end. Somewhat anti-intuitive.

We put Jennie inside the room and left. There was a long pole in the corner. Jennie explored everywhere, and it wasn't long before she peered into the tube and saw the banana. Jennie was so upset! She screamed and pointed and signed *Banana, Jennie eat banana! Give banana!* Nothing happened, so she tried to reach it. She hammered on the tube. She somersaulted and hooted. She drummed her hands and feet on the floor. We gave her an hour of this and then let her out. It took her three one-hour sessions before she solved the problem.

She was staring down the tube through her legs, and chattering grumpily, when suddenly she stopped, stood up and went directly to the pole propped in the corner, and grabbed it. *In that very instant* it was obvious to all of us that she had solved the problem. Sure enough, she went straight to the tube, pushed the banana out, and ate it with a great smacking of the lips. It was extraordinary. We could actually see when the idea occurred to her to use the pole.

Our psychologist, Dr. Sonnenblick, told us we should test Jennie for an ability called "cross-modal transfer." This is nothing more than the ability to recognize through touch something we see with our eyes, and vice versa. This was, Sonnenblick said, supposed to be a uniquely human ability.

Aha! Not so. We let Jennie feel a football blindfolded. Then we showed her photographs of five objects. Right away she picked out the football. We showed her a picture of a teacup, and then blind-folded her and let her feel five objects. Again, she picked out the teacup. The other chimps at the Barnum colony were also able to do this. Ha! You should have seen Sonnenblick's face!

I won't go into all the experiments that were done. The IQ tests showed that Jennie was smarter than the colony chimps, but not by an overwhelming margin. So, in fact, her upbringing as a human had something to do with her acquisition of language. Very, very interesting!

This was not all we discovered. The question of the chimps' IQs became secondary to what we learned from the tests themselves. And what was being discovered about chimpanzees in the wild. *I'm telling you, the sharp dividing line between man and ape has been erased.* Many of the fundamental traits that we thought distinguished humans from the animals went the way of the flat earth. Now let's see . . . I want to read you something. [Editor's note: At this point Dr. Epstein took a book down from his shelf and flipped through it.]

Aha! Diogenes. Here we are. "Plato having defined man to be a two-legged animal without feathers, Diogenes plucked a cock and brought it into the Academy, and said, 'This is Plato's man.' On which account this addition was made to the definition: 'With broad flat nails.' " [Laughs.]

You see, we've been trying to define Man for a long time. I mean in contradistinction to all the animals. We're obsessed with it. It was a ridiculous exercise then, as Diogenes points out, and it is now. But we can't help it, can we?

Many years ago they said: only human beings have the ability to make and use tools. Not so: Jane Goodall observed wild chimpanzees making and using tools. Then they said it was language that made us human. Not so again: since the late fifties chimpanzees have been learning ASL and other symbolic languages.

Well then, they said: only humans have imagination and creativity. Well, I told you about Jennie and the doll. We did other tests that showed extraordinary imagination and creativity on the part of chimps.

So they said that we human beings are the only ones who could understand and manipulate symbols. Right? Wrong. In dozens of tests, Jennie and the colony chimps showed ample knowledge of symbols and pictures. I remember Jennie putting her ear to a drawing of a conch shell, listening for the sea. We were able to show that she recognized certain letters and even two or three words. Yes indeed, whole words. The Barnum chimps used colored disks to get food and toys.

Aha! they said, but chimpanzees surely don't have the awareness of self that humans do. Wrong again. All you had to do was put Jennie in front of the mirror and sign *Who that?* and she would sign *Me Jennie!* Now if you can devise a better test for self-awareness than that, be my guest.

Yes, they said, but only humans have the ability to abstract and generalize. Right? Sorry, my friend. Jennie and the colony chimpanzees all showed the ability to classify apples, oranges, and bananas into the concept of *fruit.* She could classify plates, cups, and spoons in the category of *tableware,* many kinds of insects as *bugs,* and so forth. Jennie used the *open* sign to indicate the opening of doors, cans of food, turning on the water faucet, and opening the mouth. Think about that for a moment. That alone requires a high level of symbolic reasoning, generalization, and symbolic classification.

Aha! What about lying? What about all those bad human qualities that animals supposedly don't possess? Lying, cheating, stealing, cruelty, murder? The chimps had those too. Goodall observed coldblooded murder, viciousness, and cannibalism among her chimpanzees. And lying! Jennie could lie just as well as any human. We did a fascinating series of tests that showed this.

Dr. Prentiss placed a banana inside one of three locked boxes, while Jennie watched. Then, a "selfish" volunteer came into the room and asked Jennie: *Where banana?*

The first time, Jennie pointed to the right box. Then the "selfish" assistant unlocked the box and ate the banana, right in front of Jennie, without giving her any. Jennie was outraged! The perfidity of it!

The experiment was repeated. *This* time, when the "selfish" person asked Jennie where the banana was, she lied! She pointed to the wrong box, an empty box! Had she forgotten? We had the "selfish" assistant leave the key in the empty box and leave. And Jennie grabbed the key, opened up the real box, and ate the banana.

Think about it! It gives me shivers even now.

However, when we repeated the experiment with a "nice" assistant, a person who shared the banana with Jennie, she always told the truth. Weeks and even months later, she would still remember which volunteers were "selfish" and which would share fruit with her. She would lie to the former and tell the truth to the latter.

I'll tell you something else that wasn't in the reports. It was too subjective. It was just the kind of thing that would get the ethologists up in arms. When Jennie lied, she averted her eyes from the person she was lying to. It was uncanny. It was so damn human. She'd lie to you and her eyes would slide sideways in the most guilty way.

We extended this fascinating experiment one step further. Could Jennie tell when someone was lying to her? This time, we had the "selfish" assistant hide a banana in one of two boxes when Jennie couldn't see. Then we gave Jennie the key and let her in. The "selfish" assistant was there. And he lied, telling Jennie (using ASL) that the banana was in a particular box. Did Jennie believe him? Not on your life. She went straight to the other box and opened it up. But when the "nice" assistant told Jennie where the banana was, she believed it.

You know, I would watch Jennie in action, and my skin would crawl. I was overwhelmed with a feeling of connection between me and this animal. I could feel in my very blood the relationship between us.

If you can be a little patient, let me just tell you a few other extraordinary experiments we did. Then I'll let you get back to the story.

We did this experiment with the colony chimps. We gave them colored disks, the red ones representing food and the blue ones representing toys. We taught them how to exchange the disks with assistants to receive one or the other. Pretty soon, when a chimp wanted something, he would go fetch a disk and give it to one of the staff. All right.

We took two chimps, and put one in one room and one in another, with a little hatch separating them. One chimp had been well fed, and he was put in a bare room with a pile of apples and a token representing *toy*. The other chimp was left hungry, and he was put in a room with a pile of toys and a token representing *food*. Do you follow?

What happened next was amazing. The full chimp saw the toys in the other room. So he handed his *toy* disk to the hungry chimp, and the hungry chimp gave him toys. Then the hungry chimp exchanged his *food* disk for the apples.

Think about that! That is much more than symbolic communication. The two chimps had spontaneously created a primitive *economy*.

Since the Jennie project ended, more recent experiments have shown even more startling results. Do you know the chimpanzee Washoe, who was taught ASL? Washoe recently adopted a baby and began spontaneously teaching that baby ASL. Without intervention from humans. So even transmission of learning can cross generational lines in chimpanzees.

Speaking of self-awareness, let me just end with one final experiment. This, for me, was the most startling experiment of all. We had a pile of photographs of animals, a photo of Jennie, and photos of people. We put the stack in front of Jennie and told her to separate the animals from the people. She started through them and carefully separated them.

She made only one mistake: she put herself in the human stack.

We told her she had made a mistake and asked her to do it again. Again, she put herself with the humans. So I said to her that she had made another mistake, and I took the photograph of her and put it in the animal stack.

I signed, *Jennie you are an animal.*

And do you know what happened? Jennie hooted and laughed and did a somersault. Great joke, huh?

We insisted that Jennie sort through the pictures again. This time she started to become annoyed, but she still placed herself in the human stack. Once again, I corrected her. I took her photograph out of the human stack and put it in with the animals.

This time Jennie wasn't so amused. She picked up the photographs and threw them across the room.

That wasn't all. Next, we added photographs of other chimpanzees to the stack. Jennie started sorting, again putting pictures of herself in the human stack and the animals in the other. Then she came to another chimpanzee. She stared and stared at it. Then she blithely threw it across the room and continued sorting. "Not classifiable" seemed to be her decision! Think about it! Whenever she came to a photo of a chimp she would just throw it across the room.

So you see, Jennie had a real identity problem, even then. For the life of me, I don't know why we didn't see it. No, we saw it, but we just didn't take it seriously. It seemed . . . *cute* that Jennie thought she was human.

My friend, man does not stand in glorious isolation, the crowning jewel of evolution. Man does not stand proudly on one side of a great divide with all the animal kingdom on the other. Hell no. The difference between us and apes exists only in degree. When you look at the sweep of evolution, the great magnificence and variety of life, from paramecium to dung beetle to man, the chimpanzee is a mere whisper away from us. *A mere whisper.* We must get over this idea that man is a special product of creation.

I will tell you a strange experience I had. I was eating in the curators' dining room and this powerful feeling started to grow on me. A kind of *jamais vu*. I looked around at all the people talking and eating. And it suddenly seemed to me that all these people were apes: chattering, masticating, perambulating, gesticulating apes. Big grotesque hairless apes, with comical tufts of hair sticking out on top. Wearing these bizarre, ritualistically colored strips of cloth. We were a big gathering of apes, like apes in the forest gathering at a tree that had dropped its fruit. The sound, I tell you, it was like the sound in the ape house, this loud, meaningless chattering. And suddenly everything seemed so comical, so ridiculous and trivial . . . so bizarre and utterly without importance . . . that I found myself leaving the room in a panic.

Try it some time, in an airport or restaurant. Close your eyes and listen, and think of the ape house at the zoo. And then open them to watch the people ingesting their food, their lips moving, their joints rotating, their digits manipulating small objects, their appendages gesticulating, their faces contorting into various expressions, and then listen to the glottal eruptions that signify their laughter. . . .

[From the journals of the Rev. Hendricks Palliser.]

June 2, 1968

R. was having tests this morning in the hospital. There has been much uncertainty and agony. My heart goes out to her. There is the possibility, although remote, of cancer. We must begin praying together again, as we used to at the beginning of our marriage. God have mercy on us both. She is afraid of death.

After we came home, I was sitting in the window of my study, looking out into the garden. I saw the sod move, and a gopher emerged into the sunlight and looked about. And then it withdrew into its earthly dwelling. I went out and stamped on the ground and shouted, trying to drive it away. I feared for its safety. If R. sees traces of it she will set the lawn men on it. It is probably raising a little family there, underground.

I have not been diligent with my journal. Yesterday was Jennie's day, and I endured yet another trying afternoon. Jennie, who is so sweet and loving, can also be quite as selfish as the rest of us. All her thoughts revolve around herself, *her* requirements, *her* toys and *her* food. To be sure, children her age are considerably self-centered.

I purchased for her a coloring book of scenes from the Bible. I was trying to teach her of Our Savior's goodness and gentleness to little children. Jennie is much enamored of coloring, although her approach tends to the abstract. She scribbled in a most energetic manner without regard to the picture on the page. I gave her some blank paper and she decorated it with high enthusiasm. And if the truth be told, her efforts are quite as respectable as those of the so-called modern "artists" who splash some paint on canvas and sell it for thousands of dollars! I believe I will organize an art show of Jennie's *oeuvre* at the church. She possesses a creative "urge." When Jennie has crayons in her hand, however, one has to watch her like a hawk, or she will mark the table and walls.

July 12, 1968

Jennie and I made a major accomplishment today. Now that my signing is improved, we have devised a kind of catechism, to teach her religious concepts. When Jennie gets a right answer I give her a cookie. She has launched into the game with the utmost enthusiasm. I have started writing down our conversations. It strikes me that, where else in the universe is an animal learning about God? I have decided to preserve this for posterity.

Our conversation today went like this:

Myself: *Jennie, what God?*
Jennie: *Up.*
Myself: *Up where?*
Jennie: *Up up.*
Myself: *Who God?*
Jennie: *God God God.*
Myself: *Who God?*
Jennie: *Up.*
Myself: *No, who God?*
Jennie: *Love.*
Myself: *Correct!* (Then I gave her a cookie.)
Jennie: *God love God love God love.*
Myself: *Who Jesus?*
Jennie: *Jesus Jesus.*
Myself: *No, Jennie, who Jesus?*
Jennie: *Jennie cookie.*
Myself: *Who Jesus?*
Jennie: *Tickle Jennie.*
Myself: *Who Jesus?*
Jennie: *Jesus tickle Jennie.*
Myself: *Jesus God's son.*
Jennie: *Jesus.*
Myself: *Who son of God?*
Jennie: *Jesus cookie tickle.*
Myself: *Who Jesus?*
Jennie: *God's son God's son.*

When she signed *God's son* I was overwhelmed. The power of God is so overwhelming that I could feel His presence like a great light surrounding our little workroom. Is it possible that I have brought God to the mind of a chimpanzee? There it was, *God's son.* Jesus, the only begotten Son of God. It was her answer to the question Who is Jesus? What more could I ask for?

It was a transcendent moment.

September 1, 1968

I have now resolved to ask for a Christian commitment from Jennie. I will ask her to take Jesus into her heart as her savior. The question is, how may I guide Jennie to this next step? It may very well be impossible. But who would have thought we would progress so far? Who would have thought that Jeannie would comprehend that Jesus is the Son of God?

I have determined to accomplish this with a series of questions covering the steps to a Christian commitment: to acknowledge one's sinful nature, to acknowledge Jesus as the Son of God who has the power to forgive our sins, and to take Jesus into our hearts and ask His forgiveness. So, I will proceed as follows:

Jennie you love Jesus? Jennie know Jennie bad? Jesus love Jennie? Jesus take away Jennie's bad? I shall require her to repeat these things, or at the minimum to sign *Yes*. Understanding begins with repetition. Then there is the question of baptism. I can only imagine what the bishop might make of that. One bridge at a time. I am not one of those who slavishly hold to the necessity of baptism as a prerequisite to salvation. I shall study up on the signs.

R.'s chemotherapy is going better than expected. Total loss of hair, though. We are praying together for the first time since the early part of our marriage, and I am more filled with love for her than ever. She seems so broken and helpless; but God's love will give her and both of us strength.

[FROM an interview with Lea Archibald.]

Let's see . . . Sometime in 1968 I got a call from the Ed Sullivan show. I don't know how they got our name, probably slipped to them by Dr. Prentiss. She was a careerist. Always trying to advance herself. Anyway, there was a lady on the telephone. I've forgotten her name.

She asked, oh so sweetly, if I was Mrs. Archibald. The lady with the darling chimpanzee?

Some darling! I said yes.

She wanted to know, Would Jennie and I like to be on television? She said this as if being on television was the apotheosis of a person's life.

I told her no thank you.

There was a shocked silence on the other end. Well! She said, this was the Ed *Sullivan* show.

But, I said, I'm not interested in being on the Ed *Sullivan* show.

Her tone changed. That hard-bitten New York voice finally showed itself. Honestly, television people are such horrors. She was prepared to offer a generous honorarium. She wanted to come up from New York to meet the "precious" chimpanzee.

Well why not? She came over one evening. She wanted Hugo and me and the chimpanzee's "trainer" on the show. Oh how I wish Dr. Prentiss had been there to hear herself described as a "trainer"! We talked for a while. It was a rather unexceptionable idea and they were offering a tidy sum. Hugo—who you know had inherited gobs of money from his father—bargained and wrangled over the fee and got it way up, and then told the woman to donate it directly to the ASPCA. The look on her face! There would be no "trainer"—*poor* Dr. Prentiss—just the two of us and Jennie.

We took the train to New York. They wouldn't let Jennie fly, but we found we could just take her on a train without even asking. They put us up in the Americana Hotel. It was brand new then, a big ugly New York glass box. That day we went shopping for a new outfit for Jennie. Everywhere we went, crowds of people gathered and ooohed and aaaahed. Jennie was the center of attention and she loved every minute of it. She actually stopped traffic on Fifth Avenue! Hugo was having a marvelous time observing everyone's reactions. Always the anthropologist. But most people merely glanced at her and kept right on going. It was New York, after all.

Jennie was being so well-behaved that we decided to take a

chance and go to Bloomingdale's. A woman screamed when we tried to get on the elevator so we took the escalator. We went to the children's clothing section, and I ran down a salesperson. She was terrified Jennie was going to soil herself in the dressing room or infect the clothes with a disease.

I held up an outfit for Jennie and signed *Jennie like this?*

Well! Don't ask a chimp a question like that. She wanted everything! *Give, give, give!* was all she ever signed back.

The salesgirl watched this for a while and then asked Hugo what we were doing.

Hugo replied that we were discussing which outfit would be most appropriate for Jennie's appearance on the Sullivan show. He had a twinkle in his eye, of course.

Well! What excitement then. Oh my. The Ed Sullivan show! She ran to get the other salesgirls and they came rushing over. Pretty soon we were surrounded by people. It was like that everywhere we went: Jennie was an instant celebrity.

The outfit we bought was so cute. A red-and-white checkered blouse with a big blue bow, a pair of blue pants, and brown-and-white saddle shoes. Big shoes. She needed them big to fit those long feet that were really hands. She strutted around in front of the admiring crowd, hooting and grunting, with a big smile plastered across her face. She could be such a show-off.

That evening we were brought over to the studio in a car, and given a room all to ourselves. They called it the Green Room. We had brought some toys and Jennie played with them while we sat there, feeling more and more nervous. Neither one of us said anything, but I knew we were both imagining all kinds of horror scenes. Anything could have happened. The Ed Sullivan show was live, you know.

Then we were brought on to the set. Ed Sullivan was just as hunched and cadaverous-looking in person as he was on television. I don't remember much of what we said. I do wish I'd gotten a tape of the show. Perhaps I should write to NBC, or was it ABC?

Ed Sullivan started off with something like, "We have a chimpanzee named Jennie who speaks sign language. Jennie, say hello to our viewers."

I signed *Say Hello* and Jennie signed *Hello hello hello!* Hugo told the story of finding Jennie, how he delivered her right there in the jungle. I talked about raising a chimpanzee as a daughter. He wanted to know what our other children thought and I told them about Sandy signing with Jennie. And then Ed Sullivan asked Jennie some more questions and made some silly jokes and that was it.

Well, not quite. Jennie gave us quite a scare. In the middle of the session Jennie signed *Dirty* several times. Ed Sullivan asked, "What's she saying now?" and we had to make up something. I think we said she was asking for a banana. I'm sure there were some ASL viewers who were rolling on the floor over that one! We really didn't know whether she was going to make it, or whether she was just looking for a reaction. But all turned out well. She may have been lying. You know, she often signed *Dirty* when she wanted to cause a ruckus or get out of doing something. She knew how fearful we human beings were of her bodily functions!

The Ed Sullivan show was the beginning of Jennie's social career. Just like the Beatles. I'm exaggerating, of course, but after that everyone wanted to meet Jennie. The phone was ringing off the hook. The *Boston Globe* ran an article about Jennie. Did you see it? After that, Jennie was famous. We rode in on her coattails. Hugo was invited to join the Somerset Club, which you know is one of Boston's oldest clubs, stuffed to the gills with Saltonstalls and Cabots. A famous New York publisher telegrammed Hugo wanting a book. Invitations arrived on Shreve Crump and Lowe stationery, all from people and organizations we had never even heard of. We were invited to the annual Botolphstown Society Ball, an invitation which I, frankly, was offended to receive. It was a very anti-Semitic organization. Not to mention racist. They wanted us to bring Jennie. What a horrid organization. Can you imagine the mindset of these people? Keeping out blacks and Jews but dying to have a chimpanzee? I should have thanked her for the invitation and mentioned that Jennie was so looking forward to it, coming as it did right after her *bat mitzvah*, and would it be all right if Jennie brought her uncle Jazzbo? I never replied, even after a follow-up note arrived, and I heard later that some Cambridge biddy was dreadfully offended. We were *blackballed* forever! [Laughs.]

The crowning moment of Jennie's social career was the Museum of Fine Arts dinner at the Ritz-Carleton. Oh my goodness! It was the hundredth or whatever anniversary of the museum, and they planned a black-tie dinner-dance. It was the most sought-after invitation of the social season. Boston is terribly provincial, you know. Hugo and I would have been the last people invited had it not been for Jennie. Not only did they send an invitation, but this starchy woman called to make sure we understood that the invitation included Jennie. Well! I got the distinct impression that if we didn't bring Jennie, we should probably stay home ourselves.

This was the one invitation we decided to accept. It sounded like so much fun. We bought Jennie a lovely red satin gown, bordered with crinoline, with puff sleeves and a draped neck. It looked so elegant. We also put her in a diaper. We weren't going to take any chances after the Ed Sullivan scare, not on your life.

The night of the dinner-dance, Hugo wore the silk brocade tuxedo he got in Hong Kong, while I wore a pale blue dress. I didn't want to upstage Jennie.

As we drove up the Ritz was ablaze with light, and a string orchestra was sawing away. There was a great line of limousines when we arrived. The footmen, or whatever you call them, were opening the doors and all these terribly fashionable people were stepping out and walking up a red carpet. It was too much. A big snapping crowd of photographers were there, behind velvet ropes.

When we arrived in our '56 Chrysler station wagon, the photographers didn't even look in our direction. Who could possibly be worth photographing in that old car? When we got out, for a moment nothing happened. But then—*then,* when they realized the petite figure in the lovely red gown was a *chimpanzee,* they went absolutely wild. They surged forward and the velvet ropes toppled and we were simply surrounded by these grunting, sweating people shoving cameras in our faces. The flashbulbs were popping away and I couldn't see a thing. It was like being bombed. I could hear Hugo shouting and the security guards yelling and shoving.

Jennie became frightened, and she started to scream. I tried to lift her into my arms but the crush was so impossible that it was all I could do to hold on to her hand. Naturally in her fright she bit one or two photographers. Maybe three. And I don't blame her. I would have done the same thing. There was more shouting and pushing. The bitten photographers were crying *"Help!"* and trying to get away while others were trying to push in. It was . . . I simply can't describe it. Bedlam, absolute *bedlam.*

Finally the security guards cleared a path for us and we escaped. I could hear the most appalling language from some photographer behind me, threats to sue or some such rot. Served him right, the pushy jerk.

Once inside, Jennie was an angel. Everyone was there—Governor Volpe, Bobby and Teddy Kennedy, Senator Brooks. And the *artists*! I've always liked modern art; I don't care what they say about it. There was Jackson Pollock, Andy Warhol, Kenneth Noland, Rothko, Lichtenstein, Jasper Johns—quite a gathering.

Jennie was absolutely the hit of the party. People shoved the governor aside or elbowed a Kennedy just to shake hands with her. [Laughs.] I remember Bobby Kennedy picking her up, saying "Hello, beautiful," and I said "Keep your hands off my daughter." He laughed till I thought his sides would split.

Andy Warhol was walking around with a big sign on his shirt that said "Famous Artist." I suppose he thought he was being funny. Well! Jennie hated pompous people. She walked right up to him and ripped the sign off. Everyone roared with laughter. I never cared for his work. He had only one idea his whole life.

What? Oh yes, the party. I have to say, Jennie was a model of polite behavior. She ate a little bit from each course, although the food was rich and not at all to her liking. She did not throw any food. She even carried on a conversation. We had to translate, of course. The gentleman on our left was the president of some company, and he turned to Jennie and asked her if she liked her dinner.

Hugo had to translate, so he signed *Jennie like food?* Jennie signed right back *Food phooey!*

You want me to demonstrate again? Oh dear. Well, I'll try. Anyway, she was a sensation. Let me see if I can remember. . . .

Someone else asked if she liked the company. So Hugo translated again: *Jennie like people?* He had a rather elegant style of signing, Hugo did. Slow and precise but with a flourish. Like a symphony conductor. He looked so distinguished in that dinner jacket. I'll never forget that evening. . . . Oh dear.

Anyway, Jennie signed back *Jennie like Jennie.* That got another laugh. Honestly, I can hardly believe it now, looking back. She was just so clever, that chimp. I don't know how she knew what to say.

She loved the attention. And of course she started signing *Hug Jennie, hug Jennie.* Hugo translated again and gave her a big hug. Everyone was captivated.

Jennie then wanted a banana. She kept signing for one, and someone asked what she was saying. Hugo translated, and then immediately everyone was up and waving about for a waiter, calling for a banana. She could have been a princess. No one could find a banana and there was a terrible fuss and a waiter was thoroughly dressed down. Finally a banana arrived. I do believe they had to send someone out to the grocery store to get it.

Jennie was in rare form. Jackson Pollock was at our table—you know, the man who did those dribbly paintings—and he'd had a little too much to drink I think, poor man. And he asked Jennie, "Do you like me?" Jennie replied *You stupid.* Oh my goodness, you never asked Jennie a question like that! Our end of the table was rollicking with laughter. Everyone was looking over and you knew they all wished they'd been seated at our table. Hugo was having the most marvelous time.

Hugo signed to Jennie *Who stupid?* and she signed right back *You stupid!* So Hugo asked her, *He stupid?* pointing to Mr. Pollock. Hugo was so wicked. He started to tell Mr. Pollock that Jennie and he had something in common, in their painting styles. It so happens that I love Pollock's work, but Hugo was a bit old-fashioned in his taste for art. . . . Well, I'm off the subject again. Anyway, Jennie got excited and starting signing *Stupid stupid everyone stupid!* while she bobbed up and down in her chair. It was very amusing. Jennie was at her most charming self that night.

During dessert, Bobby Kennedy came over and squatted by Jennie's chair. I'll never forget that conversation. He wanted to know if Jennie was having a good time, and Hugo translated.

Jennie signed right back *Jennie fun, Jennie fun!* And then she asked Senator Kennedy, *Play tickle chase.*

Hugo told him that Jennie wanted him to chase her down and tickle her. Senator Kennedy laughed and said, "My wife wouldn't like that."

So Hugo had to tell Jennie, *Wife say no.*

Jennie signed right back *Wife stupid stupid.*

Kennedy laughed and laughed, and then he wanted to know who Jennie was going to vote for in the primary.

This was a little tough to translate. Hugo had to fudge it. *Jennie like him best?* he signed.

Stupid, Jennie signed. She was getting "stuck" on *stupid.* She often kept repeating a sign if everyone started laughing when she used it. She'd keep signing the one thing over and over again.

Hugo lied and told him she was voting for him.

The senator held out his hand. He gave a funny little speech, something about a banana in every pot. Jennie refused to shake his hand, though. She pushed it aside and opened her arms for a hug. When Kennedy didn't hug her right away, she signed *Hug, hug* insistently and opened her arms again. He finally gave her a hug and went on, shaking hands down the table. The poor man. He was assassinated not one or two months later. He would have made a fine president, not like that horrible Nixon.

When the dance began, Jennie's dance card was full. Everyone wanted to dance with her. Governor Volpe danced with her. Ted Kennedy danced with her. Nobody wanted to go home without dancing with the chimpanzee. Even Warhol came over to dance with her; it was the thing to do apparently. She didn't like him and cut him dead. [Laughs.] Oh my goodness, cut the man *dead*. It was so marvelously funny. It happened like this. Warhol came over and offered Jennie his hand, very languid and *recherché*-like. The man was a walking corpse, all white, you know, with that expressionless face. I would have thought he'd have frightened Jennie. Anyway, Jennie took the hand and pulled him down a little, while puckering her lips. For a kiss. Warhol bent over for the kiss and Jennie razzed him right in the ear, with a big spray of saliva. Oh my goodness! Then she scooted away and hid behind my dress while clacking her teeth and laughing. I didn't see Warhol after that and I'm sure he left in disgrace.

She was always embarrassing people like that. She knew just what to do. I still wonder, how in the world did Jennie know how to do these things? After that incident she was rather pleased with herself and started to get overly excited, so we had to take her home early. Somebody might have gotten bitten.

As she got bigger, she became quite a handful. She didn't bite that often—and she never bit us—but we always had to worry about it. We put locks on all the doors of our house. When she reached the age of three or so, someone always had to be with her when she went outside. Before that she was frightened to leave the yard, but when she got to be three . . . Well! There was no telling whose door she'd be banging at. She became a very bold girl indeed.

[AN excerpt from *Chimpanzee Sweeps Boston Off Its Feet,* from the society page of the Boston *Herald-Traveler,* September 12, 1969. Used with permission.]

BOSTON, Sept. 22—No, an organ grinder was not among the invitees to the **Centennial Celebration** at the **Boston Museum of Fine Arts** last night.

The monkey you all saw on the evening news, sashaying about like a princess, begowned and bejeweled, was none other than Miss Jennie Archibald, scion of the blue blood Archibald family of Kibbencook, adopted daughter of the renowned scientist Dr. Hugo Archibald of **Harvard University**.

It was the opinion of all concerned that the lovely Miss Archibald stole the show at the party to end all parties last evening. More than one upstaged young lady was heard to mutter under her breath, "The nerve of that chimp, coming to the party in a dress *just* like mine."

Well! The nerve!

We understand that Miss Archibald is destined for higher things than cranking a hurdy-gurdy. She is being privately tutored in diction, locution, and grammar by a professor from **Tufts University**, and she is receiving religious instruction from the venerable Dr. Hendricks Palliser, rector of the **Kibbencook Episcopal Church**. Perhaps we will soon hear of her admission to the hallowed ivy-covered halls of her father's alma pater, **Harvard University**, with— we do not doubt—a full scholarship.

Miss Archibald regaled the guests with charming witticisms and *bon mots,* delivered handily (no pun intended) in American Sign Language, which she has been learning for the past few years. She danced the night away with both **Kennedy** brothers and sallied forth arm in arm with the likes of **Andy Warhol**, the **Governor**, and various dignitaries and artists.

Other guests at the party included . . .

seven

[FROM a letter from Alexander ("Sandy") Archibald to the author, dated September 10, 1992.]

Dear Mr. Preston,

Your letter had been sitting at the Totsoh Trading Post for three weeks before I got it. Sorry for such a late reply.

I have heard, of course, about your book. I doubt I can add anything to what you've already got. As far as an interview goes, I'm willing to talk to you but you would have to get out here, and that might be difficult. The nearest town is Lukachukai, Arizona, which is on the western side of the Chuska Mountains west of the Arizona–New Mexico border. Four corners area. It's marked on most good maps. I'm about twenty miles north of Lukachukai, at a place the Navajo call *Hosh dítsahiitsoh,* which means Place of the Poisonous Giant Awl Cactus. You will need a good 4WD vehicle, and it would be unwise to come in the winter, because if there is snow on the ground you'll not be able to follow the road. It's really just two tire tracks in the desert.

I herd cattle and sheep for a Navajo family, and I don't keep a regular schedule. I'm afraid you'll just have to come out here and take your chances about finding me. And you will have to find me, because I really don't want to handle this by letter. I'm a little curious about you, too.

Yours,
S.A.

[EXCERPTS from an unpublished manuscript titled "Conversations with a Chimpanzee" by Dr. Pamela Prentiss. Used with permission.]
Setting: Archibald playroom. December 10, 1969, 10:00 A.M. Jennie is trying on hats in front of a mirror.

Pam: *That nice hat. Nice hat. Say nice hat.*
Jennie: Takes hat off and throws it across room. Holds out her hand for another hat that Pam has.
Pam: *No, Jennie no throw hat. No.*
Jennie: *Me hat. Me hat.* This is signed simultaneously, with Jennie making the sign for *me* (palm on chest) with one hand and *hat* (hand on head) with the other.
Pam: *Jennie no throw hat?*
Jennie: *Me hat!*
Pam: *Jennie be good.* Gives Jennie the hat.
Jennie: Puts hat on. It is a big hat which flops down over her eyes. She pulls it off and throws it across the room.
Pam: *No bad Jennie. No throw hat. Go get hat. Go. Go!*
Jennie: *Go!*
Pam: *No, Jennie go.*
Jennie: *Go! Hat!*

Pam: *No bad Jennie. No throw hat. Go get hat. Apple?*

Jennie: Gets up, collects the two hats, and brings them back to Pam. *Apple!*

Pam: *Thank you Jennie. Here take apple.* Gives Jennie slice of apple, which she crams into her mouth while holding out her hand for more. Pam does not respond.

Jennie: *More!*

Pam: *More what?*

Jennie: *More!*

Pam: *More what?*

Jennie: *More! More!*

Pam: *No.*

Jennie: *Apple!*

Pam: Gives Jennie another slice of apple.

Jennie: *More!*

Pam: *No! No more apple. Jennie want to play with toys there?* Points to Tinkertoy box. This is one of Jennie's favorite activities.

Jennie: *Play. Play.*

Pam: *Play what?*

Jennie: Runs over to the box (which is locked) and starts hammering on the lid with her hands and screaming with excitement.

Pam: *No. Jennie be quiet.*

Jennie: Hops up on the box and starts drumming on the lid with her feet. *Play! Play!*

Pam: *Jennie off box. Jennie play if Jennie get down.*

Jennie: Climbs down from box and waits while Pam opens box. As soon as the lid is raised she scoops out an armful of Tinkertoys and dumps them on the floor. *Play! Pam play!*

Pam: *Jennie make house?*

Jennie: *House!*

Pam: *You and me make house. Say, Jennie make house.*

Jennie: *Jennie.*

Pam: *Say, Jennie make house. Jennie . . . make . . . house.*

Jennie: *Me Jennie.*

Pam: *Make. Make.*

Jennie: Screams in frustration and whacks the floor vehemently with both hands, over and over, her sign for play.

Pam: *No. Jennie be quiet. Make. Make. Say make.*

Jennie: *Say make.*

Pam: *Good! House. House.*

Jennie: *House.*

Pam: *House. Make house.*

Jennie: *House.*

Pam: *Jennie make house?*

Jennie: *Play!*

Pam: *Say Jennie make house. Jennie make house.*

Jennie: *Jennie make house.*

Pam: *Good! Good Jennie! Good! Jennie make house!* Pam starts building a house with the Tinkertoys, fitting the rods into the wheels while Jennie watches, fascinated. Jennie's favorite time will come when the structure is finished, and she will be allowed to knock it over, shake it to pieces, and take it apart.

Jennie: Hopping with excitement. *Good Jennie! Me good Jennie good!*

[FROM an interview with Harold Epstein.]

You keep asking me about Jennie's aggressiveness. Let me see if I can explain to you what we know about chimpanzee aggression. It seems that no matter how much you discuss this subject with journalists, they just don't get it. Please don't take offense, I don't mean you necessarily. I can't understand why some people have such a hard time understanding this.

As Jennie got older, she became more aggressive. This was

normal. Mind you, this was not the kind of aggression you see in disturbed human beings. Her aggression operated according to a set of rules. It was normal chimpanzee aggression. Are you with me so far?

Second point: chimpanzees are not the gentle, peace-loving animals that people once thought. Jane Goodall spent years studying chimpanzees in the wild. She learned that chimpanzees in the wild are very aggressive. They—especially the males—are obsessed with status and their position in the social hierarchy. They're ruthless social climbers. Chimpanzees spend a great deal of time sorting out who's boss and who isn't. Goodall saw many examples of violence, deliberate murder, infanticide, and even cannibalism. Chimpanzees do not fight fair; they gang up on the weak. Sometimes male chimpanzees will beat up female chimpanzees. They fear and loathe strangers. They are territorial. A group of male chimpanzees will sometimes operate like a street gang and go cruising the edge of their territory looking for strange chimps to attack and kill. Jane Goodall, you know, was quite distressed when she realized the Gombe chimpanzees were showing more and more of the ugly traits of humans.

I'm deliberately using anthropocentric terms here. The ethologists are going to kill me when they read this. Let them! The point I'm trying to make is this: chimpanzees (and most other animals) do not live a pure, peaceful existence, killing only to eat. Nor is mankind living in a corrupt and unnatural state, as supposedly evidenced by the high level of violence in our society. I'm trying to lay to rest the notion that violence is deviant—either in chimpanzees or in humans. Aggression is built into our genes and that's that.

If you're going to write a book about Jennie, you need to understand these points. So many of these journalists who wrote about Jennie never could understand the source of Jennie's aggression. These so-called science journalists know as much about science as I know about fixing cars.

You see, like most "pop" thinkers, these writers assumed that any aggression on Jennie's part must be the result of the corrupting influence of human society. Or they said it was abuse at the hands of scientific researchers. Or the result of living in a dysfunctional family, or whatever. This is defective thinking. This idea that animals in nature are uncorrupt and peaceful, while man is corrupt, violent, and unnatural, is sheer, unadulterated, unmitigated, one-hundred-percent crap.

If the murder rate that Jane Goodall saw among the several dozen chimpanzees she studied in Gombe were extrapolated to New York City, for example, there would be over fifty thousand murders a year there. "Man is the only animal that kills for pleasure" you hear people say. What poppycock! Where do people get these ideas? That's as ignorant as asserting the world is flat. Anyone who has owned a cat—and who had two brain cells to rub together—would know this isn't true. Animal behaviorists have noted again and again that predatory species often kill when they have no desire to eat. They are killing because the instinct to kill is very strong. Whether they experience "pleasure" when killing is a moot point.

What the hell do you think's going on when you feed your dog and let him out the door and he chases a squirrel up a tree? He's not hungry, but he wants to kill. Or when your cat stalks birds for hours in the backyard. Even members of nonpredatory species, like horses and chickens, can be vicious and aggressive. Cannibalism and murder are prevalent throughout the animal world. So where does this idea come from that man alone is vicious, violent, and corrupt? It comes from "pop" thinking that is antihumanistic and self-righteous. New Age science. At bottom, it is thinking based on that most preposterous of ideas, an idea that we Jews invented but which you Christians refined to the apex of absurdity, the myth of Original Sin. Man is corrupt. Man is evil. Man is a sinner from birth. [Laughs.] What a load of rubbish!

Now I'll tell you something. You want to know what the real Original Sin is? Because there is a kind of original sin that all human beings are born with. I'll tell you! It's the aggression built into our genes by evolution. Aggression that once served a purpose. But now, with modern weaponry, it has become horrifically maladaptive—

Excuse me. Please excuse me. Thank you. I am becoming excited. Let me catch my breath. What I wish to say is, mankind has done a much better job controlling violence than most animal societies that we have studied. There have been, to be sure, spectacular failures—most notably in this century. Our capacity for violence is greater, but not necessarily our desire.

This brings me back to my original point. Jennie's aggression was built in. Nothing caused it. People have aggressive impulses. Those who can't control them either go to prison or into therapy, depending, in large part, on what socioeconomic level of society they come from. Those who overcontrol those impulses, who are passive, end up in a depression or suicidal. It's a fine line.

I believe Jennie had to walk a similar fine line. Only it was more difficult for her, because she was programmed according to a different set of rules. In hindsight, it was unreasonable for us to expect another species to understand and obey our social controls. Heck, we have enough trouble getting our own citizens to obey our controls.

You get my point? Okay, so let's talk about Jennie's aggression in this context. When Jennie became aggressive, it was almost always because of some chimpanzee idea of status, dominance, and the social hierarchy.

Let me give you an example. In Jennie's universe, Hugo was the dominant male, the "alpha" male. Nobody had higher status. Thus, if Hugo were arguing with someone (like me), Jennie would threaten that other person.

I remember well some of the scenes that Jennie caused. Once, Hugo and I were down in the basement room at the museum. We were sitting on the floor, playing with Jennie and talking about the design of some experiment. We had a disagreement—I can't even remember what about. We never raised our voices or anything obvious like that. We were merely disagreeing. While making some point, I touched Hugo on the arm, and quick as a flash, Jennie displayed and rushed over and bit me, and then signed *Angry, bite, angry.*

Hugo, of course, scolded Jennie. Jennie cowered and seemed very surprised. She held up a limp hand—you know, the pronated wrist gesture that indicates submission among chimpanzees—and signed *Sorry sorry.*

Hugo asked Jennie why she bit me, and Jennie answered *Man hurt.*

Hugo asked, *Man hurt who?*

You Hugo Hugo.

Harold no hurt Hugo. Harold friend.

Sorry sorry sorry. Harold friend Harold friend.

[Dr. Epstein demonstrated the conversation in ASL.]

The conversation went something like that. She had misunderstood our human interaction. She saw it in chimpanzee terms.

When Jennie got to be three or four, she watched Hugo's interactions with other people like a hawk. If you were talking to Hugo, and touched him or patted him on the back, Jennie might take that as a threat and bristle up and bark. She made a *Wraaa!* barking sound to indicate a threat. Once I nearly got bitten when I clapped Hugo on the back a little too vigorously, congratulating him for something. I had to speak very sharply to Jennie. That was another thing: if you showed fear or backed down, she would bite you. If you stood your ground and spoke or signed angrily to her, she usually chickened out. That's another chimpanzee behavior mode. They're just as cowardly as humans. But let us think for a moment what cowardice is in evolutionary terms. On the other hand, let's not. Back to the story!

Not everything about Jennie was cute and wonderful. She was a complex, intelligent, thinking being. She had a distinct and utterly unique personality. Like all of us, she had her unattractive qualities.

Talk about greed! Jennie got possessive as she got older. There were things lying around that she considered hers. God forbid if you should touch them or pick them up. Once, I went into Hugo's office and we were going to look over something at his desk. I started pushing that ratty old wing chair over to his desk. You know, the one Jennie used to sit in. And what happened? There was Jennie in the corner, displaying and bristling and barking at me. I was monkeying with her chair! [Laughs.] Sorry, no pun intended. Hugo then told me Jennie had to be locked in her room when the cleaning lady came, because she hated the lady moving around the furniture.

Did Lea tell you about Jennie beating up the carpet? That's a funny story. Lea had the living room recarpeted when Jennie was away at the museum one day. When Jennie came back, she ambled into the living room and suddenly all her hair was standing on end. She barked and backed out, grimacing in fear. And then she rushed back in and attacked the carpet. I mean literally *attacked* it. She stomped on it and beat it and pounded it and tried to tear it up, screaming her head off. She was furious.

The point I'm making is that I don't think there was anything unnatural in Jennie becoming more aggressive as she got older. All chimpanzees, whether in captivity or in the wild, become more assertive as they grow up. For heaven's sake, human children are exactly the same.

I suppose what I really mean to say is that chimps and humans share a great deal, including selfishness, cruelty, cowardice, greed, and a propensity to violence. Well, now, I don't mean to make it sound all bad. Chimps also show such human attributes as love of family, kindness, altruism, friendship, and courage. The very worst and the very best. *Simia quam similis, turpissima bestia, nobis!*

[EXCERPT from "Jennie Comes of Age," in *Psychology Today* magazine, March 16, 1970. Used with permission.]

In a long-running experiment at the Boston Museum of Natural History, a chimpanzee is being taught to communicate using American Sign Language. Jennie is being raised by Dr. Hugo Archibald, a curator in the Anthropology Department. Dr. Archibald found Jennie as a baby in the jungles of Africa. He brought her to America and he and Mrs. Archibald have been raising her as their own daughter. They live in a suburb of Boston. . . .

The experiment is not the first attempt to teach chimpanzees American Sign Language. According to many primatologists, it shares something in common with these earlier experiments: it is fatally flawed.

"This is a waste of NSF [National Science Foundation] money," says Dr. Craig Miller of the University of Pennsylvania, a leading critic of language training of chimpanzees. Dr. Miller assembled a team of psychologists to study a two-hour videotape of Jennie signing to her trainer, Pamela Prentiss of the Tufts University Center for Primate Research. The tape was intensively studied using freeze-frame techniques. "One of our psychologists spent twenty hours analyzing six minutes of tape," says Dr. Miller. "This was the most intensive study of chimpanzee 'signing' ever attempted."

The conclusion? Says Dr. Miller: "The chimpanzee is not using language. Period." The cognitive scientists studying the tape found that most "utterances" of Jennie's were preceded by use of the same signs by the trainer. Thus, Dr. Miller argues, the chimpanzee was merely repeating signs. A second problem is syntax. Neither Jennie nor any of the ASL-trained chimpanzees has mastered syntax. "Syntax is fundamental to the definition of language," says Dr. Miller. " 'Dog bites man' has a totally different meaning from 'man bites dog.' " Without mastery of syntax, Jennie cannot be said to have "language" according to the usual definitionoftheterm.

Dr. Miller also brings up the question of motivation. Every sign that Jennie made was aimed at the immediate gratification of some desire, usually food, a hug, or possession of a toy. "I defy these ASL researchers to get a chimpanzee to say anything that isn't motivated by the prospect of an immediate reward," he challenges. Another researcher who studied the tape termed Jennie's signing "running on with the hands until she gets what she wants."

The Miller team's analysis of the tape showed that Jennie interrupted a great deal and had not grasped the two-way nature of conversation. She rarely initiated conversations. Finally, her longer utterances did not add appreciably to the meaning and merely consisted of a multiplication of the same words.

"The basic problem," Dr. Miller contends, "is that these so-called researchers want so very badly to believe that apes have the potential for language. There is far too strong an emotional identification between researcher and subject for any kind of objective analysis. It would be like asking a mother to evaluate the intelligence of her son. What is needed here is a little rigor and emotional distance. As a start I would use a video monitor instead of a human being to teach. This would eliminate any possibility of cuing. And I would introduce rigorous double-blind controls. Finally, I would cut down on the background 'static'—the confusion and lack of structure—by keeping the animal in a restricted, controlled environment. A big noisy household with kids and neighbors coming and going is not exactly an ideal research environment."

[FROM an interview with Dr. Pamela Prentiss.]

Every time we tested Jennie, we discovered something new. Every single experiment opened up more avenues for research. It was such a heady time. The chimpanzee mind is so complex. The only thing was, we could never seem to limit the variables and create a "pure" experimental environment. We were always testing five things at once.

Our psychologist, Sonnenblick, was interested in "intentional theory." You must know all about that from *Generative Grammar and Deep Structure*. You *did* read that book, didn't you? I know, it's a little big. But how are you supposed to write about this stuff if you're too goddamn lazy to . . . Excuse me, but this is *important*. At least read this. "Intentional Analysis, Prevarication, Abstractionalization, and Generalization in the Mind of an Ape." It's a short paper. You'll find everything in there.

The question Sonnenblick wanted to know was: Do chimpanzees know that we have intentions? Let me explain. Let's say I accidentally hurt you. You will be less upset than if I deliberately hurt you. Right? Because you know my intentions. Now this is not like dogs. When you step on a dog's tail, he'll bite you whether you meant it or not. He doesn't know your intentions. And he can't know your intentions; he hasn't got the brains. Up until then, we thought only human beings could interpret the intentions of another. So the question was: Can chimps know we have intentions? If so, can they figure out those intentions?

We did this experiment to see if chimps could lie. Oh, Dr. Epstein told you about that? Good. Now listen. The experiment didn't only show that chimps could lie. Jennie knew which person would share the banana and which person wouldn't. That is, Jennie knew the intention of the person. Okay?

Sonnenblick wanted to explore this idea further. This is complicated, so pay attention. Can chimps attribute intentions to a third party? He designed a very ingenious test. The test didn't ask Jennie to solve a problem for herself. It asked her how a third person would solve a problem.

Here's what we did. We created a series of videotapes. Jennie had watched so much TV at the Archibald house that it was second nature for her to view a monitor. That was at least one good thing from all that television she watched. Mrs. Archibald would just park her in front of the TV. It was such a bother to her, having

Jennie around. It was television that ruined her son, Sandy, too. Let me tell you—

I'm off the subject. These videotapes showed people confronting a problem. Then we'd ask Jennie to solve the problem for them. For example, one tape showed a man trying to reach a bunch of bananas hanging from the ceiling. Shown nearby was a chair. When the tape was over we showed Jennie photographs illustrating two possible solutions to the problem. In one, the man was lying on the floor with the chair on its side. He had fallen off the chair, you see. The second showed the man stepping up on the chair, which was now under the bananas. She was given the photographs and told to place the "right" one in a certain place and ring a bell when she was done. Then we would leave the room. This was to prevent any unconscious cuing on our part.

She chose the correct solution. Naturally. So we showed her three more complex problems: a man shivering in a room with an unplugged heater, a man trying to get out of a locked cage, and a man trying to water a garden with an unattached hose. These were all things Jennie was familiar with, you see, in her home environment.

Then we gave Jennie photographs of the solutions. The first pair showed the heater either plugged in or unplugged. The second showed two keys, one bent, the other whole. The third pair showed an attached hose and an unattached hose.

Jennie got them all right. Just like that! It's all here in the paper. I think in—well, let me see that paper. In twenty-four tries she got twenty correct solutions. Now look at this. She scored twice as high as three-and-a-half-year-olds given the same set of problems!

Now we come to the most interesting example of all. Pay attention. Sonnenblick realized that there were several ways to interpret the results. Was Jennie choosing solutions because they were what she would do in the situation? Or what she would *like* to see the person do? Or what the person *should* do?

Sonnenblick had a brilliant solution to this problem. You aren't going to believe this. He used a "mean" assistant. Did Epstein tell you about this? He had an assistant dress up like a robber with a bandanna around his face and dark glasses. And the person did mean things to Jennie. Nothing physical, of course. Just mean. Like eat a banana without giving her any. Or ignore her when she signed *Hug*.

We got it so Jennie really hated this fellow. When she saw him coming, she'd scream and threaten. And he made these growling noises and slunk around. Very amusing.

Okay. So we took the "mean" person and showed Jennie a videotape of him trying to reach the bananas. Then we showed Jennie two pictures of chairs: one good, the other one broken with only three legs. She chose the chair with three legs! Can you believe it!

Then we showed Jennie a videotape of the "mean" man trying to get out of a locked cage. We showed her the two keys. And she chose the bent key! She often made these choices with glee, laughing and spinning 'round and 'round. It was *incredible*.

Do you see what was happening here? For people she liked, she chose the good solutions. For people she didn't like, she always chose the unpleasant solutions, the catastrophes. So she was indicating what she wanted to see happen.

Think about it. She was able to realize that the "mean" person *intended* to get the bananas and she was damned if he would! She was *thwarting* his intentions. Now if this isn't proof that chimps can ascribe intentions to others, I don't know what is.

We did all kinds of experiments. Let's see. You should read some of these papers here, where everything is explained. We wanted to know if a chimpanzee could count. No problem! As long as the number was small. We would put out five buttons, and then offer several trays with either five pebbles or four or six. We'd ask Jennie for the correct solution, and she'd select the five. Five was about as high as she could count reliably. When we went higher her scores dropped. By seven it was just about randomness. Although as we tested her she started to get better. If we'd worked on her I bet we could've taught her to add and subtract. No kidding.

Now get this. She could understand fractions! We filled up a glass partway with water. Then we would offer her tokens that looked a little like pie-charts. A three-quarters token, a half token, and a quarter token. Once she understood what was expected of her, she would always match the correct token with the correct amount of water in the glass. We did the same experiments with lumps of clay, with pieces of wood, and so forth.

I could talk to you all day about these experiments. Read my papers. I've dug up some more offprints for you. Here. You'll be amazed. Amazed.

[From *Recollecting a Life* by Hugo Archibald.]

Our family took an August vacation in Maine every year, at a saltwater farm originally bought by my father. It was located near a town called Franklins Pond Harbor, a fishing village along the shores of Muscongus Bay. The property had over a hundred acres of fields and woods and a half mile of rocky shoreline, with a small cove and cobble beach.

These August holidays were a vacation for all of us, particularly Jennie. She was a very busy chimpanzee during the year, with ASL lessons three days a week, going to the museum and participating in cognitive experiments two days a week, and religious lessons once a week from Rev. Palliser. Our suburban Kibbencook neighbors would have envied Jennie's schedule; had she been human, it would have been the fast track to Harvard.

Sandy and Jennie were as close as human twins. They went everywhere together. As a result, there was not a morning that Sandy went off to school that Jennie didn't become anxious and distressed. She could never understand why he had to go away. In Maine, however, everything was different. Jennie could spend all her time with Sandy. Sandy had no one else to play with, and they spent hours roaming the woods, fishing for crabs in the tide pools, looking for a rumored buried treasure on one of the nearby headlands. Jennie was allowed to run free in Maine. The nearest neighbor was half a mile away, and Jennie was far too cowardly to venture that far on her own. We could release her to play about in the fields and orchard, and we did not even have to keep an eye on her. If she broke a few branches, screamed, or threw apples, it was perfectly fine.

Jennie's freedom in Maine had a curious effect on her personality. Instead of making her more wild and difficult to control, it seemed to make her calmer and more obedient. Her life in Maine, I theorized, more closely replicated the free life that chimpanzees lead in the bush, and as a result she was happier and less anxious.

Next to the house stood an old post-and-beam barn with a loft and hay mow. The interior of posts resembled a jungle gym and Jennie spent hours in the barn, climbing around and dangling from the heights. It worried Lea a great deal, and she tried to put a stop to it, but I pointed out to her that, after all, Jennie was a chimpanzee. Sandy was forbidden to climb on the beams, and that frustrated Jennie and Sandy alike. She would scamper out on a beam and start signing: *Play, play, Sandy, play*. Sandy would sign back *No, Sandy not allowed*. The barn loft had an old bed, where Jennie slept.

The old apple orchard in the backyard was Jennie's favorite place to play. It was like a jungle gym hanging with her favorite fruit. She climbed into the crown of a tree, where she could watch the comings and goings of the family, and eat apples until she was sick. She defended and protected her apples with vigilance. One morning we heard a scream and saw Jennie pile out of the barn and head down to the orchard, where two deer had the temerity to be eating her apples. She screeched and threw a rock at them as they bounded away in terror. None of us had the courage to pick apples when Jennie was around.

I spent much time sitting on the stone porch and watching

Jennie swinging in the orchard. She was most like the ape she was when playing in those trees, hooting and chattering to herself in between stuffing apples into her mouth. She could eat enormous quantities of apples; I once counted while Jennie ate twenty apples in a sitting.

It was in the orchard where Jennie acquired a taste for alcohol. One late-summer day in 1969, we could not find Jennie anywhere, and Lea and Sandy went through the fields calling for her. They finally found her in the orchard, fast asleep in the tall grass. When they woke her up, she acted groggy and unnatural. She waddled back to the barn and got into bed, which was highly unusual in the middle of the day. She was fine the next morning, and bright and early we watched her heading straight for the orchard. There, she began scooping rotten apples off the ground and eating them, although there were many ripe apples in the tree. We wondered why, until she began to stagger around like a drunk, laughing and tumbling through the grass, and then we understood: she was becoming intoxicated on the fermented fruit.

Jennie always insisted on trying everything that we ate or drank. She had demanded sips from time to time from our evening cocktails, but she had always grimaced and spat out the liquor. Shortly after the apple incident, we were sitting around the living room, having our cocktail, when Jennie spoke up.

Jennie drink.

Jennie drink this?

Jennie drink drink.

I handed Jennie my gin and tonic. She sipped it and made a face, but to our great surprise she gulped it down. I quickly snatched it out of her hand.

Jennie drink! she signed frantically.

Lea and I were appalled. We had no idea what a strong cocktail would do to a forty-pound chimpanzee.

No, no, I signed. It looked like Jennie was working herself up to a tantrum about being denied a drink, when suddenly the expression on her face changed. She stood up straight as if she had heard a distant noise, looked around, and then a maniacal grin spread over her face.

"Uh oh," said Lea.

Jennie looked around and gave a low hoot. Then she climbed up on the sofa and sat back with that wonderful smile on her face, and watched us through half-lidded eyes.

After that, Jennie wanted to have a drink with us every night. Juice or Pepsi would not do; she wanted something stronger. Lea put up a strong resistance to her drinking alcohol, but she had developed the taste and knew perfectly well that we had something special in our glasses. She countered Lea's efforts with one magnificent tantrum after another, and finally Lea gave up.

"Go ahead and drink yourself silly," she shouted, handing Jennie her cocktail. Jennie drank it quietly and settled back on the sofa with those same lidded, contented eyes.

Lea and I had several talks about the ethical aspects of letting Jennie consume alcohol. Was it good for her? Would it damage her psychologically? Would she become dependent on liquor? In the end, it was Jennie's responsible behavior with alcohol that settled the question. Drinking seemed to affect her as it would an adult. It did not make her excited or angry, but rather calm and relaxed, and she never wanted to drink more than we drank or wanted to keep drinking when we stopped. She never had more than the equivalent of one drink, as we mixed them weak. She had all the hallmarks of a responsible social drinker.

Jennie officially joined our cocktail hour. We then heard from another quarter; Sandy did not like Jennie receiving any special privileges.

"No fair! How come *she* can drink and I can't?" he complained.

We explained it was bad for him.

He cornered us on that one. "So it's good for Jennie but bad for me? Or you don't love Jennie as much as me? Is that what you're saying?"

I could not extricate myself from my son's logic, so I finally told him the truth: Jennie's tantrums were far more intolerable than his were. That did not sit well with him either.

"You always let her do everything and I can't do anything!" Sandy cried. "She gets away with murder and if I do something I always get punished. You *stink*." And he stormed off to his room.

This was a common complaint of his as he entered his preteen years. It is perhaps a sign of their deep friendship that no matter how much Sandy complained about Jennie getting favored treatment, it never interfered with their relationship.

When Jennie began to drink, she also insisted on having a glass of wine at the table. We shortly found that our stock of expensive wine—I have always had a weakness for Bordeaux—was vanishing down the throat of an ape. I simply could not adjust to seeing a chimpanzee slurping down a full glass of my Léoville-Poyferré '56, which I had laid down ten years ago and watched mature with infinite patience.

I therefore bought a case of Cold Duck for Jennie, since I thought she would like the sweetness and, more importantly, because it cost ninety-nine cents a bottle. When we first gave Jennie the Cold Duck, she drank a little, but then she noticed that her wine was a different color from the Chateau Petrus we were drinking. A different color, and no doubt inferior, must have been her conclusion. She was outraged: we were trying to fob off a shabby product on her, while reserving the best for ourselves. She promptly set her glass down, grabbed my glass, and swallowed five dollars worth of Bordeaux in a single gulp. Then she settled back in her chair with a defiant expression on her face.

We solved the wine problem by buying Jennie bottles of cheap red and white wine of the same color and appearance as what we were drinking. As long as the bottle was the same shape, and the wine the same color, Jennie did not notice that she was getting Gallo Chablis while we were getting Puligny-Montrachet.

* * *

Just as with human siblings who are close in age, Jennie and Sarah did not often see eye to eye. Jennie and Sarah were both five years old in the summer of 1969. Their relationship could be characterized as a Mexican standoff. They had very different personalities. Sarah, even from a young age, was quite fastidious, and she objected to Jennie's rambunctiousness. Where Sarah liked order, Jennie liked chaos. Sarah liked silence; Jennie liked noise. Sarah was a thinker; Jennie was a doer. Sarah was always smiling and quiet and sweet; Jennie was loud and liked to tease. They did not have much in common. Sarah had not learned ASL with the enthusiasm of Sandy, but she knew enough to scold, insult, and threaten Jennie, and set her firmly in her place.

Sarah, for all her sweetness, had a toughness underneath that intimidated Jennie. Jennie's *modus operandi* was to identify and exploit weakness, but she never could find a chink in Sarah's armor. On the other hand, Sarah knew all of Jennie's weaknesses—her greedy materialism, her fear of rejection, and her upset at seeing human beings cry. She exploited them whenever the need arose. Sarah did not go out of her way to put Jennie in her place, but when Jennie crossed some invisible boundary Sarah knew how to react.

Even at five, Sarah was adept at controlling Jennie. One time in Maine Jennie broke a toy of Sarah's and hid the pieces under a chair in the living room. Sarah found them and, without saying a word to anybody, went up to Jennie's loft and scattered the pieces in Jennie's bed, carefully pulling up the covers. Another time Jennie stole one of Sarah's favorite shirts and got it filthy playing in the dirt. Sarah caught her, but instead of trying to get the shirt back (which would have been impossible), she went up to Jennie's room, took out a shirt of hers, and flapped it around in Jennie's face. Jennie was protective of her "things," and when she saw Sarah waving her shirt about she tried to take off Sarah's and get her own back, signing *Give shirt! Give shirt!* Sarah just signed *Phooey* and walked away, while Jennie screamed in frustration, whacking the ground with both hands.

Jennie always seemed to know when the Maine vacation was coming up, and she became restless in the weeks leading up to August. When we started packing the car for Maine, she became almost uncontrollable. She would race about the house, scurrying up and down the stairs, out to the car and back in, signing *Go! Go! Go car! Hurry!* Sometimes she would pound on the car parked in the driveway and sign *Bad car! Bad!* as if the car itself were holding things up.

Jennie knew every landmark on the drive, and as we neared the farmhouse Jennie would become more and more excited. A large wooden Indian outside a shoe factory outlet always set her off, because it meant we were about to turn off the highway. Ten minutes later, as we turned in the driveway and the barn loomed into view, Jennie would lose control entirely and begin a pant-hoot that would build in intensity until it ended in a drawn-out scream of magnificent intensity.

[FROM a telephone call to Sarah Archibald Burnham of Manhattan, October 23, 1992.]

I got your letters, I got your messages. You can call me until the end of time, and I won't talk to you. I just won't. I have nothing to say. I don't think you or anybody else has any business prying into our family's private affairs. I will not read a letter; I will not answer a letter. So please don't bother. I don't mean to be rude, and maybe you're even a nice person, I don't know.

I will say one thing, just one thing. I've never said this before. But why not. My father's dead and it can't hurt him now. It should be said. It took me a long time and a lot of help to figure this out. I want at least this one thing in your book, if you have the guts to print it. I mean it. Print whatever garbage you're going to print, but put this in there somewhere:

I *hated* that chimpanzee. And I'll tell you why. My father loved that chimpanzee more than he did me.

So now it's said. Good-bye.

[FROM an interview with Lea Archibald.]

The truth is that by the time Jennie reached four or five our lives had become—how shall I say it—anarchistic. When you've got a chimp living in your house, you find out soon enough who your real friends are. Many of our friends stopped visiting. Some of them were afraid of Jennie. Others found her noise or activity too trying. But we had many friends who loved Jennie. You had to love her to enjoy a visit to our house, particularly because you were likely to go home with broken glasses, a soiled tie, or a mussed hairdo. If you were lucky. Jennie's ability to create mischief knew no bounds.

People talk about the terrible twos with children. With chimpanzees, I'd call it the terrible twos, threes, fours. And fives and sixes. Oh, when I think about the things she did! I'll just give you a few examples. She'd climb up to the kitchen cabinets, take out a jar of honey, eat a few mouthfuls and then leave it sideways on the living room carpet. Open. I would be furious, but Hugo would say, "Did you see how she unscrewed that lid? Isn't that amazing?" He didn't have to deal with the mess. Or the time Jennie removed the back of the television set and ripped out the tubes and wires with a great shower of sparks. She could have burned down the house. You see, Hugo, in one of his experiments, taught Jennie how to use a screwdriver. What a mistake that was! We took away the screwdriver, but she found one later and hid it. We found that one, but a few weeks later she'd gotten another one. We started finding handles unscrewed, and door hinges dangling, and locks removed from doors. I was beside myself, but for the life of me I couldn't find where she had hidden that darn screwdriver.

I tried signing to Jennie: *Where screwdriver?* But she was a little liar and kept saying, *Don't know.* That's another thing she learned from those experiments, how to lie. I got mad and signed *Angry! Phooey! Where screwdriver?* But she stayed cool as a cucumber. *Don't know don't know,* with a guilty look in her eye. Wild horses would not drag that information out of her. This went on for a few days, and then there was a quiet spell, and we thought maybe she had lost the screwdriver. Well! One day, the screws on the liquor cabinet were removed and the bottle of gin gone. I went running up to her room and, sure enough, there she was, lying on the floor, giggling and clicking her teeth. Dead drunk! She'd taken a bottle of gin and a tube of toothpaste, and a dish, and she'd squeezed out a little toothpaste, and mixed it with gin, stirred it around with her finger, and slurped it up. And then repeated the process. She reeked of Crest and gin. It was revolting.

When she saw us, she tried to get up but she fell back laughing. And then she was sick all over herself. I was wild, but Hugo found the whole thing fascinating. Why, he says, do you see what this means? Jennie has the ability to deceive! To plan ahead! Or some such rot. I can't remember what it proved, except that it proved Jennie needed a good licking. So I locked her in the bathroom, which coincidentally happened to be where she had hidden the screwdriver, and the little vixen unscrewed the doorknob and escaped. That's how I found it. It was in the bathroom cabinet. Here I had turned the house upside down and there it was, in plain sight.

That was the way it went. Jennie would find ever more clever ways to get into mischief, Hugo would go on and on about her ingenuity while I cleaned up the mess. Do I sound a little resentful? I suppose I am. Hugo had all the fun, while I was mopping the floor.

Sometimes we gave dinner parties. Less frequently as Jennie grew older. It was a special guest who could enjoy a meal with Jennie. Some of them were disastrous. Oh dear, I remember one time we had President Julius Whitehead of Harvard University over for dinner. With his wife. My goodness. This wasn't long after

Jennie's triumphal coming-out at the Museum of Fine Arts benefit. Hugo had been given an adjunct professorship at Harvard, you see, and we felt an obligation to invite President Whitehead over for dinner. Besides, Whitehead and his wife had read all about Jennie in the society columns and just had to meet her. Well! They met her all right.

First, we had cocktails. President Whitehead had a daiquiri, and Jennie a gin and tonic. I think the Whiteheads were a bit scandalized to see Jennie drinking in the first place. We only put a tiny bit of alcohol in Jennie's drinks. Anyway, Jennie took one look at her boring glass and another at Whitehead's nice green drink, and made a decision. She sidled up to Whitehead and handed him her drink. He said, "Oh, is this for me? How nice!" while he put his drink down to accept it.

That's what Jennie had been waiting for. Her hairy hand flashed out and swiped his drink, and she scurried under a table and drank it with a great slurp while Hugo scolded in his usual ineffectual manner.

"Oh my," was all President Whitehead said. He was a rather stiff person, you know. He should have objected more strenuously. If you were a stranger to Jennie, you had to show her who was boss right away. Or she would test you again and again. So, at dinner, Jennie ate her fruit cocktail very fast and reached over and took his, before the poor man had even lifted his spoon. He was so busy pontificating he hadn't begun to eat. I tried to tell her, *No, Jenny, give back*. But she just signed back *Phooey!*, which was a rather vulgar gesture. Then she opened her mouth, and dumped the fruit in, spilling it all down her shirt and on the table. Then she started picking up each piece with her lips. Oh dear. President and Mrs. Whitehead just sat there. There was a . . . a passivity or weakness about him that Jennie sensed and took advantage of. It was his upper-class Boston upbringing, you know, being a member of a dying class. He didn't last much longer and then Harvard wised up and hired that wonderful fellow, I forget his name. Bok. At any rate, I signed *No! Bad Jennie, leave table next time.* She hated to leave the table and I thought that would make her obey.

The next course was steak. Jennie didn't like steak, so I felt Whitehead's meal would be safe. We'd prepared her a bowl of oatmeal, fruit, and honey, which she loved. But no, she had to have President Whitehead's steak, so she reached over, grabbed it off his plate, and shoved it into her mouth. Then she made a face, pulled it out, and threw it into the kitchen! I was just mortified.

We sent her from the table, screaming piteously, and locked her in the bathroom. For the rest of the dinner we had to endure a screaming tantrum, with the whole house shaking from her pounding. Naturally, the Whiteheads couldn't wait to leave. I was so embarrassed, but Hugo thought it was rather funny. He thought Whitehead was a bit of a stuffed shirt. I was worried it might get him into trouble at Harvard, but Hugo said he was just a figure-head, a fund-raiser.

What else can I tell you about those years? Jennie loved to drive in the car. She was like a dog. She'd stick her head out the open window into the wind. She screamed and pounded on the outside of the car when she saw something interesting.

When we stopped at a light, and Jennie saw something interesting in the car next to us, she would scream with delight and start signing and hooting and waving her hands. All heads in the car would turn and stare. The utter *shock* on those people's faces! People are so unimaginative. Anything slightly out of the routine upsets them so. And heaven forbid if there was a dog in the car! Dogs went crazy at the sight of Jennie.

One time, I think it was around 1970, we were driving and Jennie had her head out the window as usual. She pulled back in and signed *Go, go,* pointing down a street. I couldn't for the life of me understand what she wanted. But I was curious, so I turned. From then on Jennie directed me, signing *Go* and pointing. We turned and turned and finally we drew abreast of an Ice Cream Palace and Jennie signed *Stop! Stop!* and let out a gust of food sounds, hooting and grunting. She tumbled out of the car and scooted up to the window, cutting the line, of course, just shoving everyone aside. Oh my goodness. Then she started pounding on the counter and reaching in the window, making her hungry-hoot sound. The girls behind the window were squealing "The chimp's back! Jennie's back! Hello, Jennie!" They made a terrific fuss over her. I asked Hugo about it later and he said that the weekend before he had taken Sandy and Jennie to the Ice Cream Palace. She remembered how to get there! Isn't that remarkable? She was quite a genius.

She got to know the location of many of the fast-food places around town, and after this success she was constantly signaling *Go!* and *Stop!* while we were in the car, and pounding on the door in frustration when we drove by a Howard Johnsons or an Ice Cream Palace, or even a vending machine at a gas station. It became a rather annoying habit, to tell you the truth.

Sarah was six at this time, and she and Jennie had reached a kind of understanding. Sarah had her room and Jennie was not allowed in. That chimp respected her. Oh yes. Sarah wasn't going to take any guff from Jennie, and Jennie knew it. Sarah was no la-di-dah little girl. Once in a while they had their clashes, but Sarah always won. Jennie took some food off Sarah's plate once, some noodles. Sarah was only five, but as calm as you please she picked up a fistful of noodles and mashed them down on Jennie's head. Jennie was so surprised, and really quite humiliated when we all started to laugh. That was the last time she ever took food from Sarah. Another time she got into Sarah's room—which we usually kept locked, but somebody must have forgotten—and stole a great armful of toys. She hid them in her own toy box.

Well! Sarah wasn't going to take that lying down. She went into Jennie's room—which made Jennie nervous because Sarah never went into her room—opened the toy box, and proceeded to take her toys back and all of Jennie's toys. Normally Jennie would have been furious, but she knew she was guilty and sat there. I think

Sarah made four or five trips, stealing every one of Jennie's toys, while Jennie sat in the corner, signing *Bad, bad!* and whimpering. It was only after Sarah left that Jennie started a commotion, screaming and banging on her toy chest. And then Sarah, still calm, proceeded to return Jennie's toys. Keeping her own, of course. It showed Jennie that Sarah was in control, and it was a brilliant little ploy on Sarah's part. Jennie almost never touched any of Sarah's toys after that. In some ways I think Sarah handled Jennie better than any of us.

[EXCERPTS from an unpublished manuscript titled "Conversations with a Chimpanzee" by Dr. Pamela Prentiss.]

Setting: Archibald yard, under the crab apple tree, 4:00 P.M. Wednesday, April 16, 1970.

> Pam: *What's that?*
> Jennie: *Bug.*
> Pam: *What kind bug?*
> Jennie: *Bug bug.*
> Pam: *Butterfly. Sign butterfly.*
> Jennie: Attempts to sign. Butterfly is a sign Jennie knows but has not learned well.
> Pam: *Butterfly.*
> Jennie: *Red butterfly.*
> Pam: *Pretty butterfly yellow not red.*
> Jennie: *Red butterfly yellow.*
> Pam: *Yellow.*
> Jennie: *Red.*
> Pam: *Yellow.*
> Jennie: *Yellow, yellow, phooey.*
> Pam: *Phooey to you.*
> Jennie: *Chase tickle Jennie.*

Pam: Ignores request and points to ant. *What's that?*

Jennie: *Chase tickle Jennie!*

Pam: *What's that?*

Jennie: *Bad bug.*

Pam: *Ant. Sign ant.*

Jennie: *Black bug.* Squashes ant with her foot.

Pam: *Ouch! Ant dead.*

Jennie: *Ant.* (*Dead* is not a sign Jennie knows.)

Pam: *Sign dead. Dead.* Molds Jennie's hands in the sign for "dead."

Jennie: *Dead. Dead.*

Pam: *Ant now dead.* Pam picks up dead ant, shows to Jennie.

Jennie: *Ant.*

Pam: *Ant dead.*

Jennie: *Ant ant.*

Pam: *Sign dead. Ant dead.*

Jennie: *Dead.*

Pam: Pam puts ant down.

Jennie: *Banana.*

Pam: *Not now. Banana later. Jennie climb tree?*

Jennie: *Climb!* Jennie swings into tree and climbs up.

Pam: *You like tree?*

Jennie: Ignores question.

Pam: *Jennie like tree?*

Jennie: Continues to ignore question, climbs higher.

Pam: *Jennie climb higher.*

Jennie: Finally stops and sits on branch, looking down. *You climb climb.*

Pam: *No. I can't climb tree.*

Jennie: *Sorry.*

Pam: *Humans can't climb tree.*

Jennie: *Climb!*

Pam: *No. I can't climb tree.*

Jennie: *Sorry.*

Pam: *Jennie come down.*

Jennie: Looking away, deliberately ignoring Pam.

Pam: *Play chase-tickle.*

Jennie: Immediately descends. Jennie and Pam play "chase-tickle" for a few minutes.

Pam: *Jennie want banana?*

Jennie: *Banana! Banana!*

Pam: Gives Jennie banana.

SETTING: playroom of Archibald house, 1:00 P.M., Monday, April 19, 1970. Jennie has just been given a locked wooden box, which has a live mouse in it.

Pam: *Present for Jennie.*

Jennie: Stretches out hands.

Pam: *What Jennie say?*

Jennie: *Please please please.*

Pam: *What's this?* Points to box.

Jennie: *Please.*

Pam: *What's this?*

Jennie: *Apple.*

Pam: *No, box.*

Jennie: *Sorry, please box.*

Pam: Gives Jennie the box. *Open box.*

Jennie: Lifts box up and smells the air holes. Then Jennie tries to peer inside.

Pam: *Open box.*

Jennie: *Open open.* Tries to hand the box to Pam.

Pam: *No, you open box.*

Jennie: Fumbles with box, turning it over and over. She puts box down and pounds on it in frustration.

Pam: *Jennie cannot open box?*

Jennie: *No. Jennie no.*

Pam: *Jennie want key?*

Jennie: Stretches out hands.

Pam: *Jennie want key?*

Jennie: *Give give.*

Pam: *Give what?*

Jennie: *That.*

Pam: *What's that?*

Jennie: *Key.*

Pam: Gives Jennie the key. Jennie immediately unlocks and opens box and the mouse peers out, rather shaken from its ordeal. Jennie picks up the mouse and puts it in her mouth.

Pam: *No!* Takes mouse out of Jennie's mouth and holds it in hand, so Jennie can see it.

Jennie: *Give give!*

Pam: *What's this?*

Jennie: *Give.*

Pam: *This is mouse. Mouse. Sign mouse.*

Jennie: Bangs on box.

Pam: *Mouse. Mouse. If you sign mouse, I give you mouse.*

Jennie: *Give me Jennie.*

Pam: *Mouse, Mouse.*

Jennie: *Jennie! Jennie! Give! Phooey!*

Pam: *Sign mouse. Mouse. Mouse.*

Jennie: *Give!* Bangs on box again, picks box up and throws it.

Pam: *No, bad Jennie. Do not throw. Sign mouse. Mouse. Mouse.*

Jennie: *Mouse.*

Pam: *Good! Do not eat mouse. Play with mouse.* Gives Jennie the mouse.

Jennie: *Play, play.* This is signed at the mouse. She then picks up the mouse and holds it very gently to her chest, looking down at it with pursed lips. Then she kisses mouse.

Pam: *Kiss mouse.*

Jennie: *Mouse Jennie me.* Kisses mouse again and tastes it with her tongue.

Pam: *Mouse taste good?*

Jennie: *Good. Apple.*

Pam: *Mouse taste like apple?*

Jennie: *Give apple.*

Pam: *No apple now. Jennie ate apple. Jennie like mouse?*

Jennie: *Mouse.* Jennie smells the mouse and turns it over and pokes it in the stomach.

Pam: *Nice. Be nice to mouse.*

Jennie: *Nice mouse.*

Pam: *Nice mouse.*

Jennie: *Jennie's mouse.*

Pam: *Yes that is Jennie's mouse. Put mouse in box.*

Jennie: Puts the mouse in the box. *Jennie eat apple.*

Pam: *Jennie already ate apple.*

Jennie: *Apple!*

Pam: *No. Jennie play with word board?*

Jennie: *Dirty.* Jennie does not like the word board, a board with pictures on it that represent words. The word board is used to teach Jennie word concepts in pictures.

Pam: *Jennie go toilet?*

Jennie: *Dirty, dirty.*

Pam: *Jennie lie.*

Jennie: *Dirty.*

Pam: *Jennie not dirty. Jennie go toilet already.*

Jennie: *Dirty.*

Pam: *Jennie play with word board now.*

Jennie: *Dirty! Dirty! Dirty!*

Pam: *No, Jennie not dirty.* Brings out the word board.

Jennie: *Phooey phooey phooey!*

SETTING: backyard of Archibald home, Wednesday, April 23, 1970, 3:30 P.M. Sandy is just arriving home from school. Words not printed in italic were vocalized but not signed.

Sandy: Jennie! I'm home!

Jennie: [Stops in the middle of a lesson and runs toward the hedge, vocalizing.]

Sandy: Where's Jennie? Where's Jennie?

Jennie: [Vocalizes loudly, mostly screams and hoots.] *Hug!*

Sandy: I can't see Jennie. Where's Jennie? [Sandy crouches behind the hedge. Jennie forces her way through the hedge and grabs Sandy around the waist.] *There Jennie. Hello Jennie. Help help hairy ape got me.*

Jennie: *Hug hug hug me.*

Sandy: [Hugs Jennie.] *Where Pam?*

Jennie: [Points toward me.]

Sandy: Hi, Dr. Prentiss.

Pam: Hello, Sandy. Go ahead and keep playing. I'll watch.

Sandy: Okay. *Jennie play tickle-chase?*

Jennie: [Screams with anticipation and runs toward brook. Sandy follows and grabs her. She rolls on her back and he tickles her while she screams. Then she jumps up and runs away, letting Sandy catch up to her. Again she rolls, fending off Sandy with hands and prehensile feet. They wrestle for a while, and then Sandy stops the play.]

Sandy: *Jennie go house, get two apples from Mom, give me one, Jennie eat one.*

Jennie: [Goes into house. She returns five minutes later with one apple.]

Sandy: *Where two apples?*

Jennie: *Jennie eat.*

Sandy: *This apple for me?*

Jennie: *Give Jennie.*

Sandy: No way, José. You ate yours, gimme that. *You eat apple already, give me apple.*

Jennie: [Gives Sandy the apple.] *Give apple.*

Sandy: *I give you piece.* [He gives Jennie a piece.]

Jennie: *More.*

Sandy: *No, apple is mine,* you hairy ape, you.

Jennie: *Phooey.*

Sandy: *Phooey to you. Jennie ride tricycle?*

Jennie: *Tricycle.*

Sandy: *Let's go. Ride tricycle. Go get tricycle.* Yeah!

Jennie: [Runs to the garage and heaves up on handle, opening door. Goes inside and comes out riding tricycle. Sandy gets his bicycle and rides past her, shouting "Faster, faster." The two ride down the driveway and Sandy waits for her at the corner. When she catches up they ride around the corner and disappear.]

[FROM interviews with Lea Archibald.]

For years, we wondered when Sandy would lose interest in Jennie. They were very close, but at a certain point, we figured, a boy moves on to other things. If you know what I mean. Pretty soon he'll be thinking about girls, and getting his driver's license. And Jennie would have to find another friend.

Our other worry was with the teenage years in general. We anticipated some trouble. Mix this with an excitable chimpanzee and heaven only knows what will happen. It was the tail end of the sixties, and some of our neighbors had had a lot of trouble. The Millers' son, down the street, died of a drug overdose, and there was the Newcomb girl's suicide. The Hoyt boy was killed in Vietnam, of course, and there were so many dreadful car accidents. Oh dear, there are so many things that can happen to a child in the world! When you have children, that's when you realize the world is a dangerous place. You really do.

I was always so worried about Sandy. He was vulnerable, in a way that Sarah wasn't. He was sweet and innocent, even when his hair stuck out like a rat's nest. He had good values. And good values are the best protection in a world like this. You see, a lot of those other families hadn't raised their children with any decent values. They were so focused on success and money, and having manners, that these kids had no foundation. When they rebelled, they had nothing to fall back on. They had gone to a restrictive country club and Boy Scouts and ballroom dancing classes and sworn their allegiance to the flag every morning, year after year. Well, I ask you, what kind of a value system is that? They had done everything their parents wanted. When they hit eighteen and saw their country was sending them to die in a jungle on the other side of the world, well! No wonder they rebelled. You can imagine the shock.

We raised our children differently. We encouraged them to think on their own. We didn't tell them what to do, or make them cut their hair. If they wanted to look ridiculous, well why not? We let them make their own decisions. So when Sandy rebelled, he could reject us and our life-style, but he still had something to fall back on. Today he may not be the outward success that society labels as important, but he's always had strong values. That, to me, is what really counts. When he finds his niche in the world, he'll do something worthwhile.

Sandy turned fourteen on August 15, 1971. Jennie was six. The first thing that happened was when Sandy stopped playing chess. He was a very good chess player, you know, and he won several school tournaments. And then he suddenly lost interest. He became sullen and slouchy. And his room! You've never seen a mess like it. Hugo and I knew the teen years had arrived.

The curious thing was, as Sandy got older he and Jennie remained just as close. He would go to a party and Jennie would go with him. When Sandy stayed out late and I was beside myself with worry, Jennie would be with him. When Sandy went to the bridge, Jennie went along.

Oh dear. The bridge was a place where all the teenage kids hung out. It was down there past the Kibbencook Golf Course, where the old Boston and Albany railroad crossed the Charles River. The trestle itself was closed off but the kids would gather under the bridge, alongside the river. They would light a fire and sit around and drink beer. I'm not sure exactly what went on there but none of it was good. There were girls there too. I worried terribly when Sandy went there. I didn't want to forbid him from going there, because of course that's the worst thing you can do with a teenage child. He would have gone anyway and that would have encouraged him to be deceitful. The only thing we absolutely demanded from our children was honesty. And you know, the easiest way to make something attractive to a teenage child is to forbid him from doing it.

So when Sandy was thirteen or fourteen he started going to the bridge. It was just across the golf course, within walking distance. Even at thirteen, Sandy was turning into a radical intellectual. He had started to grow his hair and he had some books by Russian anarchists, Bakunin or something, that he pretended to read and understand. He hung a burned and torn-up American flag over his bed, with a big peace sign painted over it. He was starting to spout a lot of nonsense. He sold his coin collection and gave the money to the Black Panthers. It happened so fast, as fast as it took to grow his hair. I mean, what were we going to do with this genius fourteen-year-old kid who was spouting Trotskyism and sending money to the Black Panthers?

You'd think a chimpanzee would be a bit of a "drag" to a budding young anarchist. Not so. What we hadn't realized was just how attached Sandy was to Jennie. Sandy didn't outgrow Jennie as we expected. On the contrary. And Sandy's friends, far from rejecting Jennie, all decided Jennie was the "coolest." [Laughs.] That's what happened. Jennie became totally "hip," the hippest of the hip. She drank beer, I'm sure she smoked pot with them, and heaven only knows what other drugs they gave her. She went along with everything they did. I shouldn't say "went along"; I'm sure Jennie demanded to participate in whatever they were doing. I hate to think what went on at the bridge. I really *hate* to think about that. We talked to Sandy, we educated ourselves about the dangers of drugs, and a few times when I just couldn't stand it anymore I made Hugo go out there to get Sandy and Jennie and bring them home. Hugo talked to Sandy about sex and responsibility and things like that. Or at least he said he did. Maybe I'm exaggerating, and maybe nothing really that bad happened out there. I don't know. Oh dear.

You're too young to have experienced this, but it's a terrible feeling when you lose control over your children. You can't stop them from doing something idiotic if they want to. How can you stop them from taking LSD or heroin? You can't. You can only hope and pray that you managed to drum some sense into them when they were young. All you can do is hope that they're going to be smart enough to avoid doing the really moronic things. It's a terrible feeling. And Sandy, for all his brains, was really quite innocent. So naive. I was worried sick.

I felt I was losing control of both my children at once—Sandy and Jennie. We worried about the effect of whatever Sandy was doing on Jennie—drugs, late nights, whatever. She was becoming increasingly unruly and rebellious. Harold had warned us that as Jennie got older she would get more aggressive. All chimpanzees do, whether home-raised or not. Hugo and Harold had long talks about it, and Harold felt that Jennie's aggressiveness was normal. I don't know. Jennie picked up a lot of Sandy's rebelliousness and refused to do everything we told her. Her favorite sign became *Phooey!* which she used as a kind of "go to hell" curse. As if that wasn't bad enough, someone—one of Sandy's friends, I'm sure—taught her the "finger." Do you know what I mean, the "finger"?

Oh dear. We punished her severely when she made that gesture, but in retrospect I think it only made things worse. Jennie learned it would provoke a big reaction from us. And do you know what Hugo said? "Oh, isn't it fascinating how Jennie has learned the power of the signed word." Honestly, this is what I had to deal with. Jennie giving the "finger" to some absolute stranger at a stop sign, and Hugo musing about how fascinating it was. He'd say, "Who can take it seriously? She's only a chimpanzee." But what did it say about our family? About how we were raising our children? And that chimp knew exactly when to make that gesture to horrify everyone around her.

Christmas dinner, I think it was 1972, the doorbell rang. Jennie raced to the door—she was always the first to answer the door—and opened it. There was my mother. Jennie blocked the door and made that terrible gesture. My mother burst into tears. You see, she had just lost her husband, my father, and this was her first Christmas alone. It was so grotesque. Jennie blocking her and making this hateful gesture. I don't know how she was able to hurt someone like that. And Jennie liked my mother.

Then of course the Jehovah's Witnesses came by and Jennie stole the lady's hat. When she asked for it back, Jennie made that gesture. It was so embarrassing. I suppose I should look at the bright side, because they never came back. Clearly we were beyond saving! [Laughs.]

And then Dr. Prentiss. Jennie started up on that with Dr. Prentiss, and she came marching into the house with her pinched face and said we needed to have a serious talk. As if I were some monster of a mother. She was such a—a *bitch*. Excuse me. You should've heard the mouth on her! When she lost her temper—the words that came out of her mouth! She swore like a sailor.

She was also outraged at Jennie's drinking. "Forcing liquor on a poor defenseless animal." Defenseless! And Sandy started being so rude to Dr. Prentiss. Oh dear. He was rude to everybody, of course. But he was so smart, and he knew exactly how to get under

Dr. Prentiss's skin. He would accuse her of conducting "fascistic behavior modification experiments" on his "sister." Her relationship to Jennie was "bourgeois," whatever that was supposed to mean. The accusations were, I have to admit, unfair. If I for a moment thought that Dr. Prentiss was abusing Jennie in any way I would have sent her packing. It made Dr. Prentiss wild to be accused like that. She considered herself a bit of a rebel, you see, and to be accused of having middle-class values made her hopping mad. She felt Sandy was trying to turn Jennie against her. And I think he was, but it didn't work. Jennie loved and trusted Dr. Prentiss. I don't really know why, but she did. Sandy, you know, was the first to see through that woman.

I will say this however: Sandy never said anything to Jennie that was bad about me. We had our differences, but Sandy never tried to turn Jennie against *me*. Or Hugo.

Everything seemed to change so fast. It was a very difficult time. Oh, it was so very difficult. I had this feeling that something awful was going to happen.

eight

[EXCERPTS from the journals of the Rev. Hendricks Palliser.]

February 10, 1971

This morning it was frigid. When I went for my morning walk the brook was frozen. I could hear the water running underneath the ice. But the brisk walk did nothing to shake off a lethargy that has settled on my soul since the death of Reba.

Today marks exactly one month since her passing. There is so much death in the world today, the death of fine young men in the jungles of Vietnam, the murder in our cities, the protests, the killing of college students. I can hardly accept this is my beloved country anymore. God said "Thou shalt not kill." I do not recall His mentioning any exceptions to the rule. All the great pillars of my life are crumbling. I must constantly remind myself that I am not the only grieving person in the world. And yet, the loss of Reba is a terrible cross to bear and I do not think I have the strength for it.

When Jennie arrived for her weekly lesson this morning, I felt a great weight being lifted. She is so cheerful and so untouched by the sorrows of the world that she cannot but gladden a person's heart. I watched her wander about the living room, picking objects up, smelling and tasting them, rolling them around between her palms, and dropping them on the rug when they had lost her attention. I did not have the heart to discipline her. It reminded me of how it used to irritate Reba and I shed a tear or two, and when Jennie noticed she came over with a look of great concern furrowing her brow. She embraced me with much affection and touched and patted my tears, trying to wipe them away. Kindness and love are God's greatest gifts and Jennie has them in abundance. I need look no further than this to find proof that Jennie is a child of God.

And now I wonder if my failed effort to bring a Christian commitment to Jennie's life was, in truth, an exercise of not seeing the forest for the trees. In every way, at every moment, Jennie shows kindness and altruism that reveal her to be a child of grace. Just as babies and severely retarded children are saved by grace despite their lack of intellectual understanding, so is Jennie's grace revealed by her Christian responses to those around her. If spontaneous kindness, without cunning or forethought of reward, is not proof of grace, what can be proof? I am aware that this may be a radical conclusion, perhaps at variance with my church. So be it. I seem to be at variance with so much in my church these days.

I am resolved to finally deliver that sermon on Jennie. Fear of ridicule has held me back.

After Jennie arrived, I played on the hi-fi one of my favorite pieces of religious music, Duruflé's *Requiem,* and Jennie was quieted by it and sat on the floor listening. I signed to her that the piece was about God and Jennie looked at me with interest but did not respond.

February 24, 1971

In the middle of last night, I heard a squirrel in the chimney and now I am afraid to light a fire. I was under the impression that squirrels hibernated in the winter.

Jennie was very lively today. She announced her desire to listen to music by banging on the hi-fi, and I obliged by playing Bach's Passacaglia and Fugue in C minor. She is greatly taken with loud organ music. To her great delight she has discovered the knob that controls the volume, and she turns it up whenever my back is turned, hoping, perhaps, I will not notice.

We perused the latest issue of *Pennies from Heaven* and she signed *Jesus Jesus* when we came to a picture of Jesus raising Lazarus from the dead. It showed Lazarus lying in a robe, and then him rising with a radiant light around his head. Then Jennie began signing *What that?* and pointing at the picture, and I tried to explain the story of Lazarus. The conversation was rather peculiar, and, indeed, astonishing in its own way. I will here insert the relevant sections from my Jennie notes:

Myself: *Man dead.*
Jennie: *What?*
Myself: *Man dead.*
Jennie: *What?* (By this I think she possibly meant *Why?*)
Myself: *Man dead, Jesus make man alive.*

Jennie stared at the picture with utmost interest. I thought she probably did not understand. She repeated *what* five or six times, slowly. Then she finally signed: *Dead, dead, dead, dead.* Over and over again. I repeated the story, *Man dead, Jesus make man alive.* Jennie furrowed her brow and scratched and squeaked and hooted to herself, as if lost in deep thought.

Then she signed something followed by the word "dead." Like so:—— *dead.* I could not find any meaning in the ASL dictionary for the —— sign, except *bug* which of course must be wrong. She continued signing —— *dead* quite insistently. At the same time she exhibited all the signs of puzzlement, as if the word "dead" itself held some mystery for her. As indeed it should. It is one of the oldest and most baffling questions that faced Mankind until God revealed himself through His Son Jesus Christ, and when that happened, truly then, death lost its mystery. I hope that Jennie at some point in her life can come to this realization, although it may be beyond her intellectual capabilities.

We continued our peculiar conversation.

Myself: *Jesus make dead man alive.*
Jennie: *Dead, dead, dead man.*
Myself: *Man dead.* (And I pointed to the picture)
Jennie: *What dead?*
Myself: *Man.*

Jennie became frustrated at this. *What dead?* she signed several times in rapid succession. I realized that she must be asking "What is it to be dead? What is death?" So I responded, *Death like sleep.*

She stamped on the floor and hooted loudly. *Dead! Dead!* she signed, and then signed *What dead?*

I responded by lying down and pretending to be dead. This silenced Jennie, and when I peeked out of an eye I saw that she was looking at me with a terrible grimace of fear. I had frightened the poor thing! I quickly got up and she signed *Hug, hug* over and over again. Then she picked up the book and threw it down on the floor and slapped it and kicked it across the room. Death is obviously as distasteful a subject to a chimpanzee as it is to a human being.

I did not, however, wish to leave the subject. I felt a breakthrough might be imminent. The fear of death is what brings many to God, and I have often thought that God gave us this terrible fear for that very reason. Therefore, as painful as it was to me, I introduced Reba into the conversation.

I signed, *Reba dead.*

Jennie looked at me.

Remember Reba? I asked.

Jennie signed *Reba.*

Reba dead I signed.

Jennie signed *Reba!* several times, as if she had forgotten about Reba. Then she looked about wildly. I do believe that she realized, for the first time, that Reba had been missing for a while.

Right away she turned and ran up the stairs and pounded on the door to Reba's old bedroom, which I keep shut but unlocked. Reba had spent several months there before the end. I went up the stairs after her, and by the time I arrived she had thrown the bedroom door open and was standing on the threshhold. Then she whirled around and came racing past me in the hall and went back down-stairs—myself struggling to keep up—and headed into the kitchen, the other place where Reba was often found. When I caught up with her, she was standing in the middle of the kitchen looking confused.

Where Reba? she signed.

Reba dead, I signed. *Reba in Heaven.* My heart was pounding so awfully, with a mixture of sorrow and anticipation. I felt that some very profound revelation was taking place in Jennie's under-standing. And I felt so terribly sad at the same time.

Jennie signed, *Where Reba!* again with both hands.

Reba dead, I repeated. *Reba with God in Heaven.* I pointed to the sky. *Reba dead, gone to Heaven. Reba with God.*

She looked so utterly lost that I signed *Jennie, what you think?*

She looked at me and signed again, *Where Reba?* and stamped her feet on the ground in frustration.

And then I remembered Jennie's kitten, which she owned for a short time some years ago and which died. I signed *Remember cat? Jennie's cat? Jennie's cat dead. Reba dead. Same. Same.*

Jennie became very still, looking at me. I repeated: *Jennie's cat dead. Reba dead. Same.*

At this, a most dramatic reaction occurred. Jennie remained frozen, but her hair slowly began to rise up on end, and she swayed back and forth on her knuckles, while making a peculiar squeaking noise in the bottom of her throat. A noise I had never heard before, but clearly one of profound distress. I do not know whether she was affrighted or grieving. I suspect the former.

She then signed *Jennie's cat* several times and went and sat in the corner, facing the wall, hugging herself and squeaking. She would not allow me to approach or comfort her, which was very unlike her. My heart was in turmoil. I was divided between thinking that Jennie was sharing in her own way my grief, and wondering if what Jennie was actually experiencing was that terrible and unassuagable fear of death that often strikes nonbelievers in the middle years of life. I could hardly breathe.

I attempted to comfort her in my own limited way. *Reba happy. Reba in Heaven. Reba with God and Jesus.* Jennie continued signing to herself *Jennie's cat* and *Reba Reba Reba* and rocking back and forth, lost in her private and powerful emotion, without paying me the slightest attention. I finally took her hand and led her home. She was passive and unresponsive.

Knowledge of death—which is, in a peculiar way, also the knowledge of good and evil—is the most terrible burden that we human beings must bear, and I wonder now if it wasn't cruel to force that knowledge on Jennie.

[FROM *Recollecting a Life* by Hugo Archibald.]

By the fall of 1971, we noticed that Jennie was growing up fast. Every day she seemed to get bigger and stronger, more self-assured and less dependent. She abandoned many of her childish ways. She stopped hoarding her toys and guarding them obsessively. She became more at ease with strangers. She was less likely to throw a tantrum, but when she did her tantrums were more prolonged and violent.

At the same time our son was going through the throes of adolescence. He grew his hair long and participated in a protest of the Vietnam War in Kibbencook Square. It was a tame protest—a candlelight March for Peace—and we insisted on coming along, partly because we agreed with the protesters, but mostly because we did not want to see Sandy arrested or injured if the police should overreact. Jennie, naturally, came along as well.

The marchers gathered at the high school parking lot at sunset and proceeded down Grove Street to the clock tower in Kibbencook Square. There were several hundred marchers, mostly young people from the high school, along with a number of worried parents. Sandy and his young friends wore flowers in their hair and they carried candles. Lea and I followed behind, keeping one eye on them and another on the police. We were worried that one of Sandy's less-intelligent friends would light up a marijuana cigarette and give the police a reason to arrest everyone.

They linked hands and sang "Give Peace a Chance," with Jennie right in there with the thick of them. She had no idea what was going on, but she loved the crowd, the singing, and the undercurrent of excitement. She was in her element.

The police and a National Guard unit lined the marchers' route, but there were no pointed guns or tear gas. The police were well behaved and the only unpleasant note came from a group of working-class men in black leather jackets, who were protesting our protesting with jeers and catcalls. Kibbencook was not a hotbed of radicalism, and even antiwar marches were organized with a certain decorum. It was a thoroughly suburban protest.

During the march, Jennie behaved herself beautifully. She did not start a riot, attack the police, burn the flag, or spit on the National Guardsmen. It was an odd sight indeed seeing these young teenagers treating this ape as a friend—albeit a rather special friend. Jennie would sign away until she was blue in the face with Sandy's friends, but none of them understood what she was saying without Sandy translating. This never seemed to matter much to them or to Jennie. She made herself understood in one way or another.

The local press was there, and the next day there was a picture of Jennie and a line of protesters, hands linked, on the front page of the Kibbencook *Townsman*. There were several nasty letters to the editor making crude comparisons between Jennie and the marchers. The letters made Sandy angry and he responded with a letter to the editor pointing out that chimpanzees were perhaps more intelligent than certain American politicians, since war was unknown among apes. This was, of course, before Dr. Jane Goodall's observation of a deadly conflict between two chimpanzee groups in Gombe.

The march deeply impressed me. It was a moving experience, seeing young people so earnestly concerned about the morality of our involvement in Vietnam. While many of their ideas may have been naive or youthfully excessive, their hearts were in the right place. It was one of the first times in the history of America where a large segment of the population had questioned the morality of war—not just *a* war but *any* war. They were not going to accept blindly the values of their parents.

Sandy had just turned fourteen. I felt that I was witnessing the beginnings of a great sea change in America. I was deeply moved. Through this terrible ordeal of Vietnam, I believed, we might finally see America becoming what the founding fathers had envisioned, a nation with a moral purpose in the world and a nation that cared about all its citizens. We might see the end of the cynical Nixon-Kissinger version of *realpolitik*.

It hasn't turned out that way, but then we are all a little older and wiser.

Not long after the march I purchased a Trans-Lux eight-millimeter silent movie camera, a projector, and a set of lights. I hoped to capture on film her childhood playfulness before it vanished completely. I was almost too late.

I began to film Jennie at home, doing the things she normally did: eating, squirting the hose, running around the house, playing with Sandy. When the first batch of film came back from the developers, we set up the screen and settled in for an evening of home movies. We were curious what Jennie's reaction might be to seeing herself on the silver screen. She had a streak of exhibitionism, a necessary prerequisite for movie stardom.

When the lights darkened and the moving picture flickered on, Jennie became still and attentive. Her image suddenly appeared on-screen, squatting on the piano stool and pounding away at the keys of our old Weser "cabinet grand." When Jennie saw herself on the screen, she let fly a short scream and stood up, hopping up and down in excitement and pointing at the screen. Then she began to sign *Jennie* and point again. If ever there was proof of self-awareness, this was it.

Yes, Sandy signed, *that's Jennie playing piano.*

Me Jennie! signed Jennie. She went up to the screen to examine her image more closely. Her shadow obscured the screen, and she began poking at her shadow, grunting with puzzlement. Then she went over to the projector and tried to look into the lens, but the light was so bright she backed away with her face wrinkled up and her eyes blinking. We tried to persuade her to sit down and watch, but whenever her image appeared on-screen she sprang back up and hopped up and down, squealing with excitement.

It was curious to see her reaction. With each change of scene Jennie signed what was happening: *Jennie eat* or *Jennie wet* or *Fire fire* when she was shown pulling roasted apples out of the fire. When we filmed Jennie chasing one of the neighbor's dogs she jumped up with a screech of derision and raced to the screen, signing *Bad! Go away!* In another scene we gave her a hamburger loaded with pickles and ketchup, so we could record for posterity her dinnertime manners. When she threw the hamburger in the film,

Jennie laughed and whirled about on the floor, signing *Bad Jennie! Bad bad Jennie!*

One of the truly interesting sequences occurred when Sandy brought home a milk snake he had caught in the fields in Maine. We knew Jennie had an irrational fear and hatred of snakes. We put the snake in a shoebox and left it on the coffee table in the living room. I set up the camera in a strategic place to record the action and Sandy called Jennie in from the orchard.

She came tumbling into the house and raced to the living room. Jennie had extraordinary powers of observation and always noticed when something new had been added to a room. She immediately saw the shoebox and stopped dead. She reached out to touch it, and quite suddenly she jerked her hand back and her hair rose in fear. To this day I do not know how she knew there was a snake in the shoebox. Chimpanzees do not have a sense of smell keener than humans, and milk snakes are clean and do not have a detectable odor.

She took Lea's hand and whimpered loudly and stamped on the floor a few times, but she did not retreat. Her curiosity was too strong. Pulling Lea by the hand, she advanced on the shoebox, swatted it, and scurried back behind Lea.

The box did not open.

She signed *Box open box* to Lea, but Lea merely signed back *Jennie open box.*

Jennie took another quick step toward the box and gave it a harder swat, which sent it tumbling to the floor, spilling the snake on the rug.

At this Jennie let fly a terrific scream and ran to the door, where she stopped and stood swaying on her knuckles, screaming and drumming on the floor with her feet. She ran halfway to the snake, pounded and stamped the floor in a display of anger, and retreated back to the doorway. Her magnificent performance was lost on the poor snake, who was either dazed from his fall or merely half asleep on the soft rug.

She signed *Bad! Bad!* and made another charge and retreat at the snake, to no effect. The snake just lay there, flicking its tongue. Sandy fetched the snake and eventually persuaded Jennie to touch it from a distance, which she did with her arm stretched out and her face averted with a grin of fear. I recorded the entire encounter on film, and Harold Epstein and Dr. Prentiss both watched it with great interest. We concluded that chimpanzees must have a genetically programmed fear of snakes, as well as the ability to detect them when they are hidden, something that we humans have lost.

During that next year I took several thousand feet of film of Jennie and Sandy: the two of them roasting marshmallows and dancing around a campfire in the field behind the farmhouse; Jennie and Sandy riding their bikes around the neighborhood; Jennie and Rev. Palliser waving at the camera. The camera revealed one limitation in Jennie's intelligence: she never made the connection between the camera and the home movies that we later viewed. As a result she was never self-conscious in front of the camera. This was a great contrast to Sandy, who became increasingly irritated at being filmed. He had turned fifteen and, like most teenagers, was agonizingly self-conscious.

Jennie was nearing the age of puberty. Just as Harold Epstein had warned, she was becoming increasingly unruly. She had always "tested" the limits of her power, but as she reached the age of eight her testing of us became more strident and aggressive. We found ourselves quite unable to oppose her at times.

Jennie's rebellion at eight paralleled Sandy's at fifteen, and the two of them often defied parental authority together. It was a conspiracy: each would undermine our efforts to discipline the other. It was not uncommon that when I became angry at Sandy for some reason, Jennie would start bristling up, barking and swaggering toward me, in a classic threat. When we tried to discipline Jennie, Sandy would often say "Leave her alone" or "Come on,

Jennie, let's get out of here," and Jennie would drop her contrite expression and stare at us with sheer insolence.

I particularly recall one time when Jennie had been pounding on the piano for too long while I was trying to work, and I shouted at her to stop. Sandy was in the room reading a book. Jennie stopped and got off the piano stool, crouching and looking guilty. Then Sandy said, "Why don't you quit picking on her. You're always at her, trying to control her every little move, make her do this and not do that."

As if she understood what Sandy said, Jennie hopped back on the piano stool and pounded several times on the keys. When I shouted at her again, she started spinning on the rotating stool, signing *Phooey* with each turn. And then she pounded once more on the keys in a most insolent way, to make sure I got the message.

Looking back over the calming gulf of years, I see the humor in this scene of a rebellious chimpanzee and teenager making a father's life miserable. At the time, however, I was very angry. It is difficult for a parent—particularly a father—to understand and react appropriately to a rebellious son, but when you have two who are reinforcing each other, it is intolerable. The two of them, through their defiance, made me feel powerless, rejected, and superannuated. They made me feel like a useless middle-aged man.

[FROM an interview with Dr. Pamela Prentiss.]

This shitty tape recorder of mine seems to be broken. Will you send me a copy of your tapes? Thank you.

Frankly, I'm disappointed you haven't read these papers. How can you write a book about Jennie without reading this stuff? You've had a whole month. I know it's a lot, but you need to know all this.

Let's see . . . I have one thing for you here. This is what we call a matrix analysis. It's a three-dimensional computer plot. I did this myself using the old IBM 3000 mainframe at Tufts. You could do this graph today with a little Macintosh powerbook. Anyway, it shows Jennie's progress in language. This should go into your book. It's very important.

You see the x-axis is time, and the y-axis is the number of times each individual sign is made per unit of time, and the z-axis is the average number of words per utterance. Isn't this fantastic? Look at how her language ability just *exploded* after eighteen months. See that big bump? Looks like Mount Everest!

And here, by 1972, you see she's already using one hundred and forty signs regularly in two- and three-word utterances. Blows your mind. . . . No, that's the z-axis. See, it's *three*-dimensional. . . . No wonder, you're holding it *sideways*. Each point consists of three degrees of freedom. Three variables. If you can't see it I can't explain it to you. Sometimes I don't know why I bother.

By 1972, the project was four years old. Jennie had learned over one hundred and fifty signs. It was unbelievable how she was signing. Now you see this trough? This dropoff? No, look, it's right there in the graph. This was a disappointment. We hoped that as she learned more signs her utterances would become longer and more complex, until she was creating sentences. If that had happened this, here, would be a smooth surface. Not this big drop. Looks like a canyon, here. See? Even as her vocabulary increased most of her utterances remained one to three words long. Four-word utterances were rare. She was able to get out a five-word statement only with a lot of prompting.

She had difficulty creating the subject-verb-direct object form that human children naturally take up. In English, of course. Other languages are different. It's all there in the papers I gave you.

Jennie, you see, had trouble going from *give ball* to *give me ball*. The concept of the indirect object—like *give ball to Sandy*—was beyond her abilities. She could understand it, but not say it.

Her syntax was weak. It was terrible. We did statistical analyses of her utterances and found only a slight correlation with correct syntax. What I mean is, she would sign *Ball give* almost as often as *Give ball*. Of course, our enemies—I mean that jerk Craig Miller at Penn—seized on this and said that without syntax there wasn't language. Well that's a lot of shit. Excuse my French. I mean, not all human languages even use syntactical constructions. Like Latin, for Christ's sake. Miller was a real shithead. He was out to get us. Oh, you've still got that tape recorder on. Well, don't put that in. [Laughs.]

Don't get me wrong. We weren't disappointed in Jennie's progress. It was just that our hopes had been raised by the incredible rate of learning in the first three years, and we had expected ever more complex sentences to result. It didn't happen. We noted the same "plateau" among our colony chimpanzees, though at a lower level of vocabulary. This was a big divergence from the way human children learn language, and that itself was interesting. But it wasn't the big deal that Miller made it out to be.

Did you read those transcriptions that I gave you? "Conversations with a Chimpanzee"? Good. You know, I can't get that book published. Nobody'll touch it after that Proxmire shit. Anyway, from reading that you can see how incredible the communication was between us. Jennie and I communicated like you wouldn't believe. What you don't see from those transcripts is the body language. For example, in ASL a question is not noted with a special sign, or even syntax, but with a pause and a quizzical expression, a lifting of the eyebrows. Just like in Italian. Like this: *Jennie eat.* And *Jennie eat?* [Dr. Prentiss demonstrates.] See? It's signed the same way, but the question is in the body language.

If you have ever watched a fluent ASL person, you'd see immediately that the entire body and face are involved. Watch me. I'm going to tell you a story about Jennie. In ASL. Oh, I hope I can remember it after all these years! But instead of just mouthing the words—like real ASL translators do, to help lip readers—I speak them. See? Here goes. [Dr. Prentiss stands up and demonstrates.]

A-little-while-ago Jennie and Pam go walk. We walk, walk, walk to brook. See water there. Jennie like go swim? No! Jennie no like water! Jennie and Pam go tree. Jennie climb, climb, climb tree. Jennie see everything! Jennie queen of everything! Jennie hoot. Entire town hear Jennie. Pam cannot climb. Pam stay at bottom. Pam cry, cry, cry.

See what I mean? The whole body is involved.

One of the great myths of ASL is that it is an "artificial" or "invented" language. Not so. ASL has biological and evolutionary roots just as surely as spoken language does. Did you know that research on gorillas has shown that they communicate using gestures? Now listen to this. An ASL-like language may very well have preceded spoken language in human development. A kind of language with gestures and vocalizations. Gradually the vocalizations took over from the gestures, because it's so much more convenient to speak than gesture. I mean, this stuff is *unbelievable.*

With me and Jennie, so much was beyond just signing. So much more was exchanged between us than what you see in those transcripts. There was no way to quantify the incredible level of communication we had.

Jennie and the other chimpanzees had this ability to convey information through facial expression, gesture, and body language. While the utterances remained mostly one to three words, the facial expressions and body language became more and more sophisticated. You see, the problem is that this result was very difficult to quantify. It was mind-to-mind, in a way. But of course, none of that is scientific or quantifiable. If I said anything like that at a meeting, they'd laugh me out of the room. Nobody knows what language is. It isn't just speech, that's for sure. But try to explain that to some of these reductionist structural linguists.

Anyway, I have a theory. I believe that we humans, in teaching chimpanzees and gorillas ASL, stumbled upon a natural communication system already in use. We just enhanced it. This is just my opinion and I wouldn't dare put it in a paper. See, with this vicious attack against the Jennie project, we never had a chance to look at some of these things.

We had planned a six-year project. It ended up being about five years. Toward the end Jennie and I had quite a bit of trouble. The inconsistent and chaotic atmosphere in the Archibald home was starting to take its toll. Jennie became very disobedient. She picked up a lot of Mrs. Archibald's ways. Very aggressive.

I am very sorry to report to you that the Archibalds began giving Jennie liquor to drink. They were drinkers in the evening, having a cocktail before dinner and then a glass of wine at dinner. They actually allowed Jennie the same. Almost every night. I tried to put a stop to it but was unsuccessful. I know this will sound shocking to you but it was no secret to anyone. I must report it as the truth. So you can see that Jennie's home situation was not exactly ideal.

When Sandy was young, we had a great relationship. Sandy was a brilliant child. He is, if I may use a tired world, I mean word, a genius. Where did that Freudian slip come from?

As he became a teenager, he developed an antagonism toward me. He picked this up from his mother. He made all these outrageous and silly accusations against me. He kept Jennie out late at night. She was bleary and irritable in the mornings when I arrived. He interrupted our sessions. He talked about me to Jennie behind my back. Jennie never did reject me, however. Oh no. She loved me to the very end. Her love for me was more powerful than anything the Archibalds could undermine.

When Sandy reached adolescence he rebelled. He was a terrible role model for Jennie. You see, Sandy affected the pose of an SDS Yippie "radical." Of course, he wasn't a real radical, just a spoiled white middle-class teenager. He was never in danger of being drafted, either. But this didn't stop him from protesting and calling for the burning of the banks.

Jennie picked up a number of terrible habits from Sandy. I'm almost positive she smoked pot, and it's possible she even took LSD with Sandy or his friends.

The real blow to the project came in 1973. I expected a renewal of my NSF grant for 1973. This was automatic. The NSF rarely cuts off funding in the middle of a research project, especially when the results are as spectacular as ours were. But there were other forces afoot. Do you remember Senator William Proxmire and his "Golden Fleece" awards? That shit Proxmire found he could get votes by criticizing government-funded scientific research that he didn't understand. Proxmire had about a fifth-grade knowledge of science. Every year he would select a few projects that he felt had no merit and would award them a golden fleece. As in "fleecing" the taxpayers.

Oh my God, I'll never forget the morning I unfolded my *New York Times* and found that our chimpanzee linguistic project "won" a golden fleece. Right on the front page. I felt like throwing up. Proxmire said the American taxpayers had wasted $550,000 teaching five chimpanzees to talk sign language. What could a chimpanzee have to say that might be of interest? Proxmire asked. Well, he said, here it is in black and white, here are the earth-shattering comments from these chimps, after a half million dollars of English lessons: "Gimme banana!" and "I gotta go potty!" He was reading from one of my papers on the Senate floor! The big fat pompous asshole. I should've sued the bastard. Then he went on and on about how our young people can't afford the five thousand dollars to go to college while millions are being spent teaching chimpanzees. As if this money had been taken away from deserving students. The big fat sack of shit.

So, despite outstanding results and excellent peer reviews, the funding was killed. Losing our NSF funding wouldn't have been the end of the world, except that after Proxmire no private foundation would even touch the project. All our funding was withdrawn. We were the lepers of science. It was that fellow at Penn, Craig Miller, who was behind it. Miller got ahold of some videotape of Jennie signing on some pretext and then analyzed it. They concluded that everything she said was cued. They felt that almost every sign of Jennie's was a repeat of a sign that had just been made by the trainer Then there was that absurd syntax business again. No language without syntax. Well, what about Latin! These assholes didn't even know Latin! Where did these guys go to school?

Anyway, these conclusions came from people who had never spent any time with chimpanzees. You can't tell anything from a two-hour videotape. I spent five years with five chimpanzees. There are so many modes of communication between human and chimp that can't be quantified. Body language. Vehemence and speed of gesture, facial expression. You had to be there with Jennie to understand the depth of communication. With our enemies out there, and a Senator against us, we got hammered.

This research had been extremely expensive. Maintaining the Barnum estate, paying for teachers, trainers, and keepers twenty-four hours a day for the colony chimpanzees, my time teaching Jennie, and the thousands of hours spent analyzing and processing the data. A humane research environment for chimpanzees is very, very expensive. I'm sure Miller would have been much happier if we'd locked all the chimps in four-by-five cages. When we lost our funding, we had to shut down the project immediately.

This was a terrible loss to science. I can't even begin to tell you. But it also affected Jennie. It was the beginning of the end.

[FROM an editorial in the *Boston Globe,* February 1, 1973. Used with permission.]

Every year, Congress and the public eagerly await Senator William Proxmire's "Golden Fleece" awards. Sen. Proxmire, the watchdog of the scientific community, has tracked down and reported tax-payer-financed scientific research that is redundant, unnecessary, or just plain silly. Those projects that represent an egregious waste of taxpayer money are given his highest award, known as the Golden Fleece. Many of the projects that win the award seem amusing, until one examines the cost.

This year Sen. Proxmire gave his uncoveted award to a project going on right here in Boston, a joint effort sponsored by Tufts University and the Boston Museum of Natural History. Over half a million dollars of National Science Foundation monies have supported this project since its inception in 1967. The nature of the project? Teaching chimpanzees to "talk" using American Sign Language.

The question is, do we really need talking chimpanzees? The supporters of the project tell us they are unlocking the secrets of human language. But Sen. Proxmire—backed up by an eminent scientist from the University of Pennsylvania, Dr. Craig Miller—has called that idea into question. The project has yielded nothing more than elaborate imitative behavior on the part of the apes. Nothing approaching real communication—that is, language—has resulted. And all this after spending half a million dollars of public money. When our inner cities are crumbling, when children go hungry, and when people shiver in freezing tenements because they can't afford to buy heating oil, surely there are better ways to spend a half million dollars.

So we say to Sen. Proxmire: Bull's-eye! Or should we say, Chimp's-eye!

[From a letter to the editor, published in the *Boston Globe* on February 11, 1973.]

Dear Editor,
    So you think the world doesn't need talking chimpanzees. Well, have any of your smart-aleck editorial writers bothered to come here to Kibbencook and see our "talking" chimpanzee? Her name is Jennie and

she's a member of our family and communicates with those around her a lot better than most human children her age. I open your paper in the morning and I can hardly wade through all the gobbledygook that you try to pass off as "news." If you call that "communication" then you deserve a Platinum Fleece. As for Craig Miller, not once—not *once*—has he ever met Jennie! So what does he know? Or as Jennie would say, "Phooey to you!"

I think what the world doesn't need are talking editorial writers.

Sincerely,
Mrs. Hugo Archibald

[FROM an interview with Lea Archibald.]

At the age of fifteen and a half, Sandy got his learner's permit. God save us. Of course, he had to have an adult in the car until he was sixteen, or something like that. That didn't stop him. He began taking the car out when he wasn't supposed to, and Jennie of course went with him. Jennie loved to ride in the car. She would hang out the window and make big vulgar noises and give people the "finger." I just cringe when I think about it. Hugo was not a stern disciplinarian, and I had more than I could handle.

That winter, the winter of 1973, the big "event" occurred. That was what made Jennie famous all over again. There was an ice storm and everything was covered with a layer of ice. I was out shopping and Hugo was holed up in his study, where he always was. Sandy snuck out the Falcon, and they went down to the high school parking lot. Well, I came home and the car was gone. I thought, That's funny, Hugo didn't say he was going out. And just then Hugo came out of his office. I said, "Where's Sandy and Jennie?"

He said, "Why, aren't they right here?"

As if on cue, the telephone rang. Oh my goodness. It was the Kibbencook town police. They were in an uproar down there. We were told to come down immediately. I could hear in the background this appalling sound that could only be simian in origin. The policeman was hopping mad. He started yelling at me over the telephone, all about how I was going to get a big bill for damages and the animal control people were there because Jennie had bitten a policeman and she would have to be destroyed.

Oh my goodness, you can imagine what we were thinking. We rushed down there. The whole place was in a shambles. The dog-catcher had arrived to get Jennie. The poor man was scared to unlock the jail cell where Jennie was shut in. Jennie was tearing up the place. Oh dear. Forgive me for laughing. It seems funny now but at the time we weren't at all amused.

It seems that Sandy had been skidding around the parking lot, I think they called it "doing donuts." Making the car spin around in circles on the ice. The police arrived and this one officer ordered Sandy out of the car. The man was angry and acting like a bully, as policemen do. His name was Russo. Bill Russo. Well, I'd known Bill Russo for years, and he was a bit, shall we say, limited. He knew Sandy, or should have known him, but I guess he didn't recognize him with the long hair. Thought he was some kind of crazed hippie. So he ordered Sandy up against the car with his arms out, and started searching him. Well, you know how protective Jennie was. She tumbled out of the car with a scream and gave Russo a good bite on the leg, really opened it up. That chimp was strong.

Like the complete ass that he was, Russo drew his service revolver and pointed it at Jennie. Sandy, of course, went berserk, screaming and grabbing at the gun and wrapping himself around Jennie. He called Russo the most horrid names, fascist pig and that sort of thing. It must have been just awful, thinking this moron was going to shoot Jennie. I'm sure he would have if Sandy hadn't stopped him. Sandy saved Jennie's life.

So they threw Sandy and Jennie in the back of the car and brought them down to the Kibbencook police station over there on Washington Street. Even though Sandy quite reasonably asked that he and Jennie be put in the same cell, they were separated. And Jennie—who *hated* cages—Well! she just destroyed that cell, tore open the mattress, broke the toilet, unscrewed everything and busted the sink. The dogcatcher arrived and he was this horrid fat thing who was afraid to open the door. He was getting ready to shoot Jennie with a tranquilizing dart. Sandy told him Jennie was part of a secret government scientific project and that if they did anything to her the FBI would put him in jail. Can you imagine? Honestly, it was so funny. I don't know whether this idiot of a dogcatcher believed it, but the police chief had read about Jennie and the research, so he asked the man to wait until we came down.

When we arrived, Bill Russo was just getting into his car to go down to the hospital. He was all red and just furious that this chimpanzee had gotten the better of him. He said that Jennie should be destroyed and that Sandy was a menace to society and what was the matter, did his barber die or something? Or was he trying to be one of these hippie radicals who wanted to make America Communist? Why, he said, if his kid grew his hair like that he'd show him the raw side of a belt. Imagine. He spoke like that to me. Well! I told Bill Russo that what he just said was slander plain and simple and that one more word out of his big fat mouth and I'd see him in court. He said that we'd be in court first for raising a vicious ape that nearly tore his leg off. My goodness! I was so angry.

When we got inside, Jennie was raising cain, screeching and banging on the bars. You couldn't hear a thing it was so loud. Hugo went to the cells—there were just three little rooms down the hall—and told Jennie to shut up and she did. We had to pay bail for Sandy, and the dogcatcher gave us a citation. He said we'd have to go to court. In the meantime, he said, he would have to take Jennie down to the pound.

Hugo was magnificent. Very cool and patient. He explained to the man who Jennie was, what she was, and why it was impossible to even think of putting her in the pound. He dropped hints about Jennie's strength and how she could escape from any cage made for an animal. He frightened the poor man half to death. He said, well, under the circumstances it would be acceptable if Jennie were kept at home, fully restrained at all times, until the court date. If she bit anyone else, well, that would be a very serious matter indeed.

We drove home in silence. Hugo was angry. So was I, for that matter. Sandy and Jennie were both subdued; I guess they knew they were in big trouble. Hugo said to Sandy: Come up to my office. He signed to Jennie: *Bad Jennie, go to bathroom.*

Jennie pretended not to react, but as soon as the car doors opened she jumped and hid in the garage. Hugo was madder than ever and shut the garage door, and made Jennie spend an hour in there. It was cold in there, and all she had was her Donald Duck T-shirt and pants.

Sandy spent quite a few weekends shoveling snow to earn money for his fine. Then the judge took away his learner's permit and he wasn't allowed to drive until he turned sixteen and a half.

Jennie's hearing was a more serious matter. You see, the town really did have the right to destroy her. Kibbencook had very strict animal control laws, and a dog that bit someone and drew blood was required to be destroyed. First time; no second chances.

Hugo actually hired a lawyer, he was that concerned. Of course, we would never have given Jennie up. We would have moved away if it came to that.

The lawyer Hugo got was magnificent. His name was Alterman. Arthur Alterman. He cost a hundred dollars an hour, but he was worth every penny.

It was a very funny trial. There was nothing in the history of jurisprudence like it. It wasn't a real trial, though. Just a hearing.

There was no "prosecutor," just an administrative law judge running things, a little Italian fellow named Fiorello. Even so, the end result could have been horrible. It was a *capital* case.

Russo testified, and his partner. And then the dogcatcher, all sweating and red-faced, gave his little song and dance. Then Alterman got up and put Jennie on the stand.

I noticed that there was a young reporter in the hearing room, sleeping in the back. When Jennie came in he woke up right away. He was falling all over himself looking for a pencil and taking notes and getting on the telephone trying to get a court artist down.

Alterman had hired a professional ASL interpreter from the Somerville School for the Deaf. Her credentials were impeccable. She was terrific and we had very carefully coached Jennie and rehearsed her testimony. For days on end we rehearsed what Jennie was to say. If she were human I am sure it would have been illegal, coaching the witness the way we did.

Alterman didn't put Jennie on the stand for her testimony alone. He explained it all to us. The minute the judge saw Jennie in her little blue suit with the big red bow, and saw her signing back and forth with the interpreter, he would never, ever, in a thousand years, find her a menace to society and order her destroyed. How could he? She was just like a little person!

The interpreter led Jennie and Hugo up to the stand and the two sat there together, since somebody needed to control Jennie if something happened. God forbid that she should bite the judge or a lawyer!

Alterman was marvelous. He was a showman. He explained that the witness couldn't swear on the Bible because she wasn't a Christian. There was a big laugh at that one. If Rev. Palliser had been there I'm sure he would have taken exception! The judge explained to the court, I suppose for the record, that Jennie's testimony was meaningless to determine the facts of the case, but that he was allowing it anyway. The judge wanted to see the signing chimpanzee in action.

So Jennie was installed in the witness stand. She looked so funny, sitting in that big oak chair with her little feet sticking out, looking around with the utmost interest. Her little black eyes were just twinkling. I wish you could have been there. She looked so small and helpless in this grand room with the flags and oak paneling and the judge in his robes. Let me see if I can remember how it went. Do you want me to demonstrate the signing again? It's surprising how little I've forgotten, really. I suppose it's like riding a bicycle.

[Editor's note: At this point Mrs. Archibald stood up and as she described the questions, she demonstrated the signs at the same time.]

Mr. Alterman spoke to the interpreter only. He said to ask Jennie—he called her "the witness,"—what happened on the afternoon of February such-and-such 1973. So the woman signed to Jennie, *What happen?* When Jennie replied she would immediately translate.

Jennie of course immediately demanded an apple or something. *Apple! Give apple!* Right away she was off the script. My heart just sank. But the interpreter was required to translate everything.

Well! The judge banged his gavel and assumed a very serious face, and said, "No eating in the courtroom." And everyone laughed. I was so relieved. I knew at that moment that we were going to win the case. The judge was already having a wonderful time. But then he said, "Tell the witness to respond to the question."

So the interpreter signed: *Jennie, no apple. Later. What happen?* And Jennie signed back, *Hurt.*

Who? signed the interpreter. *Who hurt?*

Man, Jennie signed.

Where man? asked the interpreter.

Jennie kept saying *Man, man!*

The interpreter asked her to point to the man several times, and finally Jennie pointed right to Officer Russo.

At this point Mr. Alterman thundered: "Let the record show that the witness has identified Officer William H. Russo!" It was so thrilling. Now I hate to admit this, but we'd rehearsed for days with Jennie using a blown-up photograph of Russo that Mr. Alterman had managed to find, I don't know where. Every single question had been rehearsed a dozen times.

Well! When Jennie pointed to Russo, a great Ahhhhh! went up in the courtroom and I could see the reporter scribbling away as if his life depended on it. I suppose for him it was the scoop of a lifetime. Here he'd probably been sitting around for months doing the Kibbencook courthouse "beat," and seeing nothing more interesting than a drunk driver. And now, isn't it funny, but I wonder if Mr. Alterman didn't have something to do with getting that reporter into the courtroom? I hadn't thought about that before, but this case made Mr. Alterman famous. He was in *Time* magazine even.

Let's see now. Mr. Alterman asked the interpreter to ask Jennie who the man hurt and why. So the interpreter asked: *Man hurt who?* and Jennie replied: *Sandy.*

Another murmur rose up in the courtroom and the judge was banging on his gavel. It was so thrilling, just like that television show, "Ironsides," you know, the Perry Mason show. Jennie stood up and started bobbing and hooting with excitement, and Hugo had to sit her down fast. I suppose the whole thing was highly irregular from a legal point of view, but it was great fun. And nobody was having more fun than the judge. It wasn't a real trial, you see, so he didn't have to worry about all the legal niceties.

The interpreter asked again, *Man hurt Sandy?*

And Jennie repeated it, *Man hurt Sandy,* a perfect witness. At this Russo jumped up and got all huffy with the judge. He was outraged. It was ridiculous, he said. Was the judge going to believe this monkey over him? Who was on trial here? What kind of kangaroo court was this anyway? He certainly made himself look like the fool that he was.

By this time the judge was completely on our side. He leaned back with a smile and said, "Correction, Officer: What kind of chimpanzee court is this?" That got a great laugh. So then the interpreter asked, *How man hurt Sandy? What man do?*

Well! Jennie departed from the script again. She signed *Bite. Man bite.* But when had Jennie ever kept to a script? If there was a way to create excitement, Jennie would find it.

Russo jumped up again. The poor man didn't know when to keep his mouth shut. He hollered out, "Your Honor! I didn't bite anybody! It's a lie!"

Oh my goodness, that just brought down the house! Everyone was helpless with laughter. The judge was trying not to laugh but he couldn't help it. Finally he banged his gavel and assumed a grave face, and asked Mr. Alterman what the relevance of all this testimony was. He said, "Surely you weren't going to allege that Officer Russo bit the ape?" He was laughing before he could even get out the question! Honestly, I'd never laughed so hard in my life. Russo and that horrid dog catcher sat there with these sour expressions on their faces. Fiorello was banging his gavel and laughing at the same time, but then he finally got mad and threatened to clear the court.

Mr. Alterman explained that he was merely trying to establish Jennie's "state of mind" at the time she nipped the officer. So the judge let him continue.

Jennie signed *apple, give apple!* You see, we had coached her by feeding her apples, so she kept expecting a reward. From her point of view, she was answering the questions right but no one was giving her an apple! The interpreter signed *No, apple later. Bad Jennie. No eat now. Man do what to Sandy?*

Jennie signed *Hurt!*

The judge interrupted and said that he was giving Mr. Alterman one more minute to elicit information from the witness. So he said to the interpreter: "Could you please ask the witness *why* she bit the police officer?"

Why Jennie bite man? the interpreter signed.

Jennie replied, *Man hurt Sandy.*

At that point Mr. Alterman was all smiles. He said, "That is all, thank you, Your Honor. And thank you, Jennie!" And the whole courtroom broke into applause, while the judge banged away.

When Mr. Alterman summed up, he said something like, let's see if I can remember it. He said that Jennie obviously believed the policeman was hurting Sandy, even though he wasn't. Jennie mistakenly thought that her best friend and brother—that is, Sandy—was being hurt or attacked by a strange man. She responded to protect her friend and brother. It was a mistake. But it was a noble mistake. She was protecting someone she loved. Did the judge really want to destroy this kind, loyal, and brave chimpanzee for making a mistake? Of course not. He went on and on like that. I think the judge found her not guilty in about a minute. I don't mean to say not guilty, because she was guilty. It was really a hearing to determine whether Jennie was dangerous and should be destroyed. She was guilty of biting Officer Russo but not guilty of being dangerous.

And then! Oh my goodness. That little reporter's story got everyone else interested. The *Globe* and the *Herald Traveler* and the Kibbencook *Townsman* all carried the story on their front pages. And then the television stations carried it and it got picked up and was even written up all over the country, in the *Los Angeles Times,* the *Chicago Tribune, People* magazine, the *New York Times,* everywhere. Actually, the *New York Times* ran a very good article on Jennie. It was the only intelligent thing written about Jennie during all those years. What was that reporter's name? He was such a nice man. Sullivan. Walter Sullivan. Anyway, all the talk shows called again. We were offered unbelievable sums by some of these drugstore newspapers. We turned them all down. We were a little shaken up by the incident. We didn't want to risk more public appearances by Jennie. She was getting toward puberty and becoming unruly and difficult. And strong. She could twist a heavy metal doorknob right off a door. Actually, she was becoming a major problem. It wasn't a laughing matter.

Setting: under the crab apple tree, July 20, 1973, 1:00 P.M. Jennie has just had her lunch and is hanging off one of the lower branches. She climbs down and sits in front of Pam. [Editor's note: This was the last session between Dr. Prentiss and Jennie.]

> Jennie: *Chase-tickle. Chase-tickle Jennie.*
>
> Pam: *No, Pam tired.*
>
> Jennie: *Chase-tickle.*
>
> Pam: *Jennie, sit down. Jennie talk with Pam now.*
>
> Jennie: *No.* She stands up and stamps her foot.
>
> Pam: *Jennie please be good. Pam talk to Jennie. Important. This is important.*
>
> Jennie: Continues to stand.
>
> Pam: *Pam going away. Pam going away for long time.*
>
> Jennie: Sits down.
>
> Pam: *Pam going away for long time. Jennie understand?*
>
> Jennie: No reaction.
>
> Pam: *Jennie understand? Pam going away for long time. Jennie not see Pam for long time.*
>
> Jennie: *Bad.*
>
> Pam: *Pam going away for long time. Jennie understand?*
>
> Jennie: *Bad Pam.*
>
> Pam: *Pam love Jennie.*
>
> Jennie: *Bad bad.*
>
> Pam: *Pam love Jennie. Jennie love Pam?*
>
> Jennie: *Bad.*
>
> Pam: *Jennie understand? Yes or no? Pam going away for long time.*
>
> Jennie: *Jennie bad.*
>
> Pam: *Jennie good. Jennie very good. Pam love Jennie.*
>
> Jennie: *Bad.*

Pam: *Jennie good.*

Jennie: *Bad bad.*

Pam: *Pam love Jennie. Jennie hug Pam?*

Jennie: Doesn't move. *Bad.*

Pam: *Please Jennie hug Pam?*

Jennie Doesn't move. Hair gradually goes into piloerection.

Pam: *Please Jennie hug Pam.*

Jennie: *Jennie bad. Sorry sorry.*

Pam: *No, Jennie good. Jennie good.*

Jennie: *Bad angry.*

Pam: *Please Jennie hug Pam. Pam hurt.*

Jennie: *Bad bad bad bad.*

Pam: Stands up and takes Jennie by the hand. Jennie brushes away the hand and turns away. Pam sits down and starts grooming Jennie's back. Jennie gradually relaxes her hair and finally rolls over to have her tummy scratched.

[Editor's note: The transcription ends with the following exchange, which took place next to Dr. Prentiss's Jeep.]

Pam: *Jennie hug Pam?*

Jennie: Opens her arms for a hug. Pam hugs Jennie. Jennie holds on to Pam for a long time before letting go.

Pam: *Pam love Jennie.*

Jennie: *Go?*

Pam: *Pam go away.*

Jennie: *Bad bad Pam dead.*

Pam: *Pam not dead. Pam go away. I know. Bad bad. Pam go away very bad. Pam love Jennie.*

Jennie: *Pam Pam Pam sorry sorry Pam. Jennie bad. Bad bad bad bad bad dead dead dead.*

nine

[FROM *Recollecting a Life* by Hugo Archibald.]

The fall of 1973 stands out in my mind as one of the most difficult periods in my life.

The first blow came when Dr. Prentiss unexpectedly lost her funding for the Jennie project. We did not quite realize how dependent we were on her until she ceased coming three days a week. The withdrawal of funding also ended our work with Jennie at the museum. Harold had reached retirement age, and I had to move on to other projects. All the additional care for Jennie fell on Lea's shoulders. At the same time, Sandy was in full rebellion against constituted authority and a disruptive influence in the house.

The fall made a sorry contrast to the August vacation we had just passed at the farmhouse in Maine. It was a wonderful summer, one of the best of our lives, and it was Jennie's last summer in Maine.

I will never forget that summer. As we drove up, at least an hour from our destination Jennie was hooting and drumming on the seat with her hands. When she saw the wooden Indian, she let out a screech of joy, and as we turned into the driveway she rolled down the window and jumped out, even before the car had stopped. We saw her black form racing through the meadow to the apple trees. She sat in her favorite tree, screaming with delight, shaking the branches and clapping her hands. Sandy, at sixteen, was also happy to get away from Kibbencook, which he found oppressive and "middle class."

Sarah was nine years old that summer. Her passions were reading and music. Sarah devoured books, sometimes two a day. Lea had to check her every night to make sure she turned out her light, or she would read to all hours and drag herself down to breakfast with dark circles under her eyes. She also loved classical music. She had started piano lessons and played tolerably well. We bought her a plastic portable record player that summer, and she set it up in the living room and listened endlessly to Chopin's preludes, until the record became worn and scratchy. In Maine she could indulge in music and reading without the interruption of schoolwork.

Music was the only interest Jennie and Sarah had in common. Unfortunately, their respective ways of appreciating music were very different. As soon as the sounds of a Chopin prelude floated out of the living room, Jennie would appear out of nowhere and sit on the sofa with her eyes half closed, her lips pursed. As the music swelled to a climax, Jennie would begin to make unpleasant noises. We charitably called her noises "singing," although they sounded more like the wheezing of a dying poodle. Sarah could not tolerate noise while she listened to her beloved Chopin. She had many clever ways of dealing with Jennie. Sometimes she stopped the record, went to the kitchen, and rattled the padlock on the refrigerator. Jennie could never resist the sound of an opening refrigerator, and she scurried toward the kitchen. Meanwhile, Sarah quickly returned to the living room via the back hall, locked the door, and started the record again, while Jennie banged on the refrigerator and rattled the doors. (Like the Kibbencook house, our farmhouse in Maine had locks on both sides of all the doors, as well as on the refrigerator and cupboards.) If that ruse failed, she would take a banana and throw it on the lawn; when Jennie raced out to get it she would lock the door.

That spring I bought a boat, a secondhand Boston Whaler with an eighteen-horsepower engine. It was not a big boat, but it was seaworthy. We took it out for the first time that August. Jennie, naturally, insisted on coming. After we felt comfortable with the boat we allowed Jennie to steer it. She sat in my lap while I controlled the throttle. She weaved about the ocean, turning the wheel this way and that, hooting with pleasure and hopping up and down. She became so excited at one point that she let go of the wheel and whirled around and around, her ultimate expression of joy. Handling the wheel gave her a sense of power and control, which she found enormously exciting.

We took the boat to a place called Brackett's Ledge, which was covered with seals at low tide. It was a low spine of rock, black with seaweed, which the waves pounded incessantly. Jennie had never seen a seal. We pointed them out to her and she looked and looked, but she could not distinguish the seals from the rocks. When we got too close and they all started to shimmy into the water, Jennie squeaked with fright and crammed herself under the seat, whimpering. The seals began popping up in the water around us, curious, and we eventually coaxed Jennie out to watch them.

Jennie stared at them intently, a look of deep interest in her face. After a while she lost her fear and signed *Play, play!* at them. We didn't know what the sign for seal was, and we did not have the ASL dictionary with us, so we made up a sign and taught it to her.

From then on, all we heard from Jennie was begging to *Go seal! Go seal! Go boat seal!* She became a fanatic seal watcher.

After that we often took the boat out to Brackett's Ledge and from there went on to Hermit Island. Hermit Island was an ideal playground for Jennie. One could not have created a better environment for a rambunctious chimpanzee. It was deserted, and Jennie could race around, climb trees, pull up plants, throw stones, beat sticks on the ground, scream, and break branches, all activities we had tried to discourage at home. The boat was anchored in a cove offshore, beyond Jennie's reach. Jennie could be herself on the island without our having to keep track of her or worry about her.

On the northern end of the island was a thick stand of black spruce trees, which Jennie climbed. When she reached the top she sometimes held on by one hand and swayed back and forth, howling with abandon at the sea, drunk with freedom. When she came down she had sap all over her arms and legs. She ran through the meadows screeching with joy, and she spent many hours whirling around trying to catch the monarch butterflies that floated among the milkweed and chokecherries. When she caught them, she cupped them in her hands and smelled them, as if they were flowers. When she released them, some would drop to earth traumatized or crushed, while others flew off in a spiraling panic while she watched, her hands and nose dusted with the orange powder from their wings.

The island was named for an old hermit who once lived there, and his house still stood in the center of the island. It was made of beachstones cemented together, with a wooden roof. The walls were almost two feet thick and a fireplace was built in a corner. Other than a few holes in the roof it made a perfect place to spend the night. It sheltered us from the wind and the salt spray off the rocks and the soaking fogs of the mornings.

The hermit's name was John Tundish, and he had a curious history. According to the locals, Tundish had been born on a farm on the mainland. He was a simple, friendly boy. The farthest he had ever been from his house, they said, was Blacks Cove, about five miles to the south. When World War II broke out he enlisted, and was sent to Fort Pendleton in California, and from there shipped to the South Pacific.

Little was heard from him. When he returned from the war in 1945, he had stopped speaking. Not a word would he say to anyone. He bought Hermit Island—it was called Thrumcap Island at the time—for twenty-five dollars and moved there, where he lived for ten years.

He shopped at a store on the mainland once a month. One month he did not appear. When he failed to show up the following month, some locals went to the island to see if he needed help or was sick. They found his boat, carefully pulled up on the beach, his bed made, canned goods stacked in a corner, clothes folded in a trunk. There was no sign of him, and he was never seen again. He had completely disappeared.

Some said he was caught in an undertow while taking a morning swim, while others said he inherited money and went to Boston. He had no family and title to the island was eventually acquired by the state of Maine.

The odd thing about it, or so the locals said, was that Tundish had been posted well behind the front and had never seen combat. Shell shock or the horrors of war were not the reason for his silence. The townsfolk had no explanation for what had happened to him, except to nod and say, "Well now, they was all a little crazy in that family."

When we camped on the island, we sometimes took the boat out in the afternoon to catch a dinner of fresh mackerel. The first time we went fishing, Jennie watched intently the preparations, but when the first flapping fish was hauled in she screamed and dove under the seat. She soon got over her fright, and one day we let Jennie take the rod. Almost immediately she had a strike. Sandy hollered "Reel it in!" but at first Jennie was so excited all she could do was scream and hop up and down while the rod jerked and twitched. We finally got her reeling it in, and when the fish arrived she was beside herself with excitement. She grabbed it and banged it on the bottom of the boat and slapped and stomped on it. Jennie had seen us killing and cleaning fish, and this was her way of helping out. As soon as the fish was safely in the creel she started signing frantically *Fish! Fish!* and grabbing at the rod. She became a true fanatic.

Jennie reeled in one mackerel after another. It was a good year for mackerel and one could be certain of catching a fish by dropping a line in the water and trolling for a few minutes. As much as she liked to catch them, once they were dead she lost all interest in them, and she did not relish eating them. When we fried them up for dinner she made terrible grimacing faces at the smell and often moved as far away from the fireplace as she could.

She slept curled up in her blanket against Sandy in his sleeping bag. Lea took a photograph of them one morning as the light came in the cabin windows, a photograph which is now framed in my office. Sandy's long hair is sticking out in all directions, and his mouth is open and drool is on the pillow, just like a little boy. All his radical trappings seem stripped away, leaving his innocence. Jennie lies next to him with her arm thrown around his shoulder and a look of deep contentment on her brown face. When I look at that picture I can still hear the gulls crying outside, the sound of the surf, and the smell of seaweed and salt air coming in through the broken window frames. It was a magical summer.

On a visit to the island near the end of the summer, Sandy made an extraordinary discovery. He was cleaning out the fireplace (under protest) and he discovered a loose stone in the back. He pulled it out and found a secret hiding place. In the hiding place was a small, hexagonal wooden box.

He called us all inside and we watched him open it up. We were hoping for South Sea jewels or a stack of gold doubloons, but instead the lid crumbled in his hand, revealing a long letter and a bundle of photographs. Folded up in a piece of paper were a Morgan head silver dollar and a blue turquoise bead.

We were disappointed when we inspected our treasure. The photographs were completely ruined by time, water, and rot. One could see nothing. The letter, also, had rotted and the pages stuck together. Furthermore, the ink had been leached out by rain coming down the chimney. The silver dollar and the bead were the only items relatively unscathed by time. Sandy kept the silver dollar, but I do not know what happened to the rest.

After Labor Day we returned to Kibbencook. That was when Dr. Prentiss regretfully informed us that she could no longer tutor Jennie. Jennie had been very fond of Dr. Prentiss, and she took her departure hard, waiting on the appropriate days for her car, sulking all day long.

The most difficult change was yet to come. In October or November, Jennie went into estrus for the first time. This was not a full-blown estrus, but an early, pubescent version. Female chimpanzees, when they cycle, show a dramatic change in their genital region, which swells up and becomes pink. The sexual impulses of a female chimpanzee in heat are far more powerful than those of a human.

Jennie did not understand what was happening to her and had no idea how to deal with it. During this first estrus, she became restless and almost impossible to control. She acted in ways that were embarrassing and socially inappropriate. She became particularly irritable toward me and Sandy. She would not allow us to approach her, let alone touch her, and she often broke into loud screams if we approached. She also became curiously incommunicative and ignored many of our efforts to sign to her. Lea and I knew well that chimpanzees become difficult when they reach puberty. And yet, we had managed to persuade ourselves that Jennie would be different. We felt we knew Jennie even better than we knew each other. We were wrong.

While in estrus she found being confined intolerable, even though she had always slept in a locked room. We had to listen to her screaming and pounding much of the night, and one night during that first estrus she managed to break the lock and get out. She wrought havoc in the kitchen, and even overturned the refrigerator in her efforts to wrench off the padlock. We had to hire a man to build a steel door to her room and put bars on the windows. We hated to see her room turned into a cage, but there seemed to be no alternative. We did not want her to hurt herself or anyone else.

During estrus Jennie also became incontinent. She seemed to have trouble retaining her urine, or for some behavioral reason she began urinating in various rooms of the house. Harold Epstein, Dr. Prentiss, and I consulted on this, but we could find no research on chimpanzees that indicated how or why this kind of problem might have occurred.

Up to this point, Sandy and Jennie had a true sibling friendship. Jennie's cycling disrupted even this. She lost interest in being around Sandy, ceased to obey him, and became irritated when he tried to play with her. Sandy was sixteen and Jennie's behavior angered and puzzled him. Sixteen-year-old boys are often quite inflexible in the way they relate to others, and Sandy could not understand that it was a natural change in Jennie. It caused a minor estrangement between them, and Sandy began going out without Jennie.

All this had one unfortunate result: it threw a great burden on Lea's shoulders. Jennie could no longer come to the museum; she could no longer spend time with Dr. Prentiss; and she was going out less with Sandy. Instead, she stayed at home all day, fretted, grumped, and got into trouble. For her own sanity Lea was forced to lock Jennie in her room for hours at a time, where the chimp screamed and carried on. We even had to discontinue Jennie's visits to the old Reverend Palliser's house. Palliser had become increasingly forgetful, and we feared for his safety. Jennie was wild.

When she came out of that first estrus, her personality did not entirely return to normal, although things settled down. There were still cool relations between Sandy and Jennie. Several months later she cycled again and the difficult period started all over, only worse.

I was being called home from the museum by Lea again and again to handle one crisis after another. My work was suffering badly. Sarah found Jennie's presence even more odious, and she began spending inordinate amounts of time at a friend's house.

By the beginning of 1974, it was starting to look as if our family was falling apart.

[FROM an interview with Harold Epstein.]

We live in a nation of ignoramuses. The average American knows nothing about science. A man asked me once if the stars went away when the sun rose, or if they were still there but you just couldn't see them. He was a stockbroker I had the misfortune of employing, a man who made over one hundred thousand dollars a year! Well, I took my investments away from him, damn quick! And then the market climbed five hundred points. Oh well, that's another story.

I do not begrudge the average American his ignorance. It's a free country. But when you have elected officials, people who wield enormous power, who flaunt their ignorance, that is a different matter.

Senator William Proxmire was one of those people. Here we had a man of colossal ego and great power who was as ignorant as a—a *poodle,* who destroyed the scientific careers of many good people. Every year, the whole country would read about the Golden Fleece awards and laugh and snicker about these silly scientists with their absurd experiments. Now some experiments were trivial. It is a fact that most science is pedestrian. But Proxmire usually missed the real target—that is, faulty research—and demolished something important and worthy.

This was what happened to the Jennie project. Here we were, spending all this taxpayer money teaching chimps a few hundred signs. They had no clue as to how this would illuminate our understanding of human linguistic development. Or the evolution of language. Proxmire had no idea that this research might enhance the way we teach language to retarded or handicapped children. There was no understanding of the revolutionary results of our work, and how it revealed for the first time the mind of an ape— and how it helped us understand what it means to be human. No thought was given to what it would mean to be able to communicate for the first time with another species! No. It was framed as, "So, after half a million, what did the chimps say?" Well, not much, when you really analyze it. That wasn't the point, for God's sake! And the scientists who supported us were afraid to object. They didn't want to attract Proxmire's attention. Cowards, every one.

Anyway, going into 1974, things got very tough for Hugo and Lea. Hugo and I had had many discussions about what would happen when Jennie went into puberty. I was far more worried than Hugo. I tried to tell him that no family had ever kept a home-raised chimpanzee much past puberty. I emphasized that Jennie was not like a dog or cat, that she was a wild animal. Hugo didn't believe it. He was optimistic and naive. He said that they had been through a lot with Jennie. They could weather anything. She was part of the family forever. He would never abandon her.

I pointed out to him that chimpanzees can live to be forty or fifty years old. Well, I said, who's going to take care of Jennie after he and Lea became too old? Hugo sweated a little over that one but finally said that Sandy would probably take care of her. And what about Sandy's future wife? I asked. How will she feel about a chimpanzee in the house? Had Sandy agreed to this?

Hugo then said that the problem was no different, say, than having a mentally retarded child. But (I pointed out) you can't put Jennie in an institution. There are no social services for Jennie. She won't qualify for governmental assistance, welfare, or Medicaid. She's an animal, I said to Hugo. An animal. Was he financially able to create an endowed facility that would take care of Jennie for the rest of her life? Did he know how much principal it would take to yield, say, an income of one hundred thousand a year? Or was he going to put her in a zoo?

Hugo became defensive under this kind of questioning. Angry, even. He accused me of being a Cassandra, of always looking at the bad side. I hated to make him face these issues, but who else was going to do it? At least, I thought, Hugo will be somewhat prepared. Or so I hoped.

The inevitable happened. Jennie reached adolescence and went into estrus. Her whole personality changed. This was a very sudden change. Very sudden. While things had been worsening for a while, this was a whole new ball game. You know how traumatic it is when human children suddenly find themselves with these strange and powerful new feelings. It was worse for Jennie, operating on a foreign biology. Female chimpanzees are much more promiscuous than human females.

Hugo came into the museum, and almost every day I heard another disaster story. Jennie was running Lea ragged. Every week there was another uproar, another crisis. Meanwhile, Sandy, who had been a stabilizing force for Jennie, was slipping away from the family and becoming more involved in radical causes and going around with unsavory friends. He refused to consider college. He refused to take his SAT tests. Hugo and Lea were sick with worry. The sixties might have been over and Nixon gone, but there was still a lot of radicalism around in the early seventies. People have forgotten that the so-called sixties, as a political era, was really the period from about 1964 to 1974. Sandy came of age at the tail end of that era, but he rebelled just as thoroughly as if he'd been born five years earlier.

I'm getting off the subject. I remember one morning Hugo came into my office, looking haggard. He had not slept at all the night before. Jennie, he said, had refused to go to her room for the night.

It had proved physically impossible to force her. You understand, although she weighed only seventy pounds, she was five times stronger than a grown man.

They tried everything. They tried coaxing her with food. They snapped a lead on her and tried to drag her in. They signed to her until they were blue in the face. She had learned a sign from somewhere, an obscene gesture. The middle finger extended. You know what I mean. She started using the finger almost continuously in lieu of other signs. She used it to frustrate any attempt to communicate with her. You'd sign *Jennie be quiet* and she'd jab her hand in the air with her middle finger extended! It was outrageous! You'd say *No bad Jennie!* and she'd stick her finger right in your face. Imagine that! I saw this on several visits to the house. Anyway, getting back to this particular night. They finally gave up and tried to go to bed, leaving her outside. But she started running around the house, breaking things and knocking over the refrigerator. They spent all night trying to control her.

When Hugo finished telling me this story, he put his head in his hands and he broke down and wept. I was . . . I was quite taken aback. I was shocked. I had *no idea* just how far things had gone. He told me that this wasn't the first time this had happened, and what was he going to do? We talked and talked and Hugo finally said, "Here we are, two of the world's experts on chimpanzee behavior, and we have no idea how to control this one animal." And he laughed bitterly. For the first time in my life I felt at a total loss. I had no idea what to do, no answer for him. I felt only dread for what the future might hold.

And then, later that year—well, did you know that Sandy and Jennie had an upset, a— No? They had a disagreement, an upset. . . . I'd rather not discuss it. In fact, I don't really know what happened. I really don't. You'll have to talk to Lea Archibald about that.

October 28, 1973

Last Sunday I delivered a particularly good sermon—I ask God's forgiveness for the sin of pride—on the guilt and suffering of Judas Escariot. I do not believe, however, that the congregation took to it. I asked the question: Was Judas chosen for the deed? It was prophesied, was it not? Where, then, is the guilt? But I muddled the answer. The good people of Kibbencook, indeed all human beings, want answers, not questions, from their religious leaders. No matter.

This has been one of the most difficult concepts for me to accept as a Christian, why there should be suffering in a world created by a God who is both great and good. Is it not strange that as one's suffering increases, one's understanding of the mystery and paradox of life also increases? Perhaps this is the redemptive power of suffering, as Jesus taught us. But I suffer, and I do not feel redemption.

Fall has always been my favorite season, and today was one of those incomparable glorious fall days of infinite blue skies and gusting winds carrying along the smell of burning leaves. This is the last year the burning of leaves will be allowed on the streets. I am growing old!

Today, everything brought to me sudden recollections of Reba. But not her presence. I have not felt her presence, as I had always believed I should if she should predecease me. Where is she? I am afraid for her, and for myself.

This morning, I had misplaced my shoes. After a long and frustrating search, I discovered them behind the commode. How in the world did they get there? Am I starting to become feeble-minded? How could that be, when I am delivering the best sermons of my life?

I miss Reba. I miss Jennie. God has taken from me everything I love. Why is Jennie staying away?

November 2, 1973

But what I find unaccountable in the autumn of my life is an irrational and growing fear of death. Not a fear of the pain of death, which any sensible man must fear, but an apprehension of the thing itself. How can this be? I do not question the existence of God or my savior Jesus Christ. No, I do not. Then why should I fear death so? It may simply be an atavistic impulse. Indeed, I believe that is what it is, an atavism from our dim past as apes.

Jennie was in the car in the driveway and then they drove away with her hanging out the window, banging on the side of the car and laughing. I do not understand why Jennie is not coming over anymore. I think I called Mrs. Archibald. I forget what she said. Jennie has a cold? A broken leg again? I think it was the leg. Why am I so very tired?

November 5, 1973

I had a glimpse of Jennie in the window of her room, looking out at the last of the leaves flying into eternity from the crab apple tree. The look on her face was so sad and lost. I never see her outside anymore. Perhaps it is too cold? She missed her last lesson. I must call Mrs. Archibald and find out why.

January 15, 1974

The snows came last night again. I awoke late, to see the sun inside the bare branches of the birch. I heard Reba's voice in the kitchen, scolding Jennie, but then she wasn't there and Jennie had left when I descended. I was confused and disappointed. The house was quiet and the door was locked. How was that? There are some strange goings on around here indeed. My bronchitis is back. I tried to get the Archibalds on the telephone, but no one answered.

I dreamed last night of Langemarck. It was that late April afternoon. The German guns suddenly stopped. The silence was beautiful. There was that laughter. They were talking loudly out of habit. We were waiting behind the old Lycée by the ambulances, smoking cigarettes. Everything had the rust, that dreadful green tarnish. Even the faces of the men. Suddenly the rats were running through the deserted streets. So many rats! And then the greenish yellow cloud came, and that suffocation. We drove back over the dry roads, loaded, but leaving all the rest. I woke up fighting for breath, and coughing violently.

January 17, 1974

Reba's presence has arrived, yes indeed. Thank you, God. Jennie was at her window again, looking down at the snow, watching the children towing sleds toward the golf course hill. She looked so sad, as if she wanted to go with them. I wonder why she and Sandy weren't with them today? Jennie has proved very derelict in her lessons lately. What was it now, when I was in the world? I've got to write that sermon, but I can't find my notebooks or anything. That damned cleaning woman. Nothing is where it should be. My right shoe was stolen last week. I heard them come in through the window, shouting obscenely. This has got to stop. And then every night, they're in my room, suffocating me. I've called the police and they do nothing. Everything has that green rust again. The coins in my pocket turned green. Will you look at them? What was it? I am sorry, I cannot swim. I shall rest in the house, thank you. Water frightens me. Keep the children out of the cabana, that is where they keep the chlorine. Nurse tells me to stop coughing, I will rupture my lungs. Where is she? I do not wish to keep these green coins. What was it?

[FROM interviews with Alexander ("Sandy") Archibald, January 1993, at his "hogan" near Lukachukai, Arizona.]

You've come a long way to talk to me. I'm impressed. I honestly didn't think you'd come. Tape recorder? No, I don't mind it. You've come two thousand miles to hear me talk, you might as well tape it. I wouldn't want to be misquoted, now.

Please have a seat on the "chaise lounge" over there. The packing crate. I'll stoke up the fire and get this coffee going. Would you duck outside and pick up three or four lumps of coal from that pile to the left of the door?

Thank you. Welcome to my hogan. It ain't the Ritz, but it's warm. You're the first white man I've seen in a month, except the trader in Lukachukai, but he's practically an Indian so he doesn't count. I'm impressed that you were able to follow the road in the snow. That a rental out there? I didn't know you could rent Jeeps. Smart.

I think the coffee's already boiling. Navajo coffee. You just keep adding grounds and boiling them. Change the grounds once every week or two. Out here they're so poor, they eat the grounds. They call it pan-fried coffee. Stir the grounds in a frying pan with bacon fat, fry 'em up, eat 'em. I tried it once, gives you a caffeine high all day long.

Pam Prentiss? God, what a . . . You've got that tape recorder going, I guess I better watch my language. She was very complex. Very. And like all complex people, crazy as hell. She loved children and chimpanzees, but she had no use for grown-ups. She liked me just fine when I was a kid, but when I became a teenager she lost interest. No, it was worse than that—I *betrayed* her by growing up. She felt there was something corrupt about being a grown-up. She was smart, but not as smart as she thought. In fact, when it came to human beings she was downright stupid. And in the end she didn't know anything about chimps. Oh, she was the world's *expert* in chimpanzee linguistical development, but she didn't know shit about their feelings. It was weird, because she and Jennie had a very intense relationship.

Let me try to set you straight in the beginning. What Jennie's trouble was. See, Jennie had a set of values, but she didn't realize they were different values from the rest of us. She never could understand why she was always in trouble. In the end, I mean. She didn't know what it was that made her angry all the time. I'll tell you what it was. It was very simple: it was our society trying to break her, trying to make her a nice middle-class person. Like they do to everyone.

See, Jennie had the power of language. She believed in her humanity. That's what made her different from the zoo chimpanzees. And that's what Prentiss gave her. While Prentiss may have fucked up in other ways, she gave Jennie language. It wasn't a mother-daughter relationship, or a sister-sister, or a friend-friend. No, it was a student-teacher relationship. Very profound, more like a monk-acolyte relationship. I mean that: their relationship had a spiritual dimension. Think about that for a moment. Language is power. Prentiss was like a spiritual guide. She gave Jennie power— and Jennie used it. She used it. With language, she deconstructed and reconstructed her world. She created a new world for herself. It blew my mind to see this animal acquire language. And then literally reshape her world with it.

Now I had a very different relationship with Jennie. There was a time when there was no boundary between Jennie and me. We were like Siamese twins. We didn't know where one started and the other left off. [Laughs.] Why? I don't know why. I was a lonely kid. She was the only friend I ever had who accepted me without question. She didn't judge me, or criticize me, or lay bullshit on me. She accepted me just as I was. Now that's irresistible.

Jennie taught me a lot. You know, I was a smart kid. They told me I was a genius. Now don't for a moment think I'm impressed with that kind of bullshit. Jennie taught me just how worthless that is. Being smart. Jennie wasn't smart by human standards, but she had a set of values. Real values. You see, for Jennie, freedom was the highest value. Language gave Jennie freedom. Although I didn't know it at the time, she taught me the real meaning of the word "freedom," not the bullshit meaning you get from politicians and priests.

Here's what she taught me: human beings are terrified of true freedom. Self-imposed slavery is what life is all about. Slavery is what every human being strives for. School, college, nice house in the suburbs, nine-to-five job, promotion, retirement. People are never happier than when they are making arrangements to have their freedom removed. They pile up possessions and debt and responsibilities. It's just as Dostoyevski said in *The Brothers Karamazov*. Christ offered people freedom and scared the shit out of them, so they crucified him.

Jennie was different. She fought tooth and nail for her freedom. I don't know where we white people went wrong in our evolution, or where we had to compromise, why we chose slavery. A coyote will chew off its own leg in a trap. I had a tarantula spider last year, big hairy old thing. Found it last fall cruising through the *chamisa* out there. Looking for a mate, which they do in the fall. I brought it home and put it in a big glass jar. I fed it grasshoppers, watered it, kept it warm when it was fifteen below out there. It had everything it needed. But day and night, day and night, week after week, it was trying to climb through that glass. I'd hear it faintly scratching all night long and when I'd wake up in the morning—there it was, still trying to get out. I thought, damn, even the spider, whose brain is so fucking small you'd need a microscope to see it, has that overwhelming desire for freedom. So where did we go wrong?

Jennie had that same overwhelming desire for freedom as the tarantula. She couldn't live in our society because we tried to rob her of freedom, just like we rob ourselves of freedom. We wanted to break her and make her a human slave like the rest of us. Live free or die, was her answer. Literally.

I'm rambling. Jesus, now I'm really going. Well, I suppose you might as well get it all on tape. What do you want, some stories or something? Why am I here? Why are you so obsessed with that question?

You want to know why? When we finish talking, I'll take you for a ride. Did you see those two horses in the corral as you came in? Yeah, we'll go for a ride, and I'll show you some of the sights. It's not bad out there, about fifteen degrees, with wind chill maybe five below. We'll ride up to Los Gigantes.

See, I can't tell you why I'm here. You wouldn't understand. I can only show you. Throw some more coal in the fire.

The freedom I'm talking about is a Navajo concept. The traditional Navajos look down on those who accumulate possessions, think it's a vice, a weakness, like drinking or adultery. They also think it's dangerous, makes one a target for witchcraft.

Those mountains behind us there are the Lukachukai Mountains, and that low mesa in the distance is called Black Mesa. This whole landscape is sacred. The Navajos were never expelled from their Garden of Eden. This is it. It's a harsh landscape but it's beautiful in its own way. You have to be out here at least a month before you can really understand what I'm talking about. All the bullshit of our sorry century just falls away like rotten scales, and you suddenly see the world for what it is.

Growing up with Jennie. It's hard for me to imagine what my childhood would have been like without Jennie. I hardly remember anything before she came. It was like she was this . . . this *shadow* of me that finally arrived and made me complete. We had some good times. We used to go to a place called the bridge. Jennie always came along. Did my mother tell you about that? Hah! She hated me going over there. Her brain conjured up all kinds of horrors about what went on there.

The bridge was this railroad bridge that crossed the Sudbury River. The tracks of the old Boston and Albany. A dirt road ran alongside the river and under the bridge. It was a beautiful spot, with these white clay banks and muskrats splashing about in the river. The moonlight would shine through the trestles, making crazy shadows and flickering off the water. And the stars through the trestles, millions of stars. When it got cold in the fall, we'd build a big bonfire and sit around talking. We were going to change the world. We hatched all kinds of plots, blow the world up, start a revolution. We'd get high, and our plans got ever more intricate. But it never came to anything. It was all bullshit. You can't change the world. You're goddamn lucky if you can change yourself even a teensy, tiny bit.

To change, you've got to internalize the revolution. You've got to start a goddamn revolution inside your brain. You've got to become Hamlet, a subversive in your own court. So to finally answer your question, that's what I'm doing out here. Internalizing the revolution. I'm making myself free.

There was a group of us met at the bridge. We had a feeling of infinite possibilities. Funny though, at the same time it all seemed futile. That may sound like a contradiction. I guess it was a contradiction. We'd drop strawberry fields—that's a kind of LSD, came in a pink tablet—and lie down on the sand. And we'd stare up through those old trestles, and the night sky would be boiling purple and black. And I'd think, shit—at any moment I'll see the streak of missiles heading for Boston and that'll be it. We grew up with that, thinking the world could end at any moment. Expecting the world to end. At the same time, we were going to change the fucking world, totally change it, make it an anarchistic utopia. [Laughs.] That's a teenager for you.

So we'd gather around that bonfire, singing the Internationale, drinking cheap wine and smoking pot, thinking we were actually doing something. Jennie used to come to the bridge. She followed me everywhere. She was like a kid sister, sensitive as hell about being left out. She was a founding member of our revolutionary council. While we talked she drank Old Milwaukee beer. And why not? It made her mellow and happy. Like a happy old drunk. Sometimes we'd all get drunk and stoned and stagger around laughing. Jennie would be signing *Phooey! Phooey!* and rolling around on the ground and clacking her teeth. Once she threw up all over herself and we had to wash her in the river. Jesus it was wild.

Jennie didn't like pot. She wouldn't touch it, even after she saw me smoking it. We never gave her any other drugs. My friends wanted to give her acid but I said no way. Jennie had no way of knowing what it was, or how it might affect her.

We had all kinds of outrageous stoned conversations with Jennie—me translating of course. She was confused most of the time but she loved us laughing at everything she said. I wish I'd written some of those conversations down. We asked her what she thought of Nixon and Kissinger and America. All kinds of shit. We taught her stuff like *Nixon sucks!* and *Fuck Ameri-K-K-K-a!* Spelling out the "K's" in ASL, see. She gave us her opinions on nuclear war, Vietnam, and Hubert Humphrey. They were usually one word opinions: *Bad!* or *Phooey!* Right on, Jennie!

I did a lot of growing at the bridge. We were young and naive, but real ideas were discussed there. It's where I lost my virginity. There were girls that came with us; they thought we were cool. There was one girl named Crystal. She was pretty experienced. Sometimes when we were stoned we'd roll down a grassy hill nearby and try to stand up. It made us very dizzy. One time, Crystal and I were rolling down this hill, and I ended at the bottom and she rolled up against me. We were both stoned and laughing, and her miniskirt had kind of gotten hiked up around her thighs. Well . . . it happened pretty fast. I was fifteen. When it was over, wouldn't you know it but there was Jennie, sitting nearby, staring at us. She had this look on her face—I don't know if it was fascination or horror. Her hair was standing on end. Crystal didn't care—I suppose she was used to people watching her have sex—but I was upset. It gave me the creeps, made me feel ashamed, as if my mother had caught me in flagrante delicto.

Anyway. About a year after that I got a real girlfriend. Her name was Sammie. Samantha. We both had big intellectual pretensions. I was going to be an artist; she was going to be a writer. We used to read Chekhov out loud to each other. We were together all the time.

We would drive down to a deserted parking lot behind the grade school and smoke pot and have sex. Naturally, we didn't want Jennie along. I didn't want her looking at me like that again. Jennie resented that. She hated being left out. She would throw a tantrum when I left in the car with Sammie, or she'd ignore me, pretend I didn't even exist. She was very jealous. She actually hated Sammie. When Sammie came over, Jennie's hair would stand out when she saw her.

Sammie tried to be nice to her and even learned a few signs, but Jennie would sign back *Go away, bad bad, phooey,* or *Bite angry bite.* Sammie would ask, "What's she saying?" and I'd lie: "She wants an apple." Sammie would bring her an apple and Jennie would back away, grimacing. I'd sign *Jennie be nice!* but she'd just sign back *Phooey!* It didn't take Sammie long to realize that Jennie hated her. It was a sore point in our relationship. It really hurt Sammie's feelings. I knew, deep inside, why Jennie was so rude and angry all the time, but I resented her behavior. I also felt guilty. Like somehow my relationship with Sammie was a betrayal of Jennie.

We make our lives so fucking complicated. What we value has no value. And what we don't value is priceless.

ten

[FROM an interview with Lea Archibald.]

Nineteen seventy-four. Oh dear. I'll never forget that year. It was so difficult. And so hard on poor Hugo. He was a very sensitive man. Like Sandy. They were very similar.

That was also the year that I got up one morning and found Rev. Palliser asleep in our hedge. The poor man had become rather senile. He started coming by the house, banging on the door and wanting to play with Jennie. Just like a little boy. He got her confused with some sister he grew up with. And he talked constantly to his dead wife as if she were standing next to him. He would apologize and apologize for goodness knows what infractions, saying, "Yes, dear, no dear, I'm so sorry dear." That sort of thing. It was spooky. He wandered around the neighborhood, walking into people's houses, and the good citizens of Kibbencook couldn't stand for that, so they trucked him off to the Kibbencook Nursing Home.

It was sad. He was a sweet man. These horrid new people bought the house and built a hideous modern wing on it with glass and chrome. Some fancy architect from New York. It was appalling. The construction was very loud, and they cut down the beautiful paper birch that must've been a hundred years old. People nowadays don't care anymore how long it takes to grow a tree.

Jennie watched the whole thing with terrible anxiety. She used to stare out her window, with her hair halfway up, whimpering. She was particularly upset when the new people moved in. I believe she would have gone over there and caused trouble if we hadn't kept her on a short leash.

Jennie missed Rev. Palliser. In fact, a very strange thing happened after they took Palliser away. From time to time she would sign: *Go there? Go there?* while pointing across the street, or *God* or *Jesus*. Those were signs Palliser made up, you know, in his attempt to convert Jennie to Christianity. Oh my goodness. At one point she kept signing *Go there? Jesus, God,* over and over, and she looked so sad.

I remember one day trying to explain to her what had happened. I signed *Hendricks gone.* Jennie did not like to hear that. She scowled and wrapped her arms around herself. *Hendricks gone,* I signed again.

Then the most extraordinary thing happened. Jennie suddenly screamed. I nearly jumped out of my skin. Her hair was raised up like I'd never seen it before. Then she signed *Hendricks dead?*

I was *shocked*. I'd never even seen her use the word "dead." It seemed extraordinary that she could understand it, I mean understand the concept of death. Really incredible. But I'll tell you, that scream said it all.

I signed *No, Hendricks gone away.*

She kept signing, *Where Hendricks? Where, where?* and I signed *In town.* And then she started to sign, *Go see Hendricks! Go! Go!*

I couldn't bring an unruly chimpanzee into a nursing home. I said No.

She was very upset. She threw a tantrum, and I had to lock her in her room. Oh dear, when I think of all the tantrums she had then. Every day it was something else. I thought I was going to have a nervous breakdown. You don't have children, so maybe you can't imagine what it was like. It was every minute of the day.

Even so, Jennie wouldn't leave the subject of Palliser alone. When we drove into town, she'd sign *Hendricks! Go Hendricks!* and have a fit when we wouldn't oblige. I didn't realize just how attached she was to that man. She never forgot him.

At that age, she'd throw a tantrum over anything. Like not being allowed to pick up the phone when someone called, or being told not to sit in a certain chair, or whatever. When she did pick up the phone, she would scream into it and hammer it on the table or stamp on it. Oh my goodness, it was so embarrassing sometimes, especially with people who didn't know we had a chimp in the house. What they must have thought.

We had to restrain her more and more. We couldn't let her outside except on a lead, and we had to reinforce her room and lock her in it more and more frequently. I hated to do it but there was no other way. No other way. She wouldn't listen to anybody, except Hugo once in a while. But Hugo was gone all day. What was I supposed to do? Now you tell me, what in the world was I supposed to do? I was all alone in that big house, just me and Sarah.

That was another thing. Jennie made Sarah's life unbearable. Sarah, who loved peace and quiet and order. They kept a distance from each other, but the whole environment was wearing her out. And me.

Jennie banged on the barred windows of her room and made a terrible racket. She ripped everything up. She pooped all over her room and peed everywhere when she was in heat. I had to clean everything up. Did I mention to you the trouble we had keeping a cleaning lady? Well, we'd given that up years ago.

What could I do? Handling Jennie was a full-time job. There

was nothing left of me for Sarah. She was ten and full of plans and busy all the time, and I felt I was losing this whole part of her life. And I was beginning to be afraid for Sarah's safety. Jennie was so big and boisterous, and so impulsive. Sarah was still a fearless little firebrand when it came to handling Jennie, but Jennie was so terribly strong.

And Sandy. We never saw him anymore. He had some girlfriend, her name was Sammie. Ugh. Oh dear, she was . . . she was pretty, that's about all you could say about her. Brunette, quite petite. She didn't wash and her hair looked like a rat's nest. That was the style. They spent all their time together and poor Jennie was left out. Whenever Sammie was around Jennie was nervous and upset. I remember one time Sandy came by with Sammie, and after he left Jennie ran up to Sandy's room and ripped the mattress right open. I—I expect they had done something on the bed. Oh dear, isn't it awful to remember these things? Strewed all the stuffing everywhere, and then peed on the bed. It horrifies me just to remember it. Just talking to you is bringing back all these terrible memories. . . .

Hugo and I finally had a talk. I'll never forget it. We were both awfully upset. Hugo could hardly speak . . . We decided that Jennie had finally become dangerous. She really had. I told Hugo that we had to find another way. We talked and talked. Hugo denied it and denied it. He *loved* that chimpanzee. I finally had to say, It's either me or the chimpanzee. I'm going to put Sarah in that car and take her away, and raise her where I can give her a reasonable childhood. It was really about Sarah, you see. It came down to that: Jennie or Sarah.

Hugo finally accepted the seriousness of the situation. But then we didn't know what to do. Could we hire someone? Who? Jennie was just so strong and so willful. Nobody would have been able to handle her any better than us, and none of us could control her. Whoever we hired would probably have gotten bitten. We couldn't risk that. But we couldn't just lock Jennie up in her room all day. Send her to the zoo? That was unthinkable. To see Jennie locked in a cage, gawked at by the world . . .

Finally Hugo promised he would talk to Harold and Dr. Prentiss about it. They came over one afternoon. It was in 1974, I think. In the spring.

When Jennie saw Dr. Prentiss, she went wild. She was so happy. She had this enormous pink grin and she laughed and laughed. I was touched to see it. You know, I was also very touched to see that Dr. Prentiss actually cried a little. I didn't think she had it in her. She was a terribly misguided young lady but she had feelings. They kissed and hugged and wouldn't let each other go. Then we sat down in the living room over coffee.

Dr. Prentiss offered to take her right away. She wanted Jennie. When I first heard that, I was really quite shocked. It made me angry. I almost threw her out of the house. But then she started to explain. She made it sound so wonderful.

She explained that she was director of a chimpanzee rehabilitation center down in Florida. An island where they released chimps. It was right on the Gulf Coast, near Sarasota. Here, laboratory chimps could be reintroduced into the wild. They would actually train chimpanzees to gather their own food, to hunt, to build nests.

The purpose, you understand, was not to turn them back into wild and self-sufficient animals. Just to give them full and happy lives. Many of these lab chimps were like Jennie, and they'd become too difficult to handle. They had served science and mankind well, Dr. Prentiss said, and they deserved to be cared for. Some of them had led terrible lives in medical labs and humans owed it to them to redress that wrong. It sounded so humane. We had a responsibility to these animals. Previously, they would have been destroyed or just left locked in cages. The chimpanzees from her Barnum colony were down there, very happy and doing fine, she said. There were no cages or fences, since the island was its own natural cage. It was as close as possible to their natural African environment.

She went on and on. Jennie, she said, deserved to finally become a full-fledged chimpanzee. Jennie had been a human for a long time, and it wasn't working. She didn't understand what she was supposed to do, she didn't have the biology for it, and she was unhappy. Et cetera, et cetera. She could live on the island, mate, raise a family, and finally be what nature meant her to be. Everything would be wonderful. It was all very plausible.

I really didn't know what to say. Hugo was also silent. Harold agreed with Dr. Prentiss, and urged me and Hugo to think it over. Harold said he knew this time was long coming, and he had given the matter a great deal of thought. This would be the right thing to do. He said it would be like giving up a child. Could we do it? Could we put Jennie's interests first? Could we let her fulfill her biological destiny? Could we let her go?

Oh, I sit here talking to you and I wonder: why did I ever listen to them? Why did I ever think they knew better than a mother? God *damn* them! The vile, vile, vile *scientists*.

[FROM an interview with Alexander ("Sandy") Archibald.]

That fire feels great, doesn't it? Here's your coffee. Now maybe you're starting to see what I mean. Simplicity. You don't need a three-thousand-square-foot house to be comfortable.

Hand me that kerosene lantern and we'll get some light in here. Beans should be ready in an hour. Can you hear the wind starting to blow? It's going to blizzard tonight. What the Navajos call a *yasyítsoh*. I've been learning Navajo. It's a phenomenally difficult language, maybe the most difficult in the world. For an English speaker, that is. Lot harder than ASL, that's for sure.

Where were we? Listen to the wind shaking and moaning in the stovepipe. Sounds like a dying man. Funny though, it makes you feel safe, doesn't it? That's the thing out here, you feel safe. Out there, where you came from, it's dangerous as hell. I never felt safe until I got out here.

So. What else? Hermit Island? Sure, I remember that place. Back when I was fifteen or sixteen my father bought a boat and we used to camp on Hermit Island. There was an old hut on the island where we spent the night, with a big stone fireplace. Jennie loved that island. She could run free and do whatever she wanted. I think the only time she was truly free was on that island.

One year we spent four or five days on the island, fishing every day and eating the fish for dinner. One night it was clear and we slept outside. I think we counted thirty shooting stars that night, just one after the other, whisking across the sky. It was in early August. At first Jennie couldn't figure out what we were seeing. But soon she started counting the shooting stars along with us. "Heeee!" she said when one streaked across. There were some big ones that went halfway across the sky.

The water was phosphorescent. We swam in the cove at night, and as we moved in the water sparks of phosphorescence would swirl around us. It was beautiful. Jennie never went swimming. She was terrified of water. She hated us swimming. She'd stamp around the shore and piss and moan, signing *Come! Come hug Jennie! Help! Dirty dirty!* and anything else she could think of that would get us to come to shore. She was sure we were all going to die. She was so full of love for us, it was sometimes a little frightening.

I once was cleaning out the fireplace of the old hermit's cabin and I found a loose stone in the back. Underneath it was a box full of stuff. I believe these were his sole possessions. There were some photographs and a letter, a silver dollar . . . let's see, and a piece of turquoise. See, the hermit disappeared and nobody knew where he'd gone.

This letter was *really* scary. Legible? Oh, it was very legible. And eloquent. It was the pictures that had faded. Ah! You've read my father's book. Well I'm sorry to say that was a bit of a gloss, his saying the letter was illegible. It was totally legible.

That's right. No shit. This guy, John Tundish, wrote out his whole life story. What happened when he went to the Pacific, why he'd chosen to become a hermit. It was like his farewell letter to the world. Only it was addressed to God.

I wish I could remember the letter better. He wanted to know why God had created so many people. Too many people, all cruel and unthinking and mean. He had specific complaints about various people, all addressed to God. Why did you create Freddie Hutchins? he asked. That son-of-a-gun treated me so bad, took away the only girl I ever loved. Or if you had to create him, why did you have to station him on Hooley Island? Why not put him over there on Guam? Or if he had to be on Hooley Island, how come you let me meet Tina in the first place? Why not just leave me alone? I never would have missed her, if you hadn't made me meet her. And Colonel Gault. Why did you create that so-and-so? Or if you had to create him, how come you made him so mean? Or if he had to be mean, why not make him a private and me the colonel? And God, how come you let my mum run away with Bill Hastings, that son-of-a-gun who never did anything but drink and "God damn" this and "God damn" that? And what about me, who never took Your name in vain in my life? What about me? Why haven't you done anything for me? What kind of a God are you that you treat those who love you like this? And look at what a mess the world is. If you didn't do it, who did?

I mean, this guy was just a poor, ignorant simpleton from Franklin's Pond Harbor, Maine, who didn't understand the world at all. Didn't have a clue.

It was very weird. And then at the end of the letter, he said he was coming up there. He was coming. He wanted some answers. I mean, it took a second for us to figure out what the hell he was talking about. Whew. That's when we realized it wasn't just a letter. It was a suicide note. Tundish had written it right there, and put it under the fireplace. And then he just walked into the ocean.

My father was reading the letter out loud. And when he finished, his voice was cracking, and I saw his hands were shaking. I mean *shaking*. And he put the letter down and the look on his face was awful . . . It scared the shit out of me. I'd never seen him so frightened. So he got all gruff and stuffed the letter in his pocket and said he'd give it to the local historical society. I think he probably just threw it away. No one ever said a word about it again.

In his book my father fudged that whole issue—like so many others—by saying the letter was illegible. That was my father's way. If something was unpleasant or difficult, his way of dealing with it was simply not to deal with it. To bury himself in work, or pretend it never happened.

Oh, I'll tell you, there's a lot that isn't in that book of his. A lot. And I'll tell you something else. There's a lot that isn't going to be in your book either. You can no more understand and tell the truth about Jennie than that guy from *Esquire*. No offense. Even if we did tell you everything. Which we won't. Nobody ever tells the full truth.

Damn! Listen to that wind!

[From an interview with Dr. Pamela Prentiss.]

I didn't see Jennie at all from the time the project ended in the summer of 1973 until spring of 1974. Almost a year. Without a structured environment, Jennie became very difficult. She was also starting to reach sexual maturity. Naturally, the Archibalds wanted to get rid of her. So they asked me if I would take her to the Tahachee Island Rehabilitation Center. This was a center I had started for rehabilitating laboratory chimpanzees. It was also a breeding colony of chimpanzees in the United States. There is, you see, the very real possibility of the chimpanzee becoming extinct in the wild. If things keep going on the way they are in Africa, it will be inevitable.

Now, I knew this was coming. I expected it. No family has ever kept a home-raised chimp past sexual maturity. When that happened, I was going to bring Jennie to the Barnum colony, you see, where she would have a huge area to play and be herself while she got used to the other chimps.

The Tahachee Center was a second-best option. It wasn't nearly as elaborate as the Barnum colony, but it was pretty good. I thought it would be a nice place for Jennie. Much better than the chaos of the Archibald household. The Tahachee Center was being generously funded by the MacBruce Foundation. Thank God we weren't dependent on government funding. We had the direct support of Simon MacBruce. MacBruce is a fiercely independent type, and he didn't give two hoots for the Proxmire flap. It made Miller so mad to see me get the MacBruce grant!

The center is still going, by the way, and we now have forty-two very happy chimpanzees there. While they must be supplementally fed, they've adjusted to the semiwild life of the island very well. It's been an unqualified success.

[FROM an interview with Lea Archibald.]

After Dr. Prentiss and Harold left, I remember that Hugo and I talked. The island reminded us of how much Jennie loved Hermit Island, and we talked about what a perfect environment it had been. We also talked about what it means to grow up. At a certain point, parents have to let go of their children. We felt that Jennie's problems stemmed from her efforts to become independent. But you see, the problem was that Jennie wasn't a human being so she couldn't just "become independent." She wasn't like Sandy, who could move out, get a job, and find an apartment. Her rebellion could go nowhere.

We talked, and we cried, and we talked some more. Oh dear. Hugo was terribly upset at the whole thought of giving Jennie up. I was too, but not like Hugo. To let her go was the hardest decision we ever made. We talked to Sandy and Sarah about it. Sandy was violently opposed to the idea. He was so angry at us. It was awful. He threw a chair through the picture window in the living room. Oh dear, that was a terrible moment. Sarah said that whatever we decided would be all right with her.

We didn't accept Dr. Prentiss's proposal right away. Hugo first looked into other possible research projects or primate centers. He researched everything. There were several around the country, but all of them kept the chimpanzees in cages. There was a primate rehabilitation project starting in Africa, but that was mostly for chimpanzees confiscated from poachers, and it was a much rougher setting. The chimpanzees there were wild animals, really, and we didn't feel Jennie would do well there. After all, Jennie had never seen another chimpanzee in her entire life. Not one.

Finally, Hugo and I decided to accept Dr. Prentiss's proposal. I remember when Hugo made the phone call. He dialed her number and then he couldn't even speak into the phone he was so choked up. I could hear her nasty little voice coming through the receiver, demanding to know who it was, and then Hugo just hung up. It's so painful now to remember. How I wish he'd just left it at that. But he called her right back and said that, yes, we would accept her offer. Naturally, we wanted to see the setup and the island, and meet the caregivers. They didn't call them "keepers" since they wanted to avoid the image of a zoo, you see.

So we flew down there. . . . Excuse me. . . . I'm a little upset. Look at me, already starting to cry. We flew down there and looked the place over. . . . Please forgive me. I'm just a useless old lady. It was seventeen years ago but it still seems like yesterday. It's hard for me to talk about this. . . .

[Editor's note: At this point Mrs. Archibald excused herself and the interview was resumed the following day.]

* * *

The place was so pretty. The island was about a mile wide and two miles long, quite sandy, with lots of eucalyptus trees, pines, and palmettos. The beaches were sandy and the water was so blue.

Sandy wouldn't come. He disappeared for several days. To his girlfriend's house. She had a dreadful alcoholic mother and she and her sister pretty much ran around like wild animals.

Anyway, there were about six chimpanzees living there, the four from the Barnum colony and two others. They had the whole island to themselves. A little bayou separated the island from the center's buildings on the mainland. There was a pier and a motorboat tied up. The buildings were kind of ramshackle but it had a lazy air. Pelicans lounged about on the pilings. It seemed . . . nice.

Dr. Prentiss introduced us to George Gabriel, who ran the place. He was a rugged outdoor type, you know, with the beard and khaki shorts and tan from the sun. He just about crushed your hand when he shook it. I don't like men who grip your hand like that—they're insecure. I did not, frankly, care for George Gabriel. If only I'd listened to my instincts instead of all these scientists.

Gabriel gave us a tour of the buildings first. Right away I was shocked to see a row of large cages. No one had said anything about cages.

Well, Gabriel explained those were only for temporary use. When a new chimpanzee arrives, they first put it in a cage and let it get used to them and the surroundings. They didn't want to introduce an unknown chimpanzee onto the island without preparation. The others would have to get to know it first. So that's what the cages were for. That's what he said.

See, he used the word "it." Do you see what I mean? He didn't look on these chimpanzees as anything but things! Animals! The signs were right there, staring me in the face!

Well. It sounded reasonable to me and Hugo at the time. Then George took us to the island on the motorboat. As soon as the engine revved up the six chimps on the island came bursting out of the foliage and to the gate at the front of the pier. They knew when they were going to get fed, you see. They waited for us on the pier, making a great lot of noise, hooting and stamping on the dock and so forth. I really wondered how Jennie would fit in with these big, aggressive apes. But some of the chimps were actually signing to us and each other in ASL, and I found that comforting. They weren't completely wild.

I was still concerned that Jennie had never seen another chimp. You know that was Prentiss's doing. She wanted to keep the research "pure." I had suggested once that Jennie be taken to the Barnum colony to see the other chimps, to play with them. As a diversion for her. But she said Oh no! It would contaminate the research or some such rot. George Gabriel was just so confident that Jennie would fit in. He kept saying, "Imagine if it were you. Growing up in the wild never having seen a human being. Surely you would adjust, eventually?" How the devil could he know? Later I came across a story about this child that had been raised by wolves in the mountains of France. In the eighteenth century. The wolfman of Aveyron or something like that. This is a true story; you can look it up. When they finally got him out of the woods he had to be locked in an asylum for the rest of his life. He never did adjust to being human. So how could Gabriel know? It was all a pack of lies.

When we landed, the chimps came down and searched our pockets. We gave them some treats and Gabriel put out a stack of melons and bananas for them, so that we could walk around the island without being bothered.

There were trails worn through the brush. You could see where the chimps had built their nests in the trees! It was very exciting for Hugo and me to see these things. Their tracks were like little human handprints, all over the place.

The seaward side of the island had a lovely beach, and you could see where the chimps had been digging and playing, just like kids. Not making sand castles but digging great holes for no reason, just like children do at the beach. For some reason the beach made me think about just how Jennie was going to fit in, whether the other chimps would like her, whether she would become pregnant and have children and raise them on the island. I suppose I thought about the kind of things that all mothers think about! It was a little frightening, but exciting at the same time.

Gabriel told us that their only research objective at the center was to see if the chimps continued using ASL and taught it to their young. He said the place wasn't for research. Although if someone from time to time wanted to observe the chimpanzees they could. The point was, there would be no experimenting or anything of that sort. Just observation. The chimps, he said, had already done their service to mankind.

At the time it just seemed . . . so right. A perfect answer to our problem. It was as if Jennie were going away to college. Hugo and I were taken in by the beautiful setting, the blue sky, the water, and George Gabriel's smooth tongue.

Sandy, you know, had a different view. After we got back, he said that Jennie didn't care about blue sky and a nice island, that she cared only about people. He said we were sending her off to prison. He thought it was just horrible and disgusting that we wanted her to mate and have a chimp family. We dismissed it as teenage hysteria. He kept repeating, "Yes, but you don't know her like I know her."

[FROM *Recollecting a Life* by Hugo Archibald.]

In April of 1974, all the arrangements had been made for Jennie to take up her new life in Florida. Dr. Prentiss suggested we have a surprise farewell party for Jennie, with all her friends, teachers, and relatives in attendance. Both Lea and I thought that a wonderful idea, and we began planning an Easter Sunday celebration. Jennie was scheduled to fly to Florida the following Wednesday.

The weather had warmed up from an unusually cold winter,

and we planned an outdoor barbecue and Easter egg hunt. Jennie did not care for barbecued food, but she loved an Easter egg hunt. In addition to eggs, which Jennie loved to eat raw, we planned to hide all of Jennie's favorite fruits and vegetables. It would be a one-chimp Easter egg hunt.

When the day came, everyone turned out. Dr. Prentiss and Harold Epstein had rounded up all the volunteers and assistants who had worked with Jennie during the Jennie project. Lea had gone to the nursing home and arranged for Rev. Palliser to come with his nurse. Lea's mother came over, as did my mother. There must have been twenty or thirty people from the museum—curators, secretaries, and technicians, retired and current, who had befriended Jennie during her years there. I sent a blanket invitation to all museum employees, past and present, and even Will, the cranky old Scottish elevator operator, showed up, proudly driving a new Lincoln Continental.

We wanted the party to be a genuine surprise for Jennie. That morning Harold and I took Jennie out for a drive to Lake Kibbencook while Lea and Dr. Prentiss made the preparations and received the guests.

We drove on the circle drive around the lake. The leaves were budding on the trees, like a green mist in the branches, and the daffodils along the lake shore were in full bloom. It was a soft, warm day. We stopped at the Lollipop Gardens, a park along the lake where the trees had been trimmed into fanciful shapes. The lake was very still and cold, and the trees and sky were mirrored in its surface, another world trembling on the surface of the lake, darker and more mysterious than our own.

As we walked along the balustrade by the lake, a pair of swans came gliding by, the ripples shattering the reflected images into a confusion of blue and green and black. Jennie was excited to see the swans. She signed *Play, bird play* at them, murmuring and squeaking with interest. The swans ignored us and soon disappeared around the shore. Jennie was disappointed and signed *Phooey bad bird.*

We continued, each of us holding one of Jennie's hands. Jennie was in high spirits and she shook our hands free to climb up one of the lollipop trees. It was a yew cut into two stacked boxes, and Jennie sat on the top box screaming with joy, clacking her teeth and shaking branches, as if proclaiming her presence to the entire world. "I am here!" she seemed to announce. "I exist!" Her voice echoed across the lake and came back faintly from the far shore, transformed into something distant and sad, like the cries of a lost animal.

For some reason her boisterous happiness depressed my spirits. It occurred to me that this was probably the last time I would walk along this lake with Jennie, and the last time Jennie would see spring in New England. Harold was also subdued. I consoled myself with the thought that Jennie would be far happier in Florida with her own kind than forever imprisoned in the world of human beings.

At one point I turned to Dr. Epstein and said, "Harold, do you think we're doing the right thing?"

He had been so positive about this decision that I expected—and was hoping for—some reassurance, but instead he was silent, looking out over the lake.

"You know, Hugo," he said, "I don't really know." He looked to the Kibbencook Hills, blue beyond the water, as if looking for some kind of answer. Then he said quietly, "All I know is, I'm going to miss that chimpanzee."

We drove back to the house without speaking.

Everything had been carefully planned beforehand. The guests would arrive at noon, and we would be there a half hour later.

As we pulled into the driveway, Jennie was instantly excited by the shining crowd of cars lining both sides of the street all the way to the corner. I honked a warning that we had arrived. Harold and I walked Jennie around to the backyard, where everyone had lined up to greet her, all sixty of them. When we turned the corner and saw the people, Jennie stopped dead and stared. Everyone shouted in unison, "Happy Easter, Jennie!" and began to cheer.

Jennie was so overwhelmed she did not move. Then she saw Rev. Palliser, and she let out a shriek of joy and ran toward him. He was in a wheelchair and his nurse from the nursing home looked more than a little apprehensive. Jennie hopped into his lap and hugged and kissed him, while the old Reverend sobbed, the tears rolling down his wrinkled face. He knew who she was, in a vague sort of way, and he patted her on the head, saying over and over again, "Good girl, that's my girl. Good girl."

Everyone crowded around. I had never seen Jennie so happy. Every person she recognized—and many she hadn't seen in a year or two—she hugged and kissed.

At one point Will bellowed out, "You bluidy rude ape, you haven't shook me hand yet!" and Jennie rushed over to get another hug. Finally the excitement was too much and she sat cross-legged on the ground, grinning from ear to ear, while everyone gathered around and applauded.

Dr. Prentiss acted as the master of ceremonies. All the treats had been hidden around the yard—apples, oranges, bunches of grapes, bananas, eggs, papayas, cooked yams and sugar beets, pineapples, pieces of sugarcane—all of Jennie's favorite foods.

She sat Jennie down and signed: *Jennie go Easter egg hunt?*

Jennie hopped up and down and whirled about, so excited she could not get a sign out.

Easter egg hunt? Dr. Prentiss signed again.

Hunt! Hunt! she signed frantically, and whipped off to the crab apple tree with everyone in hot pursuit. She immediately found a banana, and then began discovering more treasures in the gnarled roots. With each discovery she gave a short scream or hoot and stored it in the crook of her arm. Soon she was carrying so many fruits that she could barely walk, and with every step fruits would tumble to the ground and she would stop to gather them up, losing more in the process.

It was comical to watch. When she finally could not move with all she was carrying, she sat down and screeched with frustration.

Dr. Prentiss gently signed *I hold food for Jennie. Jennie give me food. I give food to Jennie later.*

After a long moment agonizing over the offer Jennie dropped the armload of fruit and continued her search, bringing each armful back to the growing pile. Everyone had a marvelous time trailing after Jennie and giving her hints as to where things were hidden.

When the hunt was over Jennie sat at her pile and began to eat, stuffing the fruits into her mouth, with the juice dribbling down her chin. When she ate fruits like oranges she often spat out the fruit pulp, a practice we had tried to discourage. Soon the ground around her was littered with wads and boluses of chewed fruit, but this was Jennie's day and we were determined not to discipline her.

While the barbecue was cooking Jennie took turns playing tickle-chase with various people, and soon almost everyone had joined in the chase. I brought out my movie camera and filmed Jennie having the time of her life.

When the party was over, I had everyone line up and wave good-bye and blow kisses, while Jennie waved back. As people left, Jennie stood at the front door and shook their hands or kissed and hugged them. I was surprised to see just how many people became emotional and even wept as they said good-bye; Jennie had touched many lives.

Harold, Dr. Prentiss, and I had discussed for some time how best to bring Jennie to Florida. We ruled out the car, because the drive was over twenty-four hours and would be exhausting to us and

Jennie. A commercial plane was out of the question, since airline regulations required Jennie to be in a crate in the cargo hold. We did not want Jennie to arrive at her new home traumatized.

We decided to charter a light plane, a six-seater Beechcraft. Jennie, we regretfully decided, would have to be sedated for the journey; in a small plane, a rambunctious chimpanzee could be dangerous. The flight was scheduled for that Wednesday. Dr. Prentiss, Lea, and I would accompany Jennie to Florida and see her settled in her new home.

On Wednesday morning we arose at five o'clock. Jennie was grumpy, having been woken up much earlier than was her wont. We brought along her favorite blanket, a thick cashmere throw, much chewed and threadbare, which had been a wedding present from an old college roommate of mine. We also brought a duffel bag packed with her clothes and favorite toys.

We had worried about what Jennie might make of these preparations, but she was too sleepy and grumpy to pay them much mind. As soon as we were in the car she wrapped herself in the blanket and fell asleep.

We arrived at Nobleboro Field just as the sun broke through the ground mist. We were the only people there. Frost lay on the tarmac and the sky was a flawless ultraviolet. The pilot taxied to the runway, and we wrestled Jennie's duffel bag of toys into the cargo bay and climbed aboard. Jennie became quite alert when she saw that we were getting into a plane. Dr. Prentiss signed *Jennie fly?* and Jennie gave a low hoot and signed *Fly* back.

We got Jennie buckled into her seat. Dr. Prentiss took out a syringe and needle and administered an injection of Sernalin, a mild sedative, in her right arm. Jennie had always been cooperative about shots and this was no exception. As soon as she fell asleep the pilot revved up the engines and took off. He banked away from the sun and we flew right over Kibbencook, over our house, over the golf course and the meandering brook. The Kibbenbook Episcopal Church spire threw a long, blue shadow across the town square, and then the town was gone, and we were droning over the endless inner suburbs of Boston, jammed with traffic. The town had looked so peaceful, and I wondered if Jennie would ever again see that small, unimportant place on the earth, her world.

Dr. Prentiss and I took turns sitting near Jennie, ready with another dose of sedative in case she should wake up. Lea sat in the front. We were worried that Jennie might take fright at her surroundings, but she slept through the entire five-hour flight.

George Gabriel met us at the airport in his Jeep, and during the ride to the Tahachee center Jennie finally roused herself. She was groggy and irritated at first and gave a short scream of anxiety when she saw we were traveling. Lea soothed her and stroked her forehead, and she calmed down.

We had discussed in almost endless detail the best way for Lea and I to help Jennie make the transition to her new life. Dr. Prentiss, Dr. Gabriel, and I felt a quick departure would be better than a long good-bye, but Lea objected. She wanted to stay and make sure Jennie had begun adjusting to her new surroundings before we left. She also wanted to see how Jennie was going to react to meeting other chimpanzees. We decided to stay for two days, during which we would be with Jennie at the center, play with her, and allow her free run of the place.

We drove down a long, dilapidated road. The palmettos gave way and we passed through the center's rusted iron gates into a large expanse of green lawn sprinkled with buildings. Like the Barnum property, it had once been an estate, and it retained a parklike feeling. The main house, a stuccoed Spanish hacienda, had been converted to offices and living quarters. A long barn housed the chimpanzee cages, each with an outdoor run. The caretaker's and gardener's cottages had been converted to bungalows for visiting researchers, and we stayed in one of those with Jennie.

The first, and most critical, part of Jennie's adjustment would be her meeting other chimpanzees. We planned to introduce her to a small chimpanzee named Fred, a former Barnum colony animal.

Fred was very gentle and the lowest-ranking male in the chimpanzee hierarchy. As she learned to trust Fred, then she would be introduced to the others. When Dr. Gabriel felt assured there would be no conflicts, she would be released on the island to begin her new life.

We could not avoid putting Jennie in a cage when we left, because we all knew she was going to have a difficult time seeing us go. She had never, during her entire life, been separated from all the family members at once. How long she would take to calm down we did not know. In the meantime, Fred would inhabit the cage next to hers, and we expected they would soon become friends.

We spent the first night with Jennie in the bungalow. She was alert and excited, and a little apprehensive. Nothing like this had happened to her, and she did not quite know what to make of it. During the night she was restless, and around midnight wandered into our bedroom and snuggled under the covers between us. The next morning we ate breakfast with her at the main house and walked over the grounds. At noon, it was time for Jennie to meet her first live chimpanzee.

Fred was in a cage, where he would be safe should Jennie take a dislike to him. We brought Jennie around to the back of the complex, where the cages had outdoor runs. We were walking along, each holding one of Jennie's hands, when we rounded the corner and Jennie saw Fred.

She stopped and froze. Instantly all the hair on her body was standing on end. Fred glanced at her and continued with his business, sucking on a banana peel, not terribly interested.

But Jennie *was* interested. I heard a sound rumble up from deep in her throat, a sound I had never heard before. It was almost a growl, such as one might hear from an angry tomcat. Then she slowly backed up and went behind Lea's legs and crouched down, gripping her legs, trying to make herself as inconspicuous as possible.

We sat down about ten yards from the cage. Jennie was, I believe, terrified of Fred, and continued to hide behind our backs, sometimes peeping around the side to take a surreptitious look. We tried grooming Jennie—which usually soothed her—but she shook us off. She ignored the banana we offered her. All she did was stare at Fred and growl.

I pointed to Fred and signed *What's that?*

She stared for a long time and then signed, slowly and clumsily *Black bug, black bug.* We sat there for a good part of three hours without any visible change of behavior. Jennie had received a deep shock to her psyche.

After seeing Fred, Jennie's behavior changed dramatically. Wherever we went in the compound she was quiet and alert. When we tried to play with her on the lawn she pushed us away and sat down, looking all about her, as if afraid Fred would suddenly materialize from behind the palm trees. At the squawk of a bird or the rustle of wind she was up and looking about, her hair bristling, issuing a soft *"Wraaaa"* bark. She completely lost her appetite.

Dr. Gabriel reassured us that Jennie's reaction was not unusual. He said that chimpanzees are suspicious of each other when they first meet, even if they are used to being with their own kind. The main point, he felt, was to give the relationship time and not push it. Jennie would set her own schedule, and when she was ready to meet Fred on friendly terms she would. When we left, he would put Jennie in a cage next to Fred and let them get used to each other over a week or two.

Lea was uneasy about putting Jennie in a cage, but Dr. Gabriel explained that there was no alternative. The cage was huge—almost as big as a small house, with both outdoor and indoor facilities. Jennie would have all her toys and lots of good food. Dr. Gabriel and the staff would visit and play with her every day. With Fred in the adjoining cage, the two chimps could have continuous contact with each other without danger. He expected a quick adjustment.

Our last night in the bungalow, Jennie hardly slept at all. She crouched on the foot of the bed, looking around and sucking on her fingers, sometimes rocking back and forth. There is no doubt she sensed a big change was coming in her life. The thought of leaving Jennie was weighing heavily on us, and, if the truth be told, we all passed a grim night. I remember telling myself that this was only an animal, that we had two lovely children, but for the first time in my life my intellect could not communicate with my heart. I could hardly bear the thought of giving her up. I wondered then, and I wonder today, what the biological basis of such an attachment could have been. She was, after all, not even a member of my own species. Lea was very quiet, but I felt she was as upset as I was.

We rose at 6:00 A.M., before sunrise, and walked down to the bayou with Jennie. It was a cloudy day and instead of a sunrise the gray light seemed to come up out of the water. At 7:00 A.M. we brought Jennie to Fred's cage again, but her reaction was unchanged: she growled and bristled up her hair and hid. She made every effort to get us away from Fred's cage, pulling on our hands and stamping with anger, trying to swagger off but soon scurrying back with a grin of fear. She signed *Dirty, dirty* repeatedly in a transparent effort to get us to take her to the bathroom, and then she signed *Chase Jennie chase-tickle Jennie* in another effort to lure us away from the cage. When none of these strategems worked she sulked behind Lea, gripping her with one hand and sucking miserably on some dry leaves with the other.

We ate breakfast with Dr. Gabriel in his quarters. Jennie continued to refuse food. Dr. Gabriel suggested that it would be better in the beginning if Jennie and Fred were separated by an empty cage, so that Jennie would not be unduly upset by Fred's close proximity. We discussed over breakfast the best way to get Jennie into the cage before we left. We were scheduled to fly back to Boston that afternoon, and we had to leave for the airport about 11:30 A.M.

When it came time to bring Jennie into the building where her cage was, she refused to enter. We tried luring her in with food, but she ignored all treats. One of the center's workers, a man named Finney, snapped a lead on her and tried to pull her in, but he ended up in a tug-of-war that anyone would have known he would lose. Lea felt that it was counterproductive to try to force Jennie into the building, and she made a suggestion. We went inside the building and began playing with Fred through the bars of his cage. As soon as she saw this, Jennie came swaggering in, her hair standing up, and gave Fred her most threatening *"Wraaaaa"* bark. Dr. Gabriel quickly shut the door.

We then faced the problem of getting her into the cage itself. It was a huge cage with metal bars on the bottom and chain link on top. It had both an indoor and outdoor area, so it did not, we felt, resemble anything she might associate with imprisonment. We brought her duffel bag of toys and dumped them on the floor of the cage, and both Lea and I went inside and began playing with them, while Dr. Gabriel and Finney waited outside. Soon Jennie had come in and was driving her toy fire truck around. The presence of her familiar toys seemed to relax her. We played for a few minutes until Jennie had become engrossed.

Then Dr. Gabriel said quietly: "I think it's time now," and gestured toward the cage door.

We nonchalantly edged over.

Dr. Gabriel said, "Please leave quickly. Now."

We both ducked out and Finney slammed the door shut and locked it.

That was the last time Lea or I saw Jennie, and it was the end of her delightful, fascinating, and effervescent presence in our lives.

I will never forget you, Jennie.

[Editor's note: this rather abrupt ending is presented here exactly as written by Dr. Archibald. It is the last mention of Jennie in his memoir.]

It was just awful when we had to say good-bye to Jennie. I feel so ashamed. We tricked her into the cage. She was so trusting, so . . . I can never forgive myself for what we did. Poor Hugo; I think it just about broke his heart.

We were in the cage, playing with Jennie's toys. It was my idea. They said she would only be in the cage for a few days. So Hugo and I were in there, and Jennie came in. We played. Or we tried to. Right in the middle of it I saw that these . . . Oh dear . . . [At this point Mrs. Archibald began to weep.]

While Hugo was playing with one of Jennie's toys . . . I saw that a *tear* was trickling down his face. . . . It wasn't anything dramatic, just a single tear. . . . Hugo never cried, you see. He was old-fashioned in that way.

Gabriel then told us to leave.

So then we got up quickly and left. Before Jennie knew what was happening. And Gabriel slammed the door of the cage and locked it.

Right then Jennie *realized*. She knew exactly what had happened. How she had been betrayed by us, the two people she trusted most in the world. . . . Oh dear God. . . . Do we have to go through this? . . . I'm sorry. No, no, I'm quite all right. I'm just a useless old lady. Jennie started to scream. It was a *terrible* scream. We were walking to the exit of the barn. And suddenly I realized Hugo wasn't with me. I looked around. . . . He had stopped and turned. Jennie's arms were straining through the bars of the cage. She was reaching toward him, toward us. . . . And . . . Hugo held out his arms to her, and then he made this sound, like he was choking, and I realized he was sobbing. . . . And he said, "I'm so sorry, Jennie. Please forgive me. Oh God, forgive me, Jennie, I'm so sorry. . . ."

We had to help him out; he could hardly walk. . . . It was my fault; I'm the one who made him give up Jennie. . . . I just can't . . . no more . . . Please . . .

eleven

[FROM an interview with Dr. Pamela Prentiss.]

After the Archibalds left, I stayed on. Jennie knew me, and we felt that someone from her old life should help her make the transition. Despite a heavy teaching load at Tufts and several research projects, I made the time.

Jennie wasn't like the other chimpanzees we had had at the center. She presented terrible difficulties. Her erratic and chaotic upbringing had not prepared her for her new life, which by its very nature would be more regimented. Now everyone keeps talking about Jennie being put in a "cage." This is a misnomer. The cage was enormous. There was a jungle gym, tire swings, climbing platforms, dead trees, a sandbox, and a little pool of water. The ceiling was a good twenty-five feet up. It was much larger than her room back in Kibbencook. Which, by the way, had been virtually turned into a prison by Mrs. Archibald. Her new area was nearly the size of a small house. It had a 400-square-foot indoor space and a 200-square-foot outdoor run. These "cages" were the largest primate enclosures that had ever been built outside of a zoo habitat. So let's get over this business of "Jennie being locked up in a cage," okay? I'm so tired of hearing that shit. This cage was a lot larger and nicer than the apartment in Boston that *I* lived in for over ten years. She had all her toys, favorite clothes, and favorite foods. She lacked nothing.

Jennie suffered terrible separation anxiety. She screamed day and night. She was used to getting her way with the Archibalds by acting up. And separation from friends appears to be even more difficult for chimpanzees than for humans. She'd been with the Archibalds all her life. She'd never been away from them for even a day. No wonder she was upset!

We decided we shouldn't let her out of the cage until she calmed down, since it would seem like a "reward" to her and only make her scream louder when she was put back in. We did not want to reward bad behavior. Instead, we planned to start taking her out after she calmed down. You understand? I mean, if we started taking her out every day, that would reinforce her bad behavior. You see what I mean?

Even after three days she had not settled down. There were periods of silence. As soon as she saw someone she would begin screaming again. And hammering on the bars of her cage. When Dr. Gabriel fed her, she threatened him and often threw the food back at him. She took a marked dislike to Dr. Gabriel. I think she associated him with her change of life. Certainly it had no rational basis, this dislike. Except perhaps that Dr. Gabriel was a little intimidated by her. Jennie often acted badly toward those who were afraid of her.

She didn't threaten me, but my presence made her unbelievably shrill. It was like she was begging me to help her. Oh! It was hard to listen to that! But what you have to understand is that the best thing for Jennie was to adjust as quickly as possible to the presence of other chimpanzees. Listen to me. It would've done her no favor at all to release her every time she screamed. And then of course we never would have gotten her back in. The sooner she adjusted to other chimps, the quicker she could be released on the island. Everything we did was right.

Jennie hated the other chimps. We were shocked. Although fear and aggression is normal when strange chimpanzees meet each other, I'd never seen anything quite like it. Really. She *hated* them. This would have changed, eventually. I've never seen a chimpanzee that didn't adjust to others of its own kind.

Now that magazine writer criticized me for not having the Archibalds come down. Mrs. Archibald told a lot of lies to him. But you see, this was important for Jennie's adjustment. Jennie had to make a clean break from her old life. Any contact with the Archibalds would have been devastating. You saw what happened. We were absolutely right. Naturally, when she got used to her new life the Archibalds would have been welcome to visit.

We couldn't have just let her go on the island. Once Jennie tried to kill another chimpanzee. You see, when Jennie rejected Fred we tried her with another. Sallie. A juvenile female, very submissive. We put her in the adjacent cage.

For a while Jennie continued to scream. But later we heard her screaming stop. There was a one-way viewing mirror in the building, and Dr. Gabriel happened to be watching when he saw this terrible thing. Jennie had calmed down. She was at the bars separating her from Sallie. Of course Sallie had been terrified by Jennie and was on the other side of the cage, but Jennie started to act real friendly. She waited there with her arms through the bars, occasionally signing *Play, play* to Sallie, who did not, by the way, know ASL. She fooled Dr. Gabriel and she fooled Sallie. Dr. Gabriel was getting excited, thinking the breakthrough was at hand. Sallie began edging over until she got within Jennie's reach. All of a sudden Jennie grabbed her and, quite literally, tried to kill her. Sallie managed to get away, but she had suffered a sprained arm and a deep bite wound on her hand.

It was awful. Just awful. This was the kind of thing we had to deal with every day.

Jennie was so upset when I was around that I couldn't communicate with her. She was too busy screaming. I went to her cage several times a day and patiently tried to initiate a conversation. I kept signing *Jennie be nice, please* and *Jennie be quiet,* and *If Jennie play with Fred, Jennie go for walk.* I also tried in a crude way to explain to her that she was a chimpanzee, not a human, that Fred was also a chimpanzee, and that Fred wanted to be friends. None of it sunk in.

On the third day I finally got a reaction from Jennie. After signing for half an hour while Jennie screamed, she finally signed vigorously *Bad bad!*

I quickly signed *What bad?*

She signed *Bad Pam bad.*

Why Pam bad? I signed.

Bad Pam bite angry.

Then she began screaming and banging again.

I was so full of hope at this point! Dialogue is the first step toward understanding. I tried to encourage her by signing *Why Pam bad?* and *If Jennie be quiet, Jennie go for walk.* I tried to tell her in every way that if she quieted down, we would let her go for a walk.

It made no difference. It was so discouraging. She had started up again and worked herself into such a frenzy that she couldn't focus on what I was signing. It was like the outside world ceased to exist for her, she was so mad.

George and I had many discussions. I finally persuaded him that maybe we should allow Jennie outside for a few hours. Just to see what would happen. This was, I think, the fifth day or sixth day. Let me see my notes here. . . . No, it was on the seventh day.

So I entered Jennie's cage and snapped a leash on her. She was quiet all of sudden. I was so hopeful. For a moment there I thought it would work. We left the building, Jennie's hand in mine. Jennie immediately took the lead. She pulled me by the hand, and we went all over. Retracing the paths on the compound, down to the pier, in and out of every building. Finally we ended up at the bungalow the Archibalds had stayed in. I let her go where she wanted. It was a very purposeful exploration. Jennie had no interest in playing or in signing. I'm positive she was looking for the Archibalds.

Then a terrible thing happened. Jennie was very disappointed when we got to the Archibalds' bungalow and they weren't there. She looked under the bed, in the bathroom and closet, behind the doors. I could see she was disappointed, but she remained calm and quiet. She looked so . . . depressed.

I wasn't prepared for what happened next.

When we left the bungalow, there was Dr. Gabriel walking across the lawn. Jennie saw him through the bushes in front and gave a low bark of aggression and suddenly lunged toward him. The leash was jerked out of my hand and Jennie rushed at Dr. Gabriel. Her hair in full piloerection. As she ran through the bushes she tore a branch off one and continued on, dragging and shaking the branch as she approached.

I called out to Dr. Gabriel, but he had already seen Jennie coming. Dr. Gabriel knew chimpanzees well. He knew immediately that Jennie was heading for an attack.

He turned to face her. You never run away from a chimpanzee. Jennie came straight on and veered past him at the last moment, whacking him across the shins with the branch. The branch cut one of his legs and gave him a nasty set of bruises.

She raced on to a eucalyptus tree and climbed it, still carrying the branch. When she was safely beyond our reach she sat on a limb and barked and screamed at us. I signed *Jennie come down!* But she continued to make a fuss, and threw the branch down at me.

I signed *Bad Jennie come down now!*

Jennie finally calmed down enough to respond. She signed *Phooey*, then she signed *Bad bad angry phooey* and every other bad word and obscene gesture she knew. It was quite a remarkable string of utterances, I daresay one of the most complex of her entire life. *Bad phooey fuck you bad angry bite dirty dirty fuck you.* Excuse my French. Sandy taught her how to give people the finger.

Dr. Gabriel was understandably angry. It had been an unprovoked attack. He stood underneath and shouted at Jennie, until I told him that maybe his presence was not going to encourage her to come down. I suggested he go back to his office, which he did.

At a certain point Jennie began mocking me by repeating every sign I made to her. She would sign back *Bad Jennie! Jennie come down!* imitating me. It made me really angry, until I realized, yet again, just how sophisticated Jennie's understanding of human psychology was. How she could get under your skin!

So we spent a terrible two days trying to get Jennie out of the tree. She endured thirst and hunger rather than descend. We finally—and I hated having to do this—we finally had to tranquilize her with a dart. We lured her to a lower branch with food and we piled some mattresses around the base of the tree. Then Dr. Gabriel shot her, and she fell. She was of course unhurt.

We could only conclude that until Jennie was ready to be released on the island—that is, until she could learn to get along with other chimpanzees—she would have to stay in the cage. In her space.

When Jennie woke up from the tranquilizer, she was furious. She was angrier than ever. She worked herself into such a rage that she choked and spluttered for hours, unable even to scream. She had diarrhea all over herself and we had to spray the hose through the bars while she screamed and thrashed around. I felt so sorry for her.

[FROM an interview with Lea Archibald.]

What makes me so angry about this whole thing was that nobody told us what was going on down there! Dr. Prentiss never called to say that Jennie was having trouble adjusting or anything. And we called! We called almost every day. "Oh, everything's as expected," she sang out. "There are a few problems but nothing we can't solve." That kind of thing. All very vague and evasive.

Nothing about how she was screaming day and night. Nothing about having to shoot her out of a tree. Oh no. Everything was just hunky-dory. Those—I won't even dignify them with a word—they were treating Jennie like a common criminal. I don't know what scientific theory they were operating under that kept Jennie in a cage, but you don't have to be a Harvard scientist to realize that that was going to upset her. And Prentiss kept telling us not to visit, because that would disrupt Jennie's adjustment.

When Hugo and I returned to Kibbencook from Florida, Sandy was gone. He hadn't gone with us to Florida, and as you know he was awfully against the whole idea. He was the only one who remained loyal. He has a heart of gold, that boy. It turned out he was at his girlfriend's house, Sammie—you know, the one with the alcoholic mother. Apparently it was just fine with this woman to have her sixteen-year-old daughter sleeping with a boy right there under her roof. Poor Sandy, he was so hurt and confused.

The house was so *empty* when we returned. There was Sarah— lovely, comforting Sarah, of course—but everything seemed so quiet. In the morning it was as quiet as the grave. No more yells from a hungry chimpanzee, no more banging on the door. Gone were the squeals and hoots from a happy Jennie. No more endless requests for an apple or a tickle. When we lit a fire, there was no Jennie to roast the apples for us. There was no Jennie hammering away on the piano. The silence was eerie. It was like . . . like an unwelcome presence in the house. I complained to Hugo, but he had his office and his work, and I had to bear the empty house alone. Once again, the burden fell on me. Hugo just buried himself in his work after that. He was . . . changed.

After a week Sandy came home. He gave us the silent treatment. He was very upset, the poor boy. I wanted to enfold him in my arms and just hold him, but of course at his age that was impossible. For a long time he wouldn't even talk about it. Finally one night he and I had a talk.

He kept saying "Why? Why did you have to do it?"

I tried to explain as best I could that it was the only option left. I talked about how beautiful the island was and so forth, but he interrupted. He asked me if she was in a cage.

I had to admit she was. At the time, I believed all the claptrap from Dr. Prentiss and that George Gabriel. I was defending them! To my own son!

All Sandy wanted to know was how long she was going to be in the cage.

I explained again that she would be released on the island as soon as she got used to being with other chimpanzees, and that Dr. Prentiss had said it would take about two weeks.

"And what if she doesn't adjust to other chimpanzees?" Sandy wanted to know.

I explained to him that Dr. Prentiss had told us that never in the history of chimpanzee research had such a thing happened. She told us that chimpanzees recognized their kind, even if they were home-raised and hadn't seen another chimp since they were infants.

Sandy didn't believe a word of it. He said that maybe seeing a chimp as an infant makes all the difference. When in the history of chimpanzee research has there been a chimp that really and truly thought it was human? Who had never seen one of its own kind ever? What about that? This is what he said.

I had no answer for that. Just hope. All I had was hope. That was my answer.

[FROM an interview with Alexander ("Sandy") Archibald.]

Jennie hit puberty with a bang. If there's one really big difference between chimps and humans, it's in the sexual response. Forgive me for saying this, but when she was in estrus she was the horniest thing that ever prowled the streets of Kibbencook. When she went into heat, the whole area around her sex organs would swell up and become pink. And she became impossible. Her whole sexual response was directed at human men. When a man came to the house—it didn't matter who it was—she would jump him. Really. Jump into his arms and—well, I know this is going to sound a little disgusting—rub her sex organs on the person while kissing him on the lips. I'm telling you, there could be no mistaking her intentions. The mailman got it, the salesmen got it, random visitors, colleagues of my father—everyone got nailed by Jennie. Even men that Jennie had shown a marked dislike for. Everyone except me and my father.

Now this is very interesting. When she was in estrus, she became downright unfriendly to us. Worse than that, she wanted nothing to do with us. If we tried to hug her or touch her, she screamed bloody murder, like she was about to be molested. She went out of her way to avoid us. If ever there was proof of a biological basis for the incest taboo, Jennie was it. No kidding.

Listen to this. One day, as a joke, I bought a *Playgirl* magazine for Sammie. Jennie was hanging around, in heat, in a very bad mood. When we came into the living room, she got up and went into the dining room and sat in a corner. Signing *Phooey* to herself. Really pissed off. She was always in a bad mood during her "time."

We were looking through the magazine and laughing. Jennie just couldn't resist laughter. Pretty soon she was standing in the door, still looking pissed off, but her curiosity was getting the better of her.

Finally she swaggered in, pretending to ignore us, and circled around behind so she could see what was so funny. We heard this little grunt and a hairy hand reached out and swiped the magazine. She scooted over to a corner and started looking at it. When I went over she stood up, gave that vicious little bark of hers with her hair all standing up. No way was she going to give back that magazine.

So we watched her. She turned the pages and came to a photograph of a naked man. She stared at it, her eyes popping. She reached out, and with a hairy finger started stroking and scratching at the man's penis. She rubbed and scratched until her finger had rubbed right through the paper.

She eventually turned to the centerfold, and laid it out on the ground. Staring with this—well, hungry—look. She scratched the penis a little, and then she—I'm sorry, this may sound a little gross—squatted over the centerfold and began rubbing her vagina on the man's penis. Rubbing away with this dreamy look on her face. Then she got up, walked around in a little circle, squatted down over the picture again, and peed! Just a little pee. All the time ignoring us completely. Finally she got up and left, leaving this disgusting, wet magazine lying on the floor. We were both totally grossed out.

Her behavior drove my mother up a wall. It mortified her to have this ape attacking every man who appeared in our house. And she started to masturbate. My mother couldn't get her to quit it. She would sit on the sofa playing with herself! It was worse than having one of those dogs that hump your leg all the time. So my mother started keeping Jennie locked up when she went into estrus. Jennie screamed nonstop when that happened. Jesus, our house was like the C ward at Fernald, where they keep all the guys in straightjackets. I was so wrapped up in Sammie and the fucking revolution that I didn't care or do anything to help. So I got what I so richly deserved in the end, a little memento to last me the rest of my life. I thought Jennie had betrayed me, but it was really me who betrayed Jennie.

What memento? I mean my finger. This. [Editor's note: At this point Sandy held up his hand, which was missing the little finger from the second joint.] My pinky. In case you haven't noticed, it's gone. What, you mean no one told you about this? Jesus, what kind of a journalist are you anyway? Jennie bit my little finger off one day. That's why she was sent away, for chrissakes. I mean, you don't think she was dumped in a prison just because she'd become a little difficult, do you? My father and mother loved that chimpanzee. For my father to get rid of Jennie—it was like getting rid of his own child. Really. I didn't quite realize it at the time, but my dad was totally hung up on that chimp. But my mom was just terrified that Jennie might hurt Sarah. Because Sarah was a bold little kid. I mean, she didn't let Jennie get away with shit.

Look at you, suddenly on the edge of your seat. Here's a real scoop. Jesus, don't make me think you're like that asshole from *Esquire*. Look, I want you to stick around here for a while before you go running off and writing some bullshit about this whole thing, how I was so psychologically damaged by losing my finger to my chimp sister that I became a hermit or some such shit like that. I'm not kidding. I'm out here for other reasons, reasons I've tried to share with you. Call me a prophet crying in the wilderness, or call me a spoiled rich white suburban kid playing Indian. Okay? But don't go writing any pseudopsychological Freudian Jungian claptrap bullshit about my missing finger. It was no big deal, and you know what? You don't need a left pinky anyway.

First of all, it was my fault that I lost my finger. Entirely my fault. But everyone blamed it on Jennie.

You see, Sammie and I were very tight. It was first love for each of us. Jennie just couldn't accept that. Sammie had a mother who was a spectacular hypochondriac. God, what a piece of work that woman was. Her father had died ten years ago. Her mom stayed upstairs all day in bed and complained about her head. Nursing a bottle of Cutty Sark. For medicinal purposes. Sammie had moved into the basement to get away from her mother, fixed up a room there, and painted the floor red and the walls black. M. C. Escher posters everywhere. Big waterbed. Black light. Collection of glass bongs on the shelf. It was such a perfect sixties crash pad, it could have made an exhibit in the Smithsonian.

Anyway, we went driving with Jennie one day. Early 1974, I think. Jennie didn't like being around Sammie, but by this time she pretty much ignored her. We drove around, with Jennie as usual

hanging out the window and scaring passing motorists and screaming at pedestrians. It was always pretty funny. Then we went by
Sammie's house. Jennie had never been to Sammie's house before,
and she was always nervous in a new house. I mean really nervous.
I think Sammie wanted to pick up her pot or something. She was
a real pothead, the poor kid.

We came in the house and there was Sammie's mother upstairs
moaning about something, yelling downstairs at Sammie. Jennie
got even more nervous. She liked dealing with people face-to-face.
And she was hypersensitive to people's moods. So the mother was
yelling downstairs, and Sammie said something like "Fuck you,
bitch" under her breath, but a little too loudly. So her mom started
yelling "What was that? What did you say, you little whore? Come
up here and repeat what you just said, you little whore."

Jennie maybe didn't understand the words, but she got the gist.
Her hair stuck out just about as far as it would go and she had this
grin of fear on her face. Sammie ignored her mom and we went
down to the basement. The problem was, although Jennie picked
up on everything that went on around her, she often didn't understand what exactly was going on. All she knew was that hostility
was in the air. So she got really nervous and hostile herself. Am I
making any sense to you? When people argued around her she often
got aggressive. It was dangerous to start yelling at somebody in
front of Jennie.

Down in the basement, the darkness of the place and all the
posters and the black light made Jennie even more nervous. I should
have done something, put her in the car. I could see she was getting
really upset.

Sammie bent down to open a drawer, and I put my hand on her
back, or I guess it might have been her ass, you know, affection-
ately, and then *Jesus*. It happened so suddenly. I heard Jennie make
that barking sound and felt this sudden rush and I turned and then
there was a shooting pain in my hand. I don't even remember Jennie
even touching me. It was so dark I couldn't see much, but I could

see this sudden sticky blackness all over my hand. Inky black under the black light. Sammie started screaming and I went upstairs and ran some water in the sink and put my hand in to wash it off. The water instantly turned *red*. I pulled my hand out and that's when I saw—I mean I had this horrible sickening feeling and I saw that, well, this had happened. My pinky was gone. Well, I said to myself, there goes my career as first krummhorn with the Boston Pops. [Laughs.]

So you see, it was my fault. It was stupid to bring Jennie along with us, it was stupid to let her in the house, and it was stupid to bring her down to the basement. I knew Jennie was getting nervous. I knew she didn't like Sammie. I knew she got worried and even aggressive when people touched each other around her. It was just plain stupid.

What? Why didn't she attack Sammie? I don't know. You know, there was something about Sammie that kind of scared her. I don't know. In the dark like that, maybe she just miscalculated. I'm sure she didn't intend to hurt me or anybody. She didn't know her own strength.

At that point I threw up. Sammie was pretty good about it. Her mother was upstairs hollering her head off and yelling about not ruining the carpet. At least that's what I remember her saying. "What happened? Is he bleeding? Don't drip on the carpet! Get that boy out of here!" She didn't even know there was an ape in the house. Sammie told her to fuck off again and got me in the car and to the hospital.

The funny thing was, we forgot all about Jennie, just left her there shut up in the house with the hypochondriac mom. I was feeling very weird and didn't really know what was going on. Shock, I suppose. Sammie was so scared it was all she could do to drive the car.

So we got to Newton-Wellesley and they got me inside. The doctor wanted to know what had happened. He was really concerned that we go get the finger. He wanted to send someone back to get it. We tried to explain that it was probably in this chimpanzee's belly, but I think he thought we were delirious. And that's when I suddenly said, "Where the hell is Jennie?"

Sammie turned white and said she was still in the house with her mom, and she jumped up and left. The doctor was saying "Go look for the finger!" But she went and called the police. I have to tell you, it was pretty funny.

See, all the commotion had finally gotten the old drunken bitch out of bed. She came staggering down the stairs, saw blood on the carpet no doubt, heard some noises, and went down to the basement. Apparently Jennie was hiding under the covers of Sammie's bed, whimpering. Her mom, thinking it was somebody, started yelling and when there was no response whipped the covers back. Oh my God. The poor old sot screamed and fainted.

The police found Jennie curled up on the bed, crying. They revived the mom. She was hysterical. She refused to leave the house so the cops searched around for the finger, couldn't find it, and left with Jennie and brought her to my parents' house. By the time the police got there my parents were on their way to the hospital, so they sat there and waited. Jennie felt terrible about the whole thing. She was so ashamed and sad. When my parents came home, Jennie went to the bathroom all by herself and shut herself in. To punish herself. She stayed in there for the whole day. Not even eating.

I really don't remember much of anything. They'd given me some shots that made me feel like I was floating about two feet off the bed.

They fixed me up pretty well. After about six months I stopped missing it, except that once in a while it itches right on the tip and I can't scratch it. Damn, that's annoying!

So that's what happened. My parents blamed Jennie and decided to send her away. End of story.

I got over losing a finger pretty fast. I wasn't mad at Jennie at all. It was my fault. But my mom kind of freaked out. She kept Jennie locked up in her room most of the time and she had bars and screens put on the windows and door. It was like a prison. And Jennie treated it as such, banging and yelling and raising holy hell when she was put in there. My mother and I had pretty bad fights about that, arguing almost nonstop. Sarah was her usual uptight self, walking around with her nose wrinkled up. Sarah was basically a good kid but she really had a thing about Jennie. My father did his usual disappearing act. Did you try to talk to Sarah? I knew it. I knew she wouldn't talk to you. You might as well forget her; she's as stubborn as an ox. When she says no that's it.

So then Prentiss came around with some kind of offer to take Jennie to Florida. Prentiss and that pompous old egomaniac Epstein. Epstein thought he had the answer to everything. My parents jumped on that. I was surprised, because my mother didn't like Prentiss. My parents pretended to have a talk with us, to let us feel that we were part of the decision, but their minds were already made up. I was against it right from the beginning. I knew exactly what was going to happen. I tried my best to stop it, but being a sixteen-year-old kid I didn't have much say.

They had a going-away party for Jennie. I thought that was the cruelest thing of all. Like giving a condemned man a last meal of steak and lobster. Jennie had no idea that in three days she was going off to prison. It was so phony, this party. I wasn't going to go to the party, but then I changed my mind and showed up near the end. I guess I'd had a bit too much to drink. They were all lined up for a picture and I just ripped into the whole lot of them. I said some pretty terrible things. I asked them how they could stand there laughing and smiling and having a good time, when they were sending Jennie to prison camp. I called them hypocrites, mother-fuckers—I mean, you name it, I said it. And you know what? Nobody said a word. Nobody defended themselves. The knew. They knew in their heart of hearts that I was right. They stood there looking guilty and then they slunk away and went home.

Here was the deal. This'll make you sick. Prentiss insisted that we transfer ownership of Jennie to the Tahachee center. Like a fucking slave. Like chattel. Oh but no, it was just a legal formality, see? Something about insurance or liability, oh yes of *course,* thank you, just a formality. Right. And my parents went along; they signed the fucking slave papers, giving these bastards *ownership* of Jennie. A clean break, a new life, they called it. How oh-so-*wonderful.*

My parents flew down to Florida with Jennie and came back a few days later. I wasn't around. I was so pissed off at that point that I'd gone to live with Sammie. I stayed there for a week and then I came home.

I have to say, I found my parents pretty broken up about losing Jennie. The only one who was happy was Sarah, who went humming and skipping around the house with her fucking dolls, having make-believe tea parties and things like that. Oh well, I can't blame her really. My mother cried just about every day. That surprised me, how upset she was. We talked a lot about it and I think that was the first time I'd really connected with my mother in years. We talked a lot about the early days when Jennie was young, about Jennie and her tricycle, about Jennie's first words. My mother really needed to talk about it. She tried to explain to me why they'd sent Jennie away. It was hard for her to defend the decision when I could see she was having second thoughts herself. I think she realized she'd made a terrible mistake. My father, he just withdrew. He was always pretty remote, but he looked . . . *ashen* after that. He was at the museum all the time. I really resented that.

The reports coming back from Florida were all bullshit. Everything was "normal." Normal what? Jennie was still in a fucking cage. It may be normal for them to sit in a cage but it wasn't normal for Jennie. What a crock.

After a few weeks my mom started getting suspicious. They had said Jennie would be released on the island in two weeks, but a month later she was still in the cage. They were evasive. They didn't want anyone to come down. Dr. Prentiss came back to Boston, but three weeks later she was back down there. No one would say why.

My father was a fool. In his mind, these people were scientists and scientists never make mistakes. He had this faith in those people, Epstein, Prentiss, Gabriel.

So here we were, everyone was sitting around the house talking about it but nobody was doing anything. Not a thing.

So I finally said to myself, the hell with this, this is a crock of shit, I'm going down there myself to see what's going on. I'm her brother. Nobody, I mean nobody, is going to keep me out.

So about a month after Jennie left, I wrapped my stuff in a blanket and I went out there to Route 128 South and stuck out my thumb.

That trip was a nightmare. It took me five days to get to Florida, and it rained almost every day. The first man that picked me up was an old guy driving a gold Cadillac, and he was so drunk, weaving all over the road, that I had to get him to stop and get out in the pouring rain. Then this busful of hippies picked me up; you know, peace and love and all that, and all they did was bitch about who was hogging the drugs, who had ripped off the pot. I spent a night with them at this KOA campground outside of Baltimore, and they split in the morning without paying and I had to pick up the tab.

It rained that morning, and an old black guy in a pickup stopped. He was only going a hundred miles, but he invited me to spend the night at his place near Richmond. His name was Dad Patterson. Dad and Muriel Patterson. I'll never forget them. Their kids had grown up and moved away, and I think they were lonely. They lived on one floor of this old crooked three-story house, looked like the porches were about to fall off. His wife cooked me a fantastic meal and I told them about Jennie. They were fascinated. They asked me all kinds of questions about Jennie and what it was like growing up with a chimpanzee, and I showed them my finger and they ooohed and aaaahed about it. We drank bottles of Colt 45.

It rained the next day and the next, and when I finally got to Florida it was still raining. It took me a day and a half just to get halfway down the length of Florida. Tahachee was on the Gulf Coast near Sarasota.

The last afternoon it cleared and I slept in a nature preserve along the coast. Snuck in and curled up in this deep sandy grove of palmettos. The night was full of stars. When I got up in the morning the sun was just hitting the tops of the trees and the birds were making an incredible racket. They were flapping and squawking through the branches. The sky was an incredible blue color, and as I lay on my back I saw a snake silently gliding along a branch above my head, so smooth and graceful and alive. It seemed like such a perfect thing. Just going about its business and living its life in a pure way. There was no bullshit or phoniness in this snake's life. No complexity, no moral agony. Just this beautiful simplicity. I wanted to be the snake, at that moment. I wanted to shed this life and just be up there, gliding over a branch in the warm sun. And then I thought, Why not? What's preventing it? I *can* be like that.

I wish I could describe to you how I felt at that moment. I suddenly felt alive, for the first time in months. It was a great moment, an epiphany. I felt free.

I was only a few miles from Tahachee. I felt that, whatever happened, everything would be okay. I don't know why I felt that, but I did. It helped me get through the next few days.

I got to Tahachee about noon. I walked into George Gabriel's office. I wasn't looking very presentable, and he looked at me and demanded to know what I wanted.

I told him who I was, and I said I wanted to see Jennie.

He just looked at me steadily. He was dressed like a great white hunter, all khaki with pockets everywhere. He had a big beard and a sunburned face, but his eyes were that Nazi pale-blue color. He was a phony through and through.

Then he stood up and shook my hand. He said, "Sit down, sit down. Let's rap."

Can you believe it? *Let's rap.* He thought he was so cool, so with-it, he wanted to rap. Not talk. Rap. What an asshole.

Then he went through this thing of crossing his legs and sighing and saying that he didn't know how to say this to me, but it wouldn't be in Jennie's interests for her to see me, and so forth. Looking all thoughtful and fatherly and paternal, and pretending to take me seriously when all he wanted was for me to get the hell out. Talking to me like I was some kind of idiot.

So I said, "Why not?"

So he started this longwinded explanation. They wanted to release Jennie on this island with other chimpanzees, but in order to do that they had to accustom her to being with her own kind. And that was a hard process for her. On and on. Jennie was very upset, she was having trouble adjusting. But she was making progress. My visiting her would undo all the progress they'd made. It would upset Jennie terribly. It was a very bad idea. It would set her back.

I listened patiently. I thought, Let the asshole talk himself out. I mean, nothing was going to keep me out of that cage.

So I asked him, very nicely, why she was in a cage in the first place.

He had another long bullshit explanation for that. She was too powerful to control on a lead. She was extremely hostile to other chimpanzees and had attacked one. Why, Jennie had even attacked him. When he said that I couldn't keep myself from grinning. Too bad Jennie didn't kill the bastard. The only way, he said, to safely allow her to be in proximity with other chimps was by keeping her in a cage. On and on. It was only temporary and then she would have a long and happy life on the island.

I started to get pissed off. I said, "Look, I've got a right to see her. Now!"

He hemmed and hawed and went into more explanations. He wanted to know if my parents knew I was there. I said that was none of his business. He said he wouldn't call them unless I wanted him to. He understood my reasons for being here, on and on. Still trying to be cool, still feeding me bullshit.

Then he went into this business about what "right" did I have to see her. My family had given up all "rights" when we gave Jennie to the center. He didn't quite put it that way, but that was the idea.

That really made me mad. I said, "I'm not talking about legal rights. I'm talking about moral rights."

Nothing would shut that asshole up. He went on and on about whose right was higher, Jennie's to become adjusted to her new life or my right to see her and possibly wreck everything. They had a "duty" to see that Jennie had a happy life. On and on. I realized that I was on the wrong track, that nobody could outtalk that scumbag.

So I tried something different. I said, "This place is going to be turned upside down if you don't let me in there."

Oh, he understood, oh sure, why I was upset. And he sympathized. But let's not do anything rash that we might regret. Oh no. Finally he said that she was very upset right now. A danger to herself and others. Even if he thought it would be a good idea to let me in, it would be too dangerous. She might accidentally, in her excitement and frustration, hurt me.

I just said, "Bullshit." Can you believe he was talking to me like that, me who had grown up with her and known her all her life? I just stared at him. I didn't know what to say.

He looked at me and said, "You, of all people, should know just how dangerous an excited chimpanzee can be," and I could see him glance at my hand.

Well, that really pissed me off. What an asshole. I stood up and said, "I'll find her on my own," and walked out the door. He rushed after me and grabbed my arm and we talked on the lawn. The sun was out and I could see a big barnlike building with a row of chain-link cages sticking out along one side. I figured that's where they had Jennie.

Oh, he knew how I felt. He sympathized. But I couldn't just go barging in there. Something might happen. I just said to him, "Fuck you. *Fuck* you." I shook off his hand and kept walking toward the building. He was saying "Just think of Jennie. For her sake. Just think how upsetting it will be. She might very well attack you. I can't be responsible for that."

I just kept walking. Gabriel kept walking alongside of me, and finally he gave in. He said he'd let me into the building. But not into the cage. It was really too dangerous. I had to promise not to go near the cage. He had to remind me I was a guest of the center. Et cetera. I didn't say a word. I just kept heading for the building.

We had reached the door. I said, "Let me in."

He was dancing around with the key, and he tried to make me promise not to go near the cage. I didn't say a word.

He stuck the key in the door. The minute his key made a noise Jennie started to scream. Jesus. I'd never heard her scream like that. It made my skin crawl. It was like . . . like she was being tortured. She was choking and hammering on the bars. When the door opened she was in the far corner of her cage, shrieking and banging on the bars. She would run out of air and there would be a choking silence and then she would scream again, her eyes squeezed shut. She started hitting herself on the head with her fists. I couldn't believe it. Jesus Christ, I couldn't believe it. She couldn't even see us, she was in such a frenzy. There were bald spots all over her where she'd been pulling out hair. And her fur was kind of a dull brown, not the usual glossy black color. And she had this big potbelly. Emaciated with a big unhealthy-looking belly sticking out, like those starving kids in Africa. God, I hardly recognized her. It was *sickening* what they'd done to her.

I was so angry, I could hardly get the words out. I told him to let me in the fucking cage.

He was saying, "Wait, you promised."

I hadn't promised a fucking thing. I started toward the cage.

He started to shout. "Stay back! She'll try to grab you through the bars."

That's when I suddenly realized that this macho pumped-up Great White Hunter was actually afraid of Jennie. He was scared shitless of her! You should've seen him.

Jennie wasn't even looking at us. She was in such a fury I don't even think she was aware of her surroundings. She didn't know it was me.

I just said, "Gimme the keys."

He was going on and on. "She'll hurt you," he said. "Look at her!"

So I grabbed the motherfucker and twisted his arm behind his back. And I shoved him toward the cage.

He really started to scream "What the hell are you doing! Help! Security!"

Look at me. I'm no big tough guy. I'm actually kind of a wimp. I've never been in a fight in my whole life. And this guy was just paralyzed with fear. [Laughs.] I suppose I did look pretty intimidating, with my long hair and scraggly beard, covered with dirt and mud. Yeah, I must've looked like some crazed biker. Gabriel didn't even struggle. He was, like, flabby with fear.

When Jennie saw us close, she ran straight to the bars. Still in a total frenzy. Slammed herself against them, she was so anxious to kill the bastard. Reaching out and screaming and baring her teeth with her big canines flashing.

He was screaming his fucking head off. "No! She'll kill us both! Let go!"

I said to him, real calm. "If you don't gimme the keys, I'll push you right up against the bars." And I started shoving him forward. I can't believe what I did. I was just *crazy* I was so upset.

He was slack with fear. "In my side pocket!" he yelled. "They're in my side pocket!"

There they were, a big bunch of keys. Dozens of them. One for every fucking cage on the place.

I yelled, "Which one!"

He was scared shitless, yelling "Number six! Number six!"

I let him go and he stepped back, but he didn't leave. He just stood near the door, sweating.

Then he said, "You little prick, I hope she bites your hand off this time." His face was red. He looked like he was about to cry.

I unlocked the door and it swung open and I went in. Jennie saw me vaguely through her ranting and rushed at me with her hair sticking up, her teeth bared. A roar of rage coming out of her throat. She came straight at me. She was ready to kill.

I said, "Jennie! It's me!" and she stopped dead and looked at me for the first time. For the first time. Then she ran toward me and threw herself into my arms.

Then she started to cry. The tears were just streaming down her face. She was silent, weeping and clinging tightly to me. Her head was pressed against my chest, and she was holding me like she was never going to let go. I could feel her skinny little body shaking with sorrow. Oh God it just—it just *hurt* so much. We just held each other for a long, long time, and I could feel this pain in my chest like my heart, it was, like, *breaking*. I was crying too, I guess, and we just held each other and cried.

I don't know how much time passed, but then there were voices and they were prying her off me and I could feel my buttons popping and my shirt being ripped right off my back by her grip. Then she started to scream that terrible scream again and I—I didn't know what was happening really— Oh shit—shit—shit— [Editor's note: At this point Sandy became distraught and the interview was suspended until the following morning.]

twelve

[FROM an interview with Dr. Pamela Prentiss.]

When I heard about the horrible incident with Sandy, I flew down to Florida. Dr. and Mrs. Archibald were also flying down. Mrs. Archibald had been unspeakably abusive to me on the telephone. I can't even repeat the things she said. I will never forgive her.

Sandy had threatened Dr. Gabriel and forced his way into Jennie's cage. It was just what I said would happen. Jennie had to be sedated, for everyone's safety, and then Sandy became violent and abusive and Dr. Gabriel had to call the police. I must say it is to George Gabriel's credit that he did not press charges.

At Dr. Gabriel's insistence they took Sandy to the hospital instead of the county jail. He should have gone to jail. It was criminal what he did. That happened in the morning, and I arrived in the late afternoon and met Dr. Gabriel in his office. He was shaken up. This was—let me see here—on May 17, 1974. He was worried about what was going to happen when the Archibalds arrived.

We had a signed agreement over the care and responsibility for Jennie. We had legal ownership of Jennie—technically, of course. Sandy had been trespassing on Tahachee grounds. Dr. Gabriel, as far as I could see, had acted properly. It was just as we had warned over and over again. We told them exactly what would happen if Jennie had any contact with the Archibald family. We were absolutely right. It was all their fault but we got blamed for everything.

What was alleged in that magazine, that we refused to relinquish Jennie, is a bald lie. It is a libelous statement and if I'd had the money I'd have taken them to court. They never *once* asked us for Jennie back.

Anyway, nobody had been hurt. Jennie was sedated in her cage, sleeping peacefully. Sandy wasn't hurt either. All in all, I pointed out to Dr. Gabriel, we'd been fortunate. He shook his head and said that he'd been searching his mind trying to see where things got out of hand.

Late that evening the Archibalds finally called from the hospital. I talked with Dr. Archibald, who was calm and collected. He apologized for what had happened. He said they would like to come by the center in the morning to discuss the situation. He hinted that he might be coming alone, and I hoped that would be the case, since Mrs. Archibald was clearly mentally unbalanced at this point. I agreed and we set up an appointment for ten o'clock that morning.

The next morning . . . The next morning . . . Did you read the *Esquire* article? Well, you can forget everything they said. Not a word of it is true. I wrote a reply but they never published it.

You know, you worry me. I really don't know what you're after. I'm just warning you that I'm not going to be the fall guy yet again for what happened to Jennie. If it was anybody's fault, it was Sandy's fault. Sandy did it. We told them again and again what would happen if they visited Jennie.

Where was I? We were supposed to have a meeting at ten o'clock that morning. But then . . . Excuse me, on second thought

I would rather just . . . finish. That's right, end the interview. I've said all I wish to say. Don't misunderstand me: I have nothing to hide. I've said all I want to say, that's all. You must have ten hours of me on that tape. And you haven't even read all the papers I gave you. Don't think that I'm going to spoon-feed you everything. Go find out the rest of the story from someone else. Ask Harold to fill you in on the details. He's the one who wants this damned book. Turn that goddamn tape recorder off. I mean it. Now.

[FROM a telephone interview with Joseph Finney, former caregiver, Tahachee Center for Primate Rehabilitation, June 1993.]

Yeah, I remember that chimp. Jesus. What, you writing a book? You get paid for something like that? How much? I heard about a magazine article once about that. I was there, and nobody else was. But nobody ever asked me anything. They didn't call me. I never told my story to nobody. Right? I mean, they didn't pay for shit at Tahachee, and then they laid me off after two years on the job. I never made a dime out of that job. And those chimps were dangerous as hell. Especially that one.

So what do you want to know?

My name is Joseph Finney, and I used to be a caregiver at the Tahachee Center for Primate Rehabilitation. Is that the kind of thing you want? That's what they called us, caregivers. That was my job title.

My address is . . . Okay, no address. I don't know when it was, when they brought that chimp down. I can't remember its name. We had a hell of a time trying to get it inside the cage. See, I'd been working over Boca Grande, cleaning swimming pools. But the guy who ran the business was a real joker. He was ripping off the customers, you know. Like most of them only came down a few months out of the year, so he'd bill them for all kinds of summer work he never did. So he got caught, and I was out of a job.

I saw this ad. Taking care of animals. Experience helpful. What the hell, I thought. See, I grew up in the Bronx, and I used to shovel monkey shit at the zoo. [Laughs.] I always liked animals, you know, dogs and cats. I like 'em. I had a snake when I was a kid. So I went in there, got the job. Mostly the night shift. Ten to six. This was before I got married. They had a bunch of guys for the two day shifts, but at night there was only me. I didn't have to do much, just go around, check the place out, you know, punch a few clocks. It was all chimps. And they slept at night, most of the time, so it was pretty quiet. I worked there about a year when they brought that chimp in.

Look, I wasn't one of those guys who sleeps on the job. Or drinks. Even with a piece-of-shit job like this, I do my best. And nobody ever said otherwise. When I was laid off, it was a budget cut or something. I got my unemployment, then I went to work for Marine Magic. Over on Long Boat Key.

When they brought down that chimp, they put it in one of the cages. It was really nuts. I mean, those other chimps'd bite you in a minute, but this one wanted to *kill* you. You didn't want to get close to its cage, or it'd reach out and try to tear off your frigging arm. No kidding. I didn't have to feed them, that was the day crew, but I saw sometimes those guys would have to toss the food in, like, from a distance. I mean, that chimp was always there. Waiting to kill you. Jesus.

It screamed all the time. Especially when people came by. On my rounds, see, I had to punch a clock in the barn. That's where they kept the cages. I'd try to sneak in, keep the light off. But see, I had to turn this little key in the clock, and when it heard the click it always started screaming bloody murder. Rattling the cage. You'd hear this *Wham! Wham!* and it'd be hitting something in there. Jesus. I was scared out of my mind it'd get out and tear me to pieces. Hey, it did get out once. Sat in a tree for two days, screaming its head off. That was one crazy animal. I don't know what they were doing with it there, or what was wrong with it. Probably got messed up in some experiment.

Gabriel? Yeah, well, he was kind of a jerk. I hardly saw him. He didn't know who I was. He didn't make an effort. Like on some jobs, the top guy makes an effort. He didn't. He wasn't my boss, though. My boss was a guy called Oscar. Oscar was okay, and most of the time he wasn't around. Like I said, I was the only guy worked the graveyard. There was another scientist that was there a lot. Blond woman, a real looker. Not too friendly.

Lemme see. I guess they had that chimp for about two, three weeks. Maybe a month. So I come to work, ten o'clock, and there's a big deal going on. Someone broke into the chimp's cage. Some kid. I don't know how he did it, I mean he must've had guts. By the time I got there, he was gone, and they'd knocked out the chimp. It was in the cage, sleeping. No problem. I'm doing my rounds, like usual. Then, like around three o'clock, I was heading for the barn. I heard this chimp scream. That wasn't anything unusual. But when I got inside, I heard this other noise. Like a flopping sound. So I turn on the light. And there's this chimp, like, flopping on the floor of the cage. You know, twitching. I thought it was from the drugs, being knocked out. Coming to, you know? But then I see this blood. Like there's a trail of blood, and this chimp's crawling, leaving this trail across the cage. And it started making this sound, like snoring.

It kind of freaked me out. But I wasn't going in there. No way. So I went over to the house and woke up Gabriel. That lady scientist had an apartment there too. So anyway she calls the vet while Gabriel comes running down.

He goes, "Who did this? Did you do this?" Like I would go and kill this chimp. "Hey," I said, "take it easy. I found it like that."

He was all over me. "You let someone in. You let that kid in, didn't you? That son of a bitch, look what he did. I'll get that son of a bitch." Saying stuff like that. I was really getting pissed off. I don't have to take that kind of shit. I told him so. Nobody had been around, or I would have seen him. I hadn't seen nobody, but he didn't believe me.

He was really ripped. And this chimp is like *snoring*, and then it starts crawling across the cage. To the door. And it gets to the door and reaches up, like, grabs the handle. And then it falls back and starts flopping again and twitches. So Gabriel tells me to stay there, and he goes back and calls the cops. And while I'm waiting, the chimp coughs or something and goes still. Like, it died.

And then, it was really weird. That lady scientist comes down, and she goes in the cage and she's holding the dead chimp and screaming her head off. Getting blood all over her. And *kissing* it. No shit. I mean, she was still in her *nightgown*. And then she's looking at her hands, with the blood on them, and slapping her own face and hitting herself. Jesus. I couldn't believe what I was seeing. I swear to God you never seen anything like it. I swear to God.

Then everyone comes, and they take it away. So the cops want to talk to me, and they're asking me all these questions like Who did this? Who was around? Did I go to sleep? Had I been drinking? I mean, it really pissed me off and I told them so. Even with a shitty job like that, I'm a responsible guy. I don't have to take shit like that.

Then the next day it was all cleaned up. It was like nothing happened. A week later they asked me a bunch of questions, but it was different. They were a lot more friendly. See, they were afraid I was gonna quit. I mean, who were they gonna get to work nights at three fifty an hour? That's what they paid, three fifty. They wanted to know what I'd seen. Hey, I said, I keep telling you I didn't see nothing or nobody. Just what I said. Like, why would I lie? And that was it. So later they told me it was an accident, the chimp fell and hit its head.

Yeah. So I worked there another year and then they laid me off because of some cutback somewhere. That's when I got the job at Marine Magic.

There isn't much to tell after that. The story's over. You can finally shut off that tape recorder. Jennie was dead. It was done. And legally they owned her, she was their property, so who could we sue? Who could we complain to? They had killed our daughter and there was nothing we could do. Nothing. Anyway she was dead.

So there was Jennie's body laid out there in the veterinary hospital, on a stainless steel table, dissected. Her whole face and skull had been opened up. I was the only one to see that. No, Sandy saw her later, I believe. I kept Hugo and Sarah out. You know, it wasn't that shocking, really—because it just wasn't her. For the first time, she looked like an animal to me. All the life was gone and she looked like somebody's big black dog run over by a car. If there is such a thing as a soul, it was long gone.

Sandy was released from the hospital that day. The psychiatrist said he was upset but in good mental health. George Gabriel, fearing a scandal, no doubt, declined to press any charges. We had Jennie's body cremated, and we took the ashes back to Boston.

Sandy had already made his peace. Learning of Jennie's death didn't throw him for a loop the way we thought it would. He accepted it with a fatalism that, well, kind of scared us at first. It was almost as if he'd already said good-bye to her. I guess he had.

[FROM an interview with Harold Epstein.]

Now where was I? You know the story. They found Jennie on the floor of her cage. Unconscious. While Dr. Gabriel administered emergency first aid to Jennie, Dr. Prentiss called Roger Kuntz, who was the D.V.M. used by the center. Although Dr. Gabriel was a veterinarian himself, Dr. Kuntz had more experience with trauma. He arrived ten minutes later and tried cardiopulmonary resuscitation, but by that time it was clear that Jennie was not merely unconscious. She was dead.

Now I know that *Esquire* reported that Jennie might have been murdered. Let me address that. This utterly ridiculous falsehood stemmed from the fact that, in her very distraught state, Dr. Prentiss made some thoughtless allegations against Sandy. Jennie had been found lying in her cage with a fractured skull. And Pam didn't see, at first, how that could have happened. She asked Dr. Kuntz to photograph and remove the body and perform an autopsy. Once made, the allegation was out, and it took on a life of its own. It was sensational. A macho red-blooded journalist like that fellow from *Esquire,* well, he just couldn't resist.

Dr. Kuntz quickly dispelled the idea that the death was anything but accidental. Mind you, they seriously examined the possibility of foul play. Dr. Prentiss insisted on it. What they found was crystal clear. The door to the building was locked. The cage was locked. There were no signs of a break-in or tampering. The night watchman had not fallen asleep or been derelict in his duty. All his clocks had been punched and this was, apparently, an unusually reliable fellow.

Sandy had quite definitely been in the hospital all night. When everyone finally calmed down we realized that it had been an accident, a freakish accident.

Apparently what happened was this. During the night she had had a fall, undoubtedly while the sedative was still clouding her mind. Normally chimps can fall twenty or thirty feet out of a tree and be unhurt. I might add, however, that Goodall did observe chimpanzees falling to their deaths from trees. Jennie fell from above and just happened to land on her head on some hard blunt object—we believe it might have been the edge of her cement water bowl. A severe cranial fracture followed by cerebral edema ended her life very quickly and mercifully, without suffering.

When Dr. Prentiss returned to Boston a week later, she came into my office. She was a changed woman. Her love for that chimpanzee was as powerful as any mother's love for her daughter. That tragedy changed her life. And you know what? She's never been the same since. Don't print this, but she's been treated for depression. That's why it burns me up to hear accusations leveled against her merely because she isn't, on the surface, the warmest and most socially graceful person in the world. I hope you will not be another one of those people casting stones. I'm asking you to have a little compassion. I also hope you'll be gentle with Sandy. He was a lovely, kind boy and he was just *crushed* by this whole thing. He is suffering terribly out there in Arizona. I think he blames himself. And Hugo's death, I think, had something to do with this whole thing. It ruined him as a scientist. He lost all perspective. He just seemed to give up on life. Of course, I'm not implying suicide of any kind, but one doesn't normally die from a simple gallstone operation. It was a routine operation; he just never woke up from the anesthetic.

Look, we're all good people here: myself, Dr. Prentiss, Lea, Sandy, and of course Hugo. Hugo was a wonderful man. We are kind people. To be sure, we're human beings, but we're not evil scientists. So, where did we go wrong? I really don't know the answer. I really don't.

[FROM an interview with Lea Archibald.]

We decided to bury Jennie's ashes on Hermit Island. It was the happiest place of her life, the only place where she could be herself. We put them in a clay jar that Sandy had made as a child, a big clunky thing colored in big green and yellow stripes. Sandy had been so proud of that jar when he brought it home. We kept it on the windowsill of the kitchen ever since. It was just about the only thing Jennie hadn't managed to break. It was indestructible.

We went to Hermit Island two weeks later. It was late May, but it was still cold and blustery. Hugo got the boat out of the barn and fixed up the engine—it had broken over the winter somehow—and we put it in the water in Franklins Pond Harbor on Saturday morning. It looked like bad weather, so we bundled up in sweaters and slickers. There was quite a chop out in the sound and I made the mistake of musing out loud that perhaps it might be just a little dangerous? Well! Sandy just about had a fit. So we loaded up the boat and set out.

The air still smelled of winter, it was that cold. On the way over it started to drizzle, and the water in Hermit Cove was black. Just as we got there the Monhegan foghorn began blowing, making these long soundings that rolled across Muscongus Bay. Ever since, I've associated that sound with burying Jennie on Hermit Island. So low and sad, like some lost lonely creature of the deep.

We hiked about the island, all through the wet grass, and got soaking wet. Sandy scattered a handful of ashes here and a handful there. He strewed some along the rocks and at the base of a spruce tree Jennie liked to climb.

We buried the jar with the rest of Jennie's ashes in the hole in the back of the fireplace where Sandy found the secret letter. We fitted the stone back in place, and then we lit a fire and made some hot tea. And we talked about Jennie, and we toasted her. We cried a little, but we tried to make it a happy moment. In a curious way it was a release. What kind of life would Jennie have had, if she lived? If she couldn't get along with other chimpanzees? And you know, she never would have accepted other chimps. I really believe that now. So what kind of a life was she going to have? Locked up in a cage? Put in a zoo? I've come to feel, over the years, that maybe her death was a blessing in disguise. She was too . . . too *free* for the world of people. Although chimps and humans are supposedly so closely related, there is still a gulf there—a vast gulf. We almost bridged that gulf, but in the end it didn't work.

So we huddled by the fire, and the roof leaked more than ever, and Sandy said a few words and we left. That was what, seventeen years ago? And we've never been back to Hermit Island. I don't imagine there's much left of the cabin, after all those winter storms.

The roof was already on its last legs. It isn't that we avoided the island, it was just that we never seemed to get around to it. We always talked about going back. Now with Hugo gone, I don't suppose I'll ever get back there. The boat was sold, Sandy's in Arizona, Sarah's in New York. I'm just a useless old lady now.

I still go to Maine, and Sarah visits every August with the grandchildren. Sometimes when I'm in the farmhouse, and the fog rolls in, I listen to the Monhegan foghorn, blowing, just blowing, and I think of the day we buried Jennie. And I think of Jennie's cold little jar there in the hermit's cabin in that secret place.

You know, I'm not a religious person, but sometimes I think I can hear Jennie hooting and laughing from a great distance when the waves are crashing on the shore. Of course it's bosh, just my imagination, but it always gives me a start. Yes indeed it does. And who knows, maybe she *is* out there somewhere in that big old strange universe of ours. Maybe when I die she'll be there waiting for me with open arms and a big halo around her head. Now wouldn't that be something?

[FROM an interview with Alexander ("Sandy") Archibald.]

It snowed last night. Did you hear the wind all night long? When it blows like that, it just sucks the heat right out of this place. Out the smoke hole. We'll go for another ride today. The desert in the snow is the most beautiful sight in the world. That coffee should be ready in a few minutes. Tortillas and beans for breakfast? Good, because that's all I've got. Unless you brought the bagels and smoked salmon from Zabars. [Laughs.]

We slept late. I'm usually up long before the sun. Throw open that door, let's see what happened. Ahhhh! Look at the snow! Stretching all the way to the mountains like a blanket of white. A blanket of forgiveness. Snow heals the earth. The Navajos, see, they believe that a living being named *Hak'az asdzáá,* or Cold Woman, brings the snow. They worship her, because without snow the land would burn up and the springs would go dry.

Pile some more coal on that fire and let's warm this joint up.

Where were we? Will you look at this, he's already got that damn tape recorder going. Sorry about last night. I still have a few things to work out. Ahhhh, well.

Anyway, they told me in the hospital that Jennie was dead. I wasn't a bit surprised. I knew it already. I knew it the morning I woke up in the nature preserve that I was going to see Jennie for the last time. It was like a death already, to see Jennie in that cage.

You know, they're gonna tell you it was an accident. That's what they all decided. She fell and hit her head. That's what they decided. Right. Let me tell you: they just couldn't face the truth. Oh, they believe it all right, but I know better. She didn't fall. I saw the autopsy report. I saw her body. But what really matters is that I knew her. Goddamnit, I knew Jennie, and I know exactly what happened that night. When I first went in that building, I saw what she was doing to herself in that cage, pounding with all her might on her own head with her fists. I saw where she'd pulled her hair out. I saw her run at the bars of the cage. I saw that she'd reached the end of the line. The morning after, when I woke up in the hospital, there were these huge bruises on my side. I was wondering just where those came from, when I realized. It was from Jennie gripping me, holding me for all she was worth. That's how desperate she was. That's how much she loved me.

That injury wasn't caused by a fall. Bullshit! There were two parallel fractures in her skull. What happened was, she woke up in the dark, all alone, silent. And she saw that she was still in the cage. She saw that even *I*, her friend and protector, couldn't save her. I was gone, dragged away kicking and screaming, and that must have scared the shit out of her, to see me dragged away like that. She thought I was God and when she saw me dragged away by Gabriel and his men she knew it was all over. I was her last hope and when she saw that she knew it was over. And so she ran full tilt at the bars of her cage with her head. Broke her skull, just shattered it. Deliberately. She killed herself. She wanted to die, and she killed herself. She was going to live free or she was going to die. There was no middle ground.

Jennie was capable of understanding the meaning of death. That crazy old minister, Palliser, taught her all about death. I mean, the poor guy thought he was teaching her about Christianity, but all he did was scare her shitless about death. Jennie and I talked about it, about death. Like about her dead cat. Man, she remembered that cat of hers for the rest of her life. She couldn't understand just what the hell death was, how someone could just disappear. The whole concept was a mystery. The fact that it could *happen* was what scared her. And then when Palliser's wife died, I remember she came back from across the street, and she was following me around, asking over and over again *Sandy dead?* See, she said *dead* but what she meant was "Are you going to die?" So she went around signing *Sandy dead? Sandy dead?* Whimpering and dragging herself around behind me, afraid to let me out of her sight. She was just as scared of death as any human being. But scared not for herself, but for *me*. Think about that.

That old Epstein, he thinks he knows everything. He keeps saying nobody did anything wrong, that it was an unforseeable accident. Okay, let me just say one thing. There was guilt here, of sorts. My father never should've been collecting dead primates in the first place. Jennie's mother never would've been killed. And Jennie'd probably be alive right now. It's that simple. That's where the whole thing started. There's something really wrong with looking at the world that way, trying to divorce science from everything else.

You see, my father was a scientist. He didn't see the human dimension of what he was doing, bringing Jennie into our family. This wasn't an experiment with one animal. This was an experiment that involved all of us, his wife and kids. Me. A very dangerous experiment.

Aside from Jennie, Dad was hurt the most by this. He was changed. You know when he had that operation, the one that killed him? When he went under that anesthetic, there was something buried in his mind. Something that just didn't want to wake up again. And so he didn't.

I think it's very ironic. With all those experiments, they were almost able to erase the distinction between man and animal. The one thing they didn't look at was Jennie's ability to understand death. The knowledge of good and evil. Now isn't it ironic that with her final act, her suicide, she obliterated this last distinction?

We buried her on Hermit Island. I gave the ceremony. I chose a passage from *A Farewell to Arms*. It was one of my favorite books when I was a teenager, and I memorized the paragraph. It's a book about death. Like your book will be. I'm not quite so thrilled with Hemingway now as I once was, but I still like the passage. My mother didn't like it at all, she said it wasn't a very happy eulogy, but I read it anyway. It goes like this: "If people bring so much courage to this world the world has to kill them to break them, so of course it kills them. The world breaks everyone and afterward many are strong at the broken places. But those who will not break it kills. It kills the very good and the very gentle and the very brave impartially."

That was Jennie. Good, gentle, and above all brave. [Sandy began to weep quietly at this point.] She was going to be a free human being or nothing. No compromise. I say human being because that's what she was and I mean that with total seriousness. She was never going to accept being an animal, living in a cage or some ape's mate on a grubby little island. Her death was noble and beautiful. And it taught me a lesson: I'm not going to let the world break me. The world can't touch me here. And when I leave this place, I'll have learned to carry my freedom in my heart—Jennie's kind of freedom. Wildness. If you're truly free, truly wild, the world can't kill you, it can't break you, it can't even touch you. When you're free, you're invincible.

After I read the Hemingway, I wrote Jennie's epitaph in chalk on the mantelpiece:

JENNIE ARCHIBALD, 1965–1974
VERY GOOD, VERY GENTLE, VERY BRAVE

[SCENES from an eight-mm silent movie, filmed by Dr. Hugo Archibald on Easter Day, 1974.]

Jennie is running across the lawn. She is dressed in overalls, saddle shoes, and a white blouse. She climbs the crab apple tree. In a crook of a limb she finds a banana, waves it over her head laughing and screaming with delight. The scene cuts to Jennie heaping fruits in a large pile, while someone offscreen hands her more fruits. She sits down next to the stack and peels a banana and crams it into her mouth, and then she sucks on the banana skin before throwing it offscreen. Then she turns and grins at the camera and signs: Me Jennie! Me Jennie!

The scene cuts to Jennie scooting over to Reverend Palliser, who is in his wheelchair. She climbs into his lap and starts kissing him on the lips. Palliser is laughing and crying, and clapping his hands like a child. An unknown woman, apparently his nurse, stands behind him with a nervous smile, clasping her hands. Jennie suddenly notices his tears and, looking concerned, starts touching and patting them away with her hands.

Another scene. We see Jennie from the back. Jennie is sitting on her heels on the grass, eating something. She looks back at the camera, turns around, and lunges forward, stealing a barbecued rib from a paper plate in someone's lap. She runs away with her mouth open, carrying the rib and laughing, and then she throws the rib over the hedge. She runs back toward the camera, signing Tickle-chase Jennie! *The camera follows Jennie as she runs across the lawn, pursued by several people. Jennie is caught by Pam Prentiss, and she rolls over and is tickled by several people at once. The camera is jostled around and we see Jennie laughing and fending them off with her feet. Then she jumps up and starts whirling around, her pink mouth open, her jug ears sticking out from the sides of her head. She hops up and down, somersaults, and races off camera, with several people in pursuit.*

Another scene. The camera is out of focus, giving the scene a dreamlike feeling. It is hard to make out what is going on at first. Jennie is waving good-bye, waving and waving, hopping up and down, waving again with both hands. She is suddenly in focus and then out of focus again. She rolls over on her back and waves good-bye with her feet, somersaults, and grins and claps her hands over her eyes. The camera pans to a blurry crowd of people waving good-bye. Everyone is waving good-bye. Good-bye, Jennie. Everyone is waving good-bye. Everyone wave good-bye to Jennie. Wave good-bye for the camera. Good-bye, Jennie. Good-bye. Good-bye.

Jennie is a novel, but a novel based on real science. The language experiments recorded in this book, the cognitive experiments, the genetic affinities between humans and chimpanzees, and Jennie's signing abilities are all based on actual research and experimental work done with chimpanzees and gorillas. The anecdotes regarding Jennie's ability to imagine and create, her insistent identification of herself as a human being, her understanding and manipulation of human psychology, her sexual attraction to human males, and her caring and affectionate nature are all based on actual events in the lives of home-raised chimpanzees. The clear dividing line between humans and chimpanzees has indeed been erased in the past few decades.

I cannot leave this subject without mentioning the grave danger that chimpanzees, and all the great apes, face in the wild. Chimpanzees, bonobos, gorillas, and orangutans are all extremely endangered, in some cases on the verge of extinction. These are the animal species closest to us. Humans and chimpanzees share 98.5 percent of the same DNA. Recent work on the rare bonobo (once called the pigmy chimpanzee but now recognized as a separate species) has shown that they are even more humanlike than the chimpanzee.

If more isn't done to save the great apes, and done immediately, they will become extinct. This would be a terrible crime against nature and against our own biological family.

I would ask the reader: What hope do we have as a species if we allow such a thing to occur?

There are a number of organizations that are helping save the great apes in the wild. I will list a few of them here in the hope that the reader will be moved enough by this book to give these organizations the support they so desperately need.

The Jane Goodall Institute
P.O. Box 599
Ridgefield, CT 06877
203-431-2099
or
15 Clarendon Park
Lymington, Hants. SO41 8AX
U.K.

Committee for Conservation and Care of Chimpanzees
3819 48th Street NW
Washington, DC 20016
202-362-1993

Bonobo Protection Fund
Language Research Center
Georgia State University
University Plaza
Atlanta, GA 30303-3083

The Dian Fossey Gorilla Fund
45 Inverness Drive
Englewood, CO 80112
303-790-2349
or

110 Gloucester
Primrose Hill
London NW1 8JA
U.K.

Friends of Washoe
P.O. Box 728
Ellensburg, WA 98926

The Gorilla Foundation
Box 620-530
Woodside, CA 94062

The Great Ape Project
P.O. Box 1023
Collingwood, Melbourne
Victoria, Australia 3066

The Orangutan Foundation International
822 South Wellesley Avenue
Los Angeles, CA 90049

Projet de Protection des Gorilles
Howletts & Port Lymphe Foundation
Brazzaville BP 13977
Republique du Congo
or
John Aspinall's Wildlife Sanctuaries
750 Lausanne Road
Los Angeles, CA 90077

Wildlife Conservation Society
The Wildlife Conservation Park
Bronx, NY 10460

World Wide Fund for Nature
World Wildlife Fund Switzerland
Forrlibuckstrasse 66
Postfach, 8037
Zurich, Switzerland

International Primate Protection League
P.O. Box 766
Summerville, SC 29484
803-871-2280

Chimfunshi Wildlife Orphanage
P.O. Box 11190
Chingola, Zambia
or c/o The Jane Goodall Institute

Many primatologists will recognize experiments, stories, and anecdotes in this book that were adapted from nonfiction accounts of raising chimpanzees in human families, observations of chimpanzees in the wild, and cognitive and linguistic studies of chimpanzees. I am obviously indebted to many works about chimpanzees, particularly the writings of Jane Goodall, Maurice Temerlin, Cathy Hayes, and Herbert S. Terrace. I would like to acknowledge my major sources here.

Goodall, Jane. *The Chimpanzees of Gombe: Patterns of Behavior.* Cambridge: The Belknap Press of Harvard University Press, 1986.

———. *In the Shadow of Man.* Rev. ed. Boston: Houghton Mifflin Co., 1988.

———. *My Friends the Wild Chimpanzees.* Washington, D.C.: The National Geographic Society, 1967.

———. *Through a Window*. Boston: Houghton Mifflin Co., 1990.

Hayes, C. *The Ape in Our House*. New York: Harper Brothers, 1951.

Linden, Eugene. *Silent Partners: The Legacy of the Ape Language Experiments*. New York: Times Books, 1986.

Montgomery, Sy. *Walking with the Great Apes*. Boston: Houghton Mifflin Co., 1991.

Nichols, Michael, with contributions by Jane Goodall, George B. Schaller, and Mary G. Smith. *The Great Apes: Between Two Worlds*. Washington, D.C.: The National Geographic Society, 1993.

Premack, David, and Premack, Ann James. *The Mind of an Ape*. New York: Norton, 1983.

Raven, Henry C. "Meshie: The Child of a Chimpanzee," *Natural History,* vol. 32, 1932.

———. "Further Adventures of Meshie," *Natural History,* vol. 33, 1933.

Rosen, S. I. *Introduction to the Primates: Living and Fossil*. Englewood Cliffs, N.J.: Prentice-Hall, 1974.

Temerlin. Maurice. *Lucy: Growing Up Human*. Palo Alto, Calif.: Science and Behavior Books, 1972.

Terrace, Herbert S. *Nim: A Chimpanzee Who Learned Sign Language*. New York: Alfred A. Knopf, 1979.

Acknowledgments

I owe a great debt to my agents, Tom Wallace and Matthew Snyder. I would like to thank my editor, Bob Wyatt, for his excellent work. I am deeply indebted to Mary G. Smith of the National Geographic Society for her enthusiastic support and excellent advice. I would particularly like to express my great appreciation to Dr. Douglas Schwartz, President of the School of American Research, for his support. I thank Stuart Woods and Lincoln Child for their helpful comments, and I am grateful for the editorial suggestions of the No Poets Society of Santa Fe. And I thank my father, Jerome Preston, Jr., for his very helpful advice, and my grandfather, Jerome Preston, Sr., for his great support.

I would like to thank Nina Root, Chairwoman of the Department of Library Services at the American Museum of Natural History, for allowing me access to the Raven papers and films. I would also like to thank the late Dr. Harold Shapiro of the American Museum for sharing with me his vivid reminiscences of Henry Raven and the chimpanzee called Meshie.

Finally, I want to thank my wife, Christine, for all her support.

The fictional characters in this novel are not based on real people and any resemblance to such is purely coincidental. As for the real people and organizations who appear by name in this novel, most of what is written about them is not true. Proxmire did not, for obvious reasons, award a Golden Fleece to the Jennie project. Walter Sullivan did not write an article about Jennie. Teddy Kennedy did not meet Jennie. Nor did the Boston *Globe,* the Boston *Herald-Traveler, Esquire* magazine, *Psychology Today* magazine, or any other magazine or newspaper report on Jennie. Jennie did not appear on the Ed Sullivan show. I apologize for any negative opinions expressed by fictional characters about real people. The reader will be able to separate fact from fiction in these instances.